25708
65⁰⁰

Olivier de La Marche

Le Chevalier deliberé
(The Resolute Knight)

MEDIEVAL & RENAISSANCE

TEXTS & STUDIES

VOLUME 199

Olivier de La Marche

Le Chevalier deliberé
(The Resolute Knight)

Edited by

Carleton W. Carroll

Translated by

Lois Hawley Wilson & Carleton W. Carroll

Arizona Center for Medieval and Renaissance Studies
Tempe, Arizona
1999

Library of Congress Cataloging-in-Publication Data

La Marche, Olivier de, ca. 1426–1502.
     [Chevalier délibéré. English & French (Middle French)]
     Le chevalier délibéré = The resolute knight / Olivier de La Marche ;
edited by Carleton W. Carroll ; translated by Lois Hawley Wilson &
Carleton W. Carroll.
        p. cm. — (Medieval & Renaissance Texts & Studies ; vol. 199)
     In Middle French with English on facing pages.
     Includes bibliographical references and index.
     ISBN 0-86698-241-8 (alk. paper)
     I. Carroll, Carleton W. II. Wilson, Lois Hawley. III. Title. IV. Title:
Resolute knight. V. Series: Medieval & Renaissance Texts & Studies (se-
ries) ; v. 199.
PQ1565.L2A6513 1999
841'.2—dc21   98–49199
                                                CIP

∞
This book is made to last.
It is set in Garamond,
smythe-sewn and printed on acid-free paper
to library specifications.

Printed in the United States of America

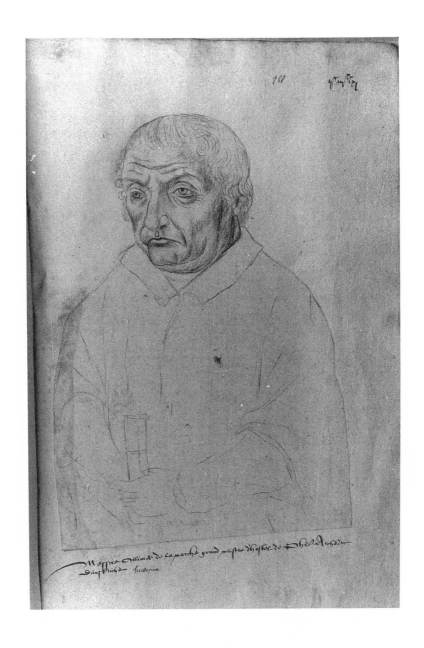

"Messire Olliuier de la marche grand maistre d'hostel de
Philippe Archiduc d'austriche historien."
Arras, Médiathèque municipale, ms. 266, folio 281.

Table of Contents

Introduction

Introduction

Le Chevalier delibere is the most important poetic work of Olivier de La Marche. In the late fifteenth century and through virtually all of the sixteenth it enjoyed great popularity, as evidenced by its reproduction in at least eighteen manuscripts and numerous printings in French as well as subsequent translations or adaptations into Spanish, Dutch, and English. There have been no modern critical editions or translations of the poem. A reprint appeared in 1842,[1] based on the undated text printed in Schiedam, Holland, near the end of the fifteenth century. The editor added the instructions for the illustration of the poem and claimed to have consulted four manuscripts and two other early editions, but he did not identify them; the work contains no notes or variants. The Schiedam text was reproduced in London in 1898[2] for the Bibliographical Society, with a brief preface, a summary of the poem, and an English translation of the author's directions for the illustration of the poem; it was again reprinted in Paris in 1923[3] with an introduction including a modern French version of those instructions and an extensive bibliography. A facsimile edition of the very imperfect 1488 Paris printing of the text was published by the Library of Congress in 1946.[4] All these facsimile editions are long out of print. As a result, the text is largely inaccessible and very little critical attention has been paid to it. This was an important text in its day and does not deserve the near-total oblivion into which it has fallen in recent times.

1.　　　*Olivier de La Marche*

Olivier de La Marche was a man of many talents who worked long and hard in the service of the Dukes of Burgundy. He "was the Burgundian

---

[1] See "Incunabula and other printed editions", Z.
[2] See Bibliography, La Marche.
[3] See Bibliography, Picot and Stein.
[4] See Bibliography, La Marche.

courtier *par excellence*. . . . everything except an official historian: page, equerry, steward and ambassador" (Vaughan, *Philip*, p. 158).

It is generally accepted that Olivier was born in 1422, in Villegaudin in Burgundy, the son of Philippe de La Marche and Jeanne Bouton (Stein, *Olivier*, p. 14). His father dying young, Olivier was given a position at court in return for services previously rendered by his father (Doutrepont, p. 445). He was made a page to Philip the Good and thereafter rose steadily: "page, stable squire, breadmaster, carver, head breadmaster, house steward, ambassador, warrior, poet, memorialist, crusade preacher, director of festivities, he belonged body, soul, and spirit to his dukes."[1] He was educated at the university at Dole, an institution established by Philip the Good; some of his expenses were defrayed by Philip's sister Catherine (Hexter, p. 60).

Molinet describes Olivier as "a man of short height, but of great prudence, plainly virtuous, rich in eloquence, with a keen and penetrating understanding."[2] Olivier did not serve solely from a feeling of duty, but also from a taste for a worldly and courtly life,[3] and was considered by some "Europe's foremost expert on noble households and etiquette" (Weightman, p. 29), even writing a treatise on court etiquette for the king of England entitled *L'État de la Maison du duc Charles de Bourgogne*. Among the various grand ceremonies that he staged was the marriage of Margaret of York to Charles the Bold (Calmette, p. 195). Olivier's epithet, by the way, for his foremost patron is not the usual one, Charles *le Téméraire*, but instead he calls him *le Traveillant*, meaning Hardworking or Assiduous.[4] Olivier is mentioned time and again leading troops in the wars waged by the Burgundian dukes. Stein comments that, when others were deserting Duke Charles and defecting to Louis XI, including

---

[1] Doutrepont, p. 446: "page, écuyer d'écurie, panetier, tranchant, premier panetier, maître d'hôtel, ambassadeur, guerrier, poète, mémorialiste, prêcheur de croisade, directeur de fêtes, il appartient, corps, âme et esprit, à ses ducs."

[2] Molinet, quoted by Stein, *Olivier*, p. 98: "Olivier de la Marche, très pieux et hardi chevalier de Bourgogne, était homme de petite stature, mais de très grande prudence, cler en vertu, riche en éloquence et de vif et pénétrant entendement."

[3] Calmette, *Grands Ducs*, p. 316: "C'est qu'il n'a pas servi par devoir seulement. Son goût le portait à la vie mondaine et courtoise." (English translation, p. 230: "He did not serve the duke from a sense of duty only; he was by nature a man who loved society and Court life.")

[4] *Mémoires*, I, 147: "pour riens n'a pas esté nommé Charles le Traveillant, car d'autant qu'il regna aultre homme ne traveilla tant en sa personne qu'il fist" ([it was] not without reason that he was called 'Charles the Assiduous,' for as long as he reigned no other man worked as hard as he did). See line 249.5. The notation "249.5" stands for stanza 249, line 5. This convention is used throughout.

Molinet who praised him so highly, Olivier remained steadfastly loyal.[5] Beaune and d'Arbaumont say that he inherited this loyalty from his family.[6]

Olivier fought and was taken prisoner at Nancy, the battle where Charles was killed. After the death of the last of the great Burgundian dukes, Olivier entered the service of Maximilian of Austria, husband of Mary of Burgundy, Charles's daughter, and performed faithfully until very old. One of his last important duties was as preceptor for Philip the Fair of Burgundy, son of Maximilian and Mary, to whom Olivier dedicated his *Mémoires*. In these, Olivier says that he has reached the point in his life where, like the deer or roebuck, it is time to lie on the fresh grass, to browse there and ruminate on and enjoy the taste of his cud. "And meanwhile, among my bitter tastes, I find an assuagement and a wondrous substance in the grass called memory, which alone makes me forget troubles, travails, miseries and afflictions."[7] He brings this same theme to *Le Chevalier deliberé* where Fresh Memory (stanzas 142–143) is described as a beautiful princess in whom all pleasure and solace can be found. Olivier concludes the poem with his motto, *Tant a souffert*, and his portrait, preserved in manuscript No. 266 of the Bibliothèque Municipale in Arras, does not seem to show a happy man. However, Christine Weightman says in her Epilogue (p. 218) that this was "the fashionable melancholia, the pious gloom which led the far from gloomy Olivier de La Marche to adopt [this] as his device...." Huizinga describes this attitude of the nobles of the time as "a sentimental need of enrobing their souls with the garb of woe."[8]

These *Mémoires*, which he describes as being written late in life (he is 61 when he says this), are famous for their descriptions of court life and particularly of the campaigns and tournaments in which its members participated. They have been of incalculable help in sorting out many of the persons memorialized in this poem, although as Weightman

---

[5] Stein, *Olivier*, pp. 51–52: Olivier "resta fidèle. ... Mettre en suspicion la bonne foi d'Olivier de la Marche nous semble impossible."

[6] Beaune and d'Arbaumont, eds., *Mémoires*, IV, XII, speaking of Olivier: "C'est de son aïeul ... qu'il tient la loyauté, le dévouement à toute épreuve, le culte de l'honneur et de la personne de ses maîtres" (quoted by Doutrepont, p. 445).

[7] *Mémoires*, I, 186: "Et toutesfois, entre mes amers goutz, je treuve un assouagement et une substance à merveilles grande, en une herbe qui s'apelle memoire, que celle seulle me fait oblier paines, travaulx, miseres et afflictions."

[8] *Waning*, p. 34. *Autumn*: "All the examples of the nobility's mood of life testify to a sentimental need for a dark costume for the soul" (pp. 33–34).

points out, "like most of the writers of the period [Olivier] was totally indifferent to chronology" (p. 30). Doutrepont declares that Olivier and Chastellain were "the two exponents *par excellence* of the knightly and worldly life of the court"[9] and Dahmus says that Olivier's writings, "although somewhat partisan and lacking the perceptivity of his contemporary Philippe de Commines, possess considerable historical value. Like Jean Froissart, he proved himself an eloquent spokesman for the tradition of chivalry" (p. 424).

When Olivier died in 1502, after a long and active life, his literary legacy included his *Mémoires* and *Le Chevalier deliberé*. The former is important for its view of the external life and times of a renowned fifteenth-century man, while the latter gives glimpses of his concern for his life in that other eternal world.

2.   *Summary and Evaluation of the Poem*

Le Chevalier deliberé is a didactic poem describing a knight's search for salvation through the vehicle of a quest. At first he is impulsive, leaving his house *par une soudaine achoison,* on the spur of the moment. He is started along the way by Thought, who brings him to a realization of his soul's unprepared state and who acquaints him with the encounters he must face with the henchmen of Atropos, Goddess of Death: Accident and Debility. The knight as Author is befriended by the hermit Understanding and eventually arrives at the house of Study where Fresh Memory begins his real instruction.

The Author sees himself as a pilgrim whose primary reward will be difficulties (25.5). In *The Epic Quest*, William Calin says, "The active external metaphor of the quest is but a representation of every man's internal struggle and growth through life ... and a pilgrimage a form of *transitus* from this life to the next" (p. 57). In order to accomplish this quest, "Man must learn to suffer, to merit grace. Without knowledge of what is expected by God, even the best intentioned will stray from the right path. Hence the importance of the 'theme of knowing' " (p. 108). In this poem the Author moves forward in his search, going from doubt and unsure direction to firm resolve and preparedness. He loses battles

---

[9] Doutrepont, p. 443: "Les deux *expositeurs* par excellence de la vie chevaleresque et mondaine de la cour."

along the way to Quarreler and Age, but continues to seek the way with Fresh Memory and Understanding.

The poem is heavily allegorical, in an age when allegory was a very real presence in people's minds: "To the men of the Middle Ages,... these [allegorical] figures had a very vivid æsthetic and sentimental value ... [and were] often called in to express a thought of particular importance.... [They] had a suggestive force which we find it very hard to realize" (Huizinga, pp. 210–11).[1] The Author takes up his lance, Venture, and sets out. His first battle is with Quarreler, whose lance is named Little Sense. Both lances are broken, a metaphor for the results of a quarrel. The Author is saved only by a final burst of returning youth in the allegorical form of a young maiden, and continues on his way.

His next meeting is with the hermit Understanding, who tells him that he too was once a knight but has retired from the "sea of inconstant life" (33.7) to a life of contemplation. He leads the author to his small chapel, *moult devote, plaisant et belle* (28.8), where all the furnishings are personifications of virtues. He shows the Author the relics he has collected, artifacts of previous violent deaths, and names the killer: Accident. The feats of Debility are deferred until another time.

During their visit, Understanding offers to give the Author a new lance, tipped with Authority (40), and with this the Author goes on his way and encounters Age. With his sword, Too Many Days, Age smashes Authority and the Author must give himself up, promising on his honor as a knight to forego youthful activities—dancing, love, courtly ambition, frivolous pursuits, and jousts—and is given liberty to continue his quest. Alas, he still has difficulty finding the right way and strays onto the path of Delusion, where everything is green and young and the future is his:

Abuz est restaurant de vie.	Delusion is the restorer of life.
La je rentray en fantasie	In fantasy I returned there
Des haulx plaisirs de mon jouvant	To the great pleasures of my youth
Et oubliay le demourant.	And forgot everything else. (105.5–8)

---

[1] *Autumn*, p. 244: "for the people of the time they [= allegorical figures] were realities clothed in living form and imbued with passion.... This was obviously the way to make an impression, something that we will find understandable if we realize that allegory still served a very vital function in the thought of those times."

The Author arrives at the Palace of Love (113.8), whose porter is Illusion. Desire comes to the gate to tempt him to enter, but he is saved by Remembrance, who asks if he wishes to forswear his knightly oath to Age (114.6–8). Thus reminded, the Author leaves, asking them to forget that he was ever there, and passes through a distressing place called Decrepitude (126.1). He finally arrives at Good Fortune (134.8), a beautiful place in which to study and remember. Here he meets Fresh Memory, who shows him the tombs of departed worthies and who once again summons Understanding to instruct him in how to prepare for his final battles.

"Medieval chivalry at its best was a sacred institution consecrated by religious rites and dedicated to the service of God and the defence of the church" (Dawson, pp. 176–77). Understanding's tutelage of the knight consists in telling him how he must arm and train himself to resist the temptations of flesh and spirit, to make himself right with the Church's teachings and with God, to prepare to die in God's grace. The armor is allegorical as well: the helm is made by Dame Temperance; obviously the perfect knight can not be hotheaded. His tassets, the lower extension of his cuirass, are of Consummate Chastity (289).

Written six years after the death of Charles the Bold at the siege of Nancy, where Olivier himself was taken prisoner, this poem salutes him as well as others of the house of Burgundy who were his patrons. Enthusiastically received, it offered, in allegorical form, "wisely moral precepts as well as particularly interesting ideas about the knightly combats and the undertakings of the principal Burgundian lords of the fifteenth century."[2] The era of the grand dukes of Burgundy has ended and the feats of chivalry that Olivier celebrates are already an anachronism, but he memorializes those he deems worthy, in lists that may seem long to the modern reader. The work can arguably be considered a lament, not only for those dead knights but also for a time that has passed.

The tone of the poem is fittingly somber and Huizinga remarks that "always and everywhere in the literature of the age, we find a confessed pessimism" (*Waning*, p. 37).[3] Furthermore, "the mind of world-denying medieval man had always liked to dwell amidst dust and worms....

---

[2] Stein, *Olivier*, p. 124: "[*Le Chevalier deliberé*] peut être considéré ... comme offrant, sous la forme allégorique, des préceptes d'une sage morale ainsi que des notions particulièrement intéressantes sur les combats chevaleresques et les *emprinses* des principaux seigneurs bourguignons du XVᵉ siècle."

[3] The text of *Autumn* is not parallel at this point; compare p. 36, "Daily reality is viewed in terms of the deepest depression whenever the childlike joy of life or blind hedonism gives way to meditation. Where is that more beautiful world for which every age is bound to yearn?"

Until late in the sixteenth century, gravestones depict the disgustingly varied notion of the naked corpse, with cramped hands and feet, gaping mouth, with worms writhing in the intestines" (*Autumn*, p. 159).[4] Olivier's style is considered by some a reflection of the tastes of the Burgundian court, which Huizinga characterizes as heavy and flowery, pompous, turgid, formal, and somewhat elephantine (*Waning*, p. 284; *Autumn*, p. 342). Elegiac in principle, the poem contains touching passages, as when the author describes the little caged bird singing to forget his troubles (132); or when he tells of the "messengers" of Debility who will come step by step: eyes that dim, ears that need to be stopped up, the flesh, which has been so tenderly nourished, needing to be propped up, etc. (330–333).

He ends by telling the reader that the book has been finished in April, with winter in exile and summer doing its work. Consequently, while the poem is a celebration of finality, it ends with an affirmation of continuity.

The surviving manuscripts of *Le Chevalier delibere* range from the hastily-scrawled and amateurish to the costly professional copy, replete with lavish decorations and colorful illuminations. Within a few years of its composition it was taken up by the still-young printing industry, both in France and elsewhere, and made known to far greater numbers of readers through subsequent printings spanning more than five decades. Finally, its popularity spread beyond the domain of the French language, as translations or adaptations into Spanish, Dutch, and English continued to be produced until late in the sixteenth century.[5] That it slipped into subsequent obscurity is hardly surprising: tastes change, and it is the rare work of literature that enjoys sustained popularity beyond a century or so following its composition.[6]

---

[4] Compare *Waning*, p. 140: "Ascetic meditation had, in all ages, dwelt on dust and worms. . . . Until far into the sixteenth century, tombs are adorned with hideous images of a naked corpse with clenched hands and rigid feet, gaping mouth and bowels crawling with worms."

[5] Picot and Stein, *Recueil*, pp. 322–45. The first printed version produced in Paris was that of Antoine Vérard, 1488; a version printed in Gouda is undated but may have been printed as early as 1486 (Mongan, Intro., p. xiv). The latest printed edition listed by Picot and Stein is *The Resolved Gentleman*, "translated out of Spanishe into English by Lewes Lewkenor, Esquier", published in London in 1594.

[6] Calin, "Inventing the Medieval Canon": "[A]s a general rule, the medieval vernacular public treasured fashionable contemporary writing and a literary heritage from the relatively recent past. With the unique exception of *le Roman de la Rose*, the canonicity, or simply the reception, of a medieval text or author lasted one century at the maximum. After a century, the work simply was no longer read, or, if read, no longer esteemed."

The comments of modern critics, when they have mentioned Olivier de La Marche or *Le Chevalier deliberé* at all, have rarely been positive. Henri Stein, author of the first and still most extensive study of Olivier's life and works, set the tone that many others were to follow: "The poet is far beneath the chronicler. Whether he devotes himself to political, epic, or lyric poetry, to while away his leisure time or to accomplish a mission, inspiration is too often unknown to him, verve is lacking."[7] Gaston Paris, in his *Esquisse historique*, groups *Le Chevalier deliberé* among the "didactic works of value only to those curious about old mores", where "*le bon Olivier de la Marche*", in the form of fashionable allegories and symbols, paints a tableau of the virtues that are to make the men and women of high society dear to God and to the world.[8] Robert Bossuat sees Olivier "cultivating in turn the epic and the lyric genre, political poetry and courtly poetry", but "despite so many efforts he achieves only mediocre results. He strove to be a poet and was barely a *rhétoriqueur*."[9] Pierre Champion, in a study with the promising title *Histoire poétique du quinzième siècle*, announces that he has "deliberately set aside Olivier de La Marche" and some other poets of the fifteenth century.[10] Similarly, one might expect that our poem might figure prominently in a work entitled *Le Thème de la mort dans la poésie française de 1450 à 1550*, but the author, Christine Martineau-Génieys, excludes Olivier's poem from her study, claiming that, at the date when he was writing, "taking up themes treated by Michault and Montgesoie was to be behind the times" and so, her goal being to see an evolution taking shape, she sets aside "those who were unable to create along with their times."[11]

---

[7] Stein, *Olivier*, p. 123: "Le poète est loin de valoir le chroniqueur. Que ce soit à la poésie politique, à la poésie épique ou à la poésie lyrique qu'il s'adonne pour charmer ses loisirs ou pour remplir une mission, l'inspiration lui est trop souvent inconnue, la verve manque."

[8] Paris, *Esquisse historique*, p. 257: "Joignons ici des œuvres également didactiques qui n'ont de prix que pour le curieux des vieilles mœurs : *Le Chevalier délibéré* et le *Parement des Dames*, où le bon Olivier de la Marche trace aux hommes et aux femmes de la haute société, sous les allégories et les symboles à la mode, un tableau des vertus qui doivent les rendre chers à Dieu et au monde."

[9] Bossuat, *Poésie lyrique*, p. 242: "Cultivant tour à tour le genre épique et le genre lyrique, la poésie politique et la poésie courtoise, il ne parvient malgré tant d'efforts qu'à de médiocres résultats. Il s'efforça d'être poète et ce fut à peine un rhétoriqueur."

[10] Champion, *Histoire poétique*, Avant-propos, p. ix: "De propos délibéré nous avons écarté Olivier de la Marche [...]"

[11] Martineau-Génieys, *Thème de la mort*, p. 258: "[*Le Pas de la Mort* d'Amé de Montgesoie] inspira [à Olivier de La Marche] son *Chevalier délibéré*. Mais nous n'étudierons pas ici cette œuvre, bien qu'elle touche à notre sujet, car à la date où écrit Olivier de la

It must be said that a number of literary historians have substantially misrepresented the work, as in the case of Geoffrey Brereton, in his *Short History*, who informs the reader that "the author's patron, Charles the Bold of Burgundy, is presented as a knight-errant moving among allegorical figures and exploits" (p. 41). The attribution of a central role to Duke Charles seems to have originated with some of the early printed versions of the text, e.g., that printed by Jean Lambert (Paris, 1493), where the title reads *Le Chevalier Delibere Comprenant la Mort du Duc de Bourgongne qui trespassa deuant Nancy en Lorraine* (*The Resolute Knight, Containing the Death of the Duke of Burgundy who Died During the Siege of Nancy in Lorraine*). According to Picot and Stein (pp. 334–38), this same wording appears in all but the first of the early French editions (Paris: Vérard, 1488), and it was reproduced in the 1842 Paris edition. Stein declared that Charles was "the hero" of the poem (*Olivier*, p. 124); this misleading affirmation is also found in Bossuat (*Poésie lyrique*, pp. 242–43), while Molinier affirms that the poem was composed "in honor of Charles the Bold" (*Sources*, V, 45, § 4746). Although Dufournet is somewhat more accurate, saying that in this work Olivier "mournfully sings the praises of Charles of Burgundy,"[12] it is nonetheless misleading to suggest that the author singles him out, since only fourteen stanzas (236–249) can be said to be devoted to the last of the dukes.[13] Finally, some studies affirm that the poem consists of 248 stanzas, but this is totally inaccurate.[14]

* * *

Marche, reprendre les thèmes traités par Michault et Montgesoie, c'est être un attardé. Or systématiquement, en fonction de notre but qui est de voir se dessiner une évolution, nous écartons de notre étude ceux qui n'ont pas su créer avec leur temps."

[12] Dufournet, *Dictionnaire*, p. 451: "A ce poète, de cour, sans grande inspiration ni beaucoup d'adresse, on doit, entre autres œuvres, *le Chevalier Délibéré* (1483) où, sous forme allégorique, il chante avec mélancolie Charles de Bourgogne."

[13] Perhaps the most extraordinary case of misrepresentation is to be found in Rosemond Tuve's *Allegorical Imagery* (p. 387). Speaking of Book III of *The Faerie Queen*, she affirms that Spenser "does a little of that rather decadent literalizing of metaphors which we find in others; the bleeding heart separated from the body is an image of late romance (the mainstay of the plan and of the illustrations of Olivier de la Marche's *Chevalier deliberé* . . .)." Similarly misleading is Charles Aubrun's statement that the poem is dedicated to Philippe le Beau (review of Clavería, p. 430).

[14] The error apparently originated with Stein, *Olivier*, p. 124: "*Le chevalier délibéré* est un poème allégorique . . . composé de 248 octaves en vers de 8 syllabes." This erroneous figure is repeated in *Chantilly, Le Cabinet des livres* (II, 105) and by Molinier (*Sources*, V, 45, 4746) and Bossuat (*Poésie lyrique*, 242–43). Brunet, *Manuel*, gives the figure 238, and Thiry, *Splendeurs*, calls the poem "une allégorie de 1968 vers" (p. 957), i.e., 246 stanzas.

Le Chevalier deliberé follows two literary traditions that marked the latter Middle Ages. The first is the taste for allegory, which can be traced back at least as far as the *Romance of the Rose*. But while our poem makes abundant use of allegorical figures, it is distinctive in that it does not anchor its narrative within the framework of a dream or vision (La Vigne, *Ressource*, ed. Brown, p. 28 and note 1). The second tradition is the widespread focus on death and dying which permeated late medieval literature and art, especially that of the fifteenth century.[15] An in-depth study of that theme would not be in order here; it may suffice to evoke such works as François Villon's *Testament* and the *Danse macabre*.[16] The primary theme of *Le Chevalier deliberé* is the inevitability of death and the best way to prepare for it in the context of the Christian religion. In this connection the poem mentions a large number of famous figures and in many cases tells how they died. These include characters from classical literature, the Bible, mythology, and medieval literature, as well as numerous historical figures, both from earlier epochs and from the author's own recent past. These vignettes constitute a veritable miniature encyclopedia, and, along with the author-narrator's philosophical musings, reveal a fascinating insight into the mentality and attitudes of the late fifteenth century.

Olivier de La Marche probably did not consider himself first and foremost a poet, and one may certainly debate the literary merits of the present work. We cannot deny that it contains some weak lines and passages of awkward syntax. But at the same time it has moments of poetic inspiration which, if they do not rise to greatness or grandeur, at least manage to touch the reader with their sincerity of expression. In his *Medieval Romance*, John Stevens affirms, "As in all our dealings with the Middle Ages—or, for that matter, with any period remote from our own—we find that the most important question to ask is *not*, straightaway, 'What is this worth to me?' but 'What was this worth to *them*?' Systems of thought, patterns of feeling, codes of behaviour, styles in literature and art—in a word, conventions—are not invented for their

---

[15] Huizinga, *Waning*, particularly Chapter I, "The Violent Tenor of Life", and Chapter XI, "The Vision of Death"; *Autumn*, Chapter One, "The Passionate Intensity of Life", and Chapter Five, "The Vision of Death".

[16] Olivier focused on this theme again in *Le Triumphe des dames* (also known as *Le Parement et triumphe des dames*), composed around 1492, particularly stanzas 161–178. Huizinga traces the development of the *ubi sunt* theme, mentioning Deschamps, Gerson, Denis the Carthusian, and Chastellain, as well as La Marche and Villon: *Waning*, pp. 139–40; *Autumn*, pp. 156–59.

own sake and do not maintain their life on those terms. They come into being because they are needed. They are needed, primarily, for explanation; they are needed to order experience, to impose meaning on life" (pp. 29–30).[17] It is our hope that this edition and translation of *Le Chevalier deliberé* will help the modern reader to better understand the world-view of the late Middle Ages.

3.   *Versification and Style*

VERSIFICATION

i. Rhyme-scheme

The poem is composed entirely in octosyllabic lines arranged in eight-line stanzas rhyming *abaabbcc*. This rhyme-scheme was fairly popular during the second half of the fifteenth century; various examples may be found in the works of Georges Chastellain, whom Molinet calls its *principal inventeur*, and in those of other poets of the time.[1] Olivier himself had already used this same rhyme-scheme in his *Complainte sur la mort de Madame Marie de Bourgongne*, a poem in octosyllabic lines (1482), and was to use it again, with decasyllabic lines, in his *Triumphe des dames* (1493 or 1494, according to Stein, *Olivier*, p. 125), in the *Doctrine et loz pour madame Alienor* (also known as *Les Cinq Sens*), perhaps composed near the end of his life (Stein, *Olivier*, p. 128), and in an untitled and undated single-stanza poem found in manuscript *L* (published by Veinant, 1842, and Stein, *Olivier*, p. 229).

---

[17] Compare Roach, ed., *Melusine*, 15–16: "[I]l est clair que pour l'histoire de la pensée et de la culture d'une époque, l'œuvre d'un poète peu doué qui a eu une diffusion importante au siècle de sa composition est beaucoup plus intéressante qu'un texte de haute valeur littéraire ignoré de ses contemporains." (It is clear that for the history of thought and culture of a [past] era, the work of a less gifted poet which was widely distributed in its own time is much more interesting than a text of great literary value that was unknown to its contemporaries.)

[1] Langlois, *Recueil*, pp. 220–21. Among Chastellain's poems composed on this model: *Le Miroir de Mort* (also known as *Le Pas de la Mort*, not to be confused with Amé de Montgesoie's poem) and *L'Oultré d'Amour*, both using octosyllabic lines, and *Le Thrône azuré*, *Le Dit de Vérité*, and two *Epistres*, all using decasyllabic lines. A portion of André de La Vigne's *Ressource de la Chrestienté* was also composed on this rhyme-scheme. H. Chatelain, *Recherches* (pp. 101, 103, 252–53, 256–57) mentions other poems using the rhyme-scheme *abaabbcc*.

ii. Rhymes

Several of the treatises gathered in the *Recueil d'arts de seconde rhétorique* mention *equivocques*, i.e., rhymes based on two meanings or uses of a single word, such as *avoir* (noun or verb, etymologically related) or a rhyme involving two homographs, such as *nuit* (noun or verb, not etymologically related). This poetic device can be traced back at least to the latter twelfth century, when Chrétien de Troyes made abundant use of it. Olivier shows a moderate fondness for these homographic rhymes. Of 1,014 "rhyme-groups" (three per stanza), 47 involve identical written forms in *C*; to these we may legitimately add another five, in which only inconsequential differences in spelling distinguish the two rhyming words. Thus, just over 5 percent of the poem's rhymes fall into this category. In three cases (stanzas 17, 36, and 96) the same form is used for three rhymes. Most of the time there is the expected difference between the words thus used, i.e., the poet does not rhyme a word with itself. Frequently this involves a noun and a verb, e.g., *soye* and *mort*, both in stanza 5. There are cases, however, where the rhyme really does seem to involve the same word used twice, as in the case of *erré*, stanza 109, or *place*, stanza 128.

Two of the treatises in the *Recueil*[2] also mention a second type of *equivocque*, in which the rhyming portion of one or both lines involves two or more words. Generally referred to nowadays as *rime équivoquée*, this sort of punning rhyme was much used by some of Olivier's contemporaries among the *Rhétoriqueurs*. We find just four examples of this technique in the present poem: 60.2:5, *Cartaige : quart age* (see the note to this line); 72.7:8, *monstra : monstre a*; 184.1:4, *Milan : mis l'an*; 265.7:8, *a fin : affin*.

On the other hand, it seems that Olivier was sometimes satisfied with more facile rhymes. In addition to the identical rhymes mentioned above, Olivier sometimes rhymes a word with a compound based upon it, as in stanza 14, where *je raconte* rhymes with *je vous compte*, or bases a rhyme on a grammatical ending, as in stanza 4: *clerement : entierement : pareillement*.

---

[2] Jacques Legrand, *Des Rimes* (c. 1405), p. 3, and Anon., *L'Art et science de rhétorique* (c. 1524–25), pp. 316–17.

STYLE

Without attempting an in-depth analysis of the style of the poem, we may say that it is generally undistinguished, perhaps because the author was concentrating more on the moralizing and didactic substance of his work than on its form. There are occasional weak lines, containing more filler than substance, such as 77.8, *Qui ressembloit estre bien grande*, and the relative clause of 150.1, *Je viz en ce drap qui fut beau*. On the other hand, there are series of oxymorons, characteristic of Renaissance poetry, as in 73.3–7, 94.3–4, and 215.4–5. The extended metaphor of *l'oisel qui chante* in stanza 132 is rather striking, and stanzas 265 and 266 reveal the depth of Olivier's personal feeling concerning the deaths of the last three members of the House of Burgundy (mentioned by Veinant in the afterword to his reprinting of the poem).

Olivier makes relatively little use of strong enjambment, but examples can be found, as in 5.6–7, 16.4–5, 33.6–7, 38.6–7, 120.4–5, 151.4–5, 170.6–7, 203.2–3, 229.4–5, 231.6–7, 244.4–5, 245.4–5, and 323.4–5. Other examples could no doubt be added to this list. In contrast, Olivier's stanzas often present a strong pause at the end of the fifth line, effectively dividing the stanza into two unequal parts. There seems to be only one instance of sentence structure continuing from the end of one stanza to the next, joining stanzas 155 and 156.

Finally, we may mention what appear to be various types of poetic license. The first of these involves two cases where a form must be given an unexpected treatment in order to obtain an octosyllabic line. In line 37.7, the word *eage* can count for only two syllables, rather than the usual three; in line 181.5, *messire* must also be read as a two-syllable word, despite the presence of an initial consonant in the following word. Second-person singular verbs constitute a particular class of words subject to manipulation: Olivier occasionally uses the expected *-es* ending (8.6, 302.7) but more frequently the verb ends in *-e*. This may be to achieve the necessary rhythm, as in *tu pense adés*, 9.6, or—and this is more often the case—for reasons of rhyme, as in 94.2 (*tu te boute*) and elsewhere; see note to 99.2.

Our poet makes more extensive use of another type of poetic license, involving lack of grammatical agreement between parts of speech, again for reasons of rhythm or rhyme, and sometimes both together. Thus we find non-agreement of verb with subject (5.1), adjective with noun (7.4), and noun with adjective (60.7). Past participle agreement is inconsistent, generally observed but sometimes not (210.7, 251.3, etc.). Many more examples could be cited of each type of non-agreement. Readers of Olivier's time may have been more tolerant of such poetic license than was to be the case for later generations.

4.   *Title, Date, Author*

Both title and date are furnished by the text itself, the former in line 337.8 and the latter—the end of April, 1483—in lines 338.1–3. The sense of *deliberé* may be revealed to some extent by its use in *Le Triumphe des dames*. In prose section XII, line 71 (p. 44, Kalbfleisch ed.), Olivier refers to Judith as *Ceste dame deliberee de afranchir la chité de sa nativité*; and Olivier begins section XVI thus: *Il n'a pas guaire de temps que je ouys ung graciëulx compte au propos de devote memoire, et suis deliberé de le couchier presentement pour exemple en l'avertissement de toutes dames et de celles qui se present volume liront* (p. 59). In her glossary, p. 116, Kalbfleisch gives *entscheiden, beschliessen* as equivalents, both of which can be rendered as "decide" or "resolve" (to do something). See also Rickard, *Chrestomathie (Glossaire)* and Greimas-Keane.

There is no real dispute concerning the authorship of the poem (although one late manuscript attributes the work to Georges Chastellain). In six manuscripts (*BCORTW*) the author's name directly follows the concluding line of the poem, in the same hand as the text. It also appears, at least obliquely, by means of word-play on the words *la marche* in stanzas 36 and 337. This word-play is present in most manuscripts, but is at least partially missing from stanza 36 in the case of manuscript *L* and printed versions *Ai*, *M*, and Lambert. Cynthia J. Brown discusses a similar phenomenon in the case of various versions of André de La Vigne's *La Ressource de la Chrestienté*.

5.   *Manuscripts and Editions;*
              Manuscript Relations

MANUSCRIPTS

For each manuscript we give the following details:
1. Siglum, city, library, manuscript number (Former identification is limited to cases where the geographical location has changed.)
2. Contents of the manuscript (complete unless otherwise indicated)
3. Foliation, material (parchment or paper), date(s) and source(s) for

same. When Picot and Stein (1923) give the same date as Stein, *Olivier* (1888) or Stein, *Nouveaux Documents* (1922/26), the source is indicated as "Stein".

For the text of *Le Chevalier delibéré* we indicate
4. Lacunae, if any; out-of-order stanzas, if any.
5. Layout, in terms of stanzas or lines per side. When the number of lines varies, the range is given. These figures are for pages containing exclusively verse text, i.e., with neither rubrics nor illustrations. Catchwords, if any.
6. Decoration, rubrics, miniatures.
7. Bibliographical references, in short-title form and in chronological order. See Bibliography for full details.

A Paris, Bibliothèque de l'Arsenal, 5117
   1r–62v OLIVIER DE LA MARCHE, *Le Chevalier delibéré*
   63r two notes concerning the poem
   I + 63 + I leaves, parchment and paper. 15th and 18th centuries (Stein, *Catalogue*).

Several leaves were removed from the original manuscript, presumably for the miniatures they contained. The missing text was supplied in the eighteenth century, copied from the version printed by Michel Le Noir (Paris, c. 1512). The folios in question, and their contents, are as follows:

Folios	Contents
1	stanza 2, missing from the original manuscript
5	stanzas 16–19
7–10	stanzas 24*a* and 26–50; rubric preceding stanza 51
15	stanzas 73–76
47–48	stanzas 248–262, including the rubric preceding stanza 256

Readings from these 50 stanzas and the accompanying rubrics are identified in the variants by the siglum *Ai* and are grouped with readings from other printed sources.

The original manuscript is generally three stanzas per side (exceptionally 22 lines). The 18th-century portions contain 29–34 lines per side (generally four stanzas).

Decorated initials (gold on red or blue background); rubrics. Ten miniatures of what was in all probability a complete program in the original manuscript (missing: Nos. 3, 4, 5, 7, and 13). The remaining miniatures are of excellent artistic quality, though a few are partially damaged. Nos. 1, 6, 9, 10, and 11 are reproduced by means of woodcuts in Lacroix, *Sciences et lettres*; photographs of No. 9 can be found in Martin & Lauer, *Les Principaux Manuscrits*, pl. LXXIX (description, pp. 56–57), and in Bossuat, *Moyen Age*, facing page 296.

References
> Stein, *Olivier*, p. 141, No. 5.
> Martin, *Catalogue ... Arsenal*, V: 67.
> Picot and Stein, *Recueil*, p. 320, No. 5.

B Oxford, Bodleian, Douce 168
> 1r–65r OLIVIER DE LA MARCHE, *Le Chevalier delibéré*
> 65v blank
> 66r–79r Amé de Montgesoie, *Le Pas de la Mort*
> 79v–83v blank
> IV + 83 leaves, paper. Perhaps second half 16th century (Madan); 17th century (Stein, *Olivier*); mid 16th century (Pächt and Alexander).
> No lacunae.
> Three stanzas per side.

Large initials and rubrics, in same ink as text. Fifteen miniatures (grisaille). Most are parallel to the written instructions (see Appendix), but there is nothing corresponding to No. 5; the fifth through seventh miniatures correspond to our Nos. 6–8; the eighth miniature corresponds to nothing in the written instructions. No. 15 reproduced, approx. 1/3 size, in Pächt and Alexander, pl. XXXIII, No. 403 (who list this among the Flemish manuscripts).

Frequent use of apostrophe and occasional accentuation. Both are sometimes mis-applied, e.g., "Q'uont", 4.7; "c'este" for *ceste*, 34.7 and elsewhere; "s'cay", 37.3; "Q'uung" 44.7; "c'est" for *cest*, 54.6 and elsewhere; "L'alain" 181.5; "D'oncq" for *Donc* 248.1; "m'est" for *mest* 251.1; "C'elle" 294.1; "Q'u Adam" 318.3; "qu'este" for *queste* 337.3; "à" for *a* as *passé composé* auxiliary: 5.8 and elsewhere; "à" for present indicative, *avoir*, 135.3, 329.4; "estés" and "escoutté" for *estes* and *escoutte*, 16.5. We have not included these misplaced apostrophes and accents in the variant readings.

References
> Stein, *Olivier*, p. 141, No. 10.
> Madan, *Summary Catalogue*, No. 21742.

Picot and Stein, *Recueil*, p. 321, No. 12.

Pächt and Alexander, *Illuminated Manuscripts*, pp. 30 and 101, No. 403.

C Chantilly, Musée Condé 507

Numbering is by page, rather than by folio.

1 blank

2 full-page miniature (unrelated to the text) featuring the arms of Louis Malet de Graville, French admiral (died 1516), an early owner of the manuscript

3–102 OLIVIER DE LA MARCHE, *Le Chevalier deliberé*

II + 102 pages + III, vellum. 15th century (*Cabinet des livres*; *Catalogue général*; Stein, *Nouveaux Documents*).

No lacunae.

30 or 31 lines per side.

Decorated initials; rubrics. A paragraph sign marks the beginning of each stanza, with the exception of stanzas 46 and 224. These are, for the most part, alternately blue with red tendrils and gold with blue tendrils, but there are frequent cases of two consecutive signs of the same color, usually preceding the last stanza on one page and the first stanza on the following page. When a page ends with the first line of a stanza and lines 2–8 are at the top of the following page, a duplicate paragraph sign occasionally precedes line 2 (stanzas 6, 142, 211, and 338, but not stanzas 42, 66, 86, 95, 123, 173, 192, 235, 244, 280, 300, 319). Complete program of 15 miniatures, in excellent condition and of very fine artistic quality ("*école de Bourgogne*"). Floral borders, incorporating either a realistic bird (six cases) or a grotesque (nine), on pages with miniatures.

This is the base manuscript for the present edition. See other sections of the Introduction for a discussion of linguistic and scribal features.

References

[Not listed in Stein, *Olivier*.]

Chantilly. Cabinet des livres. Manuscrits. T. II, pp. 103–105.

Stein, *Nouveaux Documents*, p. 16, No. 14.

Picot and Stein, *Recueil*, p. 320, No. 6.

Catalogue général, p. 111.

Murgey de Tupigny, *Principaux Manuscrits à peintures ... Chantilly*, p. XVI.

Michel, "Trois Magnifiques Ouvrages," 430–34, particularly 431–32.

Samaran and Marichal, *Catalogue*, 1: 35.

E Edinburgh, National Library of Scotland, Adv. MS. 19.1.8
   1r–56r OLIVIER DE LA MARCHE, *Le Chevalier deliberé*
   II + 56 + II leaves, parchment. Late 15th to early 16th century (*Summary Catalogue*).
   No lacunae. Stanzas 167–172 appear between stanzas 196 and 197.
   24–26 lines per side.

Decorated initials; rubrics. Ten miniatures (none corresponding to Nos. 3, 5, 7, 14, and 15); different subjects in Nos. 1 and 13. The subjects that do correspond to the instructions (see Appendix) often diverge significantly from them. Artistic quality inferior to that of *A* or *C*; some smudged or washed-out areas, particularly faces. Unidentified arms, 1r; motto, AU PERDRE GAIN, incorporated into frame of miniatures, 1r, 16r, 27r, and 36v.

References
   Meyer, "Deuxième Rapport," 139.
   Stein, *Olivier*, p. 141, No. 11.
   Picot and Stein, *Recueil*, p. 322, No. 14.
   National Library of Scotland, *Summary Catalogue*, p. 104, No. 1327.

F Cambridge, Fitzwilliam Museum, MS. 166
   1r–62r OLIVIER DE LA MARCHE, *Le Chevalier deliberé*
   62 + I leaves, vellum. 15th century (1490, *Catalogue*, Stein).
   No lacunae. Because of an error in binding, several groups of stanzas
      are out of order, as follows:

Folio	Contents
26	133–138
27	145–150
28	139–144
29	157, miniature No. 10, 158–160
30	151–156
31	161–166

Three stanzas per side.

Decorated initials; rubrics. Complete program of 15 miniatures, mostly in excellent condition and of very good artistic quality. All but No. 1 (knight in armor, holding a book, standing before lists) correspond to the written instructions (see Appendix), with some discrepancies of detail. Floral borders surround each miniature and the accompanying text. Arms of Albret, 1r.

References
> [Not listed in Stein, *Olivier.*]
> James, *Descriptive Catalogue*, pp. 366–68.
> Stein, *Nouveaux Documents*, pp. 15–16, No. 13.
> Picot and Stein, *Recueil*, p. 321–22, No. 13.
> Sutch, "Production."

G Paris, Société des Manuscrits des Assureurs Français (S.M.A.F.), ms. 80-11 (formerly Berlin, Königlichen Bibliothek, Gall. fol. 177)
> 1r–39r GUILLEBERT DE LANNOY, *L'Instruction d'un jeune prince*
> 39v–100v OLIVIER DE LA MARCHE, *Le Chevalier deliberé*

I + 100 + I leaves, parchment. 15th century (Picot and Stein); "probably within two or three years of [the poem's] composition" (Sotheby).

No lacunae. This manuscript was copied from Cambridge, Fitzwilliam Museum, MS 166 (*F*) and presents exactly the same incorrect order for stanzas 139–160.

Three stanzas per side.

Catchwords, fols. 40v, 48v, 56v, 64v, 72v, 80v, 88v, 96v.

Decorated initials; rubrics. Complete program of 15 miniatures. All decorative elements are virtually identical to those of *F*.

References
> Bekker, *Bericht*, p. 13.
> [Not listed in Stein, *Olivier.*]
> Huisman, *Inventaire*, pp. 367–69.
> *Mitteilungen*, p. 11.
> Stein, *Nouveaux Documents*, p. 16, No. 18.
> Picot and Stein, *Recueil*, p. 321, No. 9.
> Sotheby, *Catalogue*, pp. 55–59.
> Avril and Reynaud, *Manuscrits*, 155, No. 79a.
> Sutch, "Notice."
> Sutch, "Production."

L Paris, Bibliothèque nationale de France, Fonds français 1606
> 1r–77r OLIVIER DE LA MARCHE, *Le Chevalier deliberé*
> 78r–80r OLIVIER DE LA MARCHE, [*Prière à la Vierge Marie*]

80r OLIVIER DE LA MARCHE, untitled eight-line poem beginning
Tant a souffert mon Dieu de mon ordure
II +80 + II leaves, paper. 15th century (*Catalogue*, Stein).
Omits stanza 144.
18–24 lines per side.

Large initials in same ink as text; rubrics. Large alternating red and black letters at the beginning of each of the five parts of the poem. Instructions to artists for the illustration of the text (see Appendix) replace the fifteen miniatures.

References
B.n.F., *Catalogue*, tome premier.
Stein, *Olivier*, p. 140, No. 1.
Picot and Stein, *Recueil*, p. 319, No. 1.

M Paris, B.n.F., fr. 1667
1r–294v [epigrams and relatively short pieces, both prose and verse, by diverse hands]
295r–347r GEORGES CHASTELLAIN [*sic*], *Le Chevalier deliberé*
347v–366v [miscellaneous short pieces]
II + 366 + II leaves, paper. 16th century (*Catalogue*); 1540 or later (Veinant).
Omits stanzas 144, 329, and 330; adds one stanza between 24 and 25.
18–32 lines per side.

No decoration. Rubrics are written with the same brown-black ink as the text.

According to the closing paragraph, this text was copied from an otherwise unknown printed version of the poem. We have therefore grouped readings from *M* with those of the other printed versions, *XYZ* and *Ai*.

References
Veinant, *Chevalier delibere*, third unnumbered page following the text.
B.n.F., *Catalogue*, tome premier.
[Not listed in Stein, *Olivier*.]
Picot and Stein, *Recueil*, p. 339 (K, for the edition printed by Pierre Sergent, c. 1540).

N Paris, B.n.F., fr. 2361

   1r–65v OLIVIER DE LA MARCHE, *Le Chevalier deliberé*
   III + 65 + III leaves, paper. 15th century (*Catalogue*, Stein).
   No lacunae. Stanzas 81–86 follow stanza 87.
   Generally three stanzas per side; sometimes 18–20 lines.

Rubrics. Spaces left for decorated initials and miniatures, not executed.

References
   B.n.F., *Catalogue*, tome premier.
   Stein, *Olivier*, p. 140, No. 2.
   Picot and Stein, *Recueil*, p. 320, No. 2.

O Paris, B.n.F., fr. 4907

   1r–100v OLIVIER DE LA MARCHE, *Mémoires* [incomplete; beginning
      and end missing]
   101r–103r *Cest le triste reuel de Messire Oliuyer de La marche en son
      temps cheuallier dhonneur de madame marie duchesse de Bour-
      goingne dit le chevalier delibere.*
   103v–104v blank
   105r–120v [short works by diverse hands, numbered 3–26 in the
      Catalogue]
   V + 120 + V leaves, paper. 16th century (*Catalogue*; items 19 and 20
      are dated 1536).
   Fragment, 46 stanzas: Nos. 167–182, 182*a*, 183–205, 207–210, 216,
      338.
   Two columns, generally five stanzas per column.

No decoration (there are no rubrics in the represented portion of the
text). Written entirely in red ink, apart from *S*-shaped symbols, in black,
preceding and following stanza 182a and between stanzas 216 and 338.

References
   [Not listed in Stein, *Olivier*.]
   B.n.F., *Catalogue*, tome quatrième.
   [Not listed in Picot and Stein, *Recueil*.]

P Paris, B.n.F., fr. 15099

   1r fragment, post-medieval hand; 1v is blank
   2r–63r OLIVIER DE LA MARCHE, *Le Chevalier deliberé*

II + 63 + III leaves, parchment. 16th century (*Catalogue*, Picot and
  Stein); end 15th century (Stein)
No lacunae.
Three stanzas per side.

Decorated initials; rubrics. One miniature (knight in armor, holding a
book, standing before lists, virtually identical to No. 1 in *F*); spaces left
for other miniatures, not executed. Inscription, following opening ru-
bric: *Ex dono Ioannis Armandi De Mauuillain, A.R.S.H. 1671.*

References
  Stein, *Olivier*, p. 140, No. 3.
  B.n.F., *Catalogue général.*
  Picot and Stein, *Recueil*, p. 320, No. 3.

Q Paris, B.n.F., fr. 24373
   1r–3v blank, with some librarians' notations
   4r–50r OLIVIER DE LA MARCHE, *Le Chevalier deliberé*
   51 blank except for notation "12 miniatures"
   I + 51 leaves, parchment. 16th century (*Catalogue*, Stein)
   No lacunae.
   Basically four stanzas per side; sometimes 31 lines.

Decorated initials; rubrics. Twelve miniatures (none corresponding to
Nos. 3, 7, and 15), beautifully executed but contents do not always re-
flect the text.

References
  Barrois, *Bibl. protypographique*, p. 318, No. 2250.
  Stein, *Olivier*, pp. 140–41, No. 4.
  B.n.F., *Catalogue général.*
  Picot and Stein, *Recueil*, p. 320, No. 4.

R Paris, B.n.F., Rothschild 2797 (IV.1.14) (formerly Ashburnham
   Place, T. Barrois, No. 478)
   1r–15v AMÉ DE MONTGESOIE, *Le Pas de la Mort*
   16 blank
   17r–77v OLIVIER DE LA MARCHE, *Le Chevalier deliberé*
   78 blank
   79r–231r *Bien advisé et mal advisé*
   III + 231 + III leaves, paper. 15th century (Stein, *Catalogue*, Mongan)

Missing stanzas 86–89 (one leaf removed, between folios 33 and 34). Three stanzas per side.

Rubrics. Fourteen miniatures (watercolor without gouache) of what was presumably a complete program: No. 8 would have been removed along with stanzas 86–89. Arms of Josse de Lalaing, ff. 1 and 79.

References
> Stein, *Olivier*, p. 141, No. 9.
> *Catalogue ... Rothschild*, pp. 99–101.
> Stein, *Nouveaux Documents*, p. 16, No. 15.
> Picot and Stein, *Recueil*, pp. 320–21, No. 7.
> Mongan, in *Chevalier délibéré ... 1488*, p. viii.

S Paris, B.n.F., Rothschild 2806 (III.6.8)
> 1r–62v OLIVIER DE LA MARCHE, *Le Chevalier deliberé*
> I + 62 + I leaves (mostly unnumbered), vellum. 16th century (Picot and Stein); late 16th century (Stein); late 16th or early 17th century (*Catalogue*).
> No lacunae.
> Three stanzas per side.
> Catchwords, fols. 16v, 24v, 32v, 40v, 48v, 56v.

Decorated initials, rubrics. Thirteen miniatures (none corresponding to Nos. 3 and 7); the subjects sometimes have little or no apparent relation to the instructions (see Appendix). No. 1 is reproduced (photogravure) in the *Catalogue ... Rothschild*, facing page 126. A floral border surrounding No. 1 includes the arms of Paul Pétau (d. 1614), 1r.

References
> [Not listed in Stein, *Olivier*.]
> *Catalogue ... Rothschild*, pp. 126–27.
> Stein, *Nouveaux Documents*, p. 16, No. 16.
> Picot and Stein, *Recueil*, p. 321, No. 8.

T Turin, Biblioteca Nazionale Universitaria, L.V.1
> 1r–61v (formerly 12r–72v) OLIVIER DE LA MARCHE, *Le Chevalier deliberé*
> 62 blank
> 63r–125v [four shorter courtly works]
> 126r–131v OLIVIER DE LA MARCHE, *Vie de Philippe le Hardi*

132r–158v OLIVIER DE LA MARCHE, *Traictie des nopces de Monseigneur le duc de Bourgoingne et de Brabant*
159r–186v [five anonymous works relating to the house of Burgundy]
186 leaves, paper. 15th century (Pasini, Sorbelli, Selvaggi).
Missing stanzas 231–235 and the beginning of the instructions for miniature No. 12 (one leaf removed, between folios 53 and 54).
Three stanzas per side.

Large initials, apparently in the same ink as the text; rubrics. Instructions to artists for the illustration of the text (see Appendix) replace the fifteen miniatures.

Badly damaged in the fire of 1904. The opening leaves are in particularly poor condition, so that very little is legible and one can only guess an occasional word. The text of the poem itself is generally legible from stanza 15 on, though in the rubrics and the instructions for the illustration, written in long lines, words are often missing at the beginnings and ends of lines.

Rather than indicate that the manuscript is illegible, we give variants from *T* when this can be done with confidence. Bracketed readings and the siglum itself in brackets indicate a lesser degree of confidence but that the reading can at least be guessed.

References
Pasini, p. 465.
Stein, *Olivier*, p. 141, No. 8.
Sorbelli, *Inventari*, vol. XXVIII, p. 166.
Picot and Stein, *Recueil*, p. 322, No. 16.
Selvaggi, personal communication

V Vienna, Österreichische Nationalbibliothek, Cod. 2654
1r–14v and 16r AMÉ DE MONTGESOIE, *Le Pas de la Mort*
15r–75v OLIVIER DE LA MARCHE, *Le Chevalier deliberé*
V + 76 + II leaves, parchment. 16th century (*Tabulae*, Stein); c. 1520 (Unterkircher).
No lacunae. Stanzas 5–10 (fol. 15) precede stanza 1.
Generally three stanzas per side; 20–22 lines per side, fols. 53v–55r; 18–22 lines per side, fols. 65r–75r. Fols. 43v, 52v, and 56v are blank.

Large initials, apparently in the same ink as the text; two decorated initials, stanzas 169 and 219. No rubrics.

References

> *Tabulae*, II, 112.
> Stein, *Olivier*, p. 141, No. 6.
> Picot and Stein, *Recueil*, p. 321, No. 11.
> Unterkircher, p. 61, No. 90.

W Vienna, Österreichische Nationalbibliothek, Cod. 3391
   Contains 62 works in all; those by OLIVIER DE LA MARCHE are as
      follows:
   5r–10r *Doctrine et loz pour Madame Alienor d'Austrice* [also called *Les
      Cinq Sens*]
   77r–79v *Lettre(s) enuoyee avecques le present traictie* [*Le Triomphe des
      dames*] *a la ... princesse la contesse de Charolais ...*
   80r–81r *Presentation faite du present traictie* [*Le Triomphe des dames*]
      au ... duc de Bourgogne et de Brabant ...
   81v–89r *Le Debat de Cuidier et de Fortune*
   142r–191r *Le Chevalier deliberé*
   200r–200v *Ces vers furent donnez par La Marche a mon seigneur
      l'archiduc* [Philippe Le Beau] *pour sa nouuelle escolle*
   201r–204v *Ces vers nommez les vers dorez donna La Marche a son
      maistre* [*l'archiduc Philippe*] *en l'eage de xv ans*
   205r–206v *Ces vers furent faiz a la requeste de Monseigneur de
      Rauestain et donnez par la marche a son maistre larchiduc en
      l'eage de xviij ans*
   207r–209r *Ces vers et petit traictie fu fait a la requeste de Madame
      Margueritte d'Austriche princesse de Castille et donnez par La
      Marche a mon seigneur l'archiduc Philippe en l'eage de xx ans*
   561r–567r *Complainte sur la mort de Madame Marie de Bourgongne*
   567v–578r *Predestination des sept fees et leurs dons a l'empereur Charles*
   III + 584 leaves, paper. 15th century (*Tabulae*, Stein); 1500–1520 (Unterkircher).
   No lacunae. Stanzas 144 and 145 are inverted.
   Basically four stanzas per side; line-count varies from 28 to 34.

Large initials, apparently in the same ink as the text; rubrics. Instructions to artists for the illustration of the text (see Appendix) replace the fifteen miniatures.

References
>   *Tabulae*, II, pp. 272–76.
>   [Not listed in Stein, *Olivier*.]
>   Stein, *Nouveaux Documents*, p. 16, No. 17.
>   Picot and Stein, *Recueil*, p. 321, No. 10.
>   Unterkircher, pp. 2–3, No. 2.

In addition to the foregoing, the following manuscripts may be mentioned:

1. Turin, Biblioteca Nazionale Universitaria L.V.9 (formerly e.III.44). Presumed lost in the fire of 1904.

References
>   Stein, *Olivier*, p. 141, No. 7 (*"copie médiocre de la fin du XVe siècle, in-folio, papier, 62 feuillets."*)
>   Picot and Stein, *Recueil*, p. 322, No. 15 (*"In-fol. de 62 ff., sur papier, XVe siècle."*)
>   Selvaggi, personal communication

2. Chalon-sur-Saône, Bibliothèque Municipale, manuscrit n° 123. Not consulted for the preparation of the present edition.

References
>   Stein, *Olivier*, p. 141, No. 12 (*"copie sans valeur faite en 1873."*)
>   Picot and Stein, *Recueil*, p. 322, No. 17.
>   Guelon, personal communication

INCUNABULA AND OTHER PRINTED EDITIONS

We give only minimal bibliographic information. For complete details of these and other early editions, see Picot and Stein, *Recueil*, pp. 322–45.

X   Paris, Antoine Vérard, 1488.
     In-quarto, unpaged (36 leaves). Thirteen woodcuts (No. 4 is repeated). 20–24 lines per side.

References
>   Brunet, *Manuel*, tome III, col. 779–80.
>   Stein, *Olivier*, p. 141, Éditions, No. 1.

Picot and Stein, *Recueil*, pp. 322–24 (*A*)
Facsimile edition, Washington: Library of Congress, 1946.

Y Schiedam, c. 1498.
  In-folio, unpaged (34 leaves). Sixteen woodcuts (frontispiece and full
    program of fifteen illustrations). Spaces left for initials, not exe-
    cuted. Two columns, six or eight stanzas per side.

References
  Brunet, *Manuel*, tome III, col. 780–81.
  Stein, *Olivier*, p. 142, Éditions, No. 4.
  Facsimile edition, London: Bibliographical Society, 1898.
  Picot and Stein, *Recueil*, pp. 330–32 (*D*); facsimile edition, pp. 239–
    306.

Z Paris: Silvestre, [1842]. Reprinting with Gothic characters of Schie-
    dam (*Y*).
  In-12, unpaged; signatures A.1 to P.1, followed by a four-page after-
    word. One woodcut, reproducing the frontispiece of the Schie-
    dam edition.

Title page: Le cheualier delibere comprenant | la mort du duc de Bour-
gongne qui trespassa deuant Nancy | en Lorraine. Fait et compose par
messire Oliuier de la | marche. Et nouuellement imprime a Paris.

According to the afterword, the editor (A. V[einant]) also consulted four
manuscripts (including *M*; unfortunately Veinant does not specify the
others) and two other early editions. Includes instructions to artists for
the illustration of the text (see Appendix), presumably taken from *L*.

References
  Brunet, *Manuel*, tome III, col. 782.
  Stein, *Olivier*, p. 142, Éditions, No. 10.
  [Not listed in Picot and Stein, *Recueil*.]

Manuscript Relations

A few lines present significantly divergent readings and demonstrate the
existence of two distinct traditions. In order of their occurrence in the
text, they are as follows.

82.6   Et je mon glave sans demeure *CATW* <> Ma lance que je cong-
        neuz seure *BEFGNPQRSV/MXY* (+ *L/Z*)

198.1   Des Bourbounois le duc Loÿs *CABLRTVW/YZ* <> Charles duc
        de bourbon je vis *EFGNOPQS/MX*

198.2   Jut la par Debile maté *CALRT/YZ* (+ *BVW*, with minor
        variations) <> Par debile mort et mate *EFGNOPQS/MX*

205.7   Grant fut cest Amoras Bahy *CABLTVW/YZ* (+ *FGR*) <> ...
        cest Mahomet Beigny *ENOPQS/MX*

259.1   La dame de son curre sault *CBRTW/YZ* (+ *LV*) <> La dame de
        son bon gre sault *EFGNPQS/AiMX*

265.2   Assavourez ceste adventure *CABLRTW/YZ* (+ *V*) <> Pensez
        bien a ... *EFGNPQS/MX*

312.3   Mais au primes vient le plus fort *CABLRTVW/YZ* <> Mais
        maintenant ... *EFGNPQS/MX*

These contrastive readings demonstrate a grouping into two primary
families, *CABLRTVW* and *EFGNPQS*.[1] In these seven lines, *ATW*
always align themselves with *C* (apart from 259.1, where *A* is replaced
by *Ai* and consequently represents a different tradition). *BLRV* join with
C in all cases but one (and, curiously, it is always the same exception,
line 82.6). On the other hand, *FG* are in the group with *C* in only one
of these lines, and *ENPQS* share none of these readings with *C*. Many
other readings throughout the text confirm the close relationship of *A*
and *T* with *C*. Both of these are generally quite reliable texts (in the case
of *A*, this is, of course, limited to the portions where the original
manuscript is preserved), and it is all the more regrettable that these are
the very manuscripts to have suffered the most damage, *A* through
mutilation and *T* through fire.

    This is not the place for an in-depth study of manuscript relations.
Suffice it to say that the variants occasionally suggest certain sub-group-

---

[1] Heitmann, whose textual corpus did not include *G*, *M*, *O*, or *Z*, but included three
additional incunabula, arrived at a similar division into manuscript families ("Die spanischen
Übersetzer," 232–35).

ings, but these are unstable and do not follow a consistent pattern. A notable exception is the group *FG*, since it can be conclusively demonstrated that *G* was copied from *F* (Sutch, "Production").

6. *Editing Principles*

i. Base manuscript
Our edition and translation are based on Chantilly, Musée Condé 507 (*C*). One of the earliest copies, this manuscript is carefully written and free from lacunae and mis-ordered stanzas. It is axiomatic, however, that no manuscript is free of error, and *C* is no exception. We have therefore emended as seemed necessary, particularly to restore rhyme or meter and to provide greater internal consistency.

ii. Variants
Manuscripts *ABEFGLMQRSTVW* and incunabulum *X* have been examined *in toto* and all significant variants are included. All problematic lines, as well as numerous others, have been checked in the remaining manuscripts, *N* and *P*, and in incunabula *Y* and *Z*. All manuscripts except *V* and *W* have been examined *in situ*; these two were studied by means of microfilm.

But "significant variants" is a somewhat slippery term, and the distinction between mere orthographic variation and significant morphological or semantic variants is not always obvious; indeed, one person's significant variant may be another's graphic variant, and vice versa. Our approach has been to exclude what we considered to be mere variations in spelling, where we felt the same word was intended, and to include all other sorts of variants. In particular, we have included variants involving singular versus plural, *se* versus *si*, *ce* versus *se* and similar pairs involving *s* and *c*, and others which, admittedly, involve form more than substance. These decisions, like most of the work of editing a text, are only partially objective; much subjective judgement is involved as well. In case of doubt, we have preferred to err on the side of caution, and have thus included some variants which may be merely orthographic.

We have not generally listed the non-linguistic peculiarities of the various manuscripts. For *C* we have indicated what appear to be modifications to what was first written, e.g., insertions, *grattages*, and the like, but we have not included this type of detail for the other manuscripts. On the other hand, we have listed all cases where the text of another manuscript is in a different order from that of *C*. Further, we have not indicated punctuation, sporadically present in some manuscripts.

In the interest of saving space, minor variations among variants are generally not indicated. Thus, in 155.8, seven manuscripts share the same word order, different from that of *C*. The variant given as "ont este jamais *ABFGMSV*" is shared by the majority of the manuscripts in question, *FGMSV*, but it also includes the variant spellings *ont este iamais* (*A*) and *ont estez jamais* (*B*). Similarly, in 187.3, two manuscripts, *L* and *R*, have *cheualier* and one, *O*, has *cheuallier*, where our text has *chancelier*. The variants list *cheualier* for all three, *LOR*. On the other hand, variant spellings in support of an emendation to *C* are listed separately.

The indication "[?]" in the variants indicates that this is our best reading of what we see in the manuscript, but that we are not 100% confident of it.

iii. Textual notes

Lines marked with an asterisk at the end of the line are discussed in the Textual Notes. Such discussions include all emendations, except for cases of obvious misspellings, such as *necessoire* (for *necessaire*, rhyme, 11.2) *talle* (for *taille*, 20.5), *resemboit* (for *resembloit*, 31.8) *Dug* (for *D'ung*, 40.4); substitution of *ce* for *se*, *si* for *cy*, and the like; hypo- and hyper-metric lines where the other manuscripts indicate the necessary correction (6.6); non-standard forms outside the bounds of variable spellings, e.g., *ma compaignet* (for *m'acompaigna*, 1.6), *falut* (for *faillit*, 18.8), *moulut* (for *moulu*, past participle, 34.1), etc.

iv. Word separation

Word separation generally follows accepted usage. Variants involving bound vs. separate forms are not generally noted, except in the case of the three printed versions, where spacing, being mechanically constant (either there is a space or there is none; there is not the sort of "half-space" or "possible space" found in some manuscripts) can be indicated with greater confidence. Special mention should perhaps be made of *tres*, which occurs a total of 25 times in our text. Of these, *C* presents ten cases of round *s* followed by a clear space, six cases of round *s* followed by a slight (sometimes very slight) space, eight cases of long *s* with no following space (bound forms), and 1 case of long *s* followed by a slight space. Since the scribe of *C* does seem to have followed a system, writing long *s* in bound forms (with just one exception, and the space is slight) and round *s* when separating *tres* from what follows, we have decided to reflect that usage. The resulting inconsistencies reflect those of the scribe: *tres fors* and *tresfort*; *treshorrible* and *tres horrible*; *tres richement* and *tresrichement*.

v. Diacritical symbols and elision

The cedilla is used as in modern French. Elision of vowels is indicated by an apostrophe. We have, however, maintained the final *e* when it is present in the base manuscript. Thus, *me estoit* (20.8) is to be read as though it were written *m'estoit*. The acute accent indicates the pronunciation of word-final *e* (past participles, adjectives, nouns) and of final *es* (plurals, proper nouns, and a few other words). The *tréma* shows the disjunction of contiguous vowels (e.g., *haïssent*, 19.8) and the syllabic value of final *e* that would otherwise be elided. The *tréma* is not, however, used for the spellings *ia* (always representing two syllables with the sole exception of *biaucop*) and *io*, bisyllabic in all occurrences (primarily in the endings *-tion* and *-cion*).

vi. Spelling and abbreviations

We have introduced the customary distinction between *i* and *j* and between *u* and *v*. Otherwise, we have followed the spelling of manuscript *C* wherever it seemed reasonable to do so (see discussion of peculiarities of *C*). Following the lessons of Omer Jodogne (see Bibliography), we have maintained the spelling *pou-* in the plural present indicative and the imperfect of the verb and for the substantivized infinitive *pouoir*. Abbreviations have been replaced by the full forms of the words. Two particular cases merit specific mention: *xpïen* (205.1, 317.5) is transcribed as *chrestïen*, following Rickard, p. 22, and Brown (*Ressource*), p. 98; *ihūcrist* (324.1) is transcribed as *Jhesucrist*, as in manuscripts *FNRT*.

vii. Capitalization and punctuation

Proper names and common nouns with allegorical value are capitalized. Punctuation follows modern French usage and is added to clarify the reading of the text as we understand it.

7. Language of the Poem

i. Possible vestiges of the Old French case system

"As early as 1314 one sees the case system broken down. . . . Only a vague sense that an *-s* should be placed on some singular forms and omitted on some plural forms remained. Hence in the rare instances in which the declension system is found, the use is often incorrect. From the beginning of the fourteenth century, in the majority of cases, the Modern French usage was already in force" (Gardner and Greene, p. 1). At the same time, according to Marchello-Nizia (henceforth referred to as "M.-N."), "One can say that in the 14th and 15th centuries there may not exist a single manuscript that is totally devoid of traces of declension" (p. 97).[1] As is to be expected in a text of this relatively late date, such traces are very few in number and often do not reflect the "classical" declensional system. And, of course, it is impossible to tell whether the usage we observe in C (and the other manuscripts) is Olivier's own or merely that of the scribe. Some particular observations:

C consistently uses *amis* for the vocative singular (six occurrences: 16.1, 113.3, 140.6, 269.5, 283.1, and 302.2).

C uses both *nul* (five occurrences) and *nulz* (fourteen). In all but one case (313.4), *nulz* is used as it would have been in Old French. See note to 7.8.

We find *riens* (thirteen occurrences) far more often than *rien* (two), and nine of the thirteen can be seen as conforming to the Old French usage as subject of a verb or as predicate nominative. This may, however, be less telling than those figures suggest: according to Gardner and Greene, "There are occasional case survivals, but they are used haphazardly. In the fifteenth century the preferred spelling in all positions was *riens*" (p. 125).

C uses both *sire* and *seigneur*. The former is restricted to the vocative (three occurrences); the latter serves as subject (four), predicate nominative (two), and direct object (one).

In 202.6 we find *Nez* ("born"). It is uncertain whether this is a relic of the Old French nominative singular, or whether the *z* served merely to distinguish the word from *ne* (which occurs in the previous line). On the other hand, C has *ne* = *né* in rhyme-position, 247.3, and two occurrences of *nez* = "nose" (303.2, 307.1).

The form *Armoyez* occurs as a singular adjective in 220.8. It is possible that the *-z* resulted from anticipation of the word *nulz* in the same line, since no other similar forms occur in C. On the other hand, the *-ez* spelling for plural adjectives or past participles is fairly common (at least 20 occurrences).

---

[1] "Au XIVe et au XVe siècle, on peut dire qu'il n'existe peut-être pas un seul manuscrit totalement dépourvu de traces des déclinaisons."

Among the numerous proper names, the only one that seems to present the tell-tale -*s* (discounting *Charles*, which survives in that form) is *Phelippes Maria* (184.2), which we may contrast with *Phelippe* (duke of Burgundy, 225.7).

What appears to be the Old French nominative singular *hons*, 213.8, was probably chosen for purely metrical reasons.

ii. Other traces of earlier stages of the language
According to Gardner and Greene, "By the end of the fourteenth century the preposition *de* was generally used with determinative complements" (p. 6). M.-N. says that this form is not exceptional in Middle French, but that it is quite rare in fifteenth-century texts.[2] If this is so, Olivier de La Marche's usage may be considered somewhat archaic, since we find at least five instances of this construction, and it does not appear to be restricted to "fixed formulae": *l'Avenement Melusine* (67.8), *le conseil la deesse* (68.5), *le baisier Judas* (69.5), *les pas Atropos* (160.2), and [*les*] *mains Tristresse* (221.2). On the other hand, contrasting examples using *de* are plentiful: *la grant forest d'Atropos* (6.2), *le propre filz de Gourmandise* (16.8), *le peuple de Dieu* (65.6), [*le*] *trespas de la noble dame* (263.7), etc.

Other linguistic traits that suggest that Olivier's language was somewhat behind that of the late fifteenth century include the use of the bisyllabic form *vëoir* (whereas, for example, Villon uses exclusively the monosyllabic *voir*: M.-N., p. 58) and the use of *doin(s)t* in third-person *formules de souhait* (three occurrences, contrasted with one of *donne*: M.-N., pp. 207–208). The trisyllabic form *roÿnes* may, like *vëoir*, be a relic of an earlier time (M.-N., p. 61), or it may be a dialectal trait (see note to 207.3).

On the other hand, before a feminine singular noun beginning with a vowel, the possessive adjective has its modern form, *mon, ton,* or *son,* in 16 cases out of 17, the sole exception being *m'amie* in 2.1 (contrasted with nine occurrences of *mon,* with such nouns as *enfance,* 1.8, *espee,* 12.8, etc.). This supports M.-N.'s observation that the elided forms persisted before certain substantives, particularly *amour, amie,* and *ame,*

---

[2] "Le complément déterminatif absolu placé immédiatement après le substantif complété existe encore en moyen français, et il n'y est pas exceptionnel ; il est cependant très fortement concurrencé par la construction en *de* essentiellement, et par *a* accessoirement, selon les textes" (pp. 318–19). "Au XVᵉ et au XVIᵉ siècles, elle n'existe plus guère que sous forme de traces, de formules figées" (pp. 321–22). See also Rickard, *Chrestomathie,* p. 33.

whereas before others they yielded to *mon, ton,* and *son* as early as the second quarter of the fourteenth century (p. 138).

Pronoun usage before an infinitive is still in a state of flux. In C the tonic form *soy* strongly outnumbers *se,* four cases to one, but in the other two persons the balance is nearly even: eight occurrences of *moy* to seven of *me/m'*; five occurrences of *te* to four of *toy.* The figures would almost certainly be different for other manuscripts.

8. *Particular Features of Manuscript C*

i. Problematic spellings

Our aim throughout has been to reproduce the text as preserved in manuscript C. In a few cases, however, in the interest of providing a more readable text, we have felt compelled to depart from that principle.

The first of these involves the letters *c* and *t,* a traditional source of problems, particularly when the two letters occur side by side. Sometimes a given combination of pen-strokes suggests *ct,* and at other times *cc* or *tt.* The word *accident* occurs 72 times in our text as the name of the allegorical figure (and twice as a common noun, once in the plural). In very few cases does this word seem to be written with *acc-.* Many are ambiguous, but the majority really look as though they are spelled with *act-.* Similarly, there are 21 occurrences of various forms of the verb *occire* and one of the related noun *occiseur*: of these, nine look like *occ-,* four look like *oct-,* and the remaining nine are ambiguous. By way of contrast, the two occurrences of *octroy* are clearly written *oct-.*

We have therefore adopted the following general principle. Where the manuscript appears to read *ct,* that spelling has been retained when the *c* could be explained on etymological grounds and when such spellings can be considered "traditional" by virtue of their appearing in other texts of the time. The former group includes words like *amictié, droicture, practiques,* and *traictié*; the latter, words like *actaindre, barrecte, lectre,* and *mectre.* In other cases, C's apparent *ct* spelling has been replaced by *cc.* This involves the name *Accident* and the related common nouns, forms of the verb *occire* and *occiseur,* and *neccessité.*

A similar difficulty arises in the case of *sf* versus *ff.* When the first letter is written as "long" *s,* the two letter combinations are virtually indistinguishable. In cases where *ff* can confidently be assumed, the crossbar does not usually extend to the left of the body of the first *f.* Hence, many such cases are quite ambiguous, and it must be admitted that, to a considerable extent, one sees the letters one expects to see based on context and prior experience with the language. We expect *ff* in words like *affubla*, *effect*, *offendre*, and *prouffit*, and we expect *sf* in words like *satisfaction* and in compound forms such as *biensfais* and *tresfort*. On the other hand, we can accept both *desfist* and *deffist*. We have therefore attempted to reproduce what we see as *C*'s usage in all such cases, realizing that others may see something different.

The letters *n* and *u* are often indistinguishable in medieval manuscripts, just as they are in the handwriting of many people today.[1] A particular feature of manuscript *C* is the use of what looks like *ou* in words where the expected spelling is *on*. For example, the verb *donner* and the related noun *donneur* occur 28 times in the text. Twelve of these can be read as *donn-*, twelve look more like *doun-*, and three are ambiguous. In one case *donnee* appears as *dōnee*, which suggests that the scribe was **thinking** *n*, even though his pen may have been producing *u*. We have printed *donn-* in all cases. Sometimes, on the other hand, the expected spelling predominates and there are only rare exceptions. The word *bonne(s)* (19 occurrences), is almost always written with the expected *nn*, but in one case it appears as *boune* (rhyming with *persoune* and *couroune*). Since *bonne* occurs regularly elsewhere (including once in rhyme position), we have printed *-onne* for all three of these words. The verb *convient* never appears with the expected spelling *conuient*, but rather twice as *couuient* and three times as *cōuient*. This latter form suggests that the scribe intended *n* even though, in some cases, he wrote *u*.

In many cases, printing *ou* would produce a very strange-looking word. For example, in 174.3 *C* literally reads *out eu*, the second letter of the first word having almost exactly the same shape as the second letter of the second word. But since the word *ont* occurs with the expected spelling at 17 other points in the text (one occurrence is ambiguous), we have printed *ont* in this line as well. There are a number of instances where one must consider that certain letter-combinations are "orthographically impossible" (C. Reno); as in the case of emended readings, we have endeavored to reach a reasonable compromise between fidelity

---

[1] Christine Reno points out that "It is probably [due to] the fact that 'u' and 'n' have continued to be often indistinguishable in modern writing that this confusion does not appear so troublesome" (p. 7; the context is the *c/t* confusion). And in a conversation concerning the reading of *moult*, which in one manuscript looked more like *monlt*, Roger Middleton once remarked that just because something **looks** like an *n*, that doesn't mean that it **is** an *n*.

to our base manuscript and the desire to produce a readable text.

In a few cases the scribe has written *ou* where *om* is expected. This is more surprising than the *u*-for-*n* substitution, since the number of strokes is not the same. Thus, among 23 occurrences of forms of the verb *nommer*, we find *nōm-* 19 times, *nomm-* twice, and two occurrences of *noum-*. Similarly, in the case of various forms of the adjective *renommé*, there are six occurrences of *-nōm-* and one of *-noum-*. The other words so written are *soumeil* (the unique occurrence of the word), *assoumer*, and *assouma*; by contrast, we find one occurrence of *assomme* and two of *somme*.[2] We have printed *-omm-* for all of these words.

ii. Idiosyncratic spellings

Occasionally *C* presents a single intervocalic *s* rather than the expected *-ss-*: *Ausi* 95.6 <> (as opposed to or in contrast to) *aussi* (four occurrences); *laisasmes* 76.1 <> *laiss-* (seven occurrences of forms of the verb *laisser*); *mesagers* 329.1 <> *messager* 333.6; *mesages* 332.2 <> *messages* 334.1; *peuse* 15.4 <> *eusse* 81.1, *fusse* 79.4, 81.4; *resembloit* 31.8, 77.8, 238.3 (no occurrences of *ress-* forms); *resjouÿsoie* 133.1 <> *recongnoissoie* 108.5, *retondissoit* 112.2, *flourissoit* 277.5, *eslargissoit* 100.1. Such variation may be considered symptomatic of the non-standardized spelling of the time, and *C*'s spellings have been retained in all cases.

A similar situation obtains with respect to the representation of the palatal fricative ("soft") *g*: sometimes spelled *ge* or *j*, as would later become the norm, this sound is also represented by *g*. Thus we find *alegance* 271.8 <> *alegeance* 127.8 (as well as other words ending in *-geance*); verb forms *herbega* [*sic*] (rubric preceding stanza 26), *abregasse* 30.1, *auantagast* 223.4, and *obliga* 318.4 <> *logea* 27.2; *haubergon* 304.1, and *gut* 186.1 <> *jut* (three occurrences). Here, too, we have preferred to retain *C*'s spellings.

C presents just six occurrences of *-ez* instead of the usual (unstressed) plural *-es*: *Faictez* 47.3; *Oncquez* 47.6 and 60.8 (compared to 9 occurrences of *oncques*); *apprestez*, 300.3 (*apprestes* 299.2 and 329.6); *montaignez*, 303.3; *nullez*, 307.3.

The sigmatism (substitution of *s* for *r*) present in some manuscripts does not manifest itself in *C*. See variants to 286.8 and 299.3 (*armurier*, both lines), 330.2 (*bericles*), and 336.8 (*armoirie*). On the subject of sigmatism, see M.-N., pp. 85–86, and Huchon, p. 93.

---

[2] We may compare the treatment of *homme* (including *omme* and *hommes*): of 15 total occurrences, 12 are spelled with *ōm* and three with *omm*.

Similar to the use of what appears to be *ou* before *m* or *n* (see above) is the use of *ou* before *gn* in words like *Bourgougne*, *besougne*, and forms of *cougnoistre* and related verbs. In this case, however, the scribe is consistent, and the spelling *-ougn-* is to be found in all such words. We have therefore retained this idiosyncratic spelling.

iii. Elision and non-elision of vowels

C's normal practice is to elide, but there are a few cases of non-elided written forms where the line must be read as though it contained the corresponding elided form. In addition to *me estoit*, already mentioned in the section on editing principles, these include *que Herculés* (9.2), *se occist* (53.6), *que honneur* (93.8), *Que en* (120.7), *Se en* (128.5), and *que a* (242.4). See in addition the note to line 167.4. On the other hand, there are eight cases where word-final *e* has full syllabic value despite the presence of a following vowel; these are consequently marked *ë*: *Maladië a* (124.4), *D'ellë on* (143.3), *Donnë ou* (145.2), *së encoffre* (145.4), *më assista* (167.4), *princë ou* (200.2), *terrë et* (235.4), and *quë oÿrent* (331.3).[3]

9.   *The Translation*

This translation is the result of a thoughtful gift from professor to student some years ago. What began as an exercise in reading and transcription has developed into a full-scale edition and translation; what began as an inquiry has ended in a quest. Starting with a copy of the facsimile edition published by the Library of Congress, it has progressed through many discoveries. As a consequence, this translation is based on an edition based on the results of a comparison of eighteen manuscripts. Common sense and experience, combined with hope, have been the guiding principles in our work.

We have tried to stay as close as possible to what we perceive as the meaning and tenor of the poem. In order to do this, a conscious choice was made to maintain a neutral tone and closely reflect the original, hoping to seem neither archaic nor too modern. We felt it was more important to be faithful to the meaning of the text than to try to twist and torture it into some kind of metrical rhymed line. Therefore, this translation is parallel and not in poetic form.

---

[3] For an extensive discussion of the phenomenon of non-elided word-final *e*, see Piaget.

To maintain rhythm and rhyme, Olivier was obliged to pad some lines, which padding we have tried to minimize. Double adjectives were often used and have been pruned when the English flowed better with fewer. Sometimes it was more appropriate to the sense to turn a negative French phrase into an affirmative one in English. Some adjustments were made in verb tenses for continuity, to keep time sequences in order. In a few cases, lines within the poem were realigned to make the translation flow more easily, but this has been done sparingly.

Great effort has been made to identify those named in the poem, a task rendered difficult by the medieval tendency for repetition and multiplicity in name-giving. Indices, biographical dictionaries, and especially Olivier's *Mémoires* have been pored over at length. Many of the names have been anglicized and Biblical and literary names given modern spelling. The literate people of this time took great interest in the early heroes, real and literary. While the modern reader may question the value of these lists, this was not an uncommon device and the references to antiquity and the Bible had meaning for them and gave greater depth to the poem.

10.   *Acknowledgments*

It is a genuine pleasure to recognize in print the many individuals and institutions without whose generous assistance a book such as this could not have been realized.

Financial support was provided by the American Philosophical Society and by the College of Liberal Arts, the Department of Foreign Languages and Literatures, and the Library Research Travel Grant program of Oregon State University.

We thank the directors and personnel of the numerous libraries whose materials we consulted: the Fitzwilliam Museum, Cambridge; the Musée Condé, Chantilly; the National Library of Scotland, Edinburgh; the Bodleian Library, Oxford; the Bibliothèque de l'Arsenal, Paris; the Bibliothèque nationale de France, Paris; the Biblioteca Nazionale Universitaria, Turin; and the Österreichische Nationalbibliothek, Vienna, for access to original manuscripts and microfilms; Oregon State University, the University of Oregon, Southern Oregon State College (now Southern Oregon University), Jackson County (Oregon) Public Library, and an uncountable number of others whose holdings we consulted through the wonderful services of inter-library loan. Special mention should be made of the personnel of the Centre Culturel des Fontaines, whose hospitality makes any stay in Chantilly such a delightful experience.

The following individuals have helped in various ways, and we are pleased to thank them publicly for their generosity: Barbara K. Altmann, Cynthia J. Brown, Robert L. Casebeer, Sylvie Chossat, Kristine J. Dodson, Joan Tasker Grimbert, Ann Tukey Harrison, Elspeth Kennedy, Alice Kottke, Anne-Françoise Labie-Leurquin, Jean-Loup Lemaitre, Leslie S. B. MacCoull, Christiane Marchello-Nizia, Christine M. Reno, Eleanor Roach, Samuel N. Rosenberg, Delford L. Santee, Barbara Nelson Sargent-Baur, Maureen Schroeder, Diane G. Scillia, Susie S. Sutch, Jane H. M. Taylor, Claude Thiry, Richard C. West, Charity Canon Willard, and Ralph D. Worthylake. We also thank the readers who evaluated our manuscript for MRTS; we are grateful for their helpful suggestions. A special expression of thanks goes to Karen Lemiski, production manager for MRTS, whose editing and word-processing skills did much to make this a better book.

Lastly, it is a pleasure to acknowledge the support and assistance of our respective families. Paulette Carroll contributed her expertise as writer and translator on many occasions and provided unfailing moral support during the entire course of the project. Jim Wilson gave unlimited support to a wife discovering a belated passion and the rest of the family added their unqualified encouragement and tolerance.

CWC, LHW

Bibliography

Adam, Antoine, Georges Lerminier, Edouard Morot-Sir. *Littérature française*. 2 vols. Paris: Larousse, 1967.

Alexander, Jonathan J. G. *Medieval Illuminators and Their Methods of Work*. New Haven: Yale Univ. Press, 1992.

Avril, François, and Nicole Reynaud. *Les Manuscrits à peintures en France 1440–1520*. Paris: Flammarion–Bibliothèque Nationale, 1993.

Barrois, Jean Baptiste Joseph. *Bibliothéque [sic] protypographique, ou Librairies des fils du roi Jean, Charles V, Jean de Berri, Philippe de Bourgogne et les siens*. Paris: Treuttel et Würtz, 1830.

Bartier, John. *Charles le Téméraire*. Documentation iconographique réunie et commentée par Anne Rouzet. Bruxelles: Arcade, 1970.

Beaumarchais, Jean–Pierre de, Daniel Couty, Alain Rey. *Dictionnaire des littératures de langue française*. 4 vols. Paris: Bordas, 1994.

Bekker, Immanuel. *Bericht über die zur Bekanntmachung geeigneten Verhandlungen der Königl. preuss. Akademie der Wissenschaften zu Berlin*. Berlin: Druckerei der Königlichen Akademie der Wissenschaften, 1853. [Pp. 3–13: description of Berlin ms. Gall. fol. 177.]

Bibliothèque Impériale/Nationale, Département des manuscrits. *Catalogue des manuscrits français, ancien fonds*. Tome premier [Nos. 1–3130]; tome quatrième [Nos. 4587–5525]. Paris: Firmin–Didot, 1868, 1895.

Bibliothèque Nationale. *Catalogue général des manuscrits français. Ancien supplément français III, N°s 13091–15369 du fonds français*, par Henri Omont, conservateur adjoint du Département des Manuscrits. Paris: Ernest Leroux, 1896.

———. *Catalogue général des manuscrits français*, par Henri Omont [et al.]. *Ancien petit fonds français II, N°s 22885–25696 du fonds français*, par C. Couderc et Ch. de La Roncière. Paris: Ernest Leroux, 1902.

Bossuat, Robert. *Manuel bibliographique de la littérature française du moyen âge*. Bibliothèque elzévirienne, Nouvelle Série, Etudes et Documents. Melun: Argences, 1951; rpt. Nendeln, Liechtenstein: Kraus, 1971.

——. *Le Moyen Age.* (*Histoire de la littérature française*, publiée sous la direction de J. Calvet, tome I.) Paris: Del Duca, [1962].

——. *La Poésie lyrique en France au XVème siècle.* Paris: Les Cours de Lettres, 1948.

Brault, Gerard J. *Early Blazon: Heraldic Terminology in the Twelfth and Thirteenth Centuries with Special Reference to Arthurian Literature.* Oxford: Clarendon Press, 1972.

Brereton, Geoffrey. *A Short History of French Literature.* Harmondsworth, Middlesex: Penguin, 1954.

Brown, Cynthia J. "Theorizing Late Medieval Text Editing: Towards a New Codicology." Conference paper, Kentucky Foreign Language Conference, 1994.

Brown, Sydney MacGillvary. *Medieval Europe.* New York: Harcourt Brace, 1935.

Brunet, Jacques–Charles. *Manuel du libraire et de l'amateur de livres....* 5e édition. 6 vols. Paris: Firmin–Didot, 1860–1865. Tome III, col. 779–82. *Supplément* (par P. Deschamps et G. Brunet). 2 vols. Paris: Firmin–Didot, 1878–1880. Tome I, cols. 763–65.

Calin, William. *The Epic Quest: Studies in Four Old French Chansons de Geste.* Baltimore: Johns Hopkins Press, 1966.

——. "Inventing the Medieval Canon, Then and Now: Whose Middle Ages?" Oral presentation, "Peripheral Visions: Reading the Margins in the Middle Ages," symposium, The University of Oregon, Eugene, 8 April 1994.

Calmette, Joseph. *Les Grands Ducs de Bourgogne.* Paris: Albin Michel, 1949. English translation by Doreen Weightman: *The Golden Age of Burgundy: The Magnificent Dukes and their Courts.* London: Weidenfeld and Nicolson, 1962.

Carroll, Carleton W. "Representations of Death in *Le Chevalier deliberé* (Olivier de La Marche, 1483)." *Sewanee Mediaeval Studies* 9 (1999).

——. "Transformations d'un texte: les premières éditions du *Chevalier delibéré.*" *La Recherche: bilan et perspectives*, Actes du IXe Colloque international sur le moyen français, Université McGill, Montréal, 5–7 octobre 1998. Forthcoming.

Cartellieri, Otto. *The Court of Burgundy: Studies in the History of Civilization*, trans. Malcolm Letts. London: Kegan Paul, 1929; rpt. New York: Haskell, 1970.

Catalogue des livres composant la bibliothèque de feu M. le baron James de Rothschild. Tome quatrième. Paris: Damascène Morgand [. . .], 1912.

Catalogue général des manuscrits des bibliothèques publiques de France. ...
Musée Condé à Chantilly [etc.]. Paris: Plon, 1928.

Champion, Pierre. *Histoire poétique du quinzième siècle.* 2 vols. Paris: Honoré Champion, 1966.

Chantilly. Le Cabinet des livres. Manuscrits. Tome deuxième, Belles-lettres. Paris: Plon, 1900.

Chatelain, Henri. *Recherches sur le vers français au XVe siècle: rimes, mètres et strophes.* Paris: Champion, 1908.

Cotgrave, Randle. *A Dictionarie of the French and English Tongues.* 1611. Rpt. Menston, Yorks.: Scolar Press, 1968.

Dahmus, Joseph. *Dictionary of Medieval Civilization.* New York: Macmillan, 1984.

Dawson, Christopher. *Medieval Essays.* New York: Sheed and Ward, 1954.

Dees, Anthonij. *Etude sur l'évolution des démonstratifs en ancien et en moyen français.* Groningen: Walters–Noordhoff, 1971.

Delen, A.J.J. [Adrien Jean Joseph]. "De Illustraties van 'Le Chevalier délibéré.' " *Het Boek* 12 (1923): 225–32.

Di Stefano, Giuseppe. *Essais sur le moyen français.* Padova: Liviana, 1977.

Doutrepont, Georges. *La Littérature française à la cour des ducs de Bourgogne.* Paris: Champion, 1909; rpt. Genève: Slatkine, 1970.

Dufournet, Jean. Article "La Marche," pp. 450–51 in *Dictionnaire des lettres françaises, Le Moyen Age.* Paris: Arthème Fayard, 1964.

Foss, Michael. *Chivalry.* New York: David McKay, 1975.

Fossier, Robert, ed. *The Cambridge Illustrated History of the Middle Ages,* vol. 3: 1250–1550, tr. Sarah Hanbury Tenison. Cambridge, etc.: Cambridge Univ. Press, 1986; rpt. 1987.

Fowler, Kenneth. *The Age of Plantagenet and Valois: The Struggle for Supremacy, 1328–1498.* New York: G. P. Putnam's Sons, 1967.

Friar, Stephen, ed. *A Dictionary of Heraldry.* New York: Harmony Books, 1987.

Gardner, Rosalyn, and Marion A. Greene. *A Brief Description of Middle French Syntax.* Studies in the Romance Languages and Literatures, 29. Chapel Hill: Univ. of North Carolina Press, 1958.

Godefroy, Frédéric. *Dictionnaire de l'ancienne langue française et de tous ses dialectes, du IXe au XVe siècle.* 10 vols. Paris: F. Viewig (vols. 1–5); Emile Bouillon (vols. 6–10), 1881–1902.

Greimas, Algirdas Julien, and Teresa Mary Keane. *Dictionnaire du moyen français.* Paris: Larousse, 1992. [Cited as "G.-K."]

Gröber, Gustav. *Grundriss der romanischen Philologie.* II. Band. I. Abteilung. Strassburg: Karl J. Trübner, 1902. [Olivier de La Marche, pp. 1137–40.]

Guelon, Y. (Conservateur en Chef, Bibliothèque Municipale, Chalon-sur-Saône). Personal communication, 1991. [Manuscript 123.]

Hassell, James Woodrow, Jr. *Middle French Proverbs, Sentences, and Proverbial Phrases*. Subsidia Mediaevalia, 12. Toronto: Pontifical Institute of Mediaeval Studies, 1982.

Hexter, J. H. *Reappraisals in History: New Views on History and Society in Early Modern Europe*. 2nd edition. Chicago: Univ. of Chicago Press, 1979.

Hindman, Sandra. "The Roles of Author and Artist in the Procedure of Illustrating Late Medieval Texts," pp. 27–62 in *Acta, X: Text and Image*, ed. David W. Burchmore. Binghamton: Center for Medieval and Early Renaissance Studies, 1986.

——. *Christine de Pizan's "Epistre Othéa": Painting and Politics at the Court of Charles VI*. Studies and Texts 77. Toronto: Pontifical Institute of Mediaeval Studies, 1986.

——, and James Douglas Farquhar. *Pen to Press: Illustrated Manuscripts and Printed Books in the First Century of Printing*. [College Park]: Art Department, Univ. of Maryland; [Baltimore]: Department of the History of Art, Johns Hopkins Univ., 1977. [Chapter III, "Authors, Artists, and Audiences," discusses the guide to the illustration of *Le Chevalier deliberé*, p. 172.]

Hogg, O. F. G. *Clubs To Cannon*. London: Unwin, 1968.

Huchon, Mireille. *Le Français de la Renaissance*. Que sais-je? 2389. Paris: Presses Universitaires de France, 1988.

Huguet, Edmond. *Dictionnaire de la langue française du seizième siècle*. 7 vols. Paris: Champion (vols. 1–2); Didier (vols. 3–7), 1925–1967.

Huisman, Michel. *Inventaire des nouveaux manuscrits concernant l'histoire de la Belgique acquis par la Bibliothèque royale de Berlin*. Bruxelles, 1899 (extr., *Bulletins de la Commission royale d'histoire de Belgique*, 5ᵉ série, t. IX). [Description of Berlin, In-folio, n° 177, pp. 367–69.]

Huizinga, Johan. *The Waning of the Middle Ages: A Study of the Forms of Life, Thought and Art in France and the Netherlands in the XIVth and XVth Centuries*, tr. F. Hopman. Garden City: Doubleday, 1954. *The Autumn of the Middle Ages*, tr. Rodney J. Payton and Ulrich Mammitzsch. Chicago: Univ. of Chicago Press, 1996. French translation by Julia Bastin, *Le Déclin du moyen âge*. Paris: Payot, 1932; republished as *L'Automne du moyen âge*. Paris: Payot, 1975; rpt. 1989.

James, Montague Rhodes. *A Descriptive Catalogue of the Manuscripts in the Fitzwilliam Museum.* Cambridge: Cambridge Univ. Press, 1895.

Jodogne, Omer. *"Povoir* ou *pouoir?* Le Cas phonétique de l'ancien verbe *pouoir."* *Travaux de Linguistique et de Littérature* 4.1 (1966): 257–66.

Jung, Marc-René. *Etudes sur le poème allégorique en France au moyen âge.* Berne: Francke, 1971.

Kilgour, Raymond Lincoln. *The Decline of Chivalry as Shown in the French Literature of the Late Middle Ages.* Cambridge, Mass.: Harvard Univ. Press, 1937.

Lachiver, Marcel. *Dictionnaire du monde rural: Les Mots du passé.* Paris: Arthème Fayard, 1997.

Lacroix, Paul. *Sciences & lettres au moyen âge et à l'époque de la Renaissance.* Paris: Firmin–Didot, 1877. [Woodcuts reproduce five miniatures from ms. *A,* pp. 429 (Palace of Love), 485 (Cloister of Memory), 531 (Atropos), 557 (the Author and Thought), 561 (the Author and Fresh Memory in the cemetery); discusses La Marche and/or *Le Chevalier deliberé,* pp. 484, 556.]

La Marche, Olivier de. *Le Chevalier délibéré by Olivier de La Marche. The Illustrations of the Edition of Schiedam Reproduced, with a Preface by F. Lippmann and a Reprint of the Text.* London: Printed for the Bibliographical Society at the Chiswick Press, 1898. [Includes an English translation of "The Author's Directions for the Illustration of His Poem," pp. xiii–xx.]

——. *Le Chevalier délibéré by Olivier de La Marche printed at Paris in 1488. A Reproduction made from the copy in the Lessing J. Rosenwald Collection, Library of Congress.* Washington, D.C.: Library of Congress, Rare Books Division, 1946. [Includes an Introduction by Elizabeth Mongan, pp. iii–xix.]

Lancelot, roman en prose du XIIIᵉ siècle, ed. Alexandre Micha. 9 vols. Textes Littéraires Français, 247, 249, 262, 278, 283, 286, 288, 307, 315. Genève: Droz, 1978–83.

Lancelot-Grail: The Old French Arthurian Vulgate and Post-Vulgate in Translation, ed. Norris J. Lacy. 5 vols. Garland Reference Library of the Humanities, 941, 1826, 1878, 1896, 1964. New York: Garland Publishing, 1993–96.

Langlois, Ernest, ed. *Recueil d'arts de seconde rhétorique.* Paris: Imprimerie Nationale, 1902. Contents: I. Jacques Legrand, *Des rimes* (c. 1405). II. Anonymous, *Les Règles de la seconde rhétorique* (early 15th c.). III. Baudet Herenc, *Le Doctrinal de la seconde rhétorique* (1432). IV. Anonymous, *Traité de l'art de rhétorique* (composed in Lorraine, mid-15th c.). V. Jean Molinet, *L'Art de rhétorique* (between 1477 and 1492). VI. Anonymous, *Traité de rhétorique* (late 15th c.). VII. Anonymous, *L'Art et science de rhétorique vulgaire* (1524 or 1525). [Cited as *Recueil*.]

Lebègue, Jean Albert. *Les Histoires que l'on peut raisonnablement faire sur les livres de Salluste*. Introduction de Jean Porcher. Paris: Pour la Société des Bibliophiles françois, Librairie Giraud–Badin, 1962.

Lemaire, Jacques. *Les Visions de la vie de cour dans la littérature française de la fin du Moyen Age*. Bruxelles: Palais des Académies; Paris: Klincksieck, 1994.

Le Vavasseur, A[chille]. "Olivier de La Marche, historien, poète et diplomate bourguignon" (review of *Mémoires d'Olivier de la Marche*, ed. Beaune and d'Arbaumont, and Stein, *Olivier*). *Revue des Questions Historiques* 46 (1889): 590–600.

Lodge, Sir Richard. *The Close of the Middle Ages, 1273–1494*. Fifth ed. Periods of European History; Period III. London: Rivingtons, 1957.

Lote, Georges. *Histoire du vers français*, tome III, première partie, Le Moyen Age, III: *La Poétique, le vers et la langue*. Paris: Hatier, 1955.

Madan, Falconer. *A Summary Catalogue of Western Manuscripts in the Bodleian Library at Oxford....* 7 vols. Oxford: Clarendon Press, 1895–1953. Vol. IV, p. 543, No. 21742 [ms. *B*].

Marchello–Nizia, Christiane. *Histoire de la langue française aux XIVe et XVe siècles*. Paris: Bordas, 1979; Dunod, 1992. [Cited as M.-N.]

Martin, Henry. *Catalogue des manuscrits de la Bibliothèque de l'Arsenal*. Paris: Plon, 1889.

——, and Philippe Lauer. *Les Principaux Manuscrits à peintures de la Bibliothèque de l'Arsenal à Paris*. Paris: Pour les membres de la Société Française de Reproductions de Manuscrits à Peintures, 1929.

Martineau–Génieys, Christine. *Le Thème de la mort dans la poésie française de 1450 à 1550*. Paris: Champion, 1978.

Matthew, Donald. *The Medieval European Community*. New York: St. Martin's, 1977.

Ménage, René. "Le Voyage délibéré du chevalier de la Marche," pp. 209–19 in *Voyage, Quête, Pèlerinage dans la littérature et la civilisation médiévales* (colloque organisé par le C.U.E.R. M.A. les 5–7 mars 1976). Senefiance n° 2. Aix-en-Provence: CUER MA, 1976.

Meyer, Paul. "Deuxième Rapport sur une mission littéraire en Angleterre et en Ecosse," pp. 115–39 in *Archives des missions scientifiques et littéraires*, 2e série, tome IV. Paris: Imprimerie nationale, 1867. [Mentions ms. *E* in passing, p. 139.]

Michel, Etienne. "Trois Magnifiques Ouvrages, qui firent partie de la bibliothèque du château de La Bastie d'Urfé, sont aujourd'hui au cabinet des livres du château de Chantilly." *Bulletin de la Diana* 26 (1939): 430–34. [On ms. C.]

Mitteilungen aus der Königlichen Bibliothek. Herausgegeben von der Generalverwaltung. IV. *Kurzes Verzeichnis der Romanischen Handschriften.* Berlin: Weidmannsche Buchhandlung, 1918.

Moignet, Gérard. *Le Pronom personnel français, essai de psycho-systématique historique.* Bibliothèque Française et Romane, série A: Manuels et études linguistiques, 9. Paris: Klincksieck, 1965.

Molinier, Auguste. *Les Sources de l'histoire de France, des origines aux guerres d'Italie (1494).* 6 vols. Paris, 1901–06; rpt. New York: Burt Franklin, [1964]. Bibliography and Reference Series, 80. Vol. VI, Table générale, par Louis Polain.

Mongan: see La Marche, *Le Chevalier délibéré* (Library of Congress).

Morier, Henri. *Dictionnaire de poétique et de rhétorique.* 3ᵉ édition. Paris: Presses Universitaires de France, 1981.

Muhlethaler, Jean–Claude. *Poétiques du quinzième siècle: Situation de François Villon et Michault Taillevent.* Paris: Nizet, 1983.

Murgey de Tupigny, Jacques. *Les Principaux Manuscrits à peintures du Musée Condé de Chantilly.* Paris: Pour les membres de la Société Française de Reproductions de Manuscrits à Peintures, 1930.

National Library of Scotland. *Summary Catalogue of the Advocates' Manuscripts.* Edinburgh: Her Majesty's Stationery Office, 1971.

Neubecker, Ottfried, with contributions by J. P. Brooke–Little. *Heraldry: Sources, Symbols and Meaning.* New York: McGraw Hill, 1976; London: Black Cat, 1988.

New Grove Dictionary of Music and Musicians, ed. Stanley Sadie. 20 vols. London: Macmillan; Washington, D.C.: Grove's Dictionaries of Music, 1980.

Pächt, Otto, and J. J. G. Alexander. *Illuminated Manuscripts in the Bodleian Library, Oxford, 1: German, Dutch, Flemish, French and Spanish Schools.* Oxford: Clarendon Press, 1966.

Pasini, Giuseppe Luca, and Francesco Berta. *Manuscriptorum codicum bibliothecae regii taurinensis athenaei* [etc.]. [No place, no date.]

Piaget, Arthur. "*Le Chemin de Vaillance* de Jean de Courcy et l'hiatus de l'*e* final des polysyllabes aux XIVᵉ et XVᵉ siècles." *Romania* 17 (1898): 582–607.

Picot, Emile, and Henri Stein. *Recueil de pièces historiques imprimées sous le règne de Louis XI reproduites en fac–similé avec des commentaires historiques et bibliographiques.* Paris: Pour la Société des Bibliophiles françois, 1923. [Introduction et bibliographie: *Texte,* pp. 305–45; *Le Chevalier délibéré,* fac-similé de l'édition de Schiedam, vers 1498: *Facsimilés,* pp. 239–306.]

Poirion, Daniel. *Le Lexique de Charles d'Orléans dans les* Ballades. Publications Romanes et Françaises, 91. Genève: Droz, 1967.

Prescott, Anne Lake. "Spenser's Chivalric Restoration: From Bateman's *Travayled Pylgrime* to the Redcrosse Knight." *Studies in Philology* 86.2 (1989): 166–97.

Régnier-Bohler, Danielle, éd. *Splendeurs de la cour de Bourgogne: Récits et chroniques.* Paris: Robert Laffont, 1995.

Reno, Christine. "Thorny Observations on Ligatures and Glossaries." Conference paper, Kentucky Foreign Language Conference, 1994.

Rickard, Peter. *Chrestomathie de la langue française au quinzième siècle.* Cambridge: Cambridge Univ. Press, 1976.

———. *La Langue française au seizième siècle: Etude suivie de textes.* Cambridge: Cambridge Univ. Press, 1968.

Sainte-Palaye, Jean-Baptiste de La Curne de. *Dictionnaire historique de l'ancien langage françois....* 10 vols. Niort: L. Favre, 1875–82.

Samaran, Charles, and Robert Marichal. *Catalogue des manuscrits en écriture latine portant des indications de date, de lieu ou de copiste.* Paris: Centre National de la Recherche Scientifique, 1959. Tome 1, *Musée Condé et bibliothèques parisiennes,* p. 35. [Description of ms. *C.*]

Saulnier, V. L. "L'Humanisme français aux premiers temps du livre," pp. 9–26 in *L'Humanisme français au début de la Renaissance.* Colloque international de Tours (XIVe stage), conférence d'ouverture. De Pétrarque à Descartes, 29. Paris: Vrin, 1973.

Scott, Arthur Finley. *The Plantagenet Age: Commentaries of an Era.* Every One a Witness, 2. New York, White Lion Publishers, 1975.

Selvaggi, L. (Direttore, Biblioteca Nazionale Universitaria, Torino). Personal communication, 1991. [Table of contents, ms. *T.*]

Sorbelli, Albano. *Inventari dei manoscritti delle biblioteche d'Italia,* vol. 28 (Torino). Firenze: Olschki, 1922.

Sotheby Parke Bernet & Co. *Catalogue of Western Manuscripts and Miniatures,* 10th December 1980. London, 1980.

Stein, Henri. *Olivier de la Marche, historien, poète et diplomate bourguignon.* Bruxelles: Hayez; Paris: Picard, 1888. Extrait du tome XLIX des *Mémoires couronnés et mémoires des savants étrangers,* publiés par l'Académie royale des sciences, des lettres et des beaux-arts de Belgique, 1888.

———. *Nouveaux Documents sur Olivier de La Marche et sa famille.* Académie royale de Belgique, Classe des lettres, Mémoires, deuxième série. Mémoire présenté à la Classe des lettres ... dans sa séance du 9 janvier 1922. Bruxelles: Lamertin, 1926, tome IX, pp. 3–69.

———. "La Date de naissance d'Olivier de La Marche," pp. 461–64 in *Mélanges d'histoire offerts à Henri Pirenne....* Bruxelles: Vromant, 1926, tome II.

Stephenson, Carl, and Bryce Lyon. *Mediaeval History: Europe from the Second to the Sixteenth Century,* 4th ed. New York: Harper and Row, 1962.

Stevens, John. *Medieval Romance: Themes and Approaches.* New York: Norton, 1974.

Stone, George Cameron. *A Glossary of the Construction, Decoration and Use of Arms and Armor in All Countries and in All Times* ... Portland, Me.: Southworth Press, 1934; rpt. New York: Jack Brussel, 1961.

Sutch, Susie Speakman. "Notice sur l'identification d'un manuscrit « inconnu » du *Chevalier délibéré* d'Olivier de La Marche." *Romania* 114 (1996): 246–53.

———. "La Production d'un manuscrit du poème intitulé *Le Chevalier délibéré* d'Olivier de La Marche." Forthcoming.

———, and Anne Lake Prescott. "Translation as Transformation: Olivier de La Marche's *Le Chevalier délibéré* and its Hapsburg and Elizabethan Permutations." *Comparative Literature Studies* 25.4 (1988): 281–317.

Tabulae codicum manu scriptorum praeter graecos et orientales in Bibliotheca Palatina Vindobonensi asservatorum. (Edidit Academia Caesarea Vindobonensis.) Volumen II, cod. 2001–3500. Vindobonae [Vienna]: Venum dat Caroli Geroldi Filius, 1868.

Thiry, Claude. « La Mort du Téméraire. Témoignages de chroniqueurs écrits au XV–XVIᵉ siècle », Introduction, in Régnier–Bohler, *Splendeurs,* pp. 953–61.

Turnbull, Stephen. *The Book of the Medieval Knight.* London: Arms and Armor Press, 1985.

Unterkircher, Franz. *Bibliothèque Nationale d'Autriche: Manuscrits et livres imprimés concernant l'histoire des Pays-Bas, 1475–1600,* trans. M. Wittek. Bruxelles: Bibliothèque royale de Belgique, 1962.

Vallet de Viriville, Auguste. "La Marche (Olivier de)" in *Nouvelle Biographie générale* ... Paris: Firmin–Didot, 1862. Tome 29, col. 47–51.

Vaughan, Richard. *Charles the Bold: The Last Valois Duke of Burgundy*. London: Longmans, Green and Co., 1973; New York: Harper & Row, 1974.

——. *Philip the Good: The Apogee of Burgundy*. London: Longmans, Green and Co., 1970.

——. *Valois Burgundy*. London: Penguin; Hamden, Conn.: Shoe String Press (Archon Books), 1975.

Vielliard, Françoise, and Jacques Monfrin. Troisième supplément, *Manuel bibliographique de la littérature française du moyen âge*, de R. Bossuat, tome II. Paris: Editions du Centre National de la Recherche Scientifique, 1991.

Wallen, Burr. "Burgundian *Gloire* vs. *Vaine Gloire*: Patterns of Neochivalric *Psychomachia*." Pp. 147–75 in *A Tribute to Robert A. Koch: Studies in the Northern Renaissance*. Princeton: Department of Art and Archaeology, Princeton University, 1994, inc. 4 plates.

Weightman, Christine. *Margaret of York, Duchess of Burgundy, 1446–1503*. New York: St. Martin's, 1989.

Zumthor, Paul. *Anthologie des grands rhétoriqueurs*. Collection 10/18, No. 1232. Paris: Union Générale d'éditions, 1978.

The following editions of other late-medieval texts have proven useful in the preparation of the present edition:

Amé de Montgesoie. *Le Pas de la Mort*, in "Les Poèmes d'Amé de Montgesoie (fl. 1457–1478)," ed. Thomas Walton. *Medium Ævum* 2.1 (1933): 1–33.

Charles d'Orléans. *Poésies*, ed. Pierre Champion. 2 vols. Classiques Français du Moyen Age, 34, 56. Paris: Champion, 1923–27.

Chastellain, Georges. *Œuvres*, ed. Kervyn de Lettenhove. 8 vols. Académie Royale des Sciences, des Lettres et des Beaux-Arts de Belgique. Bruxelles: Heussner [etc.], 1863–66. Tome VI, *Œuvres diverses*.

Christine de Pisan. *Le Livre de la Mutacion de Fortune*, ed. Suzanne Solente. 4 vols. Société des Anciens Textes Français. Paris: Picard, 1959–66.

Coudrette. *Le Roman de Mélusine, ou Histoire de Lusignan*, ed. Eleanor Roach. Bibliothèque Française et Romane, Série B, Editions critiques de textes, 18. Paris: Klincksieck, 1982.

The Danse Macabre of Women, Ms. fr. 995 of the Bibliothèque Nationale, ed. Anne Tukey Harrison. Kent, Ohio: Kent State Univ. Press, 1994.

La Marche, Olivier de. *Mémoires d'Olivier de la Marche, maître d'hôtel et capitaine des gardes de Charles le Téméraire*, ed. Henri Beaune et J. d'Arbaumont. 4 vols. Paris: Renouard, 1883–88.

——. *Le Triumphe des dames*, ed. Julia Kalbfleisch–Benas. Rostock: Universitäts–Buchdruckerei, 1901.

La Tour Landry, Chevalier de. *Le Livre du Chevalier de la Tour Landry pour l'enseignement de ses filles*, ed. Anatole de Montaiglon. Paris: Jannet, 1854.

La Vigne, André de. *La Ressource de la chrestienté*, ed. Cynthia J. Brown. Inedita & Rara, 5. Montréal: CERES, 1989.

Taillevent, Michault. *Un Poète bourguignon du XVe siècle : Michault Taillevent (Edition et étude)*, ed. Robert Deschaux. Publications Romanes et Françaises, 132. Genève: Droz, 1975.

Villon, François. *Complete Poems*, ed. Barbara N. Sargent–Baur. Toronto: Univ. of Toronto Press, 1994.

——. *Œuvres d'après le manuscrit Coislin*, ed. Rika Van Deyck et Romana Zwaenepoel. 2 vols. Textes et Traitement Automatique, 2. Saint-Aquilin-de-Pacy: Mallier, 1974.

On the Spanish versions of Le Chevalier deliberé:
Aubrun, Charles V. Review of Clavería 1950. *Bulletin Hispanique* 53 (1951): 430–32.

Clavería, Carlos. *Le Chevalier délibéré de Olivier de la Marche y sus versiones españolas del siglo XVI*. Zaragoza: Heraldo de Aragón, 1950.

——. "Notas sobre el significado y fortuna de *El Caballero determinado*," pp. 287–311 in *Estudios dedicados a Menéndez-Pidal*, 6. Madrid: Consejo Superior de Investigaciones Cientificas, 1956.

Groult, P. Review of Clavería 1950. *Les Lettres Romanes* 8 (1954): 167–72.

——. Review of Clavería 1956. *Les Lettres Romanes* 13 (1959): 100–101.

Heitmann, Klaus. "Die spanischen Übersetzer von Olivier de la Marches «Chevalier deliberé»: Hernando de Acuña und Jerónimo de Urrea," pp. 229–46 in Karl–Hermann Körner and Klaus Rühl, eds., *Studia Iberica: Festschrift für Hans Flasche*. Bern: Francke, 1973.

Peeters–Fontainas, J. "A propos des éditions du *Caballero determinado*." *Les Lettres Romanes* 13 (1959): 69–70.

On the art–historical aspects of printed versions of Le Chevalier deliberé:
Boon, K. G. "The Life and Work of Hugo Jacobsz Before 1500," pp. 43–48 in *Essays in Northern European Art Presented to Egbert Haverkamp–Begemann on His Sixtieth Birthday*. Doornspijk (The Netherlands): Davaco, 1983.

Heitmann, Klaus. "Zur Antike–Rezeption am burgundischen Hof: Olivier de la Marche und der Heroenkult Karls des Kühnen," pp. 97–118 in *Die Rezeption der Antike: Zum Problem der Kontinuität zwischen Mittelalter und Renaissance*, ed. August Buck. Hamburg: Hauswedell, 1981.

Llompart, Gabriel. "En torno a la iconografía renacentista del 'Miles Christi'." *Traza y Baza: Cuadernos Hispanos de Simbología, Arte y Literatura* 1 (1972): 63–94.

Moffitt, John F. " '*Le Roi à la ciasse*'? [*sic*]: Kings, Christian Knights, and Van Dyck's Singular 'Dismounted Equestrian-Portrait' of Charles I." *Artibus et Historiae* 4.7 (1983): 79–99.

Olivier de La Marche

Le Chevalier deliberé
(The Resolute Knight)

Miniature No. 9. The Palace of Love:
the Author, Illusion, Desire, Remembrance.
Paris, Bibliothèque de l'Arsenal, ms. 5117, folio 22 verso.
Cliché Bibliothèque nationale de France.

Miniature No. 10.
Fresh Memory shows the Author her cemetery.
Chantilly, Musée Condé, ms. 507, page 50.
Photo Lauros-Giraudon.

Cy commence le premier chapitre du traictié intitulé *le Chevalier deliberé*.*

1. A insi qu'a l'arriere saison,
      Tant de mes jours que de l'annee,
      Je partis hors de ma maison
   Par une soudaine achoison,
   Seul a par moy fors de Pensee,
   Qui m'acompaigna la journee
   Et me mist en ramentevance
   Le premier temps de mon enfance.

2. Celle qui moult estoit m'amie*
   Prist ung propos de verité
   Et me dist : « Celuy qui s'oublie
   Fuit honneur et si l'amenrie.　　　　　[4]
   Je le tiens pour desherité

Rubric. Cy commence *not legible in T* | traictie appelle le ch. *Q*, traittie du ch. d. *S*; intitulé *om. Y. Ai**: Le titre de l'Imprimé est ainsy. Cy commence le chevalier deliberé comprenant la mort du Duc de Bourgogne qui trépassa devant Nancy en Lorraine. *M*: Le nouveau Cheualier deliberé contenant la mort du duc Philippe [*sic*] de Bourgoingne qui trespassa deuant Nancy en Lorraine Par messire Georges Chastellain [*sic*] chevalier serviteur [?] et excellent otalier [?] dudit feu duc. *Rubric precedes miniature in E/Y; no rubric, V.*
Equivalent miniature in *ABQR/XY* (female figure labeled "grace de dieu," *X*); different subjects in *EFGPS*.
1.1 Ainsy que *ESV/M*, A. quen *R* | la riuiere [*sic*] s. *X* (+*1*)
1.4 Pour *QS*
1.5 part *Q/M* | plain de pensee *M*

Part I

Here begins the first chapter of the treatise
entitled *The Resolute Knight*

1. In the autumn of both
    My life and of the year,
    On the spur of the moment
    I went outside my house
    By myself, alone except for Thought,
    Who stayed with me that day
    And made me recall
    My earliest youth.

2. As my best friend,
    She began to talk about truth,
    And said to me, "He who gives no thought to himself,
    Who shuns honor and cheapens it,
    I consider excluded

1.6 macompaigna *EFGLNPR[T]VW/MXZ* (m'accompaigna *B*)] ma compaignet [*sic*] *C*,
     macompaignoit *A*, me compaigna *QS*, macompaigua [*sic*] *Y*
1.7 me meit a r. *V*, me vint en remembrance *M* (-*1*)
1.8 mon essance *V*

Stanza 2 om. A; copied from "l'Imprimé" (Ai).
2.1 tant est. *S*
2.2 Prent *M*
2.3 dit *V/AiY*
2.4 lhonneur *V* | si *EFGLNPQSV/XY*, sy *BR*] sil *C*, cy *Ai*; sil amenrie *W* | la meurie
     EFGS; lame nuye *Ai*, lamenuye *MZ*; *T is illegible.*
2.5 Je te *X* | descherite [*sic*] *G*

Soit d'avoir ou de la santé
Ou d'espoir de grace divine,
Que chascun n'est pas d'avoir digne.*

3.   Tu vois pour la saison passee
Arbres et terres et herbaige,
L'un sans verd, l'autre sans ramee ;
Fleur et oudeur toute est cassee,
Plus n'est feulle, fruit në umbraige.
Tout tend a froidure et a neige,
Tout est secq sans nulle vigueur
Et n'est plus seve ne chaleur.

4.   Ainsi est de toy clerement,
Qui le printemps de ton enfance
As despendu entierement
Et jonesse paraillement,
Qui t'est ores en deffaillance.
Et si n'as pas telle esperance
Qu'ont les arbres pour raverdir,
Car jamais ne peulx revenir.

5.   Dois tu oublier ou que soye*
Ce traictié qui tant point et mort
Que fist Amé de Montjesoye,
Plus riche que d'or ne de soye,

2.6   Soit deuoir Y | ou soit de s. M | la om. QW/AiX (-1), de sa EFGNPS | sente P;
de sa seurte S. T is illegible.
2.7   Du despoir [sic] Ai

Only the last line of stanza 3 is legible in T.
3.1   par la BSVW, que la E, par ta s. Q; sur la s. M
3.2   first et om. L (et puis [?] h.), V (-1) | herbaiges ABQRVW. Herbes terres et tout h.
M
3.3   Lun tout mort M. Rerum vices added in left margin, M
3.4   et om. X (-1) | tost est B/M, tout est EQSV
3.5   nest fruict feulle ne E; fleur fruit FG (-1), fleur ne fruit M | ny um. M (+1)
3.6   Tout tant X
3.7   Tout est mort M, Tous secs [sic] X (-1) | nulle verdeur E
3.8   sene [sic] A. Et na plus force ne ch. M

From wealth or health
Or the hope of divine grace,
Which not everyone deserves.

3. You see the season just finished—
Trees and lands and bush:
Greenery and branches gone,
Blossom and fragrance spent;
Leaves, fruit and shade no longer exist.
Everything is moving toward cold and snow,
Everything's dry and lacking strength,
With no more sap or warmth.

4. It's clearly like that with you,
Who have totally wasted
The springtime of your childhood
And your youth as well,
Which you now sadly lack.
Nor do you have any hope
That you can wax green and young again
As do the trees.

5. How can you possibly forget
That pricking, mordant treatise
That Amé de Montgesoie wrote
(More precious than gold or silk)

4.2 Que le *EFGV* | de son *W/X*
4.3 As perdu *X* (*-1*)
4.4 Et ta j. *R* (+*1*)
4.5 Qui tes [*sic*] *W*; Mis tes *M*, Qui tost *X* | ore *R* (*-1*), aures [*sic*] *X*, c . . . tes [*?*] *M*
4.6 si tu *M* (*om.* pas) | n'a *B*, na *FGW/X* | tel *Q* | telle experiance *E*
4.8 peut *W*; Car j. tu ne peuz r. *Q* (+*1*)

Stanzas 5–10 (fol. 15) interrupt the last stanza of Le Pas de la Mort, *V.*
5.1 ou que ie soie *G* (+*1*), ou je soye *Q*, ou que soies *S*. Dois je ou. ou que je soïe *M*
5.2 Ce traictier *BEFGP*, Le traitte *QS*
5.3 Qui *W* | feist *EFGLN*, fit *BS* | Aymé *M* | mont.ie *C*, moult *BER*, monlt [*?*] *F, G*
     | *Marginal note, M:* Ayme de Montjoïe [*sic*] premier herault darmes du roy
5.4 ny de soïe *M*

Du merveilleux *Pas de la Mort* ?*
Savoir fault qui est le plus fort*
De toy, Accident ou Debile :
Chascun d'eulx en a tué mille.

6.   Ces deulx chevaliers trescrueulx*
      En la grant forest d'Atropos   [5]
      Tiennent le Pas trop perilleux,
      Tres horrible, tres merveilleux,
      Sans avoir jour ne nuit repos
      Et continuent leur propos
      De tant combatre et de ferir
      Que faire tout homme mourir.

7.   Messire Accident le Terrible
      Furnit les jones et les fors
      Et Debille le Treshorrible
      Met a mort par cops invisible*
      Ceulx dont la vigueur en est hors.
      Ilz font de tuer tous effors :
      Leurs murtres sont sy a doubter
      Que nulz ne leur peut escapper.*

8.   Scez tu pas qu'Excés le herault
      T'a pieça noncié leurs chapitres ?
      Tu scez que ce poise et que vault :

5.6   le *om.* W (*-1*)
5.7   daccident L. *Marginal note, M:* Subiect du present liure
5.8   Cchascun [*sic*] A | mil W

6.1   Tes deux [*sic*] X
6.2   En sa V | d' *om.* LR/Y
6.3   les pas QS | tropt p. V, tresperilleux B
6.4   Treshorribles QSV/M | et tresmerveilleux B, V (+*1*)
6.6   Et continuent *ABEFGLNPQVW/XYZ*] Et si c. C (+*1*), Et contiennent R, En continu-
      ant S/M
6.7   et de tant ferir W (+*1*), de *om.* V/X (-*1*)
6.8   Quilz feront M | tous hommes V

About the monstrous Tourney of Death?
You must find out which is stronger
Than you, Accident or Debility:
Each of *them* has killed thousands.

6.   In Atropos' great forest
      These two most cruel knights
      Hold the most perilous Tourney,
      Most hideous, most fantastic.
      Resting neither day nor night,
      They stick to their aim
      To fight and strike so much
      That they make all men die.

7.   Lord Accident the Terrible
      Sees to the young and the strong,
      And Debility the Hideous
      Puts to death with unseen blows
      Those whose strength has gone.
      They make every effort to kill:
      Their murders are so feared,
      As no one can escape them.

8.   Don't you know that the herald Excess
      Long since read you their judgments?
      You know their import and worth:

7.2   Fournist *AL*, Fornist *M*, Furnist *B*, Fuirent [?] *R*; Suruit *FGPS*, Suruint *E*, Seruit *Q*,
      Seuruint *X*
7.3   le *om.* *Q* (-*1*)
7.4   a fin *LR/MY* | cop *LW/Y* | inuisible *probably over-written from* inuisile, *C*;
      nuysible *V* (-*1*), inuisibles *M*
7.5   la vigne [*sic*] *V* (-*1*), vigneur [*sic*] *X*
7.6   Terribles [?] sont les [*illegible*] *M*
7.7   Leurs euures *E*, Leur murdre *V* | font cy *L*
7.8   nul *QS/X* | ne les *L/M* | euiter [?] *M*; ne leur peuent eschapper *E* (+*1*)

8.1   quepces [*sic*] *W*, Guexcez [*sic*] *X* | les herault [*sic*] *S*; Scais tu pas bien que le h. *M*
8.2   pieca nomme *E*; porte [?] *M* | le chappittre *R*, leur chapitre *V*; leurs epistres *M*.
8.3   Tu scais bien que *M* | ce *om.* *Q* (-*1*), *M* | et ce v. *V*

Accident t'a livré l'assault !
Tu as oÿ de ses epystres.
Il est temps que tu te chappitres,
Car tu as touchié a l'emprise
Depuis ta premiere chemise.

9.   Es tu plus puissant que Sanson
       Ou plus a craindre que Herculés ?
       Plus saige que fut Salomon,
       Plus beau que le grant Absalon,
       Plus subtil que Dyomedés ?
       N'as tu peur quant tu pense adés
       Que ceulx n'ont peu les cops rabatre
       De ceulx qu'il te convient combatre ?

10.   Plus vis et plus le temps aprouche   [6]
       Qu'il te convient en champ entrer ;
       Tu sens desja ung fer qui loche.
       Maladie sonne la cloche
       En lieu de trompectes sonner,
       Qui te semont de toy armer
       Et de defendre ta querelle
       Contre la bataille mortelle. »

11.   Ainsi Pensee m'enhortoit
       De ce qui me fut necessaire,
       Dont la mercyay bien estroit
       Et luy dis : « Puis qu'il fault que soit,

8.4   la liure *V*
8.5   ses chappitres *M*
8.6   te *om. G* (*-1*) | tu le ch. [*sic*] *X*
8.7   tu a *W* | as conseillie *R* (*+1*), as couche [*sic*] *X* | a leur prise *QS*

9.1   plus plus *Q* (*+1*) | plus fort que nest s. *M*
9.2   plus *om. L/M* (*-1*)
9.3   que n'est *M*, que nestoit *L* (*+1*), que ne fut *RS* (*+1*), fut *om. W* (*-1*)
9.6   paour *ALQ* | penses *AEQS/MY* (*+1*), pensez *X* (*+1*)
9.7   Telz qui *M* | nont peuz *V* | le cop *R*, les corps *AEW* | abatre *E*
9.8   qui *BEFQRSVW/M*

Accident has launched his attack on you—
You have heard his dispatches!
It is time that you take yourself to task,
For you have been approaching this undertaking
Since you were first born.

9.   Are you more powerful than Samson,
       More to be feared than Hercules,
       Wiser than Solomon,
       Fairer than the great Absalom,
       More wily than Dyomedes?
       Aren't you instantly afraid when you think
       That *they* weren't able to counter the blows
       Of those whom you must fight?

10.   The longer you live, the sooner it's time
       For you to enter the arena;
       You already hear the rattle of steel.
       Malady tolls the bell
       Instead of sounding trumpets,
       Summoning you to don your armor
       And take up your cause
       Against the mortal battle."

11.   Thus did Thought press me
       About what I needed,
       For which I straightway thanked her
       And told her, "Since it must be,

10.1   saprouche *QV/MX*

10.2   Qui *PSV* | champs *W*

10.5   Au *M* | trompette [*sing.*] *BLVW/MY*

11.1   Ainsi pensif si men. *M*

11.2   ce que *L* | me fust *L*, mestoit *M* | necessaire *ABEFGNPVW/MXYZ*, (necc- *LQRS*)] necessoire *C*

11.3   le [*sic*] merciay *RV* | mercie *E*, mercye *X* | b. estoit [*sic*] *X*

11.4   puis que *E/X*, plus qui *V* | quil soit *BLQRW/MY*, qui soit *EV*

Je feray ce que je doy faire. »
Lors je prins mon harnas de guerre
Et comme ung chevalier errant
M'armay et montay tout errant.

MINIATURE 2. The Author, two squires, a page, Thought,
and the horse Willing

**Cy s'arme, monte et enbastonne l'Acteur   [7]
pour entrer en sa queste.**

12.   on cheval s'appelloit Vouloir
     Et mon harnas je fiz tremper
     D'une eaue qu'on nomme Pouoir.
Mon escu fut de Bon Espoir,
Au moins pour longuement durer.
Mon glave fut d'Aventurer
Fait par ung merveilleux ouvraige
Et mon espee de Couraige.

13. Ainsi j'entrepris la conqueste
De mes adversaires doubtez
Et me mis tout seulet en queste
En sievant la maniere honneste
Des bons chevaliers trespassez
Et chevauchay deux jours passez
Avant que trouvasse adventure
Digne de mectre en escripture.*

11.5 doye *W* (+*1*)
11.6 Alors mon harnois je fiz traire *M*
11.7 ch. vaillant *M*
11.8 et monte *E/X*

Equivalent miniature in *ABFGR/Y*; different subjects in *EQS/X*.
Rubric. Si *X* | sarme *et* m. *R/X*, sarme lacteur monte et *S* | monte embastonne *X* | sa
    gueste *P* [?], *R*. *Rubric precedes miniature in BEFGQS/Y; no rubric, V/M.*
12.2 temprer *RVW*
12.3 quon nomma *E*, con nommoit *R*; quon appelle *L*; appellee *M*
12.4 fet de *E*, fust de *L* | bon espir [*sic*] *X*

I will do what I must."
Then I took my battle gear
And, as a knight errant,
Put on my armor and mounted up without delay.

**Here the Author dons his armor, mounts up, and takes up arms
in order to embark upon his quest.**

12.   M y horse was named Willing;
         I'd had my armor tempered in
         The waters called Power.
My shield was of Good Hope,
So as to last a long time.
My lance, of Venture,
Was made with wondrous craft,
And my sword of Courage.

13.   Thus did I set out on the conquest
         Of my dread adversaries,
         And entered all alone on a quest,
         Following the tried and true way
         Of good knights now departed.
         I rode two full days
         Before I came across any adventure
         Worth putting down in writing.

12.6   Mon glauie *Y*
12.7   par *om. W* (*-1*) | ung *om. R* (*-1*)

13.1   j' *om. W*
13.2   doubtz [*sic*] *Y*
13.3   soulet *Q*; tout seul en *X* (*-1*)
13.4   En ensieuant *R* (*+1*)
13.6–7 *inverted V*
13.6   Je ch. *V*
13.8   Disne *E*; Quest dingne m. *V* | en lescripture *E*

14. Ja n'est besoing que je raconte
     Mes sejours et mes repousees*
     Mais raison est que je vous compte
     Les adventures de ce compte
     Telles que je les ay trouvees.
     Droit a la fin de deux journees
     Je m'embatiz en une plaine
     Qu'on nomme Plaisance Mondaine.

15. Je pris en ce lieu tel plaisir
     Et m'agrëoit tant la contree
     Que je n'en pouoye partir
     Mais ains que peuse departir
     J'ay adventure rencontree
     D'ung chevalier venant la pree   [8]
     Qui m'escria de me garder
     Et qu'il me convenoit jouster.

16. Je luy respondis : « Amis chier,*
     Du moins a ma premiere jouste
     Dictes moy, s'estes chevalier,
     Vostre non et de quel quartier
     Vous estes. » Dist il : « Or escoute :
     A qui qu'il poise ne qu'il couste,
     J'ay non Hutin qui tout debrise,
     Le propre filz de Gourmandise. »

14.1 Il nest *L/M* | que je vous compte *ENPQS/X*
14.2 Mes sisiours [?] ne mes *V* | et me r. [*sic*] *F* | reposez [*sic*] *X*
14.3 je racompte *EQS*, ie raconte *NP* | vous *om. X (-1)*
14.6 en la f. *B* | des deux *Q*
14.7 Je mesbatis *ER/X* | par une *ENPQS/X* | pleine *N/X*
14.8 no*m*moit *M*

15.2 magrayoit *Q*
15.3 n'en pouuois pas yssir *M*; pertyr *V*
15.4 peuse *CRV*, peusse *ABEFGNPQTW/XY*, peusses [*sic*] *S*; quen peusse *M*, que en puisse
      L | despartir *ES*
15.5 recontree [*sic*] *V*; Jaray laduenture racontee *R (+1)*
15.6 ch. parmy la pree *M*

14.   There's no need for me to list
      My stops and stays,
      But it's only right to tell you
      The events of this story,
      Such as I found them.
      Right at the end of two days' ride
      I suddenly entered upon a plain
      Called Worldly Pleasure.

15.   I took such satisfaction in that place,
      And the region delighted me so,
      That I could not leave it.
      Moreover, before I could depart,
      I met up with adventure
      From a knight coming through the meadow,
      Who called out to me to defend myself
      And that I must joust with him.

16.   I answered him, "Dear friend,
      At least for my first joust
      Tell me, if you are a knight,
      Your name and from what region
      You hail." Said he, "Then listen,
      Whomever it harms or costs,
      I am Quarreler, he who shatters everything,
      True son of Gluttony.

15.7   de marrester *M*
15.8   qui me *V*

Stanzas 16–19 missing, A; copied from "l'Imprimé," fol. 5ʳ⁻ᵛ.
16.1   amy *BEQRS/XY*, Amy *M*
16.3   cestes *EF/Y*, cestez *GNP*, faictes [*sic*] *X*
16.4   Voustre *Q* | nom ne de *EFGNP/X*
16.5   dit *V* | escoutté [*sic*] *B*, esconte [*sic*] *X*
16.6   quil qui p. *FGNP*, qui qui *V* | pose *W* | ne qui c. *EFGNPV/AiX*, et quil c. *S* (*-1*)
16.7   Jay mon [*sic*] *X* | tout brise *Ai* (*-1*)
16.8   Le poure filz *W*

17.   « Comment, dis je, n'estes vous pas
Debile ou Messire Accident,
Qui tiennent d'Atropos le Pas ?
Quant je vous vis venir le pas,
Je le cuiday appertement. »
Il dist que non certainement,
Mais qu'il estoit de leur mesnye,
Premier persecuteur de vie.

18.   Lors baisse sa lance ferree
D'un fer qu'on nomme Peu de Sens
Et fiert en ma targe doree
Tel coup et de telle boutee
Qu'encores certes je m'en sens !
Et moy de mon meilleur assens
Couchay mon glave si appoint*
Que nulz de nous ne faillit point.*

19.   La furent nos lances brisees
Mais nous gardasmes les arsons
Et mismes les mains aux espees,
Toutes de folies trempees.   [9]
Donnans terribles horions,
La frapoient les champions

17.1 Comme dis si n'estes *Ai* | dist il [*sic*] *X*
17.5 appartement *BEFG/M*
17.6 dit *GLV/AiXY*
17.7 Mais qui *V*

18.1 besse *GPQ*, baissa *RV/AiM*, baisa [*sic*] *X* | la lance *V* | ferree *EFGLNPQRSTVW/XYZ* (ferreé *B*, ferrée *AiM*)] ferre *C*
18.2 qui nomme *S*
18.4 boute *Y*
18.5 Que encore c. *L/Ai*
18.6 essciens *FGNP*, essiens *E/X*, essient *QS*. et moy acoup a luy j'entens *Ai*, Et moy aussi a luy j'entend *M*
18.7 Cousche *Q*; Couchant *M*, Couche *X*; touchay *Ai* | ma lance *L/AiM*; mon glauie *Y* | cy a point *Ai*

17.   "What," I said, "you are not
      Debility or Lord Accident
      Who hold the Tourney of Atropos?
      When I saw you coming
      I distinctly thought you were."
      He said certainly not,
      But that he was of their household,
      The principal persecutor of life.

18.   Then he lowered his lance,
      Tipped with a steel called Little Sense,
      And he struck on my shield
      Such a blow and of such force
      That truly I can feel it still!
      And I, as best I knew how,
      Set my lance so properly
      That neither of us missed.

19.   Our lances were splintered there,
      But we stayed in our saddles
      And put hands to swords,
      All steeped in follies.
      Dealing terrible blows,
      There the champions struck

18.8   nul *LQS* | ny f. *BV* | faillit *BEFGLNPQSW/AiMXZ*] falut *C*, failli *R*, failly *Y*, failliz *V*. [Que] tous deux ne faillismes point *T*

19.1   nous lances [*sic*] *Ai*, noz lanche [*sic*] *W* | brisiez *R*

19.2   nous *om.* *Q* (-*1*) | gardismes [*sic*] *E* | noz arcons *M*

19.3   Et meismez *R*, Et meismes *Y*

19.4   desoulies *E*, de foulies *G* | temprees *R*; actrempees *S* (+*1*). En follies toutes trempees *M*. *Following 19.4 X adds the erroneous line:* Tant quilz estoient fort estonnees (+*1*)

19.5   Donnasmes *L*. Tant donnoient grans h. *X*

19.5-8   *AiM present divergent readings (spelling and capitalization from Ai):* Et donnasmes grands horions / La frapasmes sur chapperons / Destoc de trauers et de taille / Comme chevaliers en Bataille

19.6   frapoiens [*sic*] *Y* | les compaignons [*sic*] *BV*

Cops de bancqués et baigneries
Comme s'ilz haïssent leurs vies.

MINIATURE 3. The Author, Quarreler, Remnants of Youth

**Cy se combatent l'Acteur et Messire Hutin et
Relicques de Jeunesse les depart.**

20.   CD ais Hutin faisoit vaillanment
         Et me livroit forte bataille*
         De cops d'esteufz d'eschaufement —*
      Courir, saillir, refroidement —*
      Par son espee qui bien taille,
      Et ne fust advenu sans faille   [10]
      Que la vint une damoyselle,
      La journee me estoit mortelle.

21.   La damoyselle qui survint
      Ce fut Reliques de Jounesse,
      Qui receut des cops plus de vingt
      Sur ung grant tergon qu'elle tint.
      Par sa bonté et gentilesse
      Tant exploicta qu'elle mist cesse
      Au tournoy que vous m'oez dire,
      Ou je cougnois avoir le pire.

19.7   b. en b. *LV/YZ*, et de b. *N* (+*1*) | baignieres *S* (-*1*), baigueries *B/YZ*, bragneries [*sic*]
        V
19.8   *Line om., X.*

Equivalent miniature in *BFGR/Y*; none in *EQS/X*; presumably removed, *A*.
Rubric. se combat *F* | a messire h. *F* | relicgue [*sic*] *F* | le [*sic*] depart *R*. *Rubric precedes
    miniature, BFG/Y; presumably removed, A. No rubric, EMNPQSV.*
20.1–2 Cestoit hutin qui vaïllamment / Me liura tres forte bataille *A*
20.3   cop *S* | d'esteufz *ABW* (destoeufz *T*)] desteusz *C/Y*, desteus *Z*; desceuz *FG*, de
        sueur [?] *N*, descens [?] *R*; deculz *QS*, de cuz *EP*, descuz *X*; destocz *L*, destoc *M*,
        destochz *V* | deschauffemens *RV*, de chausement *X*
20.4   refroidemens *R*, tresfroidemenr *E*, refroissement *underlined, followed by* froidesse-
        ment, *M*

Blows for banquets and bathing parties*
As if they despised their lives.

Here the Author and Sir Quarreler meet in combat and Remnants of Youth separates them.

20. **B**ut Quarreler strove valiantly
And gave me a mighty fight,
With volleyed blows of heat
Running and leaping cold
From his sword that slashes well,
And undoubtedly it would have come about
That the battle would have been fatal for me,
Had it not been for a damsel who came there.

21. The damsel who arrived
Was Remnants of Youth.
She took more than twenty blows
On the great shield she held.
Through her goodness and kindness
She performed so well that she put an end
To the tourney I am telling you about,
In which I know I was getting the worst.

20.5 taille *ABEFGLNPQRSTVW/MXYZ*] talle *C*
20.6 Et me *R/M* | fu *R*, fut *EFGPVW/MX*, feust *Q*; ne fust *L* | aduenue *W* (*+1*) | sans fialle [*sic*] *X*
20.7 Qui *FGN/X*, Quand *M* | vint la *N*
20.8 me *om. X* (*-1*). Que la j. estoit *M*

21.1 seruint *Y*
21.2 relicque *FGNPQSVW/MX*
21.4 torgnon *R*
21.5 sa beaute *R*
21.6 quel' fut maistresse *M*
21.7 Du t. *X* | que je vous veulx dire *M*
21.8 du pire *M*

22.   Jeunesse pour nous departir
       Dist : « Sire Hutin, souffrez a tant :
       Adventure me fait venir
       Ce chevalier errant querir
       Pour voir du monde plus avant. »
       Hutin respond : « Je suis content :*
       Plus loings portera son escu,*
       Plus tost se trouvera vaincu.

23.   Mais pour memoire de sa paine
       Je lui donne de ma livree*
       Une barrecte de migraine
       De telle vertu faite et plaine
       Qu'elle sera renouvellee
       Chascune lune de l'annee. »
       Ce present Hutin me laissa
       Et picque cheval et s'en va.

24.   Ainsi je portay cest assault
       Par ce qui me fut demouré
       De Jeunesse qui biaucop vault,
       Mais je la perdis en soursault,   [11]
       Dont je me trouvay desolé,
       Si me partis tout aseulé
       Et pris une petite voye
       Sans sçavoir en quel lieu j'aloye.

22.2 Dit *EFG/MY*, Du *V* | a h. *EQ*
22.3 me feit v. *M* | venir ce cheualier *V*
22.4 ch. tyrant [*sic*] *V*
22.5 veoir *ABEFGLNPQSV/MX* | du monde plaisant [*sic!*] *L, Y* (*-1*)
22.6 jen *ENPQSV/X*

23.2 luy donnay *N*
23.3 de mygarnie *S*
23.4 Qui de telle v. est plaine *M*
[*No significant variants, ABEFGLPQRTVW/XYZ.*]

22.   In order to separate us, Youth said,
       "Sir Quarreler, hold off a bit.
       Chance brought me here
       To seek this knight errant
       To see more of the world."
       Quarreler answered, "That suits me fine:
       The longer he carries his shield,
       The sooner he will find himself defeated.

23.   However, for a reminder of his pains,
       From my livery I will give him
       A scarlet cap
       Concocted and filled with such power
       That it will be renewed
       Each month of the year."
       Quarreler left me this present,
       Spurred his horse and went off.

24.   Thus I endured this assault
       From what I had left
       Of most valuable Youth,
       But suddenly I lost her,
       Whereby I felt myself bereft.
       Therefore, all alone, I left
       And took a small track,
       Not knowing whither I was going.

24.1   Je portay ainsi *V* | partiz de lassault *M*, porte ce a. [*sic*] *X*
24.2   ce quil *BLQ*, ce que *V/M* | me fust *L/X*, le fit *M* | deliure *Q*, demeurer *M*
24.3   Lors *M*
24.4   je le [*sic*] *QS*
24.5   trouue *E/MX*
24.6   pertis *V* | tout assemble [*sic*] *X*
24.8   sauoi [*sic*] *Y*
*M inserts an additional stanza at this point, not found in any other manuscripts. See Textual
   Notes.*

25.   Je cheminay le plain chemin
       Aiant Pensee en souvenir,
       Qui me fist d'armes pelerin
       Sans vouloir partir au butin
       Des paines qu'il me fault souffrir.
       Et droit au point du jour faillir
       J'apperceuz de loing ung hermite
       A l'uis de sa maison petite.

MINIATURE 4. The Author, the hermit Understanding,
a novice, Willing

**Comment l'ermite herbega l'Acteur et des
devises qu'ilz eurent ensemble.**   [12]

26.   **S** y me tiray droit celle part
           Et luy dis : « Se Dieu vous doint joie,
           Pour ce qu'il est meshuy bien tard,
       Me ferez vous de vos biens part,
       Ainsi que pour vous je feroye ? »
       Il me dist que bien venu soye
       Et traicta moy et mon cheval
       Comme ung amy espicial.

27.   Lui mesme si me desarma,
       Me logea en son propre houstel
       Et d'un grant mantel m'affubla

25.1 cheuauchay *EFGNPQ/Z*, cheuaulche *S/X* | le droit ch. *QS*
25.2 P. et Souuenir *M*
25.3 Quil *M* | me fut *E*
25.5 me feit fault *V (+1)*
25.6 de jour *W* | failly *FGP*
25.8 A lhuy de *V*

Equivalent miniature in *BEFGRS/Y*; different subject in *Q/X*; presumably removed, *A*.
Rubric. Comme *S* | diuisa [*sic*] lacteur *X*. *A is illegible between* Comm *and* et des. Et
    aussi des deuisez *R. No rubric,* V/M; *rubric precedes miniature,* BEFGQS/Y; *presumably
    this was the case in* A *as well, since the rubric directly follows stanza 25.*

25. I rode along the level road
     Remembering Thought,
     Who had made me a pilgrim in arms
     Without wishing to share in the spoils
     Of difficulties that I must undergo.
     And, just at the waning of the day,
     In the distance I saw a hermit
     At the door of his small house.

How the hermit lodged the Author and about their conversations together.

26. So I made straight in that direction
     And said to him, "May God give you joy.
     Since it is so late today,
     Will you share your goods with me
     As I would do with you?"
     He said that I was indeed welcome
     And treated me (and my horse)
     As he would a special friend.

27. He himself removed my armor,
     And lodged me in his own house.
     He wrapped me in a great cloak

Stanzas 26–50 missing, A; copied from "l'Imprimé," fols. 7ʳ–10ᵛ.

26.1 Ci *B*, Cy *EFG* | me tray *R* (*-1?*)
26.2 dist *W* | ce *FGNPR* | diz que d. *M* | dieux *R* | luy d. *M* | doient *V* (*+1*)
26.3 trop t. *T*
26.6 me *om. V* (je soye) | dit *BELV/AiX*
26.7 Et bien me traitta et *R* (*+1*)
26.8 special *Q* (*-1*), especiael [*sic*] *Y*

27.1 mesmes *BEL/AiXY*, meismez *R*
27.2 Et me logea en son hostel *L/AiMZ*, Et me ... son propre h. *Y* (*+1*)
27.3 D'ung grant mantel il m'affubla *L/Z*

Que Pourvëance luy donna
Qui fut de soye riche et bel.
Oncques mais je n'oz hoste tel,*
Car chere me fist si dehet
Que je fus logié a souhet.*

28.   Si fist a toute diligence
L'eaue naictement apporter
Par ung jone filz d'apparence
Que l'on appelloit Bonne Enfance
(En ce point l'oÿz je nommer).
Puis me voult mon hoste mener
En une petite chappelle
Moult devote, plaisant et belle.*

29.   La je fiz ma devocion
Devant l'autel qui fut paré
D'un drap de Satisfaction
Armoyé de Contriction ;
Penitance l'avoit ouvré.
L'ermite m'a cecy monstré
Par ung gracïeux exemplaire,   [13]
Car sans ce je ne puis bien faire.

30.   Il me pressa que j'abregasse
Mes oraisons pour celle foiz
Puis me mena en une place
Ou il luy pleut que je soupasse

27.5 Et fut *Q/X*
27.6 je *om. Q* (*-1*) | hostel tel *RVW*
27.7 chiere *GQR*, chier *W* (*-1*) | fit et d. *Ai* | deshayt *V*
27.8 longie [*sic*] *Y*. Que fuz loge et a s. *X*, Et si fuz seruy a s. *AiM*

28.1 Ci *E*, Cy *B*
28.2 Leau *X* (*-1*), De leaue nette ap. *AiM* (*-1?*). | appourte *V*
28.4 Que on ap. *Ai* (*-1?*), Qui fut appelle *M* | bon *Q*
28.5 Car ainsi *M* | point lay je ouy n. *E*; je *om. W* (*-1*)
28.6 me vault *R*, me vint *V*, me veult *W*, me voulut *X* (*+1*)
28.8 deuot *T* (*-1*) | plaisante *FGNPVW/AiMXYZ*

Which Prudence had given him;
It was made of rich and lovely silk.
I have never again had such a host,
For he welcomed me so warmly
That my every wish was met.

28. Then he promptly
Had clean water brought
By a young man of presence
Named Good Youth
(I heard him called that then).
Next my host wished to lead me
Into a small chapel
Most holy, pleasing and fine.

29. I said my prayers there
Before the altar which was draped
With a cloth of Atonement,
Bearing the arms of Contrition;
Penitence had worked it.
The hermit showed me this
As a gracious exemplar,
For without it I cannot succeed.

30. He urged me to cut short
My prayers for that time.
Then he led me to a place
Where he wished me to eat

29.1 fist *W*
29.2 fust *L*
29.3 Du drap *Y*
29.4 Armee de *X*
29.5 lauoit aoure [*sic*] *X*
29.6 Lermire [*sic*] *Y* | cecy *BEFGLNPQSTV/AiMXYZ* (ce cy *R*, checy *W*)] ce sy *C*
29.7 Pour ung *T*
29.8 sans se *X* | riens f. *FQ*, rien f. *G/X*

30.1 me pria *AiM*
30.2 ceste fois *T*
30.4 lui plait *M*, lui plout *Y*; Ou me pria que *E*

Avecques luy comme courtoys.
Il avoit du lart et des pois
Et d'autres biens si largement
Que je deubz estre bien content.

31.   Souvent mes yeulx j'entregectoye
Pour voir de mon hoste la geste ;
Et certes, plus le regardoie,
Tant plus voulentiers le voyoie,*
Car son maintien estoit honneste.
Blanche fut sa barbe et sa teste ;
Homme de bel et grant coursaige
Et resembloit bien estre saige.

32.   Je ne me pos oncques tenir
Que son nom ne lui demandasse,
Qui le meut d'en ce lieu venir,
Lui priant par son bon plaisir
Que son nom de lui emportasse.
Il le m'accorda de sa grace,
Disant : « Je vous cougnois assez
Et veul bien que me cougnoissez. »*

30.5   Auec *BEFGLNPRV/Y (-1)*
30.6   Il i auoit *AiM (om.* et)
30.7   largemens *G*
30.8   iay deuz *X* | ie doibz *FG*, je deuse *R*, je devoye *Ai (om.* bien). Que jen eus grant contentement *M*

31.1   mes oeilx *Q* | j' *om. QR/AiX* | je regetoie *M*
31.2   veoir *BEFGLNPQS/AiMXY.* Pour de mon h. veoir *L*, Vers mon hoste pour veoir sa g. *AiM*
31.4   Et plus *AiM*
31.5   sont [*sic*] maintien *Y*

With him, as courtesy dictates.
He provided bacon and peas
And other goods so unstintingly
That I was bound to be well satisfied.

31.   I often glanced about
To take the measure of my host,
And, certainly, the more I looked at him,
The more delightedly did I see him,
For his actions were honorable.
White of beard and head,
He was a large and handsome man
Who seemed to be very wise.

32.   I could no longer restrain myself
From asking him his name,
What had prompted him to come to this place,
Entreating him that by his pleasure
I might win from him his name.
This he kindly granted me,
Saying, "I know you well enough
And wish that you should know me."

31.8 resembloit *as in 77.8 and 238.3* (ressembloit *BFGNPQS/Z*, ressambloit *L/Y*, resambloit *RT*, resembloit *EVW/X*)] resemboit [*sic*] *C*, si sembloit *Ai*. Entre les autres le plus sage *M*

32.1 puis *L*, sceu *FGNP*, sceuz *EQS*, sus *X*
32.3 Et qui *R* (+*1*) | meult *GNPR* | dans *E*. *Line om.*, *AiM*.
Following 32.4 AiM have Mais quil nen eust point desplaisir
32.5 jemportasse *BVW*
32.6 le *om. FG/X* (-*1*) | le me octroia *M*, le moctroya *Ai*
32.8 veult *Ai* | congnoisses *S/X*, cogniossez [*sic*] *Y*

Comment l'ermite dit a l'Acteur que on l'appelle Entendement,
et des divises qu'ilz eurent ensemble.

MINIATURE 5. The Author, Understanding, a novice   [14]

33.   « Je traveillay moult longuement,
        Chevalier errant par le monde,
        Et suis nommé Entendement.
        Mon nom est cougneu plainement
    Des meilleurs de la Table Ronde.
    Mais vëant que ce n'est q'une onde*
    De mer de la vie incertaine,
    J'ay fait de ce lieu mon demaine.

34.   Mon pain est molu de Sobresse,
    Mon vin trempé de Bonne Vie ;
    Mon repas se fait en Lïesse ;
    Souffisance c'est ma maistresse ;
    J'ay repos sans merencolie.
    Cëans ne peut entrer Envie ;   [15]
    Et s'appelle ceste maison
    La Demeurance de Raison.

35.   Droit cy veul je vivre et mourir,
    Droit cy vel je mes jours passer,
    Querre Dieu, le monde fuïr,
    Servir l'asme et le corps pugnir

Rubric. Cy apres sensuyt comment *X* | dist *RS/X*, dict *BW*; parle *P* | que lon *BLR/Y*
    | appeloit *EFGNPQRS/X* | et des ... ensemble *om. B. Rubric follows minia-*
    ture in BRS; follows instructions in LW/Z. No rubric, TV/AiM.
Equivalent miniature in *FGRS/Y*; subject is that of No. 6 in *BQ/X*; none in *E*; presumably
    removed, *A*.
33.1 trauillay *R*, trauaille *Q/X*; Jay travaille *V/AiM*, Je trantillay [?] *T*
33.2 Ch. par le monde errant *R*
33.6 voyant *Q/M* | ce ne nest [*sic*] *W* (*+1*) | qu' *om. R* | qung [*sic*] vnde *S*
33.7 Dayme^r la vie *Q* (*-1*), Damer *X*
33.8 fait *om. X* (*-1*) | ma demaine *V*

34.1 molu *EFLPV/MXYZ* (mollu *BRS*, moulu *GNQ/Ai*)] moulut *CW*, molut *T*

How the hermit tells the Author that he is called Understanding
and about their conversations together

33.   "I labored a long, long time
      About the world as a knight errant,
      And I am called Understanding.
      My name is well known
      By the best of the Round Table.
      Yet, seeing that that was but one billow
      In the sea of inconstant life,
      I have made this place my domain.

34.   My bread is milled with Temperance,
      My wine steeped with Good Life;
      My meal is made with Gladness;
      Sufficiency is my mistress;
      I have rest without sadness.
      Envy cannot enter here,
      And the name of this house is
      The Dwelling Place of Reason.

35.   I want to live and die right here,
      Right here to spend my days,
      Seeking God and fleeing the world,
      Tending my soul and mortifying the flesh

34.2 tempre *RV*
34.3 ce fait *GL/X*
34.4 c' *om. ELPV/AiM (-1)*
34.5 sens *X*

35.1 Dr. sy *E*, Dr. si *X*, Droicy *R*
35.2 Et si y veulx mes *AiM* | Dr. sy *E*, Dr. si *X*, Droicy *R* | passez *EFGP*, passes [*sic*]
      N
Between 35.2 and 35.3 M inserts Sans jamais plus ailleurs courir.
35.3 Querir *V/Ai*, Querrir *Z* | et le m. *R* (+*1?*)
35.4 le corps fuir *Ai. Line om., M.*

Qui m'a fait trop plaisir aymer :
Riens ne m'est que peché amer,*
Si pri la Vierge d'excellence
Qu'elle me doinst perseverance.

36.   Ton nom, ton cas et ton emprise*
J'ay par memoire clos en marche.
Riens ne vault que l'on se desguise,
Je voy et sçay tout quant g'y vise,*
Ou que l'on tyre ne qu'on marche :
Du paÿs es et de la marche*
Ou Fortune, Douleur et Rage
Ont entreprins de faire rage.

37.   Or t'ay de ton nom devisé
Ce que j'en veulx maintenant dire
Et sçay que tu as proposé
Com vaillant, hardi et osé*
De livrer ton corps au martire
Devant ceulx que nulz desconfire
Ne poult en nulz eages passez*
Mais ont tous murtris et cassez.

35.5   tout *ENPQSV/X* | amer *LRT*, amer *or* a mer *E*
35.6   Rien *RS*
35.7   prie *BLQSVW/AiXY* (+*1*), prye *R* (+*1*) | la verge [*sic*] *W*
35.8   me donne patiance *AiM*

Preceding 36.1 L/AiM have (with minor differences in spelling) La chevalerie ne deprise. *Between 36.1 and 36.2, in the left margin, M has 6 or 7 words, possibly ending in* marche, *the rest illegible, with a horizontal line seeming to indicate that they should be inserted between those two lines.*
36.1   ne ton em. *M*
36.2   *Line follows 36.4, L/AiM.* memore *R* | lotz en m. [*sic*] *AiM*, cloux *N* | cloz *et X* | merche *V/X*
36.3   Rien *RS* | ne vault *om. M* (-*2*), ne me vault *V* (+*1*) | quon *Q* (-*1*), que on *S* (-*1?*) | se y d. *N*
36.4   scay ton [*sic*] quant *S* | tout tant que *X* (+*1*) | et je scay tout que je v. *Ai* (-*1*), Et je ne scay que je y v. *M* (-*1*)
36.5   tire ou quon *E* (-*1*), tire ou que lon *T*, tire ne que lon *L* (+*1*) | merche *V/X. Line om. AiM.*

Which made me love pleasure too much:
It is nothing to me but bitter sin,
And I pray to the most excellent Virgin
That she may give me perseverance.

36.   Your name, circumstances, and undertaking
      I have close filed in memory.
      There's no use of anyone dissembling,
      I see and know everything when I focus on it,
      Whether coming or going:
      You are from the country and of the marches*
      Where Chance, Misery and Rage
      Have set about to wreak havoc.

37.   Now I have said about your name
      What I wish to say at this time
      And know that you have purposed
      As someone bold, worthy, and daring
      To deliver your body to martyrdom
      Before those whom no one
      In ages past could vanquish
      But who have crushed and killed everyone.

36.6   p. est *E/X* | et la demarche [*sic*] *E*, et de la merche *V/X*. *Line om., L/AiM.*
36.7   O fortune *G*
36.8   afaire *or* affaire *R*

37.1   Or iay *M*; t' *om. V* | de mon *R* | nom aduise *V*
37.2   Et que *M* | j' *om. AiM (-1?)*, que ten *T* | veult *AiM*
37.3   Ce que *M (-1)*, Et que *Ai (-1)*; Et scay bien que *R (+1)*
37.4   Comme *B (om. et)*, *RV (+1)*; Quon *S* | hardy vaillant *BLRTVW/Z*; comme v. et
       ose *Ai (-1)*; hardi *om. M (-2)*
37.5   Desliurer *E*, Deliure *X* | a martire *BEFGLNPQSV/AiMX*
37.6   *Reading from BEFGNPQRSTVW/XY; a crease in C makes most of this line illegible.*
       D. c. que nul de nature *L*, Davant tous ceulx de nature *M (-1)*, Devant ceulx de
       nature *Ai (-2)*
37.7   Nont peu *BE*; Ne peult *FGNPQVW/X*, peut *Ai*, peust *S*, peulx *M* | nul eaige *L*,
       nulle eaige *V*, nulz aage *MX* | passer *Q*; et casses *S (+1)*
37.8   tout *R*. *Line om., S.*

38.   Accident est tousjours sus bout,*
       Tout prest a cheval et armé
       Pour tuer et affoller tout
       Et Debile tient l'autre bout,   [16]
       Crueulx, sans mercy ne pité.
       Mais pour ung qui aura passé
       La ou Debille prent sa rente,
       Accident en a tué trente.

39.   Je t'ay declaré ton affaire,
       Ton nom, ton vouloir et ton cas.
       Rien n'y vault fuïr ne retraire :*
       Il te fault ton emprise faire.
       Va toy presenter a ce pas :
       Assez d'honneur tu conquerras
       Et feras oultraigeusement
       Se tu vains Messire Accident.

40.   Et afin que soyes plus digne
       De soustenir ceste advenue,
       Toy donner ung don je m'encline
       D'ung glave ferré de Regime*
       En lieu de ta lance rompue.
       De ce poulse, fiers, frappe et rue,
       Car par ce tu rebouteras
       Accident la ou tu vouldras.

38.1 surbout *FGNP/X*, sur bout *ELQRS/AiM*, sur boult *BV*; sus [?] boult *T*, sus rout [?]
       W
38.3 et *om. M* (-*1*)
38.5 Cruel *L/AiM* | marcy *Y* | pitie *EFGNQS/AiMX*
38.6 par vng *T*

39.1 d. de ton aff. *Y* (+*1*). Je tay declairay ton office *M*
39.2 ton valloir *S*
39.3 Riens *BFLNQRVW/AiXYZ*, Ryens *G* | ne v. *EFNPQS/X* | fouyr *P*, fouir *AiX* |
       ne *om. FGS* (-*1*)
39.4 Il fault tout em. *M* (-*1*)
39.5 Va ten *M*, va te *Ai* | au pas *FG* (-*1*)

38. Accident is always up at one end
    All ready, mounted and armed
    To kill and mangle everyone;
    And Debility maintains the other end,
    Cruel, merciless and without pity.
    But for *one* who has passed that place
    Where Debility collects his due,
    Accident has killed *thirty*.

39. I have stated your case,
    Your name, your desire and cause.
    It's useless to flee or retreat:
    You must undertake your adventure.
    Go present yourself at this tourney:
    You will win ample honor
    And acquit yourself inordinately well
    If you defeat Lord Accident.

40. And so that you may be more capable
    Of sustaining this adventure,
    I'm inclined to make you a gift
    Of a lance steel-tipped with Authority
    In place of your broken one.
    With this thrust, strike, and strike again,
    For with it you will repulse
    Accident anywhere you wish.

39.6 dhonneur *LPQTV/AiYZ*, d'honneur *B* (donneur *EFGSW/X*)] d' *om. CN, R* (*lined out*); A. donner [*sic*] *M* | conqueras *N*

39.8 Si *EFQ/Z* | tu *om. W* (*-1*) | vaincq *W*, viues [*sic*] *X* (*+1*)

40.1 que tu s. *W* (*+1*) | soye *BFGV*, soyez *AiMX*

40.2 celle *BEFGPQSVW/X* | celle venue *EV*, ceste adventure *AiM*

40.3 Tay donne *V* | le m. *FGQS/X*; ung don ne mengine [*sic*] *E*

40.4 Dung *FGLNPS/MZ*, D'ung *B/Ai* (Dun *EQRTVW/XY*)] Dug [*sic*] *C*

40.5 de sa *M*, de la *AiX*

40.6 poulsa [*sic*] *X* | fiers *om. Q* (*-1*), fiet [*sic*] *Ai*, fiert [*sic*] *S/M* | fiers pousse *R* | et tue *Ai*

40.7 Ca par [*sic*] *S*

40.8 Ac. ou que tu *R*

41.   Pour ce dois a ton reveillier
       Toy saigner de la bonne main,
       Priant Dieu qu'il vueille veiller
       Et ton bon ange traveillier*
       Pour toy en ce voiage humain.
       Dont je pri le Dieu souverain
       Et luy rens graces de bon cueur*
       Des biens dont il nous est donneur. »

42.   Ainsi nous levasmes de table
       Aprés graces a grant loisir ;   [17]
       Et trouvay mon hoste notable
       En son propos tant agrëable
       Que g'y prenoie grant plaisir.
       Puis me dit : « Vous irez dormir,*
       Et demain je vous montreray*
       Les beaux reliquaires que j'ay. »*

43.   Lors me mena pour moy logier
       En ung lieu paré a propos
       Si gentement qu'a souhaitier.
       Il me fist couvrir et coucher*
       Sur ung materas de repos.
       Oncques mes si bon logis n'oz
       Ne lieu de si plaisant sejour,*
       Si m'endormis jousques au jour.

41.2 Bien s. *T* | seigneur [*sic*] *M*, seignyers [*sic*] *W*
41.3 Et en d. *E* | Pr. a d. *L/AiM* (*om.* qu'il) | qui *BEFGNV* | vueille *FNPQST/XYZ* (veulle *BEV*, voeulle *R*, voelle *W*)] ueille *C*; vouloir veillier *L/Ai*, voullant veiller *M*
41.4 A ton *AiM* | ange *BEFGLNPQSV/AiMXYZ*] angel *C*, angle *RTW* | traueillier *BLPTW*, -ueill(i)er *R*, -ueiller *FGNV*, -uellier *Y*, -uailler *EQS/X*, -ueilher *M*, -vailler *Ai*. *C is legible only through* tra; *the rest is obscured by a crease.*
41.5 ce *om. AiM* (-*1*) | ce veuaige *V*
41.6 Dont je prie *BV/Ai* (+*1*), Et je prie *Q/X* (+*1*), Et je pry *EFGS*, Et jen pry *P* | dieu le s. *V*, le roy s. *LQS/AiZ*; Il prie le roy s. *M*, Dont je prie le seigneur s. *W* (+*2*)
41.7 grace *BEFGLPRW/MX*
41.8 De biens *Ai* | il *om. M* (-*1*)

42.1 leuasme *P*. *Line om.*, *M*.
42.2 grace *M* (-*1*) | et grant *BV/Y*

41.   For this, on awakening you must
       Cross yourself with your right hand,
       Beseeching God to keep watch
       And your good angel to busy itself
       For you in this human journey.
       So I pray to Almighty God
       And willingly render thanks
       For the benefits He gives us."

42.   Then we arose from the table
       After leisurely thanksgiving,
       And I found my host excellent
       In his most agreeable conversation
       Wherein I took great pleasure.
       Then he said to me, "You shall go sleep,
       And tomorrow I will show you
       The lovely relics that I have."

43.   Then he led me to my lodging
       In a place tastefully prepared
       As nicely as one could wish.
       He saw to it that I was given covers and put to bed
       Upon a restful mattress.
       Never again have I been so well lodged
       Nor had a more pleasant place to stay.
       I slept until it was day.

42.4 Et son *X*, A son *L/AiMY*, De son *R*
42.6 Il me *AiM* | dist *NQRSTW/MX* | yrer *FGN* [*sic*]
42.7 je *BEFLNPQRSTVW/AiMXYZ*] om. *C* (*-1*)
42.8 Les beaux r. *EFGNPS/X* (Lez biaulx *S*, Les beaulx *EFG*)] Le reliquaire que iay
      CBLRTVW/YZ (*-1*), Les beaux reliques *Q* (*-1*); Toutes les reliques que j'ay *AiM*

43.1 par moy *S* | pour me *X*
43.3 Si saigement *X* | que au s. *YZ*
43.4 fit *BEFGNP/Ai*, feit *V*
43.5 Sus *YZ* | materalz *X*
43.6 logeiz *Q* | neuz (: repoz) *M*
43.7 plus plaisant *BEFGLNPQRTVW/AiMYZ*
43.8 *Line om., M.*

44.   Grant heure fut quant m'esvellay
       Si oÿs sonner la clochecte,
       Pour quoy a haste me levay,
       Me vestis et mes mains lavay,
       Honteux par negligence faite.
       La messe trouvay toute preste,*
       Q'ung Cordelier de l'observance
       Chanta, qu'on nomme Obedïence.

45.   L'aube dont il ot revesture
       Estoit de Bonne Volenté,
       L'amyt fut tissu par Mesure,
       Le saint fut de Chasteté Pure,
       L'estolle fut de Charité,
       Le maniple de Loyauté
       Et la chasuble par maistrie
       Fut pourtraicte de Preudhommie.

46.   L'ostie fut de Vraie Foy   [18]
       Et le calice de Crëance ;
       Les canectes de Bonne Loy
       Et la lumiere, quant a soy,
       Fut de Grace signifiance.
       Le benoictier fut d'Ignocence ;
       La cloche fut entierement
       Toute de Bon Enhortement.

44.1 fust *L* | mesueillays *V*; me levay *AiM*, quant men alle *X*
44.2 Et ouys *AiM* | clocquette *V*
44.3 Parquoy *BEFNPS/AiMX*, Par quoy *G* | en haste *B*
44.4 vestir *V* | laue *FG*, lauays *V*. Line om., *X*.
44.5 neligence [*sic*] *S*
44.6 trouuay *BEFGLNPQRSTW/MXYZ*, trouvay *Ai* (treuvay *V*)] trouue *C*
44.7 dobservance *M* (*-1*)
44.8 Chante *X* | quon dit *V*

45.1 eust *EFGPS*. Laube la premiere vesture *V*
45.2 la bonne *E*
45.3 fust *L* | messure *W/X*
45.4 Et le s. de *L* | de chaste [*sic*] pure *M* (*-1*)

44. It was late when I awoke
     And I heard the church bell's ring,
     Wherefore I rose in haste,
     Dressed and washed my hands,
     Shamed by my laziness.
     I found the Mass all ready,
     Celebrated by an Observant Friar*
     Who was called Obedience.

45. The alb in which he was clad
     Was of Good Will,
     The amice was woven by Moderation,
     The girdle of Untainted Chastity,
     The stole of Charity,
     His maniple of Constancy,
     And the chasuble most skillfully
     Fashioned of Valiance.

46. The host was of True Faith
     And the chalice was of Credence;
     The candles were of Good Law
     And as for the light,
     It signified Grace.
     The holy water basin was of Innocence;
     The bell was wholly made
     Of Good Exhortation.

45.5 fust *L*

45.6 La m. *SW* | manipule *FGNPQS/AiMX* (+*1*), magnipule *E* (+*1*), manipol *L/YZ*, manipul *R*, manipel *V*

45.7 Et le ch. *X* | par *om. M* (-*1*) | maistrise *FGQS*, mestrire *E*, maistresse [*sic!*] *X*

45.8 Fust *L*

46.1 Loste [*sic*] *X* (-*1*) | fust *L* | vray foy *B* (-*1*); Lautel fut de bonne et vraye foy *AiM* (+*1*)

46.2 Et la c. *W* | clemance *L/Z*

46.3 chauvettes *Ai*, chauetes *X*; Les potequins *V* | bonne foy *EFGNPQS/AiMX*

46.4 lumiere *BEFLNPQRSTVW/AiXY*, lumyere *M*] lumire *C*

46.5 de grand s. *R* (-*1*)

46.6 benoittie *L*, benestier *S*, bonetie [*?*] *V* | fust *L*, *om. X* (-*1?*) | dignorance *EQS/X*; fut en [*?*] trempance *M*, fut atrempance *Ai*

46.7 fust *L* | fut entendement [*sic!*] *AiM*

47.   Toutes les nappes de l'auté*
      Se monstroient par grant richesse
      Faictez par une grant cherté*
      D'un ouvraige de Verité ;
      Le messel estoit de Promesse.
      Oncquez mes ne viz tel noblesse*
      Ne lieu ou Dieu fust mieulx servy.
      Je le louay quant je le vy.*

48.   La paix fut faite de Union,
      Les chandeliers tous de Concorde,
      Le marbre de Perfection ;
      Aussi de Bonne Intencion
      Les verrieres, quant le recorde.
      Et si fut de Misericorde
      Par tout tres richement paree
      La sainte chappelle sacree.

49.   Aprés la messe celebree,
      Mon hoste, qui ot aouré
      Devotement la matinee,
      Me donna la bonne journee
      Et m'enquist doulx et en privé
      Comment j'avoie reposé.
      Je lui dis : « Bien » et me louoie
      Du logis que par lui j'avoie.   [19]

47.1 l'auté *BL/Z*] lautel *CEFGPQRTVW/XY*, laustel *N*, lautier *S*; des autelz *AiM*
47.2 Ce m. *E*, Demonstroient *S* | grande r. *EFGNPQ* (+*1*) | richesses *V/M*
47.3 Faicte *V/X* | ung [*sic*] gr. *W* | grande chierte *EFGP* (+*1*), grant cherite *Q* (+*1*),
      grande cherite *X* (+*2*). Oncques n en avoye veu de telz *Ai*, Quonques nen auoir veu
      de telz *M*.
47.4 De verite sont ouvrages *AiM*
47.5 de prouesse *AiM*
47.6 mes *om. QS* | telle n. *QS, R* (+*1*)
47.7 fut *EFPV/Ai*, fu *W*, feust *BQ* | ou fut dieu *E* | seruyz *QV*
47.8 le loue *E/X* | vey *BFGP/X*, vyz *Q*

48.1 fust *L*
48.2 tout *MX*

47.   All the linens of the altar
      By their great richness showed themselves
      To have been made at great cost
      Of Truth's workmanship;
      The missal was of Promise.
      I've never since seen such splendor
      Nor place where God was better served.
      I praised it when I saw it.

48.   The pyx was made of Peace,
      All the candlesticks of Harmony,
      The marble of Perfection;
      And also of Good Intention
      The window glass, as I recall.
      The holy, sacred little chapel
      Was richly furnished everywhere
      With Divine Clemency.

49.   After the celebration of the Mass,
      My host, who had worshipped devoutly
      The whole morning,
      Bade me good day
      And quietly inquired in private
      How I had slept.
      "Well," I told him and praised
      The lodging he had given me.

48.5   barrieres *EFGNPQS/X*, verriers *Y* (*-1*) | que le *M*
48.6   Et si fust *L*; Si furent de *V/AiMZ*
48.7   pauee *BEFGNQS/X*

49.2   adore *EFGQ/M*, dore [*sic*] *X* (*-1*)
49.4   donnat *V*
49.5   menquis deulx *M*, menquist deulx *X* | en *om. AiM* (*-1*) | et empriue *V*
49.6   Comme *V/AiM* | lauoie *Y*
49.7   bien *om. V* (*-1*) | bien je me *E*
49.8   logeiz *GQ*, logeix *X* | qua par *V* | j' *om. LRTVW/Y*

50.   Lors me dist : « Il fault que je tienne
      Promesse d'ouvrir mon tresor, »
      M'enhortant fort que je retiengne
      Et que des pieces me souviengne*
      Qui ne sont ne d'argent ne d'or.
      L'uys ouvrit qui fut de Remor :
      La clef fut Desir de Sçavoir
      Et la serrure d'un miroer.*

**Comment l'ermite Entendement monstre ses relicques a l'Acteur
et luy devise des oeuvres de Messire Accident et de son pouoir.**

MINIATURE 6. The Cloister of Memory: The Author, Understanding

51.   C e lieu fut ung cloistre longuet   [20]
        Paré d'estranges pourtraitures.
        Or pensez se je fiz bon guet
      Pour sçavoir de ce lieu que c'est
      Et mieulx cougnoistre les figures.
      Entendement fist ses droitures
      Et me dist : « Entens et applicques
      Et tu cougnoistras mes relicques.

52.   Vecy le soc d'une charrue
      Dont Accident Abel occist
      Par Caÿn, et de sa main nue

50.1 L. il me *E* (*om.* il) | dit *ENPV/Ai* | il *om. MY* (*-1*)
50.3 fors que [*sic*] *X* | que je tiengne *W* (*-1*). Il est force que je tienne *AiM* (*-1*)
50.5 *Second* ne *om. Q/M* (*-1*)
50.6 Luisse *W* | ouuris *V* | fust *L* | remors *W*
50.7 le chief *X* | fust *L*
50.8 de m. *EFGQS/AiMX*

Rubric. Comme *FLS* | luy deuises *W* | les euures *QS*, de euures [*sic*] *X* | oeuurez
    messire *R* | et de son pouoir *om. R. Rubric follows miniature in FGQRS; follows in-
    structions in LTW/Z; follows stanza 51 in P/M and in "l'Imprimé" on which Ai is
    based. No rubric, V.*
Equivalent miniature in *AEFGQR/XY*; different subjects in *BS*.*

50.   Then he said to me, "I must keep
       My promise to reveal my treasure,"
       Urgently pressing me to bear in mind
       And remember the objects
       Which were neither silver nor gold.
       He opened the door, which was of Remorse:
       Its key was Desire for Learning
       And the lock was made from a mirror.

**How the hermit Understanding shows the Author his relics
and tells him about the pursuits of Lord Accident and about his power.**

51.   *T*his place was a longish cloister
           Hung about with unfamiliar portraits.
           Now, you may believe that I paid close attention
       To discover what this place was,
       And better know the faces.
       Understanding made clear his rules
       And said to me, "Listen and apply yourself
       And you will learn about my relics.

52.   Here is the plowshare
       With which Accident had Abel killed
       By Cain, and with his bare hand

The original text of A resumes at this point.
51.1   Le *EFGPQSV/X* | fust *L*
51.2   estrange [*sic*] p. *V*, estrange pourtraicture *M*
51.3   pense *V*, penses *G* | je filz [*sic*] *W*. Or pense ie foys b. g. [*sic*] *X* (*-1*)
51.4   de celluy *X*
51.6   ces dr. *X*
51.7   dit *LV/Y* | etendz [*sic*] *M*
51.8   me r. *A*

52.1   Veez cy *ENPQ* (*+1?*), Voyez sy *X* (*+1*)
52.3   et *om. Q/X* (*-1*). Car cayn tout de *M*

Par une envïeuse advenue
(Celui premier la terre ouvrit),
Dont il fist mal et si mesfit,
Car il murtrit, chascun le juge,
L'un des bons devant le Deluge.

53.   Ce pillier d'estrange grosseur
Est celuy que Sanson ploya
Dont il abatit par vigueur
Le grant palais et sa haulteur.
Pour sa fame qu'on maria*
Il se occist et moult en tua.
Ce fut bien Accident terrible,
Prouvé ou texte de la Bible.

54.   C'est cy la chemise enfumee
Dont Dyamire (et n'en pot mes,*
Cuidant amer et estre amee)
Occist et brula en la pree
Le preulx et vaillant Herculés.
Accident fist cest entremés :
Lire le pouras en mains lieux
En *la Nativité des dieux.**   [21]

55.   En cest estuy troveras mis
Les greffes de quoy fut tué

52.4 Par vne enuye ad. *X* (*-1*), Et par une enuie ad. *M*; Par enuieuse rancune *L* (*-1*)
52.5 premiers *T/Z*
52.6 et si me fis [*sic*] *L*
52.7 meurdrist *Q/M*, murdry *R*
52.8 Vng des *S* | auant le *MX*

53.1 Le p. *BE*, De p. *M* | pille *L*, pellier *Y* | dextreme *BEFGLNPQS/XYZ*, dextre [*sic*]
      R (*-1*) | p. et degrousseur *M* (*-1*)
53.2 s. brisa *M*
53.3 il *erased*, par grant rigueur *E* | vigour *Q* (: grosseur, haulteur)
53.7 Ce fust *L* | Ce fut ac. le t. *MX*
53.8 Prouue est ou *Q* (*+1*) | au teste de *X*

Through a spiteful stroke
(He was the first to open up the earth),
Whereby he did wrong and so misbehaved,
For he murdered, each so judges,
One of the good men who lived before the Flood.

53. This pillar of singular size
Is the one which Samson bowed;
Through his strength he brought down
The great palace and its arrogance.
Because of his wife, whom someone had married,
He killed himself and many others.
This was indeed terrible Accident,
Verified in the text of the Bible.

54. This is the smoke-blackened shirt
In which Deianira (and unable to help herself,
Thinking herself loved and who loved in return)
Burned and killed in the meadow
Noble and courageous Hercules.
Accident staged this performance;
You can read about it in many places
In *The Origins of the Gods*.

55. You will find placed in this little box
The small styluses with which*

54.1 Veez cy *ENPQS* (+*1?*), Veecy *FG* (+*1?*), Vecy *BVW*; Voyez cy ch. *MX*
54.2 dyamis *N*, dyanus *EFG*, dyamie [*?*] *L*, dyamiee *Y*, dyanae *P*, dyamus *QS/X*, diamus [*?*] *M*, dyamore [*?*] *V*, deianira [*?*] *W* | si nen *MX* | pot *LR/YZ* (polt *BT*)] peult *CVW/M*, peut *AENQS/X*, peust *FGP*
54.3 C. armer *F*
54.5 Hegercules [*?*] *M*
54.6 ces *Q*, ses *SV/MX*
54.7 pourrez *M*, pourres *X* | main [*sic*] lieux *V*
54.8 de dieux *M*

55.1 ceste [*sic*] estuy *M* | trouuerez *M*, trouueres [*sic*] *X*
55.2 Le gresfe *M*, Le greffez *E*, Le greffes *Y*; Les greffe [*sic*] *V* | fust *L* | fut time *X*

Cesar par esperez amis
Qui l'ont en leur senat occis.
Par merveilleuse cruaulté
Accident a ce cop hurté :
Ces choses cy nous sont certaines
Selon les histoires romaines.

56.   Ceste boiste te veulx monstrer
Sans y advenir ou toucher :
Antipater la fist ouvrer
A tenir poisons et porter
Pour Alixandre despeschier.
Accident ouvra du mestier*
Et fut mort et empoisonné
Du monde le plus renommé.

57.   Ce grant fust, afin que tout voie,
C'est la lance dont Achilés
Tua le preux Hector de Troye,
Le plus a craindre dont on oye,
Le plus vaillant qui fust jamais.
Telz sont d'Accident les droiz mes :
De ce fait plaine mention
De Troye la destruction.

58.   De cest arch et trais tant aguz
Fut occis et mis a outrance
Achilés, par ung grant mesuz,

55.3 par espees amis [sic!] S, par ses expers amis V
55.4 Quil ont L, Qui sont [?] M | Qui la en son s. FG | seant [sic] M
55.7 cy FGLRSV/Z] si CABEPQTW/MX, sy N, icy Y (+1)

56.1 Ceste bouuette M, boeiste Q, boette S, bouette X, boit [sic] Y (-1) | je veulx M
56.3 fit ouurir E
56.4 poissons [sic] ER
56.5 dez peschier R, depeschie [sic] V
56.7 emprisonne [sic] W

Caesar was killed by trusted friends
Who murdered him in their senate
With wonderful cruelty.
Accident cast this blow:
We know these things for certain
From Roman stories.

56.   This box I want to show you
       Without your coming near or touching it:
       Antipater had it made
       To contain and carry poisons
       In order to dispatch Alexander.
       Accident plied his trade
       And the most renowned man in the world
       Was poisoned and died.

57.   This great shaft, so that you may see everything,
       Is the lance with which Achilles
       Killed mighty Hector of Troy,
       The most feared man ever heard of,
       The most valiant who ever was.
       Such are Accident's direct fruits:
       It is clearly mentioned
       In *The Fall of Troy*.

58.   With this bow and well-honed arrows
       Was Achilles defeated and put to death
       By great ill use

57.1   Le gr. *B* | fut *VW/M*, fustes *X* | tu voyes *ENP*, tu voye *FGQS*, le voye *V*; affin
       quon le voie *M*, affin que voyes *X*
57.4   quon sauoye *S*, dont on ouyt *V*. Line om., *M*.
57.5   que *YZ* | fut *BEFGLPQSVW/MXY* | iamz [sic] *Y* | Et le pl. v. de jamez *R*
57.6   drois mais *V*, droibmes [?] *W*
57.7   fat *NP*, font *B*

58.1   ce arc [sic] *F/X* | traict *V/M* | bien aguz *FGNPQSW/MX*, b. agus *BEV*
58.2   fust *L* | occist *M* | mis a la mort *M* | a oultrage *P*, a oultraige *FGNQ/X*
58.3   par vingtz [sic] grant *M* | mesbus [sic] *A*

Ou devot temple de Venus,
Par Paris qui fist ceste offence.
Accident fut a celle enfance   [22]
Et fist finer par sa rudesse
Le plus vaillant qui fust en Grece.

59. Celle espee qui la fait giste
Est celle dont morut Pompee
Par le desloial roy d'Egipte
Qui l'occist en lieu de merite
Et lui a la teste coupee.
Accident fut a celle armee
Qui deffist le pillier et l'omme,
Soustenal de l'onneur de Romme.

60. Vois la l'aneau envenimé
Ou prist Hanibal de Cartaige
Le fort venin dessaisonné
Dont mesmes s'est empoisonné
Avant qu'il eust tiers ne quart age.*
Accident mesla ce buvraige
Dont mourut l'un des vaillans prince*
Qui oncquez gouverna province.*

61. Voiz aprés le glasve tresfort
Dont le roy Marc de Cornuaille*
Navra lachement a la mort

58.4 Au *MX*
58.5 cest offense *FGPT*, cest offence *AN/X*, cest esfort *M*; qui co*m*mist loffence *R*, qui
   co*m*mist offence *L/YZ*
58.6 fust *L*; fut *om. X (-1)* | en celle *S* | celle offence *LV*; Ac. y besongna fort *M*
58.8 fut *BEFGLVW/M* | de grece *EFGNPQS/MX*

59.1 quil a *V* | qui la fist geste *M*
59.2 Cest *EFGLNPQW/MXZ* | moru *R*
59.3 le desloay [*sic*] roy *Y*
59.4 desmerite *E*
59.7 de lomme *Q*, et bourne [*sic*] *V*
59.8 Soustenant du pillier de R. *MX*

At Venus' holy temple,
By Paris, who committed this offense.
Accident was in on this game
And by his churlishness brought to an end
The most courageous of the Greeks.

59. That sword placed there
Is the one with which Pompey was slain
By the treacherous king of Egypt.
Instead of pay, he did him in—
Chopped off his head.
Accident was in this army
Which brought down the pillar and the man,
The mainstay of Rome's honor.

60. See the envenomed ring
From which Hannibal of Carthage took
The potent deadly potion
With which he poisoned himself
Before his life was a third or fourth over.
Accident mixed this brew
From which died one of the most valiant princes
Who had ever ruled a province.

61. See next the mighty sword
With which King Mark of Cornwall
In cowardly fashion mortally wounded

60.1 Veez la *EFGNPQS* (*+1?*), Voyez la *MX* (*+1?*) | laigneaul *L*, laigneau *M* | cuncu-*m*ine [*?*] *L*

60.2 Ou praint [*?*] *M*

60.4 cest *EGLPS/MX* | emprisonne [*sic*] *W/X*

60.5 ou quart *M* | aage *AS/MX* (*+1?*), eage *FGNPR* (*+1?*), eaige *BLQV* (*+1?*); ne cartaige *W*; eust ne tiers ne quart aage *X* (*+2*)

60.6 cest b. *S*

60.7 vaillant *LV/YZ* | princes *FG/MX*, princhez *R*

60.8 gouuernast *T/MX* | prouinces *V/MX*

61.1 Veez *ENQS* (*+1?*), Voyez *MX* (*+1*)

61.2 marc *ABEFGLQRSTVW/MXYZ*] mar *C*, mart *NP* | cornoualle *X*

Tristran, dont il ot vilain tort
Et fut deshonneste bataille.
Accident ne fist pas la faille
D'occire, l'istoire le fonde,
L'un des bons chevaliers du monde.

62.   De cest espieu tranchant et bon
       Fist tuer comme traiteresse
       Jadiz le roy Aggamenon
       Sa femme de mauvais renon   [23]
       De son paillart par subtillesse.
       Ce roy conduisoit l'ost de Grece
       Et sa femme traiteusement
       Le fist mourir par Accident.

63.   De ce branc d'acier inhumain*
       Occist Mordret remply de mal
       Le roy Artus son souverain
       Et aussi Messire Gauvain,
       Non pas comme ung hardy vassal,
       Mais par ung aguet desloyal
       Dont Accident fut conduiseur
       Sur deux princes de grant valeur.

64.   Du badelaire la bouté
       Fut ja Olofferne le grant

61.4 eust *LS*, ost *V*
61.5 fust *LQ* | la bataille *S* (+*1*)
61.6 fu *R* | le [*sic*] faille *W*, la saille [*sic*] *X*
61.7 Doccir *V* (-*1*) | le hystore [*sic*] *R* | de fonde *V*
61.8 Ung *Q* | des bon cheualier [*sic*] *V*

62.1 trenchan *V*
62.2 traistresse *AES* (-*1?*), traitresse *BV/X* (-*1?*), treistresse *Q* (-*1?*), tristresse *FGR* (-*1*); F.
       occire c. tristesse [*sic*] *M*
62.3 Jediz *Y*
62.4 La f. *A/MXZ* | du m. r. *M* | regnon *X*
62.6 Se roy *FG*, Le roy *V* | conduisant *A* | loost [*sic*] *L*; cond. hors de gr. *MX*

Tristan, whereby he wronged him basely
And it was a dishonorable fight.
Accident did not miss the chance to kill
(History bears it out)
One of the best knights in the world.

62.   With this good keen-edged pike
His wife of ill repute
Traitorously caused the death of
King Agamemnon of old,
Through a ruse of her lover.
This king used to lead the Greek army
And his wife traitorously
Had him slain by Accident.

63.   With this barbarous steel two-handed sword
Did Mordred, evil-filled, kill
His sovereign lord King Arthur
And also Sir Gawain,
Not in the manner of a bold vassal,
But through a dishonest ruse
Of which Accident was the instigator
Against two princes of great worth.

64.   With the scimitar placed there
Great Holofernes was

62.7   sa femme par accident *T*
62.8   morir trayteusement *T*

63.1   branc *BEFGLNPQRSW/MXYZ* (branch *AT*)] brauch *C*, brant *V* | br. desir [*sic*] *MX*
63.2   meurdrit [*sic*] *FG*, Mordree *Q* (+*1?*), mordritz *V*, mordresse [*sic*] *X* (+*1*)
63.5   comme hardy *ABT*
63.6   Mais pour *S*
63.7   Fust *L* | conducteur *EFGNPQS/MX*, condiuseur *Y*
63.8   Sus *R/Y*

64.1   De ce b. *A* (+*1*), De b. *MX* | brasselaire *L*, basselare *Y*; Au bas de laire [*sic*] *E* | la
      bonté [*sic*] *B*, la bonte [*sic*] *AR/MY*, la bouttee *S*
64.2   fust *L* | alofferne *X*

Par Judich a la mort bouté,
Dont elle sauva sa cité
Et de l'armee et du tirant.
Accident hurta bien avant
Quant par la main d'une pucelle
Mist amours en euvre cruelle.

65.   De ce clou et de ce martel
Occist Jabel, la femme honneste,
Zizaren le tirant cruel ;
Ce cop fut divin et moult bel.
Quant ce clou lui mist en la teste,
Le peuple de Dieu en fist feste.
Accident faisoit telz deluges,
Prouvé par le livre des Juges.

66.   De ces deux glaves par excés
Se sont deux freres entreoccis   [24]
Pour ce que ja Ethioclés
Ne voult rendre a Polimicés
Le regne qu'il lui ot promis.
Accident s'est ou debat mis :
Les escriptures en sont plaines
Es fais de Thebes et d'Athaines.

67.   De cest autre espieu Remondin
Tua son bon oncle Fromont,

64.4   la cite *V/MX*
64.5   de larme *M* (*-1*)
64.7   la mam [*sic*] *Y* | fumelle [*sic*] *BV*
64.8   amour *L*, a mort [*sic*] *V* | euure mortelle *ENPQS/MX*

65.1   se martel *X*
65.3   Zaciarem *V* | Z. tyrant et *LR/Y*
65.4   fust *L*; fut *om. S* (*-1*)
65.5   le clou *Z* | dans la t. *V*
65.6   en fist grant feste *Q* (*+1*)
65.7   fist *Q* (*-1*) | ces deluges *V*, te d. [*sic*] *W*
65.8   Prouuez *L/M*, Prouueuz [*sic*] *X* (*om.* le)

Struck dead by Judith,
Whereby she saved her city
From the army and the tyrant.
Accident went beyond the pale
When, by a maiden's hand,
He used love in a cruel work.

65.   With this nail and hammer,
       That honest wife Jael killed
       Sisera the cruel tyrant;
       This blow was divine and very fine.
       When she put that nail in his head,
       The people of God rejoiced.
       Accident used to cause such slaughter,
       As proved in the Book of Judges.

66.   With these two swords through hot temper
       Two brothers killed each other
       Because long ago Eteocles
       Refused to surrender to Polynices
       The kingdom he had promised him.
       Accident had a hand in the controversy,
       The evidence of it is clear
       In the stories of Thebes and Athens.

67.   Remondin, with this other spear,
       Killed his good uncle Fromont,

66.2   Ce sont *EQ/M*

66.4   Ne veult *W*, Ne volu *R* (+*1*), Ne voulut *MX* (+*1*) | a *om. W* | polimites *T/Y*,
       polinices *Q*, polunices *E*; appolunices *FG*, appolimites *L*, apoulimites *M*, appolimices
       N, appolimicez [*?*] *P*

66.5   qui *BEFGSV/X* | quil y eut pr. *A* | est pr. *E*, eust pr. *FG*, a pr. *V*; Le renge
       quillay [*sic*] auoit pr. *M* (+*1*)

66.6   sest *ABFLQRSTVW/MYZ*] cest *CEGNP/X* | au *BQSV/MX*

66.7   plaine *W*, plenes pleines [*sic*] *Y*

67.1   ce autre [*sic*] *GS* | espiet *W*

67.2   Occist *M* | fremont *X*

Cuidant ferir par le serin
Ung sangler qui livroit hutin
En l'espés du bois et parfont.
Cest accident regrecta moult :*
Lire le peux — je le t'assigne —
En *l'Avenement Melusine.**

68.   Ce sangler mist a la mort seure*
Le bel Adonis en jeunesse,
Qui de chasser prist si grant cure
Qu'il mist son corps a l'aventure*
Contre le conseil la deesse.
La fist Accident grant rudesse,
Car il desfist les amourectes
Des dames selon les poettes.

69.   De celle grant dague affillee
Navra Joab et par embas
Amazan en une acollee
Dont il a la vie finee.
Ce fut bien le baisier Judas ;
La fist ung ort et vilain cas.
Accident faisoit telz desrois,
Comme on list ou livre des Rois.

67.3 C. sairir [?] *M* | le serm [*sic*] *Y*
67.4 Un sanglet *M*, Ung senglier *E*, Ung sanglier *G/X*
67.5 En lespee [*sic*] *X* (+*1*) | dung bois *L* | et *om. M* (-*1*) | et du hault *S*, et perfont *W*
67.6 mont *AEFGPRT*, mont *or* mout *N*, monlt [*sic*] *X*
67.7 assaigne *R*. Je te le peulx. Je le [?] tesmoingne *M*
67.8 de melusine *B* (+*1*)

68.1 sangle *L*, sanglier *EFGP/M* | la *om. LS* (-*1*) | mort seure *ENPQS/M* (mort sure *ABFGLRTVW/XYZ*)] morsure *C*
68.2 adous *M* (en sa j.), *X* (-*1*); Adoms [*sic*] *Y* (-*1*) | adonys et j. *V* | en jouenesse *or* jonenesse *W* (+*1?*)
68.3 print sa grant *G*

Thinking in the dusk to strike
A boar that was wreaking havoc
In the woods' dense thickets.
He deeply regretted this accident.
You may read it, I direct you to,
In *The Coming of Melusine*.

68.   This boar brought to certain death
Handsome young Adonis,
Who had such great desire for the hunt
That he put himself in jeopardy
Contrary to the goddess's advice.
Accident acted most meanly there,
For he brought to naught the dalliances
Of the ladies, as the poets would have it.

69.   With this fine-honed dagger
Joab wounded with a low blow
Amasa, while embracing him,
Whereby his life was ended.
This was indeed the Judas kiss;
He committed there a brutal and ignoble crime.
Accident accomplished these massacres,
As one may read in the Book of Kings.

68.4 Qui mist *FG* | en aduenture *V/M*
68.5 c. de la d. *M* (+*1*)
68.6 la rudesse *L*
68.7 il dessit [*sic*] *X*

69.1 ceste *M* | grande daghe *W* (+*1*)
69.2 Joal *FG*, Jacob *V* [*?*], *M*, iaob [*sic*] *X* | par en bas *Y*
69.4 sa vie *QS*
69.5 le basic [*sic*] iudas *X*
69.6 fist burgot [*sic*] et *R* | et *om. W* (-*1*)
69.7 tel desroy *V*
69.8 au liure *MX*

70.   Ce caillou, celle fonde a las,   [25]
      Sont ceulx dont David par courage
      Occist le gëant Golyas,
      Qui de mal faire ne fut las,
      Në a luy në a son linage.
      Accident acheva ce gage,
      Qui se fiert par divers moyens
      Sur Catholicques et payens.

71.   De ce chevestre fut pendu
      Aman, tant riche, tant puissant,
      Pour ce qu'il avoit pretendu
      A faire destruit et perdu
      Le peuple juïf par avant.*
      Dont Hester, qui vertus ot tant,
      Le fist d'Accident estrangler
      Et Mardocheüs honnourer. »

72.   Je n'eux pas visité le quart
      De ce lieu qui fist a noter
      Que l'on nous dist qu'il estoit tard,
      Si fismes de ce lieu depart
      Et me voult mon hoste enmener.
      Entendement me fist muser
      Es relicques qu'il me monstra
      Ou ung tres merveilleux monstre a.*

70.1 Le c. *A* | Ce cailloux *V* | fronde *MZ* | f. et las *L*, f. allas *S*
70.3 Mist a mort *Q* | le tresgrand *V*, le grant gollias *S* (-*1*), le grant goleas *Q*, *X* (-*1*)
70.4 Que *FG*
70.5 Ne a lain [?] *N*
70.6 ce graige [*sic*] *G*, se gaige *N*
70.7 ce fiert *E*
70.8 Sus *Y* | payens *ABEFLQRTVW/MX* (paiens *YZ*)] poyens *C*, payans *NP*

71.1 ce senestre [*sic*] *V* | fust *L*
71.2 r. et t. *ELQ/Z* | riche et p. *M* (-*1*)
71.3 Panocque auoit *L* (-*1*)
71.4 Affaire *R* | Deffait d. *QS* (-*1*) | destruire *BELNV/YZ*

70. This stone and this sling
Are those with which David courageously
Killed the giant Goliath,
Who never tired of doing harm
To him and to his people.
Accident won this combat,
Who strikes in sundry ways
Both Catholics and pagans.

71. With this halter was hanged
Haman, so rich, so powerful,
Because he had tried to
Destroy and eliminate
The Jewish people long ago.
Therefore Esther, who had such courage,
Had him strangled by Accident
And had Mordecai honored."

72. I hadn't visited a quarter
Of this noteworthy place
When we were told that it was late,
So we prepared to leave
And my host wished to show me out.
Understanding made me reflect
On the relics he had shown me
Where there was a marvelous display.

71.5 juif *ELNPQT/M*, iuif *X*] juifz *CABFGRSV*, juyfz *W*, iuifz *Z*, iuisz [*sic*] *Y*
71.6 q*ui* eu [*?*] v. *M* (+*1?*), qui de v. *R* (+*1*) | vertu *EFGNPQRSV/MX* | eust *FNP*
71.7 La fit *S* | d' *om. Q*

72.1 visiter [*sic*] *V*, visecte [*sic*] *W*
72.2 De celluy qui *MX* | fut *FG*, fait *QS* | qui fit tant n. *E*
72.3 dit *FGV/Y*
72.4 Et f. *Q*
72.5 Et voulut mon *M*, Et me voulut mon *X* (+*1*), Et me veult *VW* | hoster [*sic*] *L*
72.6 mucer *A*, muer *E*, tarder *V*
72.7 qui me *ENV*
72.8 tresmeilleux [*sic*] *B* (-*1*), tres *om. L* (-*1*)

73.   Ainsi nous partismes tous deux
        Hors du Cloistre de Souvenance,
        Ou je prins plaisir douloureux,
        Ung aspre soulaz angoisseux
        Et ung delit en desplaisance.
        C'est ung doubter en assurance,
        C'est une seurté incertaine*
        Dont je ne fus pas sans grant paine.   [26]

74.   Toutesfoiz moult marry je fuz
        Et biaucop je le regrectoie
        Que je ne viz tout le surplus,
        Et oultre je m'esbahiz plus
        De ce que riens veü n'avoie*
        En ce cloistre dont je venoye
        Des fais de Debille le Fier.
        Ce cas me faisoit merveillier.

75.   Mais Entendement me saoula,
        Me disant : « S'a moy tu reviens,
        Le surplus se demonstrera
        Et de Debile on te dira
        Dont il fiert ne de quieulx engiens.
        Ses bastons ne sont terrïens,
        Mais fait de feblesse massue
        Dont mesme le porteur se tue. »

Stanzas 73–76 missing, A; copied from "l'Imprimé," fol. 15^(r-v).
73.3 Ou jay prins *Q* | plaisirs *M*
73.4 Apres ung solas *V* | augoisseux [*sic*] *Y*
73.6 un docteur [*sic*] *E*
73.7 seurete *QR* (+1) | incertame [*sic*] *Y*

74.3 ne *om. AiM* (-1) | tout *om. Q* (-1) | supplus *X*
74.4 Et oultreplus ie [*sic*] *FG/X* (+1)
74.5 rien *M* | veu je nauoye *EV/AiX*
74.7 De fais [*sic*] *W* | de ce debile *X* (+1)
74.8 Le cas *R*

73.   Thus we both departed
From the Cloister of Memory
Wherein I took painful pleasure,
A harsh anguished solace,
And a delight in discontent.
'Tis a doubt within assurance,
'Tis an uncertain security,
From which I was not without great pain.

74.   However, I was most unhappy
And regretted greatly
That I had not seen the rest;
And besides, I was more amazed
That I had seen nothing
In this cloister from which I came
Of the deeds of cruel Debility.
This situation made me wonder.

75.   But Understanding comforted me,
Saying, "If you come back to me,
You will be shown the rest
And will be told about Debility,
How he strikes and with what devices.
His weapons are unearthly
Since he makes a club of frailty
With which the bearer kills himself."

75.1   me salua [sic] W (+1?)
75.2   si a moy r. ENPQS/AiX, si a moy entens M | tu reuient [sic] W
75.3   ce L, te AiMX
75.4   debile lon FGS/X (+1); lon tiendra Q
75.5   f. et de S/YZ | de quel [sic] engiens EVW | moiens L
75.6   Ces E
75.7   faiz E, fais R/Z
75.8   mesmes BEFGLNPQRS/AiX

76.   Ainsi ce propos nous laisasmes*
        Si pris mes armes et m'armay.
        Des biens de lians desjunasmes,
        Dimes « A Dieu », nous embrassames.
        Sa grant bonté lui merciay ;
        Promectre me fist, et fait l'ay,
        Que par luy referay passaige
        Se je reschappe du voiage.

**Cy commence la seconde partie de ce livre et devise comment
Entendement donna au partir a l'Acteur sa lance de Regime.**

MINIATURE 7. The hermit gives the Author his lance, Authority [27]

77.   *L* ors j'ay ma lance demandee,
        Aprés que je fuz a cheval,
        Que le preudomme m'eut donnee*
        De Regime, bien ordonnee
        Contre la force de tout mal ;
        Si pris mon chemin par ung val
        Qui se tiroit en une lande
        Qui resembloit estre bien grande.

78.   Celle lande que j'ay nommee
        S'appelloit en vurgal le Temps.

76.1   Ainsi mon hoste nous *V* | Ainsi a ce *S/M* (+*1*), ce *om. Y* (-*1*) | le pr. *E*, se pr. *W*
76.3   Et des b. *FG* (+*1*) | leans nous devisasmes [*sic*] *AiM* (+*1*), l. desnuasmes [*sic*] *X*
76.4   Deismes *Q* | adieu et nous *R* (+*1*)
76.6   fat [*sic*] lay *W*
76.7   par la *BQS/AiMX*; vers lui *L* | je feray *L*, referoys *M*, referoye *Ai* (+*1*), referoy
        [*sic*] *X*
76.8   Sy *F*, Si *EGV/M* | je eschappe *E*, jeschappe [?] *M* | de ce v. *E*, dun v. *Y*

Rubric. devise comme [*sic*] *F* | au partir *om. R*; au partement *L* | la lance *BFLR/YZ. E*:
        Comment lacteur part dauecques entendement et sen va en son voiage[.] *Rubric
        follows miniature in FGR; follows instructions, LTW/Z. No rubric, NPQSV/MX.
        Rubric missing in A, along with stanzas 73–76.*
Equivalent miniature in *FGR/Y*; subject in *B* may be that of No. 8; no miniature, *EQS/X*;
        presumably removed, *A*.

76.   Then we left off this discussion
      And I took my armor and donned it.
      We shared a lunch from his goods,
      We embraced and said farewell.
      I thanked him for his great kindness;
      He made me promise, which I did,
      That I should make my way back to him
      If I survived my journey.

Part II

Here begins the second part of this book and tells how Understanding, on parting, gave the Author his lance of Authority.

77.   After I was on my horse,
          I asked for my lance
          (Which the worthy man had given me)
      Of Authority, well-ordered
      Against the power of all evil.
      I took my way through a valley
      Which lengthened into a plain
      That appeared to be quite large.

78.   This plain of which I speak
      Was called, in common parlance, Time.

77.1   Jay ja ma l. *V*
77.3   meust *BEFGLQSW* | donne *X*
77.4-5 *inverted X*
77.4   ordonne *X*
77.5-6 *inverted V*
77.5   sa force *W* | tous [*sic*] mal *W*
77.7   Qui se cy reit [?] *V*
77.8   qui me sembloit *MX*

78.1   Ceste *ENPQS/MX*
78.2   Rappelloit *X* | vulgal *BEFGLNPQSV/MXY*, vulgar *R*

Combien qu'elle fust grande et lee,
Si est elle tantost passee :
Quant plaisir y est sur les rens,
On y quert comme font les vens !   [28]
La j'apersus, pour abreger,
Que temps se passe de legier.*

79.   Mon cheval, qu'on nommoit Vouloir,
      Tiroit en ce lieu tant au frain
      Que je n'oz du tenir pouoir
      Que soubit ne fusse pour voir
      Droit au milieu de ce beau plain.
      La soubit je viz tout a plain
      Ung chevalier qui m'actendoit
      Et que combatre me failloit.

80.   Il estoit armé de Traveil
      Et son cheval s'appelloit Peine ;
      Son escu paroit au souloil
      Paint de Veillier et de Sommeil
      Si caduch qu'on le vid a paine.*
      Sa cotte fut de Souffrir plaine
      Et sembloit a le voir sans faille*
      Qu'il vint d'une grande bataille.*

81.   J'eusse voulentiers regardé
      La contenance de partie,

78.3   fut *BEVW* | grand *Q*
78.5   Quaut [*sic*] *X*, Quat [*sic*] *Y* | y *om. V (-1)* | sus *Y*
78.6   Qui y *QS*, Lon y *V* | y *om. L (-1)* | court *BELQSV/X*, queurt *AFGNPRTW/Y*
       | les *om. FG (-1)*, le vens [*sic*] *W* | c. toust comme le vent *E*
78.7   Ja *W* | iaperceu mon aberger [*sic*] *X*
78.8   se passe *ABEFGNPQRSTVW/MYZ*] ce p. *CL/X*

79.1   quon nomme v. *MX*
79.3   de tenir *BEFGLNPQSV/MX*
79.4   pour veoir *G*
79.5   ou *L* | bel *FG*
79.6   ie voyz *X*

However large and wide it may be,
It is soon passed over:
When pleasure is in the lists,
One sweeps across it like the winds!
To be brief, I noticed
That time passes swiftly there.

79.   My horse, named Willing,
Was pulling so hard on his reins there
That I couldn't hold him in,
And suddenly I was really
Right in the middle of that fine plain.
All at once I clearly saw there
A knight who awaited me
And that I had to fight.

80.   His armor was by Travail
And his horse was called Pain.
In the sun his shield appeared
To be painted with Wakefulness and Sleep
So faintly that one could scarce see it.
His coat was full of Suffering
And, on sight, it seemed certain
That he was coming from a mighty contest.

81.   I would willingly have examined
The face of my opponent,

80.1   estoit comme de *FG*; arme *repeated V*
80.2   sapelloit palme *V*
80.3   parioit [?] au ciel *M*
80.4   Plain *BR/M*, Painne [*sic*] *L* (+*1*), Plaint [*sic*] *X* | de vueiller *Q/X*
80.5   caducque *V* (+*1*), cadut *NQ* | quont *F* | veist *LQ*, vist *W*
80.6   Sa couette *S* | fust *L* | de souffeir [*sic*] *Y* | peine *S/M*
80.7   a la voix [*sic*] *QS* | voir *LNRTW/YZ*] veoir *CABEFGPV/MX* | sa f. *Q* | faille *ABEFGLNPQRSTVW/MXYZ*] faillie *C*
80.8   Que *B*, Qui *V* | venist *AFGNPQRSTW/XYZ*, *B* (+*1*); venoit *V/M* | grant *AFGNPQSTW/XYZ*, *L* (-*1*), grand *RV/M*

In N, stanzas 81–86 follow stanza 87.

Mais possible ne m'a esté :
Semblant que fusse destiné
D'esprouver sa chevalerie.
Je couchay, il ne faillit mie,*
Et tel hurtasmes noz escuz
Que tous deux fusmes abatus.

82.   Et lui qui fut bon chevalier
      Saillit sus sans faire demeure ;
      Si fi ge de l'autre quartier.*
      Il empoingne son branc d'acier*   [29]
      Pour moy fierement courir seure
      Et je mon glave sans demeure*
      De Regime qu'on me fist prendre
      Mis en mes mains pour moy deffendre.

83.   Son escu joint et si fait signe
      De moy assommer et confondre.
      Je le reboutay par Regime
      Deux ou trois fois par telle hactine*
      Qu'il trouva bien a qui respondre.
      Vaillanment me sçavoit semondre
      Et de ma part me deffendoie
      Le mieulx que faire le pouoie.

84.   Mais il me rassaillit tousjours
      Et me donnoit de son espee
      (Qui fut faite de Trop de Jours)

81.4   destinee *M*
81.5   Desprouuoir *X*
81.6   Je touchay *M* | faillit *ABEGLNPQRSTVW/MXYZ*] fallit *C*, faillist *F*
81.7   Et tant *QS*, Et telz *G/MX*

82.2   sus *om. M (-1)*
82.4   empoigna *LQS* | brant *FG*
82.6   Ma lance que je congneuz seure *BEFGNPQRSV/MXY*, Ma l. que je congnois seure
       L/Z
82.7   feit pr. *V*
82.8   pour me *QV/MX*

But this was not possible for me
Since it seemed that I was fated
To test his chivalry.
I couched my lance, he did no less,
And we so violently hit our shields
That we were both thrown to the ground.

82. He, who was a worthy knight,
Jumped up without delay,
As I did on the other side.
He grasped his broadsword
To run upon me fiercely and sure.
And I, without delay, my lance*
Of Authority, which I'd been made to take,
Put in my hands to defend myself.

83. He buckled his shield and indicated
That he would overcome and defeat me.
I drove him back with Authority
Two or three times with such passion
That he found out to whom he must answer.
He knew how to press me boldly
And I, on my part, defended myself
The best that I could.

84. But still he struck back at me
And delivered with his sword
(Which was made of Surfeit of Days)

83.1 escut *W*. Apres son escu print et joinct *M*
83.2 Pour moy *M*
83.3 reboute *MX* | par tel poinct *M*
83.4 tel *BELNPQRSTVW/XY* | tel haynne *W* | fois si bien apoint *M*
83.5 bien *om. X (-1)*
83.6 ne sauoit [*sic*] *FG* | respondre *MX*
83.8 le sauoie *LR*

84.1 rassailloit *BFGNPQSV/MXZ*, rasoilloit *E*
84.3 fust *L*; fut *om. Q (-1)*

De si grans cops et de si lours
Que j'en eulx la teste estonnee.
Ma lance si fut tronsonnee
Par la force de moy deffendre
Et convint mon espee prendre.

85.   Tant fut cest assault combatu
Que nul de nous n'ot la peau saine.*
Froissames haubert et escu :
Se l'un fiert, l'autre l'a rendu ;
Chascun a vaincre met sa paine.
Dont pour reprendre nostre alaine
Nous retirasmes d'un accord
Et le vouloit bien le plus fort.

86.   Quant euz mon alaine reprise,*
Je regarday mon adversaire   [30]
Que je crains beaucop et le prise
Si me mis ung pou en devise,
Disant : « Vassal de grant affaire,
Je vous pry que veullez tant faire
Pour moy de vostre nom me dire
Et je vous en prie, beau sire. »

87.   Sy me dist d'asseuree voix,
Doulcement et de bon visaige :

84.5   jen ay *E*
84.7   la *om. Q (-1)*
84.8   Et me conuient *V/M* (+*1*), Et couient *W*

85.1   combatuz *V*
85.2   nulz *BEFGNPS* | neust *FLPV/X* | la pel *EFGPQS/X*, sa pel *N* | seine [*sic*]
        N/MX
85.3   Froiasmes [*sic*] *X* | aubers *B*, auberx *Y* | Rompu fut aubert *E* | escuz *V*
85.4   Si *E* | fier *V*
85.5   a vaincre lautre m. *Q* (+*2*) | mest *L*
85.6   Et pour *FG* | mon alainne *L*, vostre halaine [*sic!*] *X*
85.7   retraismes *S*
85.8   Et bien le vouloit *R*

Such huge and heavy blows
That it made my head ring.
Thus was my lance splintered
By the force of my defence
And I had to take up my sword.

85.   This contest was so hard fought
       That neither of us had a whole skin.
       We pierced hauberks and shields:*
       As one struck, the other struck back.
       We put every effort into winning.
       Then, in order to recover our breath,
       We backed off with one accord
       And even the stronger really wanted to.

86.   When I had got my breath back,
       I looked at my adversary
       Whom I greatly feared and esteemed,
       And began to converse a bit,
       Saying, "Vassal of great importance,
       I beg you to be so kind
       As to tell me your name,
       I beseech you, good lord."

87.   And he said to me confidently,
       Pleasantly and with good manner,

Stanzas 86–89 missing R (1 leaf torn out, presumably to remove miniature No. 8).
86.1   Quant jeuz *ABEFGLNPQSTVW/MXYZ* | bien prise *B*
86.2   regarde *FG*
86.3   Que *om. A (-1)*
86.6   prie *BFGSVW/X* (+1), prye *E/M* (+1) | vueilles *S/X*
86.7   que v. *M* | nom ne dire [*sic*] *X*
86.8   emprie *FW/X*, en pry *Q* (-1) | beu [*sic*] sire *G*
In N, stanza 86 is followed by stanza 88.

87.1   Ci *E* | dit *LV/Y*

« Noble suys et yssu de rois
Avant Percheval le Galoix,
Cougnu par mon grant vasselaige.
Saches que nommé suis Ëage,
De rencontrer prest et commun
Au milieu du temps de chascun.

88.   Nul ne peult le Temps trespasser*
Qui ne passe par mes destrois ;
Tel me scet Ëage nommer
Qui ne me voudroit pas trouver,
Mais il abuse ses exploix :
Par moy fault passer une fois,
Tel est le chemin des heureux,
Ou morir jone doloreux.

89.   Et puis que tu es en mes mains,
Sçavoir te fault que je sçay faire :
Prisonnier te rendras du mains.
Je te deffie et ne te crains.
Deffens toy ; il t'est neccessaire. »
Je saulx avant sans moy retraire
Et recommensa nostre estour
Le plus felon de tout le jour.

87.3   et *om.* M (-1) | yssus Q, yssuz V | des roys *EGS/MX*
87.4   perceuant A
87.6   Scaichez B, Sachez *FGW/X*, Saichez M | nommez *BW*
87.8   Au meillieur E | dung chescun S

88.1   Nulz *V/YZ*, Nuulz W | trespasses [*sic*] N; trespasser le temps S, *with something like quotation marks around* trespasser, *presumably to indicate the correct order.*
88.2   Quil *BELNPQST/MXYZ*
88.3   ne scait M, ne scet X | laage [*sic*] X; scet bien saige nommer E

"I am noble and descended from kings
Before Perceval the Welshman,
And recognized for my great valorous service.
Know that I am called Age,
To be met readily and by all
In the middle of each one's life.

88.   No one can make his way through Time
Without passing through my narrow straits;
There are those who know my name, Age,
Who would not wish to find me,
But they waste their efforts:
I must be gone through once,
Such is the path for the fortunate
Or to die painfully young.

89.   And since you are in my hands,
You must know what I can do:
You will at least give yourself up as a prisoner.
I challenge you and do not fear you.
Defend yourself as you must."
I leapt forward without shrinking
And our combat began anew,
The most furious of the whole day.

88.4   Quil *B* | ne *om. M* (*-1*)
88.6   Pour moy *M*
88.8   jeune maleureux *S*

89.1   tu es es mes [*sic*] *E*
89.5   t' *om. M*
89.6   Je sault *E*, Il sault *V* | sans soy r. *V*
89.7   recommancera *Q* (*+1*)

MINIATURE 8. The plain of Time: the Author contends against Age [31]

Cy se combat l'Acteur a l'encontre d'Eage et comment l'Acteur se rendit prisonnier.

90.   Trop de Jours, qui son glave fut,*
        Me porta ce jour maint contraire ;
        Et puis Regime rompu fut,
        Qui mortellement me deceut
        Et me greva en cest affaire,
        Car pour moy oultrer et deffaire,
        Espoir, dont fut fait mon escu,
        Me fut lors des poings abatu.

91.   Quant Age si m'ot desarmé
        De mon bon escu d'Esperance,
        Il s'est du tout abandonné,
        Pour ce qu'il me sentoit foullé   [32]
        Et affeibly en ma puissance ;
        Si ne viz autre recouvrance
        Pour escapper de ce danger
        Que de moy rendre prisonnier.*

92.   Lors me rendis rescoux ou non
        A Ëage par son valoir
        Et luy promis foy et prison,
        Asseurant de payer rençon
        A son desir a mon pouoir.

Equivalent miniature in *ABEFGS/Y*; different subjects in *Q/X*; missing, *R*.

Rubric. Icy *M* | Cy combat *QS* | ce combat *B* | va a [*sic*] *Q* (va *inserted above line*) | et comme *FG*, Et qua*n*t *X* | comment l'Acteur *om. M* | se rend *B. Miniature and rubric missing (along with stanzas 86–89) R. Rubric precedes miniature in EQS/XY. No rubric, V.*

90.1   Trop des *X* | que *BQRS*. Maintesfois le glaive qu*i*l eut *M*
90.2   main *V*, mains *X*
90.4   le deceut [*sic*] *X*, me diceut *Y*
90.6   diffaire *Y*. Grant ennuy euz a me defaire *E*
90.7   Despoir *E* | fut *om. S* (-*1*)
90.8   Qui me fut des *E* | hors des *BLRV/M*

91.1   aage si *A* (+*1*) | si *om., with* eaige, eage, *or* aage, *BEFGLNPQRSTVW/MXY* | me eust *EGFNP*, meust *BS* | deserme [*sic*] *Y*

Here the Author does battle against Age and how the Author constitutes himself a prisoner.

90. H is sword, which was Surfeit of Days,
     Dealt me that day many a setback,
     And then Authority was smashed,
         Which fatally betrayed
     And injured me in that affair,
     For in order to overcome and defeat me
     Hope, of which my shield was made,
     Then was knocked from my hands to the ground.

91. When Age had thus disarmed me
     Of my good shield Hope,
     He lost all restraint
     Since he felt that I was worn down
     And weakened in strength.
     I saw no other way
     Of escaping from this danger
     Than to give myself up as a prisoner.

92. Then, not knowing if I would be rescued, I surrendered
     To Age according to his wish
     And swore him faith and thrall,
     Promising him that I would pay ransom
     According to his terms, within my power.

91.2   bon *om. L (-1)*
91.3   Il s'est *ABFLQRTVW/MYZ*] Il est *C*, Il cest *EGNPS/X*
91.4   Pouce quil [*sic*] *F* | qui me *W* | me souloit f. *L* | me s. saoule *EFGS*, saoulle *Q*
91.5   Et assaillir *L*
91.6   Et ne vois *MX* | recouuance [*sic*] *V*
91.8   de me r. *ENPQ/MX*

92.1   rescaux *M* | ou nom *BRW*, au nom *M*
92.2   De eaige par *E*, Aage po*ur M* | son grant v. *E*, *NPQ/X (+1)*, son grand v. *M*, sa grant v. [*sic*] *S*, son bon *FG (+1)* | vouloir *FG/MXZ*
92.4   Asseurent [*sic*] *NP*, Assurent *X*, Asseurement *E/Y (+1)*, Asseureement *FG (+2?)*, Asseurance *M (+1)*, Affermant *QS*
92.5   De son *EFGQS/MX* | et mon *L* | pouair *X*

Doulcement me voult recevoir
En prenant mon gantelet dextre
Comme mon vainqueur et mon maistre.

93. Puis me dist qu'il me traicteroit
En prison moult courtoysement
Mais tenir foy me convenoit
Et faire ce qu'il me diroit
Suz paine de parjurement,*
Car prisonnier estroitement
Doit faire ce qu'il a de charge
En tout, mais que honneur ne le charge.*

94. « Premier en la Terre Amoureuse
Ne veul je pas que tu te boute :*
La est plaisance doloreuse,
Doulce saveur trop venimeuse,
Et n'a pas sens qui ne le doubte.
On m'y heit, je n'y ayme goute :
Ëage n'est en Amours chier ;
Pour ce te deffens ce quartier.

95. Et puis ou val de Mariage
Ne veul je point que tu traverse :*   [33]
C'est ung trop perilleux passage.
Mal y sont tous les gens d'ëage ;
C'est terre pour moy trop diverse.
Ausi ne veul que tu converse*

92.6   veult *V/M*, *W* [?], volut *R* (+*1*)
92.7   En prenent [*sic*] *N*
92.8   Com *Q* (-*1*) | vinceur *X* | et mon maistre *ABEFGLNPQRSTVW/MXYZ*] et maistre *C* (-*1*)

93.1   *First* me *om. M* (-*1*) | dit *V* | me dist il quil *R* (+*1*)
93.3   Ne tenir [*sic*] *V*
93.5   Sur *ABEFGLPQRSTVW/X*, Sus *YZ* | de par Jurement [*sic*] *Y*
93.6   Car pour soinner [*sic*] *X*, En commandant *M*
93.7   ce quil a descharge *S*. Plusieurs choses dont je me charge *M*
93.8   mais quon ne ne le *X* | la charge *R*, le *om. S*, le cherge *W* (charge : cherge). Qui ne mest pas petite charge *M*

He agreed to receive me courteously,
Taking my right gauntlet
As my conqueror and master.

93. Then he told me that he would treat me
Most politely as a prisoner,
But that I must keep my pledge
And do whatever he told me
Upon pain of forswearing;
For a prisoner absolutely
Must do what he is told
In everything, except where honor contravenes.

94. "First, in the Land of Love
I do not wish you to thrust yourself.
Painful pleasure exists there,
Sweet relish too baneful,
And he who does not fear it has no sense.
I am hated there, I do not love it there at all.
Age is not dear to Love;
Therefore I deny this locale to you.

95. Next, into the Vale of Marriage
I do not wish you to cross;
It is too hazardous a passage:
Older people are not well-off there;
The land is too fickle for me.
Also, I do not wish for you to take part

94.1 Premiers *TW/Y*
94.2 veuz *F* | boutez *F*, boutes *E/X*. Ne te mesle poinct somme toutte *M*.
94.3 dolereusse *S* (*rhymed with -euse endings*)
94.4 saulueur *V*
94.5 pas sans *X* | qui na *V*, qui ny *M*, que ne [*sic*] *X* | la d. *BV*, faict d. *M*
94.6 L'on my *BV*, On me *S* | hait et ie *A* (+*1*), je ne my aime g. *R* (+*1*)
94.7 nest plus en *M* (+*1*) | amour *Q/MX* | chiere [*sic*] *W*

95.1 au val *V/M*
95.2 Ne vueille p. *MX* | trauerses *Q*, tenuerse [*sic*] *R*
95.3 tresperilleux *EFQS/MX*, tres p. *G*, trop merueilleux *T*
95.4 toutes gens *BV*, venus gens *M*
95.5 pour toy *T/M* | trop *om. W* (-*1*). Cheste terre est pour moy *R* (+*1*)
95.6 veult *X* | conuerses *Q*

Plus es dances në es carolles
Dont tient Oyseuse les escolles.

96.   Aussi je te deffens les cours
Des princes et des grans seigneurs :
La sont grans perilz et biens cours.
Jeunes gens y queurent le cours
Pour querir proufiz et honneurs,
Mais j'en voy revenir pluseurs
Par la sente de Malveullance,
Povres d'amis et de chevance.

97.   En la forest de Temps Perdu
Ne va plus querre tes deduis :
Tu as trop longuement vescu
Pour plus chasser a l'esperdu
En perte de jours et de nuys.
Ce lieu me desplaist et g'y nuys.
A mectre en prouffit ton temps veille :
Ce point Ëage te conseille.

98.   Joustes, tournois, jeulx de traveil
Te sont d'eulx mesmes deffendus.
Tous les matins a ton reveil
Penses et fais ton appareil
Afin que soyent combatus*
Ceulx qui tant d'aultres ont vaincus.

95.7   en d. *B* | ny es *EFGSV/X*
95.8   aysance *M*, oysance *X* | les es. *om. X*. Dont oyseuse tient les es. *FG*

96.1   je *om. R* (*-1*) | te *om. S* (*-1*)
96.2   des gra*n*t seigneurs [*sic*] *S* | seignours *FG*
96.3   La ont *M* | grant perilz [*sic*] *VW*; grans *om. M, X* (*-1*) | bien cours
        BFGLNQRSW/X, grans cours *E*; et mains faulx tours *M*
96.4–5 *inverted FG*
96.4   Jeune gens [*sic*] *S* | ilz q. *MX* | quierent *EV/MX* | les cours *ER/M*, leurs cours *V*
96.5   proffit *FG* | honnours *FGL*
96.6   Mais l'on uoit *B*; Mais il en reuient pl. *M* (*-1*) | parvenir pluseurs *S*.
96.7   la sante *X*
96.8   Povre [*sic*] dauoirs *W*

97.1   la foirestz *E* | du t. *BEFG/X*
97.2   pas *XZ* | querir *EQSV/X*, mectre *M* | tes *om. W* (*-1*); telz *Q*; des *G*

Any more in the dances and reels
For which Idleness holds her schools.

96. In addition, I forbid you the courts
Of princes and of great lords;
Great perils are there and quick wealth.
Young folk go the course there,
Seeking profits and honors,
But I see many of them coming back
By the Path of Ill Will,
Poor in both friends and money.

97. In the Forest of Time Lost
Go no more seeking your pleasure:
You have lived too long
To chase any more like a lost soul,
Squandering days and nights.
This place displeases me and I am a nuisance there.
Age counsels you this way:
Take care to put your old age to profit.

98. Jousts, tourneys, exercises of skill,
These of themselves are forbidden to you.
Every morning when you wake,
Think and make your preparations
In order that they may be fought,
Those who have vanquished so many others.

97.3 trop *om. A (-1)*
97.5 pertes *M* | jour *V/M* | nuit *M*
97.6 Le lieu *L/M*, Ce jour *EFGQ/X* | my d. *Q* | jy nuytz *B*, si nuyctz *V*, et gemis [*sic*] *X*. Line *om.*, *S.*
97.7 A *om. R (-1)* | a pr. *LNV/M* | tout temps *M* | vueille *Q*
97.8 En ce poinct *M (+1)*, Ce point cy. aage *S (+1)*

98.1 Joustez et t. *R (+1)* | *Originally* tournois et jeulx, *the word* et *subsequently deleted* (*grattage*) *C* | jeux et trauail *QS*, jeu a trauail *M*
98.2 Ce *X* | deusmesmes *FG*
98.3 Tout les [*sic*] *V* | raueil *FG*
98.4 Pence et *L*, Pense et *QTV/X (-1)*
98.5 que tu ne s. *Q (+2)*, que tu s. *S (+1)* | soyent *V* (soient *M/Z*)] soyes *CAPQRT*, soies *LNS/Y*, soiez *EW*, soye *BFG/X*
98.6 De ceulx *F (+1)*, Conps [?] qui *L* | vaincu *R*

Ton corps par adventure au lieu
Et garde l'ame pour ton Dieu.

99.   Or t'ay ordonné les limites   [34]
Que je ne veil point que tu passe.*
Me croire beaucop tu prouffites ;
Du rebours tu te desherites
Et pers de verité la grace. »
Si dis : « Ne doubtez que je face
Riens contre ce que j'ay juré,
Mais tiendray foy et verité. »

100.   Puis me dit qu'il m'eslargissoit*
Afin de tenir ma promesse
Et me conseilla et vouloit
Que prensisse ma voye droit
Par my le desert de Viellesse.
C'est le chemin, la seulle adresse
Selon la raison de Nature
Pour actaindre mon adventure.

101.   Cheval et armes me rendit
De sa liberale franchise
Et en prenant congié me dit :*
« Je te donne pour ton prouffit
Ce gorgerin fait de tel guise
Qu'il est meslé de barbe grise,

98.7   par *om. F* (-1) | en lieu *L.* T. c. pour durer en ce lieu *M*

99.1   Je tay *R* | tay donne *GM* (-1)
99.2   passe *ABFGLNPTVW/XYZ*] passes *CMQRS*, passez [= passes?] *ER*
99.3   A me *M* (*om.* tu) | du proffites *X*
99.5   Et si pers de vertu *M*
99.6   Se dit *M* | doubte *G/M*, doubtes *QS/X*
99.7   j' *om. L* (-1?); ce que ie niray [*sic*] *X*
99.8   tiendre [*sic*] *E*

100.1   dist *ABFGLQRSTW/MX* | qui *V* | meslargiroit *E*
100.4   Que je prinse *B/M*, Que je prenisse *L* (+1) | voie droitte *RV*

Put your body at risk instead
And save your soul for God.

99.   Now I have prescribed the limits
Beyond which I do not want you to go.
You will profit greatly from believing me;
Otherwise you will disinherit yourself
And lose the grace of truth."
I answered, "Have no fear that I may do
Anything contrary to what I have sworn,
But I will keep faith and truth."

100.   Then he said that he was setting me free
So that I might keep my promise
And wished and counselled me
That I should make my way straight
Through the middle of the desert of Old Age.
That is the road, the right road,
According to Nature's design,
To accomplish my adventure.

101.   He returned my arms and horse
From his liberal generosity
And on taking leave said to me,
"For your profit I am giving you
This neck piece made in such a manner
That it is mixed with grey beard

100.5 desirt *G*

100.6 le ch. et la *Q* (+*1*) | la seure *EFGLQRS/MX*

100.8 Pour attendre *LQS/MX*, P. attandre *RV*

101.1 Hheual [*sic*] *A*, Cheuaulx *M*

101.2 liberable [*sic*] *W*

101.3 dit *ABFGLNPTV/MXYZ*] dist *CEQRSW*

101.4 pour toy pr. *V*

101.5 gorgery *Q* | fait *om. M* | de telle guise *E* (+*1*), *M*

101.6 Qui est *SV/M* | meslay *FG*

Faite de nature si franche
Que plus vivras plus sera blanche. »

102.   Doncques Ëage me donna
Le present de barbe meslee.
Je partis et il demoura
A garder ce dont la charge a :
C'est le Temps en celle contree.
Ainsi j'ay la face tournee
Vers Viellesse qu'on veult fuÿr
Et si la devroit on querir.   [35]

103.   Ainsi la montaigne montay
Que l'on peult le my temps comprendre,
Mais certes je la devalay
Biaucop plus tost que je n'alay :
Plus poise monter que descendre
Et me fallut tirer et tendre
Contre Viellesse le desert
Qui chascun destruit et desert.

104.   Mais je n'eux gueres cheminé,
Que, droit a ung chemin croisié,
Je me suis ainsi qu'oublié,
Hors de la voye destourné
Qu'Ëage m'avoit enseignié ;
Si pris comme mal conseillié

101.8   viueras *R* (+*1*), viuera [*sic*] *W* (+*1*) | plus seras *M*, tu seras *X*

102.1   Doncqnes [*sic*] *X*
102.2   Le prouffit *Q*
102.3   Je porte *V* (*-1?*) | et y *EFV/X* | demourra *V*
102.4   ce *om. X* (*-1*) | la *om. L/M* (*-1*)
102.5   ceste c. *V*, telle c. *X*, icelle c. *M* (+*1*)
102.6   Aussi *W* | A. ieuz *FG* | tournaye [*sic*] *W*, trouuee *R*
102.8   deueroit *ERW/X* (+*1*)

103.2   Que on *RW* (*-1?*), Que len *X* | peust *Q* | le mien t. *M* | apprandre *L*
103.3   ie le d. *FG* | la deuale *X*

Made of such a hearty nature
That the longer you live, the whiter it will be."

102.   Thus Age gave me
        The present of a grizzled beard.
        I went off and he stayed
        To watch over that for which he was responsible,
        Which is Time in that country.
        So I turned my face
        Toward Old Age which one wishes to flee
        And yet one should seek it.

103.   Thus I went up the mountain
        By which one can represent middle age,
        But certainly I went down it
        A great deal faster than I went up:
        It is much harder to go up than come down
        And I needed to draw back and take aim
        Against the ravager Old Age
        Which destroys and ruins each one.

104.   But I had scarcely gone any way at all
        When right at a crossroad
        I rather forgot myself and
        Turned away from the route
        Which Age had designated for me,
        And as though badly directed took

103.4–5 *inverted S*
103.4   Plustost beau cop *S* | que je ne lay *M*, que ie ne le [*sic*] *X*
103.5   Plus prise m. [*sic*] *X*
103.6   me faillit *AEFGNPQV/X*, me falllust [*sic*] *B*, me faillut *L/M*, me faillir *S*
103.7   le dessert *VW*; la deserte *R*. *Line om.*, *X*.
103.8   Que *EFGNPSVW/MX* | et deserte *R*. Que chascun desseruy et dessert *V* (+*1*)

104.3   Je *om. M* (-*1*) | qu' *om. V* | ainsy comble [*sic*] *X* (-*1*)
104.4   Lors de la *A*, Et hors la *EFG/X*, Et hors de la *QS* (+*1*) | et destourne *V*
104.5   Ou aaige *S* (+*1*) | mauoit conseillie *R*. *Line om.*, *M*.
104.6–7 *inverted M*
104.6   Je prins *BEFGQSVW/X* | mal enseigne *Q*, mal enseignie *R*.

Le sentier qu'on appelle Abuz
Ou pluseurs se treuvent abuz.*

105.   Le chemin me sembla tout vert,
        Et si estoit saison faillie,
        Le paÿs bel et descouvert ;
        Feulles et fleurs tout y appert :
        Abuz est restaurant de vie.
        La je rentray en fantasie
        Des haulx plaisirs de mon jouvant
        Et oubliay le demourant.

106.   Lors me rassaillit souvenance
        De tout mon jone temps perdu ;
        Viellesse fut en oubliance,
        Prison, serment et obligeance
        Plus n'en fut en riens souvenu.
        Je fus tout nouvel revenu   [36]
        Ou temps certes que je cuidoie
        Avoir ce que je souhaitoye.

107.   Armes, amours, chiens et oiseaux,
        Tout fut soubmiz a mon plaisir ;
        La fiz en Espaigne chasteaux*
        Et de chardons souhaiz chapeaulx.
        Tout conquis sans riens retenir !
        Abuz me faisoit raverdir

104.7   que lon nomme abus *LR/M*
104.8   se tiennent *X* | deceuz *QS/Z*

105.1   sembloit *FG*
105.5   retorant [*sic*] *LW* | de la vie *L* (+*1*)
105.6   je entray *M* (-*1?*)
105.7   de mo*n*t *V* | mon couuent *M*

106.1   me saillit *S* (-*1*), massaillit *Q* (-*1*)
106.2   perduz *V*
106.3   V. me fu *W* (+*1*)
106.4   serment et o. *EQV/X*] et *om. CABLRTW/MYZ* (-*1*), serement et o. *FGNP* (+*1*). Pr.
        suruint en ou. *S*

The path that is called Delusion,
Where many find themselves deceived.

105. To me the way seemed wholly green,
      Even though the season had waned,
      The country fine and open;
      Leaves and flowers all appeared there:
      Delusion is the restorer of life.
      In fantasy I returned there
      To the great pleasures of my youth
      And forgot everything else.

106. Then remembrance surged through me again
      Of all my lost youth;
      Old Age was forgotten,
      Captivity, oath, constraint
      No longer remembered in any way.
      I had turned back anew
      To the time when I seriously used to believe
      That I could have anything I wished.

107. Arms, love, hounds and birds:
      Everything was subject to my pleasure;
      I built castles in Spain there,
      Made wished-for hats from thistledown.
      I took everything and kept nothing!
      Delusion made me grow young again

106.5 rien *BRS/M*. Plus en riens nen fust souuenus *V*
106.6 Il fut *M* | reuenuz *V*
106.7 Au t. *QS*, Du t. *M* | ont ie c. *F*, ou ie c. *G*
106.8 je *om. W* (-*1*)

107.1 Armes armures *M* (*om.* et)
107.4 souez *V*, souhay *W*, souuent *M*
107.5-6 *inverted B, with marginal letters A and B to indicate correct order.*
107.5 Tant conquis *L*, Bien congnuz *FG*, Bien congneu *E/X*, Bien cougneuz *QS* | rien
        B/M; suys rien [*sic*] *X*
107.6 Quabuz *EFGQS/X* | retenir *Q*

Et croire de moy l'impossible
Par sa desvoyance nuysible.

108.   Je ne tins plus bride ny frain,*
       Mon cheval s'en aloit sa voye.
       Plus ne viz montaigne ne plain ;
       Je fuz de cuyder si tres plain
       Que je ne me recougnoissoie.
       Ou j'aloys, je ne le sçavoye.
       Abuz me mascha celle oublie :
       Ainsi chemine qui s'oublye.

109.   Tant ay cheminé et erré
       Par la sente Peu de Prouffit,
       Sans cognoistre que j'ay erré,*
       Qu'en soubit me suis embarré*
       Ou plus bel lieu qu'onques Dieu fist.
       La ung palais est fait et sist,*
       Le plus bel qu'on pourroit choisir ;
       Et sembloit lieu pour non morir.

110.   Les cresteaux estoient d'or fin
       Flamboiant contre le soulail ;
       Les murs sont d'argent methalin,
       Les fenestres de cristalin   [37]
       Et le comble, dont me merveil,*

107.7 Et de moy croire *EQS/X* | de moy tout limpossible *F* (+*1*), de moy tant
       limpossible *G* | cr. imposible [*sic*] *E* (-*1*)
107.8 Par la *QS*, Pour sa *E* | inuisible [*sic*] *GS/Y*, nussible [?] *W*

108.1 tiens *B* | puys bride *M* | ne frain *ABEFGLNPQSTVW/MX*, ne frains *R*
108.2 alla *X*
108.3 montaignes *V*
108.4 culdier [?] *W*
108.6 Ou ialoyez [*sic*] *FG* (+*1*), Ou jalay *ABELNPQRSTVW/X*, Ou je alloye *M* (*om.* le)
       | ne le cognoissoie *Q* (+*1*)
108.8 Ainsi chemme [*sic*] *Y*

109.1 erray *EFG*

And believe the impossible of myself
By its harmful misleading.

108. I no longer held on to bridle or rein;
My horse went his own way.
No longer did I see mountain or plain;
I was so filled with thought
That I lost my bearings
And knew not where I was going.
Delusion prepared this oblivion for me:
Thus rides one who forgets himself.

109. I rode and wandered so much
Along the Path of Little Profit
Without realizing that I strayed,
When suddenly I was brought up short
In the most beautiful place God ever made.
A palace was made and seated there,
The most beautiful that one could see—
It seemed a deathless place.

110. The battlements were of fine gold
Flaming against the sun;
The walls were of silver metal,
The windows crystal,
And the roof, at which I marvelled,

109.3 que je erray *E*, que ie erre *X*

109.4 Que s. *BV/M*, Quant *X* | subit *BEFGLNPQSV/X* | en barre *E*

109.5 Au *V* | lieu *om. M* (-*1*) | beau lieu pour no*n* morir *S* | feit *V*, fit *M*

109.6 La est ung palais f. *E* | sist *BW* (seist *L*)] fist *CAENQR/XYZ*, fit *PS*, feist *FGV*. Line *om., M.*

109.7–8 *inverted in* Y, *with period after* morir.

110.1 Le chasteau *V* (-*1*); Les carneaulx *Q*, creneaulx *ES/M*, tresteaulx *X*, creasteaux *Y*

110.2 Flamboyent *EG*, Flamboyans *LS/MYZ*, Flambayans *Q* | comme le s. *Q*

110.3 dragent [*sic*] *Y*. Et les murs dargent *EFGNPQS/X*

110.5 dont mesmerueil *QR/MX*

Fut couvert d'un ambre vermeil
Qui rendoit clarté et lueur
Sy grant qu'on ne scet la valeur.

111.   Les fenestres furent parees
De dames et de damoiselles
Si tres richement aournees
Qu'onques mais furent atournees
En une grant feste pucelles ;
Et pour entretenir icelles
Mains gorgias et bien en point*
En ce lieu ne failloient point.

112.   Trompettes, menestriers sonnoient
Si hault que tout retondissoit.
L'un chantoit, les autres dansoient,
Les autres de leurs cas parloient :
Chascun du mieulx qu'il pot faisoit.
Par Abuz fuz en tel destroit
Qu'il me sembloit, se g'y estoye,
Que bonne adventure j'aroie.

113.   Si m'addressay vers le portier,
Que l'on nommoit Abusion,
Et lui dis : « Tresdoulx amis chier,
Ce palais si grant et si chier

110.6 Fust *L*; Furent couuerz *R* (+*1*) | dun marbre *Q*, dun antre [?] *W*, dun abre *M*
110.8 qu'on *om. X* (-*1*) | nen scet *W* | ne valeur [*sic*] *S*

111.2 et damoiselles *E* (-*1*)
111.3 Et tres *S* | et aournees *X* (+*1*) | atournees *W*
111.4 ne f. trouuees *M*
111.5 En nulle *V* | grande *B* (+*1*). En bancquet ne festes plus belles *M*
111.7 Mains *BN/X* (Maints *EQ*, Maintz *FGPS/M*)] Maint *CALRTVW/YZ* | gorgint [?]
       V | empointz *M*
111.8 failloit *V* (-*1*)

112.1 menestreux *LR/Z*, menestres *FG*, menestrez *P*, menestries *V*

Was covered with scarlet amber
Which gave off brightness and light
So great that no one knew its worth.

111. The windows were arrayed
With ladies and maidens
So richly apparelled
That never were maidens
So festively attired,
And to complement them
Many gallants, finely turned out,
Were not wanting in this place.

112. Trumpeters and fiddlers sounded forth
So loudly that everything echoed harmoniously.
Someone sang, others danced,
While others discussed their affairs;
Each one did the best he could.
Because of Delusion I was in such straits
That it seemed to me that if I were there
I should have a fine adventure.

113. So I turned to the porter
Who was named Illusion,
And said to him, "My very good friend,
This palace so grand and fine

112.3 Ungs chantoient *EFGNPQS/X* (+1) | et autres *EFGNPS/X*
112.4 En plusieurs lieulx se desduysoient *M*
112.5 qui *BEV/M*, quel [*sic*] *X* | peult *ABEFGPVW/MX*, puet *N*, peust *QS*; pouoit *Y* (+1)
112.6 Pour abus *S* | fust *L*, fut *V* | en che d. *R*. Abus en ce lieu me tiroit *M*
112.7 Qui me *RV/M* | sembla *V*, semble *M* | si *E*, que *S*; si estre pouoye *M* (+1)
112.8 y auroye *ENPQS/MX*

113.1 Ci *E*
113.3 tersdoulx [*sic*] *Y* | amy *ABEFGLNPQVW/MX*
113.4 De p. *EFG/MX*, Du p. *QS*, Se p. *N*. *This line appears in eighth position in R, with a sort of check-mark symbol in the left margin and to the left of line 3.*

Qu'i n'a point de comparison,*
Veulliez moy nommer la maison. »
Sy me respondit a motz cours
Que c'estoit le palaix d'Amours.

Comment l'Acteur s'est fourvoyé et est venu davant le palaix d'Amours ou Desir vouloit qu'il entrast mais Souvenir [38] l'en a destourné et de ses adventures.

MINIATURE 9. The Palace of Love: the Author, Illusion,
Desire, Remembrance

114.   *L* ors me retiray sur culiere,
      Car d'Amours je suys rebouté ;
      Mais Desir vint a la barriere,
Qui me faisoit perdre maniere,
Et m'a d'aler avant tempté.
Souvenir sy m'a deschanté
Qui m'escria que je faisoye
Et se parjurer me vouloye.

115.   Et me bouta devant mes yeulx
Le Miroir des choses passees,
Ou je viz Ëage le vieulx
Qui me poursuyvoit en tous lieux
Par la foy que luy otz juree ;

113.5 Quil *LNQSV/Z*
113.6 nommer *ABEFGLNPQRSTW/MXYZ*] no*m*mez *C*, nomme [*sic*] *V*
113.7 Et me *L* | respondy *Y*
113.8 sestoit *Q*

Rubric. Comme *S* | est f. *EL*, cest f. *BFNP/X* | et venu *E* | denant *X* | ou desie [*?*]
     Y | mais souuent [*sic*] *E* | len destourna *BEFGNPQSW/MX*, len destou*r*ne *T* |
     et . . . adventures *om. R. Rubric follows miniature in AFGQR/X; follows instructions*
     in LTW/Z. No rubric, V.
Equivalent miniature in *ABEFGQRS/XY.*

That none compares to it,
Would you tell me the name of this house?"
And tersely he replied to me
That it was the palace of Love.

How the Author strayed from the path and arrived at the Palace of Love, where Desire wanted him to enter but Remembrance turned him away, and of his adventures.

114.   *T*hen I drew back on my haunches
         Because I had been barred from Love,
         But Desire came to the barrier,
Who made me cast aside my purpose
And tempted me to go forward.
Remembrance broke the spell for me,
Crying out at what I was doing,
And whether I wanted to forswear myself.

115.   And he thrust before my eyes
         The Mirror of Things Past
         Wherein I saw Old Age
         Who was pursuing me everywhere
         Because of the pledge which I had sworn to him,

114.1 L. je me tiray *BV* | me retire *EFGPQ/X*, me retray [*sic*] *S* (*-1*) | costiere *E*, culliers *R*, cuilliere *V*. Lors retiray vng peu arriere *M*
114.2 je fuz *EFGNPQS/X*, je fus *MZ*
114.5 Et moy daller *MX* | moult fort t. *EFGQS/MX* | tempter [?] *V*, temple [*sic*] *M*
114.7 feroye *M*
114.8 Et ce *B*, Et si *FGSV/M*

115.2 m. de choses *Y*
115.4 poursuioit (*or* -siuoit) *W*
115.5 ay juree *V/M*, que ie luy eu iuree *X* (+*1*)

Et si viz toute figuree   [39]
Ma barbe painte de meslure :
Ce m'esbahit a desmesure.

116.   Desir si me print par la bride
        Et me voult en Amours remettre,
        Mais Souvenir si me dist : « Ride !
        Fuy ce lieu, viellard plain de ridde.
        Cy te fault ung autre commettre.
        Jamais n'estudie tel lettre :
        Au cul et con fault renoncer,*
        Car plus ne vaulx pour ce mestier. »*

117.   Quant j'eux bien pensé a mon cas,
        Combien que me temptast Desir,
        Pour le mieulx je ne le creux pas
        Mais luy dis : « Tu m'excuseras,
        Et me feras ung grant plaisir,
        Se l'on me vouloit poursuÿr
        Pour estre d'Amours retenu,
        Sy dis que tu ne m'as pas veu. »

118.   Et combien que Desir mist paine
        De me rebouter en la nasse,
        Souvenir que je biaucop ayme

115.6   viz moult toute C, *with an expunctuating dot under each letter of* moult; toutes f. M
115.7   painte *om.* R (-2) | de mesure E. Ma barbe et toute meslure M (-1).
115.8   Qui m. R/M, Et m. X | oultre mesure S

116.1   si *om.* Q (-1)
116.2   Et *om.* M (-1) | me volut R (+1), me veult VW, me voulut X (+1) | amour B
116.3   Mon souuenir S | dit BEFGNPV | rides M, ridez [= rides] X
116.4   Fuyz [sic] FG | ridde *overwritten from* ride, C; rides M, ridez [= rides] X
116.5   Il te EFGQS/MX, Il t'y B | une autre couuerte EQS/X, ung autre couuerte [sic] FG
116.6   nestudiez FG (-1), nestudies R | telle BQSV (+1)
116.7   A cul EFGNPQS/X, Ou c. L; Au *om.* M | Au .j. [?] et con T, Aux culz et cons V
        | a con X; et *om.* EFGNPQS (-1) | te f. M, X (+1) | prononcier [sic]
        EFGLNPQS; Ou amours [sic] fault aduantaigier B
116.8   le mestier EFGNPQS/MX

And also I saw fully displayed
My motley-colored beard:
That troubled me immeasurably.

116.   Desire took me by the bridle
And wished to commit me again to Love,
But Remembrance said to me, "Be off!
Flee this place, old fellow, full of wrinkles.
You need to plow another furrow.
Never study such learning:
You must renounce sex of any kind
Since you're not up to that any more."

117.   When I had fully considered my situation,
However much Desire might have tempted me,
Fortunately I did not believe him,
But told him, "You will pardon me
And give me great pleasure,
Should anyone come seeking me
As having been detained by Love,
By saying that you have not seen me."

118.   And although Desire strove
To push me back into the trap,*
Remembrance, whom I dearly love,

117.1   bien *om.* Q (*-1*) | pencer [*sic*] L | en mon BS
117.2   tempta [*sic*] FGS
117.4   mescuras V (*-1*)
117.5   me seras R
117.6   Si ENPQS/MX | poursuyuir ENPQRSTVW/MZ, poursuiuir X, pousuiuir [*sic*] FG
117.7   damour X
117.8   Se L | ma [*sic*] NW/M | point vu QS

118.1   mest p. [*sic*] E, meust pasme [*sic*] X
118.2   De moy V | masse FGNPS/X
118.3   que ei [*sic*] Y; que moult fort ie ayme [*sic*] FG (*-1*). Damours souuenir a grand peine
M

Me remist en voye plus saine*
En m'eslongant de celle place.
Abus je laissay et sa trace
Et prins la sente Bon Advis
Qui tost m'a a mon chemin mis.

119.   Si dis : « A Dieu, Amours » et celle
A qui mon service donnay.
Qui vouldra que je la decelle ?
Des belles du monde, c'est celle :   [40]
Tant de vertus ailleurs veu n'ay ;
Elle valoit et je l'amay.
Dieu scet a quel fin je tendoie :*
A lui celer ne le pouroie.

120.   En ce point je tournay le dos
A Amours et a sa sequelle,
Rentrant en mon premier propos
Pour ce qu'en tout tenir je volz
Ma foy et sauver ma querelle ;
Et fut mon adventure telle
Que en Viellesse je me trouvay
Trop plus tost que je ne cuyday.

121.   Le chemin y estoit tramblant
Et plain de parfondes crolieres ;

118.4 Me reuient *M*, Me reuint *X*
118.5 Et *G/X* | en celle pl. *M*
118.6 laisse *EFGR/X* (*-1*), lassays *V* | en sa *FG*
118.7 la sente de *L* (*+1*), la senteur de *S* (*+1*)
118.8 en mon *BFGLNPQRS/MX*; en bon ch. meut mis *E* | remys *Q* (*+1*)

119.1 Ci *E* | amours est celle [*sic*] *Q*, amour est telle [*sic*] *S*
119.3 Quil *B*
119.4 Des belle [*sic*] *V* | c' *om. RS* (*-1*), *M* | est elle *S*, est la belle *M*
119.5 vertu *FGR*
119.6 Elle le v. *A* (*+1*) | vailloit *BLV. Line om., M.*

Put me back on the safer route
By distancing me from this place.
I forsook Delusion and its way
And took the Path of Good Counsel
Which quickly put me on my road.

119.   So I said, "Farewell, Love," to her
        To whom I had given my service.
        Who would wish me to betray her?
        Of the beauties of the world, she is the one:
        Nowhere else have I seen such virtues;
        She was worthy and I loved her.
        God knows to what end I was heading:
        From Him I could not conceal it.

120.   At this juncture I turned my back
        On Love and her adherents,
        Returning to my first intent
        Because in all things I wanted to keep
        My word and maintain my cause.
        And my adventure was such
        That I found myself in Old Age
        Much sooner than I thought to.

121.   The road was shaking there
        And full of deep muddy holes;

119.7   quelle fin t. *ENPQS/MX*, quelle fin ie t. *FG* (+*1*)
119.8   A *om. M* (-*1*) | A le c. *EFGNPQS/X* | point ne *M, X* (+*1*) | le *om. M*

120.1   je tourne *F*
120.2   a s sequelle [*sic, for spacing*] *Q*
120.3   a mon *BEFGNPQSV/MX*
120.4   que tout *B* | je] luy *M*, le *X*
120.5   et tenir ma sequelle *M*, et sonner ma sequelle *X*
120.6   La fut *S*
120.7   Quem [*sic*] *S*

121.2   carrieres *E*, cuelliers *X*, ruelles [?] *M*

L'air fut bruïneux et fumant,*
Rendant flair infet et puant.
La ne croist fruit que de Miseres ;
La terre n'y prouffite gueres :
Les rentes pour toutes valeurs
Ne se payent que de langueurs.

122.   Les abres y sont tous steriles*
Et ne portent ne fleur ne fruit ;
Les feulles sont seches et villes,*
Les arbes y sont inutilles*
En ce que medicine instruit.
Brief, c'est ung paÿs sy destruit
Qu'il n'est vivres qu'on y cognoisse
Fors seulement poires d'angoisse.

123.   La sont fontaines d'Amertume
Et ruisseaux courans de Souffertes.   [41]
La ne rent point clarté la lune,
Le soleil n'y luist ou alume.*
La sont les tenebres appertes ;
Regrez de biens et cris de pertes
Sont les piteux plains et les chants
Qu'on y oit par bois et par champs.

121.3 Leau *X*, Leaue *M* (+*1*) | brugneux *S* (-*1*), brunyeux *Y* (-*1*); bruyneuse *M* | et suyuant *MX*
121.4 lair *V/M*, flay [*sic*] *L*
121.5 La ny *QRS* | croit *BLRVW/Y* | misers [*sic*] *W* (-*1*), misere *MX*
121.6 ne *FG/MX* | prouffites [*sic*] *W* | gaire *X*
121.7 par *EFG/MX* | valleur *M*
121.8 langueur *M*

122.1 sont tous st. *M/Z*] tous *om. CABEFGLNPQRSTVW/XY* (-*1*)
122.2 fleurs *S/MX*; p. fueille ne fr. *L* | fruis *S*, fruictz *V*
122.3 seches *FGPRSTW/YZ* (seiches *ABELNQV/MX*)] saches *C*
122.4 abres *V*, arbres *MX* | qui sont [*sic*] *L*
122.6 cy destruit *L*, sy *om. V* (-*1*)

The air was a cold and reeking mist
Yielding a noxious and stinking scent.
Only Misery's fruit grows there;
The land shows hardly any profit:
The rent for all its worth
Pays off only in despondency.

122.   The trees there are all sterile
And bear neither flower nor fruit.
Leaves are withered and worthless,
The grasses there are useless
In what healing art teaches.
In brief, it is such a decayed land
That there is no known food there,
Except for pears of anguish.*

123.   Fountains of Bitterness are there
And running streams of Suffering.
The moon's brightness never breaks through
Nor does the sun shine or show its light.
Shadows are manifest;
Regrets for possessions and cries of loss
Are the piteous plaints and strains
Heard there through wood and plain.

122.7   Qui *V* | viure *LV/MX*
122.8   angoisses *VW*

123.1   fonteniz *AR*, fontems [*sic*] *Y* | amertume *AFLRT/YZ*] amertumes *CENPQSV/MX*, amertunes [*sic*] *B*, amertune *W*
123.2   souffretes *FGQS/MX*
123.3   point de clarté *R* (+*1*) | cl. a lune [*sic*] *Y*
123.4   Ne soleil *L* | ne luyst *M* | ne alume *BELNPQS/MXZ* (-*1*?), ne lallume *V*; ny a. *FG*
123.5   coppertes *L*
123.6   Regretez *X* (+*1*) | et cry *G*, et cas *X*; et dures p. *M*
123.7   et *om. X* (-*1*) | leurs *V*; les *om. R* | champs *V/X*, chantes [*sic*] *W*, chanchonnettez *R* (+*1*)
123.8   Quon y ot *L*

124.   Viellesse est traveillant demaine :
        Plus y siet on, mains on repose.
        En Viellesse n'a heure saine :
        Maladië a la son regne,*
        Santé en est du tout forclose.
        L'iesse la ne vient ne n'ose
        Pour la dure Merencolie
        Qui regne sur celle partie.

125.   Pres de la en voye petite
        Siet une ysle d'Enfermeté
        Que l'on dit le lieu Decrepite :
        C'est une demeure maudite
        Plaine de grant adversité.
        Je n'y ay pas encore esté
        Mais bien si pres que de sentir
        L'air du lieu, qui me fist fremir.

126.   On ne va pas en Decrepite
        Faire seulement demourance,
        Car elle vient et si habite
        Ens ou corps jousques que on est quicte*
        De l'ame qui vit en souffrance.
        Viellesse revient en enfance
        Par la douleur de ce martire
        Qu'on ne peult nombrer ne descripre.

124.1 et trauaillante peine *V*

124.4 La a maladie *T*, M. la a *AFGLW/Y*, M. la en *ENPQS/MX*

124.5 S. y est *B* | forselose [*sic*] *G* (+*1*)

124.6 L. na [*sic*] ne *G* | ne ose *B/MX*

124.7 Par la *QV/MX*

124.8 sus *YZ*. *Line om., M.*

125.1 vne voye *V* (+*1*)

125.2 Sur une *L*, Si est une *M* (+*1*) | ung ysle [*sic*] *Q*

125.3 Quon *Q*, S (-*1*), Que len *MX* | dist *RTW* | le *om. L* (-*1*) | de decrepite *Q*, *R* (+*1*), de crepite [*sic*] *NW*

125.5 grande *W*

125.6 nay *M*; ny suis pas . . . este [*sic*] *V* | encores *ELNPQSVW/X* (+*1*), *M*

124. Old Age is a demanding domain:
      The more one stays in it, the less one rests.
      In Old Age there is not one well hour:
      Malady has dominion there
      And Health is completely excluded.
      Happiness comes not there nor dares
      Because of harsh Melancholy
      Who rules over this region.

125. Nearby along a small path
      Lies an Isle of Infirmity
      Called Decrepitude's purlieu:
      It is an accursed dwelling place
      Full of great adversity.
      I have not been there yet,
      But close enough to smell
      The place's atmosphere, which made me tremble.

126. One does not go into Decrepitude
      Only to make a short stay,
      For it comes and makes its home there
      In the body until one is freed of
      The soul which lives in suffering.
      Old Age returns to childishness
      From the pain of this martyrdom
      Which none can reckon or describe.

125.7 bien *om.* A (-*1*) | cy L, sius [suis?] Q; si *om.* M | si apres X (+*1*) | que le s. L,
       q*ue* iay sentir [*sic*] FG, que descentir [*sic*] E; pres me voy de s. M
125.8 qui *om.* L; sy *inserted above line, later hand.* | ma fait FG, me fait BV/M | *ser*uir
       M

126.1 vas [*sic*] W
126.2 Seulement faire T
126.3 Car selle L
126.4 Ens ou corps ATW/YZ (Ens au c. BV)] Ou c. C (-*1*), Ez c. R, Dans le c. FGS, Dens
       le c. EPQ, Deans [?] le c. L, Dedens le c. N (+*1*), Dont le c. MX | jusques on
       ABFGLTW/YZ, j. lon ENPSV, j. len Q, j. en MX | on en est R | soit q. Q
126.5 De la qui [*sic*] M (-*1*)
126.6 V. vient A (-*1*)
126.7 doulceur X | martir [*sic*] W
126.8 nommer M | ne escripre FG/MX (-*1*)

127.   J'entens bien que moult fait a craindre   [42]
        De Decrepite la demeure,
        Mais qui peult a ce bien actaindre*
        Le grant Purgatoire en est maindre,
        Se Pacïence la demeure ;
        Sy prie a Dieu, ains que je meure,
        Que la je face penitance
        Qui me soit a l'asme alegeance.

128.   Quant je me viz en celle nasse
        De Viellesse la ou je estoye,
        Je ne choisis lieu, trou ne place
        Pour m'eslongier de celle place
        Se en Decrepite je n'entroye.*
        En ce point je m'entretenoye
        Du mains mal que me fut possible*
        En Viellesse terre terrible.

129.   La cougneuz des gens une mer
        Faire diverses mommeries :
        L'un voult ses ans dissimuler
        Par soy de mixtions laver
        Et rere ses barbes flouries.
        Autres faisoient tromperies

127.1 Jenteng *R*, Ientend *S* | biens *V* | que mon [*sic*] f. *G* | que m. est *P/MX*, qui m. est a *E*, quil est m. *NQS*

127.2 De *om. X* (*-1*)

127.3 qui *AEGLNQRSTVW/XYZ*] quant *C*, quil *BFP/M* | bien *om. M* (*-1*) | attendre *L*, entendre *T*

127.4 p. ce est *M* | mendre *T*

127.6 Je prie *EFGNPQS/MX*, Je pry *R*; Si pry *L*

127.8 a lame elegance [*sic*] *X*

128.1 masse *FGNPQS/X*

128.2 la *om. M* (*-2*)

Between our lines 2 and 3, L has Laquelle pas je ne queroie, *lined through.*

128.3 chois [*sic*] *L* (*-1*), choisy *BQRS/X* | lieu *om. Q/MX* (*-1*)

128.4 de celle trace *M*

127. I know well that there is much to fear
From a sojourn in Decrepitude
Yet, for the person who can come through that,
Great Purgatory is less,
If Patience abides there.
So I pray to God that before I die
I may make penance there
Which might be solace for my soul.

128. When I saw myself in that trap
Of Old Age where I was,
I saw no place, way out, or situation
To distance myself from this difficulty,
Without entering into Decrepitude.
At this point I endured
With as little affliction as possible for me
In the terrible land of Old Age.

129. I recognized there a sea of people
Parading in various deceitful ways:
One wished to conceal his years
By bathing himself with compounds
And shaving his flourishing beard.
Others practiced deceits

128.5 San *RW*, Sean [*sic*] *E* | decupite [*sic*] *X* | je n'entroye *ABEFGLNPQRSTVW/MXYZ*] je *om. C (-1)*.
128.6 *Line om.*, *L;* la quelle part [?] je me queroye *added in right margin*.
128.7 Au mains *L*, De moins *X* | qui me *ABEFGQRSTW/MXY*, quil me *LNPV* | fust *A*
128.8 En vieille t. *Q (-1)* | me mys *in left margin*, terre *lined through*, *L;* tres ter. *M (-1)*

129.1 congneu *A* | de gens *TW*
129.2 nommeries [*sic*] *G*
129.3 veult *LVW/MX*
129.4 Pour soy *S* | mytterons *Q*, mixtion *V*
129.5 reres [*sic*] *W*
129.6 Les autres *FG (+1)* | f. par tr. *ENPQS/MX (+1)*

Par taindre cheveulx et parucque
Pour prendre connins a l'embucque.

130.   Mais Viellesse ne peult mentir
Ne mesconter en son pouoir.
Nature ne peult raverdir ;
Tel mehain ne se peult garir.
La ne vault charme ne sçavoir
Et n'est riens au monde plus voir
Que l'issue de telz misteres
Est de remplir les cymetieres.*   [43]

131.   Or nous tairons de ce propoz :*
C'est langaige merencolicque.
Je ne trouvay sentiers ne tros
A m'en yssir, car je ne pos.
La me faillit ma retoricque.
Je luz en la leçon anticque :
Viellesse m'aprint a souffrir
Douleur qui ne pouroit garir.

132.   Sy fiz comme l'oisel qui chante
Enclos en sa petite cage :
Combien que le cueur se lamente
Pour la prison qui le tourmente,
Dont il quiert yssue et passage,
Toutesfois il se rassouage

129.7   Pour *L* | Teindre leurs ch. *QS/MX* | perrucques *QS/MX*
129.8   connilz *QS* | alembuche *G*, a lembusche *QS/X*. Par Aage blanchies et caducques *M* (+*2?*)

130.1   Mais de v. *R* (+*1*)
130.2   mescouter *B/X* | a son *EFGQS/MXY*
130.4   Tel mesain ne ce p. *L* | se *om. SW* (-*1*)
130.6   Et si nest *M* | rien *RS/M* | du monde *BV*, ou m. *EFLT/Y* | plus *om. X* (-*1*); plus lait a veoir *M*
130.7   Pour lissue *FG* | lissues [*sic*] *W*
130.8   Est de *BL/Z*] Et de *CARTVW/Y*, Que de *FG*; A remplir tous les c. *ENPQS/MX* | de remply [*sic*] *L*

By dyeing tresses and wigs
To snare rabbits in ambush.*

130.   But Old Age cannot lie
        Nor err in his power.
        Nature cannot make young again,
        Such loss of strength cannot cure itself.
        No magic spell or knowledge avails there;
        And there is nothing truer in the world
        Than that the end result of these mysteries
        Is to fill cemeteries.

131.   Now we will leave off this conversation—
        It is melancholy talk.
        I found no opening or path
        For my exit, for I could not.
        My eloquence failed me there.
        I read in the age-old lesson:
        Old Age taught me to bear
        Suffering which could not be cured.

132.   So I did as does the bird who sings
        Shut up in his little cage:
        Although his heart grieves
        Because of the prison which torments him,
        From which he seeks a way out,
        Nevertheless he comforts himself anew

131.1 Nous noz t. *V* | tairons *ABFGLNPTVW/XYZ*, tayrons *R*] taison [*sic*] *C*, taisons
        EQS, trairons [*sic*] *M*
131.3 treuuays *V*, trouue *N/X*, treuue *M* | sentier *QRSVW*
131.4 A mon yssir *L/MX*
131.6 Je litz *B*, Je leuz *MX*, Et lutz *V* | atenticque [*sic*] *W* (+*1*)
131.7 maprent *V*, ma prins *X*
131.8 qui ne me peult g. *V*

132.1 Ci fois [*sic*] *E*, Si faitz *M*, Si faiz *X* | loiseau *V*
132.3 se *ABFGLNPQRSTVW/MXYZ*] ce *CE*
132.5 Dont y quiert *FG* | et *om.* *X*.
132.6 il sa r. [*sic*] *X* | ressonaige *Q*, ressolaige *M*

Et chante par le souvenir
Qu'il a de son passé plaisir.

133. Ainsi je me resjouÿsoie
En la Viellesse ou je me vy
Et en mes faiz passés pensoye :
L'un me fist deul et l'autre joye ;
Le temps ne fut pas tout uny.
A corps recreu et cueur failly*
Je visitay celle contree
Ou j'ay grant mervaille trouvee.*

134. Car en celle place sterille
Je trouvay ung quartier de terre,
Le plus riche, le plus fertille,
Le meilleur et le plus utille
Qui soit de cy en Engleterre.
Plus plaisant lieu nul ne sceult querre :*   [44]
La ot ung manoir en cloture
Qu'on appelloit Bonne Adventure.

135. Et peult a pluseurs gens sembler
Qu'en Viellesse n'a point de joye ;
Sy a, et je le veul monstrer,
Mais il fault a l'estude entrer

132.7 pour le *FG*
132.8 passer pl. *EFGNSV/X*

133.1 Aussi *AEGLNQSW/M*, Aussy *FP/XZ*
133.2 la *om. L* (*-1*), ma v. *EFGNPQSW/MX* | ont ie *FG* | me vey *GP*, me viz *Q*, me veiz *V* (: vny, failly), me voy *M*
133.3 en *om. V* (je pensoye)
133.5 vnyz *Q*
133.6 recran [*sic*] *ATW/Y*, recrans *B*, recrant *R*, recreans *V* (+*1?*), recrain *FGL* | failliz *Q*
133.7 Je visite *MX*
133.8 trouuay [*sic*] *W*

And sings by the memory
He has of bygone pleasures.

133.   Thus I cheered myself
       In Old Age where I saw myself
       And thought of my past deeds:
       Some brought sorrow, others joy;
       Their course was not always the same.
       With broken body and faint heart,
       I visited that country
       Wherein I found great wonders.

134.   For in this barren place
       I found a portion of earth,
       The richest and most fertile,
       The best and most useful
       That exists from here to England.
       No one could seek a more pleasing place.
       An enclosed manor was there
       Which was called Good Fortune.

135.   It can seem to many
       That there's no joy in Old Age,
       Yet there is, and I wish to prove it,
       But one must enter into study

134.1 telle place *MX*
134.2 Jay trouue *EFGNPS/X*, Jay trouuay [*sic*] *Q*
134.3 riche. et plus f. *B* (*-1*), riche et le *AQRV/M*
134.4 et le plus *ABEFLNPQRSTVW/MXYZ*] le *om. C* (*-1*)
134.5 d'icy *B*, dicy *EFGLQSVW/M*, de si *X*
134.6 nulz *BRTW/Y* | sceu *V* | nul neust sceu qu. *EFGNPQS/MX*
134.7 La eust *FGQS*, eult *V* | manoir et cl. *BV*
134.8 Quon appelle *L*

135.1 peust *S*
135.3 et *om. X* (*-1*), *M* (bien monstrer) | et si le *B*
135.4 en lestude *S/MX*

Et apprendre par toute voye,
Comme se morir ne devoye,
Et telle vie maintenir
Que l'on veult selon Dieu morir.

136.   Telle est la leçon de sagesse,
Tel est l'effet des vertueulx ;
Ce sont les moyens que Viellesse
Demande pour avoir l'iesse ;
Ce sert aux jeunes et aux vieulx.
Riens n'est tant merencolieux
Que fais de pechés et de blasme
A cil qui approuche la lame.

137.   Les murs de ce manoir petit,
Dont moult m'aggrëoit l'apparence,
Furent massonnez par Delitt
Et, qui moult ce lieu embellit,
Le portail fut plain de Plaisance.
Les fossez pour plus d'asseurance
Furent taillez parfondement
De la main de Bon Pensement.

138.   Le comble fut d'Estudïer,
Les fenestrages d'Enquerir ;
La porte fut d'Ensonnïer
Et le pont fut de Labourer.*   [45]

135.6   Comme si Q | te devoye V
135.8   Ou lon V, Que len MX

136.1   Tel est E
136.2   le fait EQS, loeuure V
136.3   Se B | moyens de v. FGLQV
136.4   Demandez F, Demandes G, Demander V
136.5   Ce BELNPQSTV/MXYZ (Che R)] Se CAFGW | fert [sic] S | jouenes W | es v. FG
136.6   Rien ST | tant aux m. X (+1)
136.7-8   inverted BV
136.7   pechie LVW, peche S/MX | blasmes N
136.8   cil quil V/X

And learn in every way
As if one were never to die,*
And live such a life
As to die in God's grace.

136.   Such is the lesson of wisdom,
        Such the success of the virtuous;
        These are the ways that Old Age
        Requires in order to have happiness.
        This works for young and old.
        There is nothing so melancholy
        As burdens of sins and blame
        For him who is approaching his grave.

137.   The walls of this small manor,
        Whose appearance pleased me greatly,
        Were laid up by Delight
        And, adding much to its beauty,
        The portal was full of Enjoyment.
        For greater safety the moat
        Was deeply carved
        By the hand of Good Thinking.

138.   The roof was of Contemplation,
        The windows of Inquiry,
        The door was of Instruction
        And the bridge of Effort.

137.1 Les meurs S
137.2 magrea B, magreoiet [sic] X, maulgreoit [sic] V
137.3 massonnees S (+1), machonne [sic] RV | par grant d. Q (+1)
137.4 Et que L | qui ce lieu moult BV (se B) | embellist S. Line om., R.
137.6 foissez Y | d' om. L
137.7 tailiet [sic] W | par fondements V

138.2 Le fenestraige L/M, Et les fenestres EFGQS/X | dacquerir M
138.3-4 inverted M
138.3 fut om. E | dessonnyer B, densoinner X | de remedier E, de souuenir M
138.4 fut om. BLV (-1) | labourier BV

Au dessus, pour mieulx resplandir,
Ot banieres de Grant Plaisir
Qui firent a chascun entendre
Que ce lieu fut fait pour apprendre.

139.   Oyseuse sy en fut banye,
Labeur se nommoit le portier ;
La ne peult entrer vilonnie*
Mais on y veult bien jalousie
Pour mieulx le temps y emploier.
Le passe temps, pour abreger,*
De ce lieu, se le vieulx sçavoir,
N'est que d'apprendre et de sçavoir.

140.   Se j'eux desir de la entrer
Et de cognoistre la demeure,
Il ne le fault pas demander.
Je laissay cheval pasturer
Et vins au portier sans demeure,
Disant : « Amis, en la bonne heure,
Donne moy cëans une entree
Pour cougnoistre ceste contree. »

141.   Le portier me fut ung peu rude
Et me dit : « Ayes pacïence !*

138.5 Ou d. *LR*

138.6 Eust *FGS* | grant plaisirs [*sic*] *W*. Et grans banieres de pl. *B/M*, Ot grans b. de pl. *LR*, Eult grand [*sic*] banieres de pl. *V*

138.7 furent [*sic*] *W*, faisoient *M* (+*1*)

138.8 Que *om. R* (-*1*) | fust *L*

In FG, stanza 138 is followed by stanza 145.

In FG, stanzas 139–144 follow stanza 150.

139.2 Labour *S* | si se *M* (*om.* le)

139.3 peult *BEFGLPRVW/M* (peut *AQS/X*, puet *N*)] poult *C/YZ*, pot *T*

139.4 voult *B*

139.5 y *om. M* (-*1*)

139.6 La passe *QS*

Over all, in order to be most resplendent,
Were banners of Great Pleasure
Which gave everyone to understand
That this place was made for learning.

139. Idleness is banished therein,
Diligence is the doorkeeper's name.
Baseness cannot enter,
But an ardent desire is wanted there
To better employ one's time.
To be brief, the time spent
In this place, should you wish to know,
Is only for learning and knowledge.

140. Whether I longed to enter there
And know that dwelling,
One need not ask.
I left my horse to graze
And came to the doorkeeper without delay,
Saying, "Friend, quickly
Give me entry inside there
So I may know this place."

141. The doorkeeper was a bit rude to me
And said, "Be patient—

139.7 si le veult *V*
139.8 de *om. Q (-1). Line om., M.*

140.1 Ci *E*, Si *FGNPQ/M* | j' *om. M.*
140.2 le demeure [*sic*] *M*
140.4 Je laisse *FG* | pasture *V*
140.5 Et vint [*sic*] *S*
140.6 amy *BELNPQS/MX* | a la *B/M*
140.7 Donnez *BV/MYZ* | une *om. M (-1)*
140.8 celle contree *X*

141.1 Se p. *A* | si fut *M*
141.2 dist *AENQRSTW/MX* | ayez *BLNPQRVW/MXYZ*

Ce n'est pas cy une begude,
C'est le lieu qui s'appelle Estude,
Le droit ennemy d'Ignorance.
Cy est le tresor de scïence,
C'est la richesse de la terre ;
Autre avoir ne debvroit on querre.

142. Ce lieu cy garde une princesse,
La plus belle qu'on peult vëoir.*   [46]
Dieu la fist par telle noblesse
Que jamais ne perdra jonesse,
Sans amendrir matin ne soir.
Mourir ne peut et n'a point d'hoir ;
Son nom est a chascun notoire
Et l'appelle on Fresche Memoire.

143. C'est tout le plaisir, le soulas,
Qu'en Viellesse trouver se peult :
D'ellë on ne peult estre las ;
Qui ne la quiert il en dit : 'Las !'
Et n'est merveille s'il s'en deult.
Tel la vouldroit qu'elle ne veult.
Memoire c'est par adventure
L'un des grans secrez de Nature.

141.3 pas vng lieu de b. *V* | vne legende [*sic!*] *X*
141.5 ennemys *V*
141.6 Si est *MX*
141.8 ne doit on *EQS/X* (*-1*), debueroit *R* (*+1?*), deueroit *W* (*+1?*)

142.1 Celluy garde [*sic*] *X* (*-1*) | lieu cy *BGTV*] si *CAFRW/YZ*, si *om. ELNPQS/M* (*-1*)
142.2 con puist *R*
142.3 Dieu le f. *X*
142.5 Sens ny auoir [*sic*] *E* | amanoir *FGNPQS*, amenoir *X* | ne main ne soir *L/M*
142.6 Mouuoir *M* | ne na *A*, ne a *M* (*-1?*) | de hoir *Q*, de choir [*sic*] *X* (*+1*); d' *om. M*
142.7 Son mon [*sic*] *Y*
142.8 Et appelle on *A/M*, Et lappellon [*sic*] *NP/X*, Et lappelle len *S* (*+1*), Et sappelle *Q* |
franche m. *M*

This is not a country inn here!*
This is the place called Study,
The true enemy of Ignorance.
The treasury of learning is here,
It is the great wealth of the world;
One ought not seek other riches.

142. A princess keeps watch over this place,
The most beautiful that one can see.
God made her in such a noble way
That she will never lose her youthfulness,
Diminishing neither night nor day.
She cannot die and has no heir;
Her name is well known to all
And she is called Fresh Memory.

143. That is all the pleasure, the solace
That can be found in Old Age:
One never tires of her;
Who does not seek her says 'alas!'
And it is no wonder if one should sorrow,
Should he want her and be not wanted.
Memory, perchance, is
One of Nature's great mysteries.

143.1 tout *om. M* (*-1*) | et soulas *L/M*
143.2 ce p. *FG*, ne se peut [*sic*] *S* (*+1*)
143.3 ne pourroit *M* | laz *FG*
143.4 Qu'il *B* | lacquiert [*sic*] *W* | il *om. EQS*; on *X* | ne dit *R*, en du [*sic*] *S*, en dis [*sic*] *W* | helas *EQS/X*, *MY* (*+1*)
143.5 merueilles *L* | se lon se deult *L* (*+1*), si sen d. *EFG/X* | deust *FG. Lines 5 and 6 are collapsed into one, M: Et merueille se on la veult* (*-1?*)
143.6 Tel la veult *E* (*-1*)
143.7 c' *om. EFGQSV/MX* (*-1*); *R omits* c' *and adds an oblique stroke, perhaps to indicate the pronunciation of the final* e *of* Memoire
143.8 des grans secret *L*, des grant secret *V*; Lung des secrets de creature *M*

144.   Et n'est Socrates ne Platon
        Qui ne faillist bien a prouver
        Dont vient de Memoire le don,
        Par naturelle portion,
        En corps corrupt et plain d'amer.
        Je croy, et la veul demourer,
        Que tel bien a la crëature
        Vient de Dieu et non de Nature.

145.   Vray est que Nature le coffre
        Donnë ou Memoire se treuve
        Par l'ame qui vie luy offre
        Par portion, et së encoffre,*
        Par quoy Memoire naist et oeuvre.
        C'est dont l'ame qui la recoeuvre,*
        Que Dieu fist ou Nature cesse.
        Donques Dieu a fait ma maistresse.

146.   Puis que dont ma maistresse est faite   [47]
        De Dieu, le Maistre des ouvrages,
        Sy digne chose et si parfaite
        Doit estre requise et attraitte
        Et honnouree par les sages,
        Et doit louer en ses langaiges
        L'omme qu'en Viellesse se treuve*
        Quant de Memoire il a recoeuvre.*

Stanza 144 om., L/M; follows 145 in W.
144.1   Et ne s. *FG*
144.2   Quil *FGR* | bien *om. A (-1)* | a prouurer [*sic*] *Q*, approuuer *GW*
144.5   corrupte *V*
144.6   et veult d. *X (-1)*
144.7   tel don *B*
144.8   D. non pas de n. *B*
In FG, stanza 144 is followed by stanza 157.

In FG, stanzas 145–150 follow stanza 138.
145.1   est ce que *M (om. le)* | de nature *V* | nature est le *EFGLNPQS,* n. est c. *X (-1)*
145.2   Donne de dieu ainsi *V,* Donne au *W/MX* | ce tr. *P*
145.3   que vie *B/MX* | acoffre *M*
145.4   et *om. R (-1)* | si *BEFGNPQRSV/X* | l'encoffre *BV* | en coffre [*sic*] *E,* encof re [*sic*] *X*

144. And neither Socrates nor Plato
Succeeded in proving
Whence comes the gift of Memory
By natural allotment
Into an impure body full of anguish.
I believe, and will stand by it,
That such a benefit comes to man
From God and not from Nature.

145. It is true that Nature provides
The coffer wherein Memory is found
Through the soul which gives it life
Proportionately and stores it away,
Whereby Memory is born and works.
It is thus the soul which retrieves
What God has made where Nature leaves off:
Thus has God made my mistress.

146. Since, then, my mistress is made
By God, the Lord of all works,
Such a worthy and perfect thing
Must be diligently sought and wooed
And honored by the wise,
And the man who finds himself in Old Age
Must praise in his discourses
When from Memory he has recourse.

145.5 Pour *MZ* | P. moy *M* | nest et [*sic*] *X* | ouure *S/M*
145.6 Cest doncques lame que requeuure *M*
145.7 Qui dit fy [*sic*] *M*
145.8 Donc *E*, *Q* (*-1*) | a fait dame et m. *E* | ma *om.* *W* (*-1*)

Stanza 146 follows stanza 147, R.
146.1 Puis doncques *B*, Puisque donc *AFGV*, Puis que donques *L* (*+1*), *X*, Puis donc que
Q, Puis dont que *R*; dont *om.* *M* (*-1*) | ma maistre [*sic!*] *X*
146.3 et *om.* *LR/M*
146.4 acquise et traite *M* (*-2*)
146.5 honnourees [*sic*] *W*
146.6 doibt toucher [*sic*] *M* | ses louenges [*sic*] *X*
146.7 L' *om.* *M* | qui en *L* (*+1*) | quen vieille se [*sic*] *X* (*-1*) | le tr. *Y*
146.8 memoir *V* | il a *ABFGLNPSTW/YZ*] il la *CEQRV/M*, il y a *X* (*+1*)

147.   Et quoy qu'elle se tient mussee,
        C'est moy, Labeur, qui la trouva*
        Par l'estude que j'ay amee.
        J'en ay la clef, je l'ay gardee.
        Nul sans vertu ne la verra ;*
        Qui Memoire vëoir vouldra*
        Apprendre fault et retenir
        De ruminer le souvenir.

148.   Mais afin que tu te conforte*
        En la Viellesse ou je te voy
        (Qui est demeure dure et forte),
        Ouvrir je te veul ceste porte.
        Va a ma dame ; je l'octroy. »
        Labeur, qui ot pitié de moy,
        Me mist en ce noble chastel
        Qui valoit ung riche chastel.

149.   Fresche Memoire promptement
        M'a bonté et doulceur monstree,
        Car elle me vint au devant
        Et me receut benignement
        Par bonne façon asseuree.
        Elle se fut ce jour paree
        D'un drap ou figura Penser,
        Grans merveilles a regarder.   [48]

Stanza 147 follows stanza 145, R.
147.1   En quoy A, Et moy [sic] V | mucee A/M, muchee R; muree L
147.2   la trouuay FGNPQS/X, lay trouuee M
147.3   que jay trouue [sic] R, que jay hantee M
147.4   les clefz EFGQ/MX | ie le gardee F
147.5   Nulz V/Y | sens [sic] M | vertuz N
147.6   m. vers vouldra [sic] X (-1)
147.8   Et BEFGLNPQRSV/MX | ruminer ABLRTVW/MZ] renuncier C, rememorer FG
        (+1), runimer [sic] Y; bien garder ENPQS/X

148.1   confortes Q/X
148.2   la om. M (-1?)
148.3   Qui test V | demeuree FG/X (+1)

147. And although she keeps herself concealed,
It is I, Diligence, who found her
Through study which I loved.
I have her key, I have kept it;
No one without merit shall see her:
Whoever wants to see Memory
Must learn and remember
To ruminate upon the recollection.

148. But so that you may be comforted
In Old Age in which I see you
(Which is a harsh and painful period),
I am willing to open this door for you.
Go to my lady, I give you leave."
Diligence, who took pity on me,
Admitted me to that noble house
Which equalled a rich possession.

149. Fresh Memory promptly
Showed me kindness and gentleness,
For she came forward to meet me
And received me graciously,
With confident good manners.
She was dressed that day
In a gown where Meditation was symbolized,
Great wonders to behold.

148.4 je *om. A* (*-1*)
148.5 dame *et* je *Q*
148.6 qui eust *EFGS*, qui a *M*
148.7 Ma mis *M*
148.8 chatel *BQT/Y. Line om., M.*

149.1 Franche m. *M*
149.2 bontee *W*, boute *X*
149.3 me vient *B*
149.6 se *om. V* (*-1*), ce fut *E*, cestoit *FGL*, sestoit *M*, se sut [*?*] *S* | se jour *E*
149.7 De ung *W/X* | ou figure a p. *L*, figure a p. *M* | pensee *W*
149.8 Grant merueilles *L*, Moult merueilleux *M*

150.   Je viz en ce drap qui fut beau,
       Entrelassé d'or et de soye,
       Moult du vieulx temps et du nouveau.
       Et sur son chief ot ung chappeau
       Qui plus me plot plus le vëoye.
       Une odeur ot que je sentoye
       Qui s'appelloit Ramentevoir :
       Le lut, l'oÿr et le sçavoir.*

151.   Je luy priay par courtoisie
       De voir ses livres de valeur ;*
       Mais pourtant si ne le fist mie
       Et me dist que qui estudie
       Lëans, il soit duit et asseur
       D'apprendre sa leçon par cueur,
       Car Memoire n'a aultre livre
       Que tel que Souvenir luy livre.

152.   « Peu prouffite l'estudïer
       A ceulx qui en Viellesse sont ;*
       Mais se doivent ensonnïer,*
       Penser et ramemorïer
       Ce qu'ilz ont veu, et qu'apris ont.

150.1 Je veis au drap qui est bien beau *M*

150.2 et *om.* Q (*-1*)

150.3 Du vieulx testament et nouveau *L/M*

150.4 Et sus *Y* | eust *EFS*, leut [?] *M*

150.5 Que plus *L* | me pleut *ABEQV/X*, plut *FG*, pleust *LNPS*. Qui me plaisoit quant le veoye *M*

150.6 Ung [*sic*] odeur *Q* | ot *om. M* (*-1*); eust *EFS*

150.7 Quel appelloit *M*

150.8 lust *S*, leu *F*, ieu *G*, lire *Q* (*+1*); La leut *AE* | le lit [*sic*] *FG*, loyer *W*. La se tient loyr et scauoir *M*.

In FG, stanza 150 is followed by stanza 139.

In FG, stanzas 151–156 follow stanza 160.

151.1 luy prie *E/X*

151.2 Veoir ses *LV/M* (*om.* De); De veoir *ABEFGNPQRSW/XY* | ces liures *M*

150. I saw in that beautiful robe,
Interlaced with gold and silk,
Much of old times and new.
And on her head she wore a hat
Which pleased me more the more I saw it.
It had a fragrance which I caught
Which was named Recollection:
Reading, listening and knowing.

151. I begged her for kindness' sake
To see her valuable books,
However, she did not allow it,
And told me that whoever studies
Therein must be instructed and sure
To learn his lesson by heart,
For Memory has no other book
Than that which Remembrance confers.

152. "There's little use in studying
For those who are in Old Age,
But they ought to apply themselves
To think about and to remember
What they have seen and learned.

151.3 si *om.* L (*-1*), M (el mye) | feis *V*, fis *W*
151.4 dit *BFGLPV/M*
151.5 y soit *EFGNPQ/MX* | duy *M* | assur *X*
151.6 De scauoir *M*
151.8 lui deliure *Y* (*+1*)

152.1 *Initial looks more like J than P, but not exactly like either, B; unidentifiable initial, A.*
152.2 viellesse *as elsewhere in* C, BLRTW/MZ (vieillesse *AEFGNPQS,* vielesse *V/Y*)]
      veullesse *C*
152.3 se doment [*sic*] *Y* | ensonnier *AFGLNPRSW/XYZ* (enssonnier *B,* ensomnier *V,*
      ensonnyer *T,* ensoignier *Q*)] en souuenir *C,* en enseigner *E,* bien enseigner *M*
152.4 En penser *E* (*+1?*) | rememorer *LV* (*-1*), et se rememorer *M*; remorier *Q* (*-1*)
152.5 *second* qu' *om. ELQS/X*; appres ont *FGL/X.* Ce quilz ont apprins en venant *M*

Ces choses au ceur joye font ;*
Pour ce dis moy qu'il te plaira*
Et Memoire te servira. »

153.   Quant oÿz la dame parler*
Si doulcement et par tel guise,
Je me pris a reconforter,
Disant : « Je vous doy honnourer,
Quant par vous puis avoir aprise
Pour parvenir a mon emprise ;   [49]
Savoir ne veul autre science,
Car ou le grief gist, le cuer pense.

154.   Je cours, je vois et m'achemine*
Contre la forest d'Atropos.
Ce souvenir me point et mine,
Car il me fault, ains que je fine,
Combatre, pour abreger motz,
Contre deulx chevaliers de lotz,*
Dont l'un est Messire Accident,
L'autre Debile le Dolent.

155.   Je demande se par histoires,
Par legendes ou par cronicques,
Par escriptures ou memoires
Ou par souvenirs transitoires,
Par soutivetez ou practiques,

152.6 Les choses *V* | ioyes *FG*
152.7 qui te *RV*

153.1 iouy *A*, joys *BNRSTVW*, joyz *Q*, je oys *L*, iouys *EFG*, jouys *M* iouyz *P*, ioyz *XYZ*
        | paler [*sic*] *G*
Lines 2 and 4 are interchanged, M.
153.2 Dy [*sic*] doulcement *M*
153.3 a reconforte [*sic*] *V*
153.4 doye *W*
153.5 Qnant [*sic*] *X* | pour vous *S* | puis *om. Q (-1)*
153.7 Scauoir je ne *M (+1)*
153.8 *First* le *om. M (-1?)*

154.1 je machemine *ABEFGLNPQRSTVW/MXY*

Those things bring joy to the heart;
Therefore, tell me what will please you
And Memory will serve you."

153.   When I heard the lady speak
So gently and in such a way,
I began to be comforted,
Saying, "I must honor you
Since through you I can be apprised
Of how to succeed at my enterprise.
I wish to know no other science,
For the heart pays heed to where trouble lies.

154.   I hasten, move along, and set out
Toward the forest of Atropos.
Remembrance of this spurs and gnaws at me,
For I must, before I finish,
Fight (to cut short my tale)
Against two vaunted knights,
One being Lord Accident
And the other Debility the Miserable.

155.   I would like to know whether in histories,
In legends or chronicles,
In written accounts or memoirs,
Or in fleeting remembrance,
In wit or experience,

154.2 foirest *E* | d' *om. LR*
154.3 Se s. *EFGL*, Et s. *V* | me print [*sic*] *MX* | et me myne *Q* (+*1*), et meine [?] *M*
154.5 abregiez *FG*
154.6 de losts *M*, de lostz *X*
154.7 Lun deux est *EQS/X*, Dung deux [*sic*] *NP*, Lung est deulx [*sic*] *M*
154.8 Lautre est d. *EQS* | d. et dolent *A* (-*1*), d. le tirant *ENPQS/MX*

155.1 Je demanday *MX*
155.2 legende *EQSV* (-*1?*)
155.3 Ou par escr. *A* (+*1*) | ou par m. *E* (+*1*)
155.4 souvenir *BRVW* | transitoire *V*
155.5 Ou par *S* (+*1*) | substiuetez *B*, subtilitez *FGQ*, subtilite *ES/MX*, subtillesses *V*,
       soubmetz *R* (-*2*)

Est il rien mis es fais anticques
Des deulx chevaliers cy dessus
S'ilz ont jamais esté vaincus,

156.   S'oncques nulz y prist avantaige,
Tant fust il de grant renommee.
J'ay en moy desir et couraige
Que je feray mon parsonnaige
Si bien a icelle meslee
Que j'auray part a la journee
Et que l'onneur m'en demourra
Ou la carougne y demourra. »*

157.   Quant Fresche Memoire entendit
A quel fin tendre je vouloye,
Moult doulcement me respondit :
« J'ay ouÿ ce que tu m'as dit   [50]
Ou volentiers conseil donroye.
De parler je t'abuseroye,
Mais a l'eul je te monstreray*
Ce que j'entens et que j'en sçay. »

155.6 riens *ABEFGLNPQRTVW/XY* | en faiz *EFN*, en fais *S*, en faitz *GPQ/X*, en faictz
M
155.7 De deux *S* | si dessus [*sic*] *X*
155.8 Silz on [*sic*] *Y* | ont este jamais *ABFGSV/M*

156.1 Doncques *E/MX* | nul *ELNPQS/MX* | ny prent *MX* | auantaiges *S*
156.2 fut *ELSVW/M*
156.3 Jay en mon *EQV/X*
156.5 celle *Q* (*-1*)
156.6 jauray *BELNQSTV/MYZ* (iauray *AFGP/YZ*, jaray *RW*, iauuray [*sic*] *X*)] iayre [*sic*]
C | par *G/M* | la la [*sic*] j. *M*

Anything has been set down in ancient accounts
About the two aforesaid knights,
If they have ever been defeated,

156.   If ever anyone has had the advantage over them,
However much he might be of great renown.
I have in me the desire and heart
To conduct myself
So well in this encounter
That I shall win the day:
Either the honor will be mine
Or my carcass will remain there."

157.   When Fresh Memory heard
The result for which I wished to strive,
She answered me most kindly:
"I have heard what you have told me
And would gladly give you counsel.
By speaking I would mislead you,
But I will reveal to your sight
What I understand and know about these things."

156.7   l' *om.* L (*-1*) | demourra *ABFGLNPQSTV/MXYZ*] demoura *CRW*, demourera *E*
        (*+1*)
156.8   demourra *ABFGLNPQRTV/YZ*] demoura *CW/MX*, demourera *E* (*+1*), y pourrira
        S
In FG, stanza 156 is followed by stanza 161.

*In FG, stanzas 157–160, including the miniature and rubric preceding stanza 158, follow
        stanza 144.*
157.2   A quelle fin tendre v. *V*
157.4   tu ma [*sic*] *W*
157.5   donroy *B*, dourroye [*sic*] *X*
157.7   a leueil *X* (*+1*) | monteray [*sic*] *X*
157.8   que je scay *RV/M*

Cy monstre Fresche Memoire a l'Acteur les sepultures
des anciens trespassés et par les escriptures voit ceulx
qui ont esté desconfiz par Debile ou par Accident.
Et cy commence la tierce partie de ce livre.

MINIATURE 10. Fresh Memory
shows the Author her cemetery

158.   ors euvre ung huys et va devant*   [51]
      Et nous mist en une champaigne
      Qui fut a sa maison tenant,
Le plus plain paÿs, le plus grant,
Qui soit de Paris en Espaigne.
La n'avoit roche ne montaigne ;
Chascun y peult choisir a l'eul
De toutes pars et a son veul.

159. Ce plain (qui fut chose infinie)
    Estoit paré de sepultures,
    Chascune faite et entaillie
    Diversement et par mestrie,
    Tant d'images que d'escriptures,
    Pour cognoistre les crëatures
    Qu'Accident avoit desconfiz
    Et par Debille les occis.

Rubric. a l'Acteur *om. R* | des sep. *A* | sepulchres *B/M* | des anciens et des tr. [*sic*] *LR*
| et par escr. veoir [*sic*] *M* | et par . . . Accident *om. R* | ont estez *W* | debile
et par *L* | par *om. M* | Et cy *B*] Et sy *C*; cy *om. AEFLNPQRSTW/MXY* | du
livre *B/M*; de ce livre *om. R*, de ce liure et dit *S. Rubric follows miniature in FGRS;
follows instructions in LTW/Z. No rubric, V.*
Equivalent miniature in *ABEFGQRS/XY.*
158.1 Lors ouvrit *L* (+*1*)
158.2 Et me meit *V*
158.4 et le plus grant *R/X* (+*1*), et plus *QS*
158.6 Qui ny ot *B*, La ny eust *FG*, La ny eult *V*, La ny ot *W* | rocho [*sic*] ny m. *G*
158.7 peust *Q*

Part III

**Here Fresh Memory shows the Author the tombs
of the departed ones of old and he sees by the inscriptions those who
have been brought low by Debility or Accident.
And here begins the third part of this book.**

158.   *T*hen she opened a door and went ahead
          And set us in an open prairie
          Which was adjacent to her house,
    The largest and most level plain
    That may exist anywhere from Paris to Spain.
    Neither rock nor hillock was there.
    Anyone can see
    Easily in all directions.

159.   This plain (which was limitless)
    Was covered with sepulchers,
    Each one made and carved
    Differently and skillfully,
    As much with images as with inscriptions,
    In order to make known the people
    That Accident had routed
    And those killed by Debility.

159.1 Le plain *E* | que fut *V*
159.2 des s. *ENS*
159.3 Chascune faites [*sic*] *W*, Chascun [*sic*] faicte *X* (*-1*) | et en taillye *E*, et entaillee *LQSV/M*, et entaillies [*sic*] *W*, et en tablie *X*
159.4 maistrise *QS*
159.7 ot d. *T* (*-1*)
159.8 debilles [*sic*] *S* | les occist [*sic*] *M*, les a occis *V* (*+1*)

160. Lors me dist : « Va et estudies
      Et note les pas Atropos:
      Cy sont les charoignes pourries
      Des grans honnourez en leurs vies
      Consumez par char et par oz. »
      Savoir le nombre je ne poz
      Par art, par sens ou retentive,
      Car c'est chose trop excessive.

161. « Ou cymetiere de Memoire
      Trouveras, ne l'oublie mye,
      Enfouÿs par le territoire,
      Ceulx dont la Bible fait histoire,
      Exceptez Enoc et Helye,
      Qui, de la puissance infinie
      Et pour fournir ce qui doit estre,
      Sont mis ou paradis terrestre.   [52]

162. Les grans desquelz escript Omere
      Sont speürs en ce cymetiere ;*
      Tous ceulx dont recite Valere
      Et de qui Turlus rent mistere
      Ne dont Orose fait matiere,
      Tous sont pourris et corps et biere,
      Tous a la terre transgloutiz
      Et pris comme ses apatiz.

160.1 dit *FGLPV* | estudie *W*; va estudier *X* (*-1*) | voy quelz drapperies *M*
160.2 le pas *ABEFGLNPQRSTVW/XY* | d'attropos *BR/M*
160.3 Ce sont *L*
160.4 Qui des grans honneurs *E*, Des grans honneurs *M* (*-1*)
160.5 Consommez *QS*
160.6 le compte *M*
160.7 Par sens par art *T* | ou par r. *R* (*+1*)
160.8 Ca c'est [*sic*] *B* | trop imposible [*sic*] *W*
In FG, stanza 160 is followed by stanza 151.

In FG, stanzas 161–166 follow stanza 156.
161.1 O cy. *V*, Au *AE/MX*
161.2 et ne *M* (*+1*)
161.3 Et fouys *M* | la t. [*sic*] *W*

160. Then she told me, "Go and learn by heart
      And take note of the tourneys of Atropos.
      Here are the rotted corpses
      Of great men honored in life,
      Consumed in flesh and bone."
      I couldn't know their number
      By skill, reason, or memory,
      For it is too excessive.

161. "In Memory's cemetery
      You will find, do not forget it,
      Buried in the earth
      Those whose story the Bible tells,
      Except Enoch and Elijah
      Who, by the infinite power
      And to fulfill what must be,
      Are placed in earthly paradise.

162. The great of whom Homer wrote
      Are buried in this cemetery,
      All those whom Valerius cited
      And to whom Cicero paid homage
      And about whom Orosius wrote,
      All are rotted, body and bier,
      All devoured by the earth
      And seized as its just desserts.

161.4 fait memoire *LT/M*
161.5 Excepte *LQRSVW/M*
161.7 f. a ce *M* (+*1*) | quil *BEFGNP/MX*
161.8 en *BEFGLNPQSV/MX*

162.1 Les gens *MX* | de quoy *ENPQSV/MX*, de qui *FG* | descript *R*
162.2 speulz *FG*, aussi *L*, icy *V*, espars *B*, esparles *W* (+*1*), espais *E*, posez *M*
162.3 Tout [*sic*] ceulx *V*
162.4 Et *om. V*, *W* (-*1*) | Tules *B*, tulles *M*, thuolus *FG*, tullius *L*, tulius *V*, titus liuius *R*
       (+*2?*), tuolus *P*, tulus *E*, troylus *QS* | fait mistere *T*. *This line is in sixth position,
       L, with a symbol ("#") to indicate that it is to follow line 3.*
162.5 Et dont *M* | oroze *BV/X*, Ozore [*sic*] *M*, orosoe *R*
162.6 et mis en b. *V* | les corps *EPQS/X*, en corps *L/M* | en biere *BEPQSV/X*
162.7 Tous en *EQS/MX*
162.8 comme es a. *V* (-*1*), c. ses a. *X* | appastis *S*, appartiz *X* | comme a elle lotis *M*

163.   Accident fiert, Debile assomme
        Et Atropos leur livre place ;
        Ilz n'espargnent femme në homme.
        Tout mectent a fin, c'est la somme ;
        La Mort tousjours rompt et deslache
        Ce que Nature queult et lache
        Et luy deschire son habit,
        Dont elle a douleur et despit.

164.   Ceulx qui firent ja les grans fais
        En Babillonne la cité,
        Les clercs d'Athenes tant parfais,
        Les Troyens dont on fait les lays
        Et dont on a tant recité,
        Chascun d'eulx a la Mort cité,
        Et les Amazonnes armees
        Sont toutes a la Mort livrees.

165.   De tout l'Ancïen Testament
        Peulx cy sçavoir, l'ueil s'y enyvre,
        Mais pour gouster plus fermement,
        Vecy ou ceulx du temps present
        Sont mis pour les premiers ensuyvre.
        Liz et retiens et cy te mire :*   [53]
        Cy sont ceulx que Mort oppressa
        Depuis l'an trente cinq en ça. »

166.   Lors me mis ainsi qu'a costiere*
        Et viz bien par les sepultures

163.2 Et *om.* MX (la place)
163.3 Et nes. *R*, Il nespargne *W*
163.4 Tous *BEFGNPQ/X* | mestent *FG*, mest *L*, mect *W* | affin *ANS/X* | et cest la
       s. *L*, sen est la s. *W*
163.5 rompt *om.* X (-1); rond *FGLP*, prent *M* | ront tousiours *V* | et delaisse *E/X*, et
       enlace *M*
163.6 cloud [*sic*] *FG*, queust *L*, creil [?] *W*, crud [*sic*] *X*; oblie *E* | lasse *FGP*, laisse *E/X*.
       Et *que* par n. se passe *M*
163.7 dessire *FG/M*, desire [*sic*] *V*

164.1 qui lors firent *V*
164.3 datheus [*sic*] *X* (-1)
164.4 les laitz *E/M*, les latz [*sic*] *X*
164.6 Cchascun [*sic*] *A* | scite [*sic*] *F*

163.   Accident strikes, Debility lays low,
       And Atropos makes room for them;
       They spare neither man nor woman—
       They finish off everyone, and that's that.
       Death always tears apart and undoes
       What Nature sews and fastens together
       And rips her garments asunder,
       Making her angry and sad.

164.   Those who once accomplished great deeds
       In the city of Babylon,
       The most accomplished scholars of Athens,
       The Trojans about whom poems are made
       And about whom so much has been said—
       Each of them was summoned by Death,
       And the Amazons in their armor
       Have all been delivered up to Death.

165.   All of the Old Testament
       You can know here, the eye drinks it in,
       But in order to savor more surely,
       Here is where those of present time
       Are placed following the first ones.
       Read and remember and reflect:
       Here are those whom Death has overwhelmed
       Within the past thirty-five years."

166.   So then I moved to one side
       And saw clearly by the tombs

164.7   amazonies *NP* (+*1*), amazonyes [?] *E*, amaisonnes *L*, amozanes *M*, amazemes [*sic*] *X*

165.1   Et tout *M*

165.2   P. si *LV* | veoir *BV* | cy e. *NPV*, ty e. *E*; s'y *om. X* (-*1*); a lueil et lire *L*, voycy
        le liure *M*

165.3   pour monstrer *S*

165.4   Veezcy *F* (+*1?*), Veez cy *EGNPQ/MX* (+*1?*)

165.5   ensieure *R*

165.6   reciens [*sic*] *Y* | cy *ABFRTW/YZ*] sy *C*, si *EGLNPQSV/MX*

165.7   Ce sont *S*, Cy sons *V* | ceulx qui *FG*

165.8   lan et trente *M* (+*1*) | trente et cinq *N*, trancteetcinq [*sic*] *X*

166.1   mis *BEGNPQS/Z* (meis *V*, miz *F*)] mist *CARTW/MXY*, meist *L* | constere *V* [*for*
        coustere?*], consistoire *M* (+*1*)

166.2   Et bien par les sepulchres *M* (-*2*)

(Qui furent de neufve matiere,
D'autre façon, d'autre mistiere),
Les armoiries, les figures,
Par les habis et escriptures,
Que les mors ou je me trouvoye
Furent du temps que je vivoye.

167.   La ot epitaphes sans nombre
        Dont oncques ne cougnuz les corps
        Sy m'en tais pour fuÿr encombre.
        La më assista et fist umbre*
        Et me monstra de mors en mors
        La dame dont je fais recors,
        Fresche Memoire, plus qu'assez
        De ceulx de mon temps trespassez.

168.   Ainsi entray en celle forge
        Dont Atropos menoit l'ouvraige.
        La viz ung seigneur de Saint Jorge
        Que Debile prist par la gorge
        Et le vainquist par vasselaige.
        Il fut tenu et grant et saige
        Entre tous ceulx de son quartier,
        Mais il est mort pour abregier.

169.   Je mis l'ueil sur ung empereur,
        Filz du puissant roy de Behaigne :
        Sigismond, prince de valeur,
        Hardy et vaillant deffenseur   [54]

166.3   Quilz *RS* | de *om. X* (*-1*) | maniere *L*, mature [*sic*] *X*
166.4   Dune [?] *M* | dautre manie*re S*
166.5   Les armonies [*sic*] *G*
166.6   Pour les *S*

*Fragment O (B.n.F., fr. 4907), « le triste revel », begins. See Textual Notes for the complete text
of this stanza in O.*
In E, stanzas 167–172 follow stanza 196.
167.1   eulx *V* | epiphes *A* (*-1*)
167.2   nen c. *EFGQS/MX* | le corps *G*
167.4   Aller *R*, Puis *M* | massista *RS*, me laissa *Q*, me assist la *M* | et me f. *QS*
167.5   m. plusi*eu*rs mors *M* (*-1*), m. de moys en moys [*sic*] *X*
167.6   Les tumbes *M* | je suis *LW*, je fuz *EFGPQS/X*; dont jay par r. *M* | recorps [*sic*]
        G, rescors *P*

(Which were of new material,
Of another style, other artwork),
And by the arms, images,
Costumes and inscriptions,
That the dead among whom I found myself
Were from the time in which I had lived.

167.   There were numberless epitaphs
Of people I never knew,
So I'll be silent to avoid idle padding.
There Fresh Memory, the lady of whom I speak,
Stood by and protected me
And pointed out to me
One person after another,
More than enough of those dead in my time.

168.   Thus I entered into that foundry
Whose workings Atropos directs.
There I saw a lord of Saint George
Whom Debility had seized by the throat
And boldly vanquished.
He was esteemed great and wise
Among all those of his district,
But, in short, he was dead.

169.   I glanced upon an emperor,
Son of the powerful king of Bohemia:
Sigismond, worthy prince,
Stout and valiant defender

167.7 plus cassez [*sic!*] *MX*
X prints *168.1*, Ainsy entray en celle forge, *as a ninth line of stanza 167, as well as in its proper place.*

168.1 jentray *BLRV*; A. entre *E* | ceste forge *V*
168.3 le seigneur *B*, vng filz *S* (*-1*)
168.4 *Line om., O.*
168.5 le *om. X* (*-1*), *M* (par son v.)

169.1 sus *TV*
169.2 Filz de *X*; Filz fut du grant roy *E*

Du grant empire d'Alemaigne.
Debille, qui mains en mehaigne,
L'a mort abatu et maté
Maulgré empire et royaulté.

170.   La je viz de Ligny le conte
Qui de Lucembourg se nommoit ;
Des vaillans fut dont on raconte.
D'Accident oncques ne tint compte
Et tousjours a luy combatoit,
Mais Debile, qui l'actendoit
Au pas pour en prendre vengeance,
L'occist a petit de deffense.*

171.   La gisoit ung Portugaloix,*
Duc de Coÿmbres, filz de roy,
De grans vertus en tous endroix,
Prince vaillant, sage et courtoix ;
Plus renommé de luy ne voy,
Mais ou milieu de son aroy*
Accident, par mortelle envie,
L'occist et luy osta la vie.

172.   Tout soubit se jecta mon oeil
Sus ung sarcueil de pierre dure,*
Ou gisoit mort Louÿs de Beul,
Qui valoit que l'on en fist deul
Et qu'il fust plaint oultre mesure.
Accident par male adventure
Faisant armes le fist mourir,
Ou plus bel de son advenir.

169.5 Dung grant *L*
169.6 maint *BEFGNPQSV/MX* | mesaigne *L*, meschaine [*sic*] *X. Line om., O.*
169.7 La mort a abatu *S* (+*1*), a batu *V/MX*

170.2 se mommoit [*sic*] *X*
170.3 fut *om. V* (-*1*) | dont en *X*
170.7 Ou *T* | emprendre *W*
170.8 petite deffence *BEFGLNOPQSV/MXZ*

171.1 La giroit *E* | portingalois *AESW/MX*
171.2 Du [*sic*] de c. *R* | coybre *S*, combre *V* (-*1*); Cuymbres *et* filz *B* (+*1?*) | du roy *M*

Of the great German empire.
Debility, who mangles many,
Thwarted and killed him
Despite his high rank and royalty.

170. I saw there the Count of Ligny
Who was called Luxembourg,
One of the valiant of whom they speak.
He never took Accident into account
And always fought against him,
But Debility, who lay in wait for him
At the lists to wreak his vengeance,
Killed him with little resistance.

171. A Portuguese lay there,
Duke of Coimbra, son of a king,
Of great merit in every quarter,
A courageous prince, wise and courtly;
I never saw one more esteemed than he.
But in the middle of his splendor
Accident, through deadly spite,
Killed him and took his life.

172. Suddenly I cast my eye
Upon a grave of harsh stone
Where Louis de Bueil lay dead.
He was worth grieving for
And limitless bewailing.
Accident, by evil chance
Waging war, made him die
At the height of his career.

171.3 Dez grans *R*

171.5 renom*m*ee.de *A* [*dot may mean expunctuation of second* e] | voye *W*

171.6 au *ABEFGLNPQRSTVW/MXY*

171.7 mortel *V/M*

172.1 Dont subit *L* | si gectay *FGNPQ/MX*, je jettay *L*, je gectay *T*; T. s. gectay *S* (*-1*)

172.2 Sur *ABEFGLNQRSVW/MX* | surqueil *S* | depre dure [*sic*] *X* (*-1*)

172.3 du bueil *FGQ/X*, de bueil *NSW/M*, de voeul [?] *V*

172.4 Qui bien v. *M* | que on *Q* (*-1?*), quon *M*, *X* (*-1*), que len fist *S* (*-1*) | fesist *R* (*+1*)

172.5 Et qui *BW*, Et que *L*; qu'il *om. S* (*-1*) | fut *LNSVW/M* | plain *VW*

172.6 malauenture *V*, maladuenture *W*

173.   Deux papes desoubz ung tombeau
       Geürent, Felix et Eugene.   [55]
       Ceulx firent ung scisme nouveau :
       Chascun pour faire son plus beau
       Voult estre pape en ung temps mesme.*
       L'Eglise en eult douleur et paine,
       Mais Debile les mist en terre
       Et fist la fin de ceste guerre.

174.   La viz deux Anglois capitaines
       Estre pourris et consumés.
       En France ont eu et bruitz et regnes ;
       En guerre firent de grans peines
       Et furent doubtez et amez.
       Thaleboth et Scalles oultrez
       Furent par Accident tous deux
       Et fussent ilz cent fois plus preux.

175.   La fut, que l'on regretoit fort,
       Par ses epitaphes escrips,
       Mis Gilles de Bretaigne mort
       Par Accident qui luy fist tort,
       Et pres de luy haultement viz,
       Par Debile mort et occis,
       Le duc Artus plain de vaillance,
       Qui fut connestable de France.

173.1-3-4: *rhymes in* -el *ENOPQS/MX*, -eaul *L*; *V mixes* -eau (*lines 1 and 4*) *and* -eaul (*line 3*)

173.1   soubz *L* (-*1*)

173.2   Gisrent [*sic*] *BV* (-*1*), Furent *Q* (-*1*); Y geurent *E* | felix aussy eu. *L*. Je vis la F. et E. *O/M.*

173.3   ung stisme *F*

173.5   Veult *VW*, Voeult *R*, Voulut *X* (+*1*); Vout oultre pape *O* | mesmez *R* | et auoir regne *M*, pour auoir regne *O* (+*1*)

173.6   eust *BFN* | eut dueil *et* p. *Q* (-*1*), eut duel et p. *S* (-*1*). Dom fut Lesglise en grande peine *M*

173.7   lez met *R*

173.8   de celle *BEFGNPQS*, dicelle *VW*, de telle *MX*

174.1   La veir [?] *S* | capitaine *X*

173.   Two popes lay under one tomb,
        Felix and Eugene.
        These two made a new schism:
        Each tried to prevail,
        Wanting to be pope at the same time.
        The Church suffered grief and pain from this,
        But Debility put them in the ground
        And put an end to that war.

174.   I saw there two English captains
        Decomposed and devoured.
        In France they had renown and sway;
        They strove mightily in war
        And were feared and loved.
        Talbot and Scales were vanquished,
        Both of them, by Accident
        Even had they been a hundred times more valorous.

175.   Most regrettably, there was,
        According to his inscription,
        Giles of Brittany, killed
        By Accident who wronged him.
        And I clearly saw dead near him,
        Killed by Debility,
        The intrepid Duke Arthur,
        Who was Constable of France.

174.2 consommez Q

174.3 *first* et *om.* BEFGLNPQRSVW/X (*-1*) | bruit *FGPQSW/X*, bruyt *LN,* bruict
       BEV/M | br. et grands r. *M*

174.4 guerres *RV*, gueres *W* | de grant [*sic*] peines *SW*. En g. de grand peine [*sic*]
       soustindrent *M*

174.6 Thaleboth *EFGN/XZ* (Talleboth *BTW*, Talebot *L*, Tallebot *M*, Tailleboth *V*)]
       Thalboth *CAR/Y* (*-1*), Talbot *Q* (*-1*), Thalbot *S* (*-1*) | et stables [*sic*] *S*. Les
       cappitaines talbot et Escalles [*sic*] *O* (*+2*).

174.8 il *E*

175.1 que on *T* (*-1?*) | que je regretay *EFGNOPQS/X*, que je regrette *M*
175.2 ces *MX*
175.3 Mais *L* | gille *V/M* | bretaignes *W*. Mis en pres le duc de belfort *O*
175.4 quil luy *W*
175.6 occhist *W*

176.   La fut ung Jacques de Bourbon,
        Roy de Naples moult a prisier.
        Le monde ne luy sembla bon
        Si voua la religion
        Et fut observant Cordelier,
        Mais Debile pour le moustier
        Ne pour royale dignité
        Ne l'a de la mort respité.

177.   Soubz une tombe de loiton   [56]
        Trouvay ensepvelis deux corps
        Dont fut honneste le diton :
        Ceulx furent La Hire et Poton,
        Des bons guerriers de ce temps lors.
        Des mains de Debile sont mors
        Maulgré leur bonne renommee,
        Qui leur est au mains demouree.

178.   Ung sepulcre parant et riche
        Je trouvay sur ung Alemant :
        C'est le duc Aubert d'Austerice.
        Celui ne fut avers ne chiche,
        Mais prince tres large et baillant.*
        Accident luy vint au devant
        Et l'occist par grant vasselage,
        Ce que l'on tint a grant dommage.

176.4   Sy voua r. O (-1)
176.6   moustier om. E (incomplete line), pour le monstrer [sic] SW/X, pour luy monstrer
        M
176.7   Ne par ENPQS/X; Que vault r. d. M | royaulte dignite S

177.1   laiton BRTVW, laton QS/MX, lecton E, letton L, leiton Y, loicton FG, locton P,
        loction [sic] N
177.2   ensepuely B, enseuely W, enseueilliz S
177.3   D. furent O (+1) | honnestes W | les ditons O
177.4   Ce BV
177.5   guerroiers FG (+1), NP; guerroieurs E/X, guerrieurs W (+1?), guerreux S; chevaliers
        M | du temps ENP/MX, BQS (-1); pour ce temps V

176. Jacques of Bourbon was there,
      King of Naples, worthy of high esteem.
      The world did not seem good to him
      So he took religious vows
      And was an Observant Friar,*
      But Debility, neither for church
      Nor for royal dignity,
      Gave him any reprieve from death.

177. Under a brass tomb
      I found two bodies buried
      Whose reputation was honorable:
      These were La Hire and Poton,
      Two good warriors of that time.
      They were slain by Debility's hand
      In spite of their good renown,
      Which at least remains for them.

178. A sepulcher of fine and rich appearance
      I found above a German:
      It was Duke Albert of Austria.
      He was never greedy or cheap,
      But a most open-handed and generous prince.
      Accident confronted him
      And killed him by great prowess,
      Which was held to be a great loss.

177.6 Des moins [sic] X | debilles M | Des mains debile ilz sont m. L (-1)

178.1 parent GN; assez noble et riche M, parut et r. S, tresgrand et r. V
178.2 Je trouue X | sus T
178.3 Ce fut M (autriche) | Obert L, haubert N | austrice V/Y, austriche BFGS,
       autriche ENQ, ostrice R, ostriche LP/X (all -1)
178.4 auer X
178.5 vaillant ABEFGLNOPQRSV/MXYZ
178.7 Qui l'occist BEFGNPQSVW/MX
178.8 que len MX | tient V

179.   En ce lieu cy ne failloit mye
       A estre mengié de vermine
       Le roy Lancelot de Hongrie,
       L'un des grans de la Germanie.
       D'estre ung empereur bon et digne,
       Accident le print en haÿne*
       Et l'occist par piteux explois,
       Au grant diffame des Pragois.

180.   J'apersus ung chevalier bon
       Qui ja fut oultré par Debile :
       C'est le seigneur de Varembon.
       Et pres ung homme de renom
       Qu'Accident murtrit entre mille :
       Ce fut le seigneur d'Esmaville.
       Devot, vertueulx et vaillant,
       Son non fut Jacques de Chaillant.   [57]

181.   La gisoit, soubz sepulchre hault,
       Ung chevalier mort en ce plain,
       Natif du paÿs de Haynnault,
       Dont le loz reluit et moult vault :
       C'est Messire Jacques de Lalain.*
       Vingt et deux fois fist de sa main
       Armes, ains trente ans acomplis,
       Et l'a Accident a mort mis.

179.1 lieu si Q; cy *om.* V (*-1*) | ny f. B | faillit W
179.2 Destre bien m. M, Destre m. X (*-1*)
179.3 dongrie S (*-1*); du lach *lined out, followed by* de hongrie, R
179.4 des grand [*sic*] V
179.5 ung *om.* Q (*-1*), M (et bon)
179.6 en grant haynne L (*+1*), prit dont a hai*n*ne V (*+1*)
179.7 exploict B
179.8 Ung gr. E, Ou gr. NPQS | de pr. M | pargoix F, pargoys N, pargois EGPS, pergoys X, pragos W

180.1 ung cheualiers [*sic*] W | ch. grant [*sic*] T
180.2 fuz W | de debille R
180.3 Barembon [?] S
180.4 Et *om.* E (de grant renom); Et *lined out,* pres lui L | regnon X

179.   In this place, without a doubt
        Eaten by worms,
        King Ladislas of Hungary,
        One of Germany's great men.
        Since he was a good and worthy emperor,
        Accident conceived a hatred for him
        And killed him through woeful acts,
        To the great detriment of the citizens of Prague.

180.   I caught sight of a good knight
        Who had been defeated by Debility;
        It was the Lord of Varembon.
        And nearby, a man of renown
        Whom Accident murdered among a thousand:
        This was the Lord of Aymeville;
        Devout, virtuous, and valiant,
        His name was Jacques de Chalant.

181.   There under a lofty sepulcher lay
        A knight dead on this plain,
        A native of the land of Hainault,
        Whose glory still shines worthily:
        It was my lord Jacques de Lalain.
        Two and twenty times he took up arms
        Before he was thirty
        And he was put to death by Accident.

180.5–6 *inverted L*
180.5 Qu' *om. QS* | occist *S*, meurdrist *MX*; a murdry *R* (+*1*)
180.6 de ma ville *LN*, de ma uille *or* de manille *R/M*, desmanville *or* -mau- *O*, s. desmanible [*sic*] *X*
180.7 Qui fut v. *M*
180.8 chalant *B*, challant *R*, saillant *FGT*

181.1 sepulcres [*sic*] hault *W*, sepulcre grant *X*
181.4 Tout le loz *R* | le lot *B* | retint *EFGN/M*, retins [*sic*] *PQS/X* | qui m. *ENPQS/MX*
181.6 Vint *X* | Vingt et deux *ABEFGNPQT* (Ving et *S*)] et *om. CR/Y* (-*1*), xxii *VW* | fist *om. X* (-*1*)
181.7 Arme *MX* (-*1*) | complis *S* (-*1*)
181.8 Mais Ac. la a m. m. *L*

182.   Accident, qui de vaincre soingne,
        Avoit fait pourir en ce pré
        Ung que je doy mectre en besougne :
        Cornille bastard de Bourgougne,*
        Chevalier preux et asseuré.
        A son escu qui fut barré
        Par my lyons et fleurs de lis*
        Cougnuz le chevalier de pris.

183.   Brézé seigneur de La Varenne,
        Grant seneschal de Normendie,
        Gisoit mort en celle garenne,
        Plat ou sablon et en l'arenne
        Comme la commune maisnye.
        La fut sa vaillance faillye,
        Son sens et son plaisant parler,
        Car Accident le fist finer.

184.   Je cougnus deux ducs de Milan :
        L'ung fut Phelippes Maria
        Mort et infett droit la gisan
        (L'escripvain n'y ot pas mis l'an),*
        Et pres couchoit et repousa
        Celui duc qui Milan gaigna,   [58]
        Le duc Francisque, filz de Sforce :
        Debile les occist par force.

182.1   songne *EFGNPRTW/Y*, songe *QS*, son gre [*sic*] *X*
182.2   fait *om. R* (*-1*) | pourry *LV*
182.3   que doye *V*, que je doye *W* (*+1*). Ung quest de mettre en la b. *L*
O inserts an additional stanza at this point, not found in any other manuscripts. See Textual Notes.

183.1   Bresse *RV*, Boexe [*sic*] *X* | de Varenne *B* (*-1*) | varanne (*rhymed with* garanne, laranne) *L*
183.3   garanne *possibly changed from* garenne *B*
183.4   la renne *E*, larenue [*sic*] *X*
183.5   la c. maysue [*sic*] *X*

182. Accident, who works hard to conquer,
Had caused to rot in this field
One whom I should put in this work:
Cornille, Bastard of Burgundy,
A noble and confident knight.
I recognized the esteemed knight
By his shield, which was barred
With lions and fleurs-de-lys.

183. Brézé, Lord of La Varenne,
Grand seneschal of Normandy,
Lay dead in that crowded burrow,
Flat in the gravel and sand
Just like the common folk.
His valor was of no use there,
His intelligence and pleasing conversation,
For Accident had brought about his end.

184. I recognized two dukes of Milan:
One was Filippo Maria
Lying right there dead and decayed
(The inscriber had not set down the year),
And nearby lay at rest
That duke who won Milan,
Duke Francesco, son of Sforza;
Debility killed them violently.

183.6 sa foiblesse affoiblye *M*, sa v. soiblye [*sic*] *X*
183.7 Son chant *Q*

184.1 Jay congneu *M* | Millam *BFG*, melan *W*
184.3 infer *W* | gisam *FG*, gisans [?] *W*; infect a son grand dan *M*
184.4 Lescripuent *L* | pas mil an [*sic*] *L*
184.5 Auprés *B*, Et apres *S* (+*1*); Et ampres de luy r. *M*
184.6 Millam *B*
184.7 Qui fut dict fr. *M* | le duc franusque duc [*sic*] *X* | de *om. M* (-*1*); deforce *A*, de force *L*, defforce *QS*, descoce *FGN*, descosse *E/X*

185. La viz Tibault de Neufchastel,
Ja de Bourgougne mareschal.
Son nom et tiltre furent bel ;
Piecza n'eurent Bourguignons tel,
Car il estoit hardy vassal.
Chevalier fut preux et loyal ;
Debile en fist la place necte
Par la Mort qui en prist sa debte.*

186. De Fribourg le conte la gut*
Et trois freres de Thoulongon.
Chascun d'eulx nommé vaillant fut,
Mais Debile si les deceut
Et les desconfist sans rençon.
Ternant, le chevalier de nom,*
En sens et prouesse acomply,
Gisoit la mort ensepvely.

187. Je rencontray en mon chemin
Ung sarcueil de grant artifice
Ou fut le chancelier Rolin.
Son tiltre, qui fut en latin,
Le monstroit parfait en justice.
Somptueux fut en edifice,
Hospitaulx et moustiers fonda ;
Et puis par Debile fina.

185.2 Jadis *QS* (+*1*)
185.3 belle [*sic*] *W*
185.4 P. ny eust bourgoingnon *F* | n'eurent bourguignon [*sic*] *BL/M*
185.8 prist *ABRTW/YZ* (prinst *F*, print *EGLNPQSV*, prit *M*)] fist *C*, point [*sic*] *X* | la debte *V* | Par qui emporta sa d. *O* (-*1*)

186.1 De faulbourg [*sic*] *M*, De fabourg *X* | jeust *B*, just *R*
186.2 hologon *M*
186.3 homme vaillant *FG/M* | fut *om. W* (-*1*); fust *R*
186.4 d. les a deceut *L*
186.5 ranchons *B*

185. I saw Thibault of Neuchatel there,
 Once Marshal of Burgundy;
 His name and title were fine;
 The Burgundians haven't had his like for a long time,
 For he was a hardy vassal.
 A noble and loyal knight,
 Debility cleared him from the field
 By Death who claimed from him her due.

186. The Count of Fribourg lay there
 And three brothers of Toulongeon.
 Each of them was called valiant,
 But Debility betrayed them
 And routed them without redemption.
 Ternant, the famous knight,
 Accomplished in wit and prowess,
 Lay dead and buried there.

187. On my way I came across
 A tomb of great artistry
 Wherein Chancellor Rolin lay.
 His inscription, which was in Latin,
 Showed him to be perfect in justice.
 He was princely in building,
 Established hospitals and monasteries,
 And then was dispatched by Debility.

186.6 Ternant *BFGLNOPQRSTW/YZ*] Teruant *CE*, Teruaut *A*, Tenant *V*, Seruant *M*,
 Ceruant *X*
186.7 En s. en pr. *Q/M*
186.8 la *om. M* (et ens.) | mort ou seuely [*sic*] *L*, m. et seueilly [*sic*] *S*, m. et seuely [*sic*]
 X, m. et enseuely *W* (+*1*)

187.1 Ja r. [*sic*] *X*
187.2 artififice [*sic*] *X* (+*1*)
187.3 le cheualier *LORW*; le chencelier *E* | Robin *L*
187.6 endeficie [*sic*] *R*
187.7 et eglises *V*, et montiers [*sic*] *X*

188.   Ung grant prince devenu riens
       La jut, si non cendres et pouldre.
       C'est le duc Charles d'Orlïens,*
       Ou tant ot de bontez et biens   [59]
       Qu'on ne le peult nombrer ne souldre.
       Et pres, que Dieu le vueille absouldre,
       Fut de Dunois le bon seigneur.
       Des deux fut Debile occiseur.

189.   Croÿ conte de Poursuan
       Mort o les autres je trouvay ;*
       Du bon duc fut grant chambellan.
       Son frere l'aloit poursievan,
       Jehan, jadis conte de Chimay.*
       Vertueux furent, je le sçay,
       Et bons chevaliers renommez,
       Mais Debile les a finez.

190.   Ung corps qui fut de grant haultesse
       Je recougnuz soudainement :
       Le roy Alphons, plain de prouesse,
       De grant estat et de largesse
       Et vault le ramentoyvement.
       Maulgré son ost et sa grant gent,
       Debile prist sur luy sa reste
       Au plus fort de sa grant conqueste.

188.2   La gent [sic] E/X, La geust LS, La ny eult V, La gisans M | cendre et V | si non
        om. Q/M | en cendres Q, fors cendres M | et en p. Q | pouldres EGQSW/MX
188.3   orliens AFGLRT/YZ] orleans CBENOPQSW/MX, orleens V
188.4   Qui t. G | Ou eut tant V | bonte BEV/X | t. de bonte eust et F, t. de b. eut et
        G | bonte et de biens R/M (+1). Ou tant de vertus et de biens L
188.5   Que ne le p. B, Quon ne les p. L; le om. W (-1) | mombrer [?] W
188.6   Et apres O/M, X (+1); Et pri LR, Et prie SV (+1), Et pries W (+1) | dieu quil L,
        dieu qui V | le om. O/M, lined out L (-1?), les RV | vueille AEFGLNPQS/XYZ
        (veulle BTV, voeulle R)] ueul C, veult O, vueil W, veille M. Line is in eighth posi-
        tion, R.
188.8   Deulx deux T

189.1   Troy S, Conte conte [sic] O | le conte L (+1)
189.2   ou les EFGNPRSVW/MX, ô les [sic] B, com les L | ne trouuay MX, ie trouue FG

188. A great prince come to naught
Lay there, only cinders and ashes.
It was Charles, Duke of Orléans,
Who had so much goodness and wealth
That none can calculate or determine it.
And nearby, may God pardon him,
Was the good Lord of Dunois.
Debility was the slayer of both.

189. I found dead among the others
Croy, Count of Porcien;
He was Grand Chamberlain of the good duke.
His brother followed after him,
Jehan, erstwhile Count of Chimay.
They were virtuous, I know,
And renowned good knights,
But Debility finished them off.

190. I suddenly recognized there
A body of most lofty rank:
King Alphonso, full of valor,
Of mighty estate and liberality
And worth remembering.
Despite his army and large following,
Debility called him to account
At the height of his great conquest.

189.3 duc y fut *V*, d. il fut *M* (grant *om. V/M*) | fut du ch. [*sic*] *X* | Du grant duc fut bon ch. *E*

189.4 poursuiuant *L/MX*, poursuan *W*

189.5 Jan *T*, Johan *Y* (+*1*) | iadz [*sic*] *X* (-*1*) | de de ch. [*sic*] *N* (+*1*) | de thunay *E*, de chinay *Y*, de chauuay *M*, de chuuay [*sic*] *X*

189.7 Et ch. bien r. *M*

189.8 Mais *om. EV* (affinez) | les a tuez *M*, les a afinez *X* (+*1*)

190.2 Je congneuz *X* (-*1*), Je congneuz la *L/MZ*

190.3 proesses *V*

190.5 le ramenement *X* (-*1*), le ramentement *M* (-*1*)

190.6 sont ost [*sic*] *F* | grant *om. R/M* (-*1*)

190.7 print *EFGQS/X* | la reste *Q*, la teste [*sic!*] *W*

190.8 Ou *BEFGNPQSVW/MX*

191.   Je trouvay Xantes et Charny
       Et maints de l'ordre du Toyson :
       Habourdin, La Vere, Crequy,
       Brimeur, Moulembaix et Auxi,
       De Lalain, Messire Symon.
       Roys, ducs et contes a foison,
       Tous mors sont en champ ou en ville
       Par Accident ou par Debille.

192.   La furent en la terre mis
       Deux hommes de grant apparance.   [60]
       L'un fut Cosme de Medicis
       Et Jacques Cueur. Ceulx ont acquis
       Et mis ensemble grant finance
       Mais n'y valut or ne chevance :
       Debile, qui tout vaintt et tue,
       Les assomma de sa massue.

193.   Je mis l'ueil sur deulx connestables,*
       Saint Pol et Halure de La Lune.*
       Puissans furent et redoutables,
       Chevalereux et honnourables ;
       Chascun ot part de la fortune.
       Accident leur monstra rancune
       Et les fist morir et finer
       Au plus hault point de leur regner.

___

191.1 La *L* | trouue *S* | santes *GL/Z*, santez *FNQR*, sante *M*, saultez *E*, sautez *P/X*,
       chantez [*sic*] *S*, pantes [*sic*] *W* | et *om. M* (*-1*), de charny *V*. Je y treuuey le conte
       de charny *O* (*+1*)
191.2 Et mains *N/MX*, Et aucuns *L* (*+1*) | de t. *MX*
191.3 la vers *W* (*-1*) | et crequy *T* | creigny *FG*, trequi *E*, coegin [*?*] *Q*, croqui *M*,
       crequin [*sic*] *X*
191.4 M. *begins line BEFGNPQSVW/MX.* | Brienne *L* (*+1*), Brymeu *B*, brimeu *ERV*,
       bruneu *FPQ*, bruneau *X*; brimeu *or* bruneu *N*, Pruncau [*?*] *M* | mouleurbaix *A*,
       Molemboix *GQS*, Malembaix *M* | et aussi *FGNQSV/MX*, et Ossy *B*
191.6 et *om. Q/X* (*-1*), *M* (*-2*) | conte *M*. Loys [*sic*] duc conte a f. *O* (*-1*)
191.7 es champs *V*, en champs *NW* | et en v. *ES/X*, et v. *Q* (*-1*)
191.8 Pour *M* | et par *FG*; ou pourille *M* (*-1*)

192.1 en la terre *ABFGLNOPQRSTW/MYZ*] en terre *CEV* (*-1*)

191.   I found Santes and Charny
And many from the Order of the Golden Fleece:
Hautbourdin, La Vere, Créquy,
Brimeu, Molembais, and Auxy,
Sir Simon de Lalain.
Kings, dukes, and counts aplenty,
All were killed in field or town
By Accident or by Debility.

192.   Placed there in the earth were
Two men of substantial significance.
They were Cosimo de Medici
And Jacques Cœur. They had acquired
And put together immense wealth.
But neither gold nor worldly goods availed there:
Debility, who overcomes and kills everyone,
Struck them down with his mace.

193.   I set eyes upon two constables,
Saint Pol and Alvaro de La Luna.
They were powerful, formidable,
Chivalrous and honorable;
Each one had his share of good fortune.
Accident held a grudge against them
And made them die and finished them
At the peak of their prominence.

192.2 grande *BV*

192.5 Comme men semble grand f. *O*

192.6 M. or *FG*, M. rien *OQS/M*, M. riens *Z* | ny vault *EFGNPQS/MXZ, L/Y (+1)*, ne vault *O* | ny or ne ch. *ENP/X*, ny mais ch. *FG*, or ny ch. *OV*

192.7 vaine [*sic*] *G*

192.8 assomme *W*

193.1 sus *Y* | sur ung c. *O*

193.2 aluere *EFGP*, N [?], aleure *QS*, Alure *B*; et autre de la lignie [*sic*] *L (+1)*; a lheure de la lune [*sic*] *M*

193.3 Puissant fust et redoubtable *O (-1)*; *singular in l. 4 also*; Puissant furent [*sic*] *RV*

193.5 eust *EFGN* | a la f. *L*, de sa f. *QS*, par sa f. *M (-1)*

193.6 monstre *M* | Ac. qui luy monstra fortune *O (+1)*

193.8 Ou *BV* | de son regney *O*

194.   Vualleran, seigneur de Moreul,
        Gisoit par les lames piteuses,
        Mort estendu en son sercueil,
        Et pres, qu'oublier je ne veul,
        Couchoit le seigneur de Saveuses.
        Pour leurs oeuvres chevalereuses
        Debile, le tresgrant ouvrier,*
        Ne les voult de mort espargnier.

195.   Vuaruick, qui tant ot de puissance,*
        Je cougnuz a la rouge croix ;
        Si fiz je le duc de Clarence.
        Accident les mist a oultrance
        Et occist deux nobles Angloix.
        Plus bas gisoit ung Escoçoys,
        Conte du Glas, en pourreture,
        Despeschié par telle adventure.

196.   Vergy, Conches et Brederode   [61]
        Vis gisans desoubz les sentiers ;
        La cougnus a l'abit et mode
        Des grans gens de Prusse et de Rode,
        Mains bons et vaillans chevaliers
        De Caletrave et de Templers.*
        Moult trouvay mors par Accident
        Ou par Debile qui tout fent.

194.1 morneil *FGPS*, morueil *X*
194.2 les larmes [*sic*] *V*
194.4 Aupres *M* | que oublier ne v. *T* (*-1?*)
194.5 Quouchoit [*sic*] *N*, Touchoit [*sic*] *MX* | saueuse *V*
194.6 Par leurs *ENQ*, Par les *S*
194.7 Debile le *ABEFGLNOPQRSTVW/MXYZ*] Le desbile [*sic*] *C* | ouurir [*sic*] *Y*
194.8 veult *EVW/M*; volu *R* (*+1*)

195.1 Varint [*?*] *E*, Varnie [*?*] *FG*, Varnier [Varuier?] *N*, Uarnicus [*?*] *S* (*+1?*), Varonic [*?*]
      M, Varu vii c. [*sic*] *X* | eust *FGNP*, ost *B* | de p. *EFGLNPQS/MXZ*] de *om.*
      CABRTVW/Y (*-1*)
195.2 Je le c. *S* (*+1*)
195.3 Si fige [*sic*] *E*, Si foy ie [*sic*] *X*; je *om. R* (*-1*) | le seigneur de cl. *Q* (*+1*)
195.4 en oultrance *EFGS/MX*

194. Waleran, Lord of Moreuil,
      Lay among the piteous slabs,
      Stretched out dead in his tomb,
      And nearby, I don't want to forget,
      Lay the Lord of Saveuses.
      Despite their chivalrous accomplishments,
      Debility, the most mighty moiler,
      Was unwilling to spare them from death.

195. Warwick, who had so much power,
      I recognized by the red cross,
      As I did the Duke of Clarence.
      Accident vanquished them
      And killed two noble Englishmen.
      Farther on lay a Scot,
      Douglas, Earl of Glasgow, rotting,
      Dispatched by such misadventure.

196. Vergy, Conches and Brederode
      I saw lying beneath the paths.
      I recognized there, by dress and style,
      Mighty people of Prussia and Rhodes,
      Many good and valiant knights,
      Calatravans and Templars.
      I found many killed by Accident
      Or by Debility who tears everyone asunder.

195.5 notables *FGQS/X* (+*1*), traistres [*sic!*] *O/M*
195.7 de glas *R*, de glase *W*, de glatz *X*, le glaix *M*
195.8 Despitie *R* | tel *RS*, tels [?] *M*

196.1 Vergey *Q* | couches *AEFGPV/XY*, couchés *B* | brederodes *V*, Brederades *M*
196.2 dessus *V*, soubz *N/M* (-*1*) | les fumiers [*sic*] *E*, les chantiers *M*
196.3 modes *M*
196.4 gens *om. M* (-*1*) | de proesse [*sic*] *V* (+*1*); du prince de R. *E/M*, du prince et rode *X* (-*1*) | rodes *M* | *second* de *om. NP* (-*1*)
196.6 caltrane *FGP*, caltraue *EQ*; caltrane *or* caltraue *NS*; caletrane *AR/Y*; caletrane *or* caletraue *LTW*; calatraue *V*, caleraues *X*, Caler auez *M* | Destaler [?] auec des templies [?] *O*
196.7 mort *BEV*
196.8 Et par *NQS/M* | tout sent *M*
Stanzas 167–172 follow at this point, E.

197. La jut des marches de Turquie
Ung bon chevalier de grant fait :
C'est Le Blanc de La Valaquie.
Sur les Turcs fist mainte saillie ;
Moult de prouesses y a fait.
Debile l'a du tout defait
Et abatu sans relever,
Celuy qu'on doit bien honnourer.

198. Des Bourbounois le duc Loÿs*
Jut la par Debile maté
Et pres de luy deulx de ses filz
Furent d'Accident mors et pris,
Dont dommage fut et pité.*
L'un fut de Beaujeu herité,
L'autre, Jasques, qui fut mainsné,
Chevalier de moult grant beauté.

199. La viz le prince d'Anthioche,
Qui ot de Chippres l'eritiere.
Contre Accident il ne tint coche
Mais l'enfouït d'une pioche*
Ou milieu de celle miniere.
Debile par autre maniere
Ot la mort de mortelle pince
Loÿs qui fut d'Orenges prince.   [62]

197.1 La gent [sic] EV/X, possibly also LST
197.3 valequie FG, velaquie B, volaquie X, volaquye M, ballaquie QS, valiquie Y
197.4 Sus Y | turcques W (+1) | maintes [sic] saillie V
197.5 proesse FG (-1?), prouesse EQRS/M (-1?)
197.7 sans reueler [sic] FG, sans releue [sic] L

198.1 Charles duc de bourbon je vis EFGNOPQS/X, Ch. le duc M (+1)
198.2 Par d. jut la m. B, Par d. geute la m. W (+1), Par d. fut la m. V; Par debile mort et mate EFGNOPQS/MX
198.3 deulx om. S (-1)
198.4 mort R
198.5 en p. Y | pite ABLRTW/YZ (possibly corrected from pitié in B)] pitie CFGNPQSV/X, pitye M, peche E

197. From the marches of Turkey there lay
     A good knight of great exploits:
     Le Blanc de La Valaquie.
     He made many sallies against the Turks,
     Performed many valiant acts there.
     Debility completely routed him
     And laid him low, not to rise again,
     One who should indeed be honored.

198. Duke Louis of Bourbon
     Lay there, foiled by Debility,
     And near him two of his sons,
     Taken and killed by Accident,
     Which was a shame and a pity.
     One was the heir of Beaujeu,
     The other the younger, Jacques,
     A knight of outstanding comeliness.

199. I saw the prince of Antioch
     Who had the inheritance of Cyprus.
     He was no match for Accident
     Who buried him with a pickaxe
     In the middle of this quarry.
     Debility in another way
     Had killed there with his fell clutch
     Louis, who was Prince of Orange.

198.6 benu [?] jeu R | heritier S/X
198.7 fut puis aisne [sic] M (+1)

199.1 La veiz ie le FG (+1)
199.2 eust EFP | des ch. EFGNPQ/X | cyprés B | lheritaige V, leriture [sic] X
199.3 tient c. M | couche V
199.4 lenfuit [sic] tout M | dune approche M (-1), dune proche [sic] X (-1). Mais la ot [?]
       mis tout dune approche O
199.5 Ou meillieu EFGN | dicelle VW, de telle m. X. Lines 5 and 6 combined, Au m. de
       telle maniere, M
199.6 Line om., O.
199.7 Eust la FGNPS | prince [sic] M
199.8 orenge AEQSV/MY, orange N

200.   La gisoit mort sur ung pesac
        Ung princë ou j'alay le cours :
        Ce fut le conte d'Armignac.
        Grant mal me fist en l'estomac
        Et me fist rendre plains et plours.
        Aussi le bon duc de Nemours
        Trouvay par Accident finé
        En ce cymetiere enterré.

201.   La fut de Cecile le roy,
        D'honneur le droit fruit et vray arbre :
        Debille l'occist par desroy.
        Et si viz mors en ce terroy,
        Gisans soubz ung tombeau de mabre,
        Deux de ses filz, ducs de Calabre,*
        Moult vertueux et renommés,
        Par Accident mors et tués.

202.   La gisoit ung roy d'Angleterre,
        Henry, qui fut plain de simplesse.
        Son escript monstroit a l'enquerre
        Qu'il ne fut pas homme de guerre
        Ne prince de grant hardiesse.
        Nez fut de tresroyal haultesse,*
        Mais Accident a definé
        Ce noble roy mal fortuné.

200.1 mort *om.* R (*-1*) | sus Y | pesat OW
200.2 Ou prince [*sic*] T | Ung grand pr. O/M | ont jalay P, ou je aloye O (+*1*) | tout le cours V
200.3 Si fut MX
200.4 a lestomac Q/MX
200.5 pleurs Q (cours : nemours)
200.7 Trouue [= *trouvé*] E
200.8 Et en M (+*1*)

201.2 vray fruit FGSQ
201.3 desray Q (roy : terroy)
201.4 mort *BEFGLMNPQRSV/X*

200.   Lying dead on a pallet there was
       A prince to whom I quickly went:
       It was the Count of Armagnac.
       It made me feel really ill
       And to utter sighs and tears.
       Also, the good Duke of Nemours
       I found, killed by Accident
       And buried in this cemetery.

201.   There was the King of Sicily,
       Honor's proper fruit and true tree:
       Debility killed him by a ruse.
       And also I saw dead in this ground,
       Lying under a marble tomb,
       Two of his sons, dukes of Calabria,
       Most virtuous and renowned,
       Dead, killed by Accident.

202.   A king of England lay there,
       Henry, who was full of simplicity.
       On examination, his inscription showed
       That he was not a man of war
       Nor a prince of great mettle.
       He was most royally highborn,
       But Accident put an end to
       This ill-fortuned noble King.

201.5   Gisant *LSV* | sur un *BER*, sus vng *T* | tombel *N*
201.6   duc *M*
201.7   Mont *L*

202.1   le roy *M*
202.3   Son dicton *B* | et lenquerre *E*, et lonquerre [*sic*] *Q*
202.4   Qui ne *BEFGNPW/M* | ne fust *S*, nestoit *V* | guerres *W*
202.5   prince *om. E* (*-2*)
202.6   Mez *G*, Mais *S*, Ne *L/X*, Il *M* | tresroyale *LV* (*+1*), tresloyal *M*
202.7   Ac. qui tout termine *O*, qui tout dermyne [*sic*] *M*
202.8   Le *S*. Luy donna trop malle fortune *O/M*; le noble roy de mal fortune *X*.

203.   Je trouvay soubz grant apparance
         Gisant mort la noble personne
         De Charles, le grant roy de France,
         Septiesme du nom d'excellence,
         Qui moult esleva sa couronne.
         Sa fin fut vertueuse et bonne :   [63]
         Debile en fut le droit murdrier
         Comme d'un simple chevalier.

204.   Le duc de Guienne choisy,
         Gisant tout mort en my la voye,
         Par Accident qui l'ot saisy
         Et, de telle mort ou quasy,
         Son nepveu le duc de Savoye.
         Le duc Jehan, que je regretoye,
         De Cleves, viz la mort gesir,
         Que Debile avoit fait finir.

205.   Tout hors du terroy chrestïen
         Viz ung qui les autres passa
         En tous triumphes sans moyen :
         C'est le Turc, ce poissant payen
         Qui douze regnes subjugua
         Et deux empires conquesta.
         Grant fut cest Amoras Bahy
         Mais Debile l'a esbahy.

206.   Se Mathusael devenoye,
         Qui vesquit plus de neuf cens ans,

203.1 Jay trouue *FG*, Je trouue *X* | grande ap. *V*
203.3 grant *om. M* (*-1*)
203.4 de ce nom *QS* (*+1*)
203.6 La fin *V*
203.7 meurtrier *M*

204.1 duc degmene [*sic*] *X* (*-1*) | g. je ch. *L* (*+1*)
204.3 qui la *FG*, qui leust *S* | choisy *FGSV/M*
204.5 Son nepueur *BLV*
204.8 avoit *BEFGLNOPQRSV/MXZ*] ot *CT/Y* (*-1*), eut *A* (*-1*), eult *W* (*-1*) | faict morir *O/M*

203.   Under much magnificence I found,
        Lying dead, the noble person
        Of Charles, the great King of France,
        Seventh of that excellent name,
        Who greatly advanced his crown.
        His end was virtuous and seemly:
        Just like a plain knight
        Debility was his real killer.

204.   I espied the Duke of Guienne
        Lying quite dead in the path
        By Accident who had taken him
        And with a like death or almost,
        His nephew, the Duke of Savoie.
        To my great regret, Duke Jehan of Cleves
        I saw lying dead there,
        To whom Debility had written finish.

205.   Completely outside Christian territory
        I saw someone who surpassed the others
        In all triumphs without measure:
        It was the Turk, that powerful pagan
        Who subjugated a dozen realms
        And conquered two empires.
        This Sultan Amurat was great
        But Debility overpowered him.

206.   If I were to be like Methuselah,
        Who lived more than nine hundred years,

205.1 Tout hault *N* | terroy *AEFGLNPSTVW/MXYZ* (teroy *R*)] terray *C*, terroir *B*,
       terrouer *Q*
205.2 qui tous autres *V/M*, qui tous les au. *X* (*+1*)
205.3 Qui tous *X*, En tout *S* | tri*u*mphe *W*
205.4 Cest ce t. *MX* | et puissant *FG/MX*
205.5 regne [*sic*] *V*
205.7 mehemet begny *NP*, mahomet beigny *E*, maho*m*met bigny *X*, mahommet banny
       O/M, mehemer begny *QS*

Stanza 206 om., O.
206.1 Ce m. *E* | mathieu sale *BLRV/X* | deuoye *M* (*-1*)
206.2 ans *om. E/M* (*-1*)

Et puis se tousjours j'escrivoye
Les mors qu'en ce lieu je trouvoye,
Si me seroit petit le temps,
Sy prendront en gré les lisans :
Chascun en peut assés pensser
Et n'est besoing de les tanner.

207.   La viz gesir desoubz les lames,
Par nombre non a extimer,
Empereïs, roÿnes, dames,*
Duchesses, contesses et fames,   [64]
Tant qu'on ne les sçaroit nombrer.
Je me passe de les nommer,
Mais beauté, haulteur ne vertu
N'y a contre la Mort valu.

208.   Les evesques et bonhommeaux,
Les papes et simples convers,
Les mendiens et cardinaulx,
Patriarches et piés deschaux—
Tous sont la gisans a l'envers.
La Mort les fait mengier aux vers
Et sont leurs os si tres semblables
Qu'ilz ne sont point recougnoissables.

206.3 Et puis si *V*, Et plus que *BEFGLNPQS/MX*, Et plus *et R* | je escriproie *L*,
rescripuoye *R*

206.4 Le mors *G* | que ie leu [*sic*] ie tr. *FG* | je *om. M (-1)*

206.6 prendrons *PW* | gres *L*, grey *V*

206.7 Ch. ne peult [*sic*] *M* | assez perser [*sic*] *FG. Line om., L.*

206.8 de leurs [*sic*] *X*, de leur *M* | nommer *ENPQS/MX*, vexer [*?*] *V. Following this line*
L adds, in a later, less careful hand, car tous ne les saroye no*m*mer (+*1*).

207.1 Ie vis *S* | veids yssir [*sic!*] *V*, veiz gisi [*sic*] *X*

207.2 non acertene [*?*] *L*, non a exciter [*sic*] *M*

207.3 Emperieres *ABEFGNPQ/X*, Empereres *S*, Empereurs *VW (-1)*; En derriere *O*, En
derrieres *M* | roynes et d. *EFGLNPQSV/MX*, roingnes et d. *O*; royennes, dames
B

207.4 *et* fememinez *R* (+*2*)

And then if I were to write all the time
Of the dead whom I found in that place,
It would be little time for me,
So the readers will be grateful:
Everyone can think of enough;
There is no need to bore them.

207. I saw lying there under the slabs
In countless number
Empresses, queens, ladies,
Duchesses, countesses and wives,
So many that no one may know their number.
I forbear to name them.
But beauty, high rank and virtue
Were of no avail against Death.

208. Bishops and friars,
Popes and simple lay brothers,*
Beggars and cardinals,
Patriarchs and barefoot pilgrims—
All lie there on their backs.
Death makes them a feast for worms
And their bones are so similar
That they are completely indistinguishable.

207.5 ne la *V*, ne le *X*
207.8 Na *EFGNP*, Ne a *M*, *QS/X* (*-1?*) | riens c. *FG* | la mort rien v. *EM*, la m. riens
v. *NP*

208.1 bons hommeaulx *RV*, et les bons hommeaulx *B* (*+1*)
208.2 Les papes, les s. *B* | *com*meres *R*
208.3 Les medians *V* | Les mendians les c. *BEFGNPSVW/X*, et les c. *Q* (*+1*)
208.4 et pied d. *M*; et peres d. *FGQS/X* (*+1*), et poytes d. *E* (*+1*)
208.5 Sont la tous g. *E* | la *om. M* | gisant *VW/M* | et lenuers *R*, a la renuerse *M*
208.6 m. es vers *E*
208.7 les os *ELR* | os *om. Q* (*-1*)
208.8 Qui ny sont *B* | pas r. *L* | recongnoissable [*sic*] *R*

209.   Les empereurs et les cocquins,
       Les mecanicques et les rois,
       Contes et ducs et galopins,
       Les bedeaux et les echevins,
       Povres, riches, sotz et adroix,
       La Mort a tout pris a la roix*
       Et n'en laira par ses cautelles
       Ung seul pour dire les nouvelles.

210.   Les converses et les prieuses,
       Les abbesses et les novisses,
       Damoiselles devocieuses,
       Mondaines et religieuses,
       Possessans et sans benefices,
       La Mort en a fait sacrefices :
       Toutes a pris, toutes prendra ;
       Tout est pourry et pourrira.

211.   Et me dist pour tout reconfort
       Fresche Memoyre pour concluire :   [65]
       « Tu voiz les euvres de la Mort :
       Riens n'y vault puissance ne port ;
       Il te fault a cela reduire.
       Le meillieur ou l'on te peut duire,
       C'est de morir tout despeschié
       Du sinderise de pechié. »

209.2 les roix *L. Line om., O/M.*
209.3 *First* et *om. E/M* (*-1*)
209.5 folz et *EFGLNPR/X,* faulx et *M,* tors et *Q;* sotz *om. S* (*-1*) | et droiz *FGQ* (*-1*), et
       edios [?] *W* | Poures sotz, riches et a. *B*
209.6 a tous pr. *BE* | rois *ABSVW,* roys *X,* roiz *ENP,* royz *Q,* rays *L* (: adrois), raitz *M*
209.7 Et ne l. pas *M* | cautalles *FG* (: nouuelles)

210.1 Et les c. *L* (*+1*) | conuers *M* (*-1*)
210.2 et les nonnesses *V*
210.3-4 *inverted R*
210.3 D. et d. *Y* (*+1*) | *Line om., O/M.*
210.4 Mondames [*sic*] *Y* | ou r. *L*
210.5 Pocessans *EG*

209.   Emperors and tattered rogues,
       Artisans and kings,
       Counts, dukes, and scullions,
       Beadles and sheriffs,
       Poor, rich, simple or clever,
       Death has snared all in her toils
       And through her wiles will not leave behind
       A single soul to spread the news.

210.   Lay sisters and prioresses,
       Abbesses and novices,
       Maidens devout,
       Worldly and religious,
       Funded and unendowed:
       Death has made sacrifices of them,
       Has taken and will take them all.
       Everything is rotten and will rot.

211.   And to comfort me,
       In conclusion Fresh Memory said,
       "You see the handiwork of Death.
       Neither power nor presence avails against it;
       You must resign yourself to that.
       The best that anyone can teach you
       Is to die completely cleansed
       Of the painful pangs of sin."

210.7   a prinses *B* (+*1*), a prises *L* (+*1*). Tous et toutes si bas pr. *V*
210.8   ou pourrira *BL*, tout p. *EFGNPQS/MX*
This is the last of the consecutive stanzas of fragment O; it is followed by stanzas 216 and 338.

211.1   me dit *BEFGPV* | par *M* | tout *om. V (-1).*
211.2   conclure *BELQV/M,* conclurre *FGP/X*
211.4   Rien *BEQS/M* | ne vault *FG* | ny port *V*, ne fort *MX*
211.5   en cela *V*
211.6   ou l'on *om. E [gap in text],* ou len *S/M,* ou on *V,* que lon *Q* | te puit [*sic*] *FG* |
        peut dire *Q* | ou lon peult desduire *L*
211.7   de memoire [*sic*] *M (om.* tout), *X* (+*1*) | tout tout *B* (+*1*), tout se *S* (+*1*)
211.8   Dit [*sic*] *E*, De *Q*, Ou *P*; De la sinderesie *R* (+*2*?)

212.   Ce qu'elle dist c'estoit raison,
        Combien que ce fust fort a faire,
        Si rentrasmes en sa maison
        Ou il ot des biens a foison
        Pour nous desjuner et refaire.
        La dame, qui fut debonnaire,
        Me sceut si bien araisonner
        Qu'il valoit mieulx que le disner.

213.   Les choses qu'elle me monstra
        Me firent penser a loisir.
        Tout conclud ce mot s'en ala :
        « Ma dame, quant est a cela,
        Plus ne fault mon penser couvrir.
        Adviegne que peut advenir,
        L'aventure veul esprouver
        Qu'oncques hons ne pot achever. »*

214.   Lors me dist : « Et je le t'octroy
        Et si te menray celle voye. »*
        Lors demanda son pallefroy.
        Je la menay et elle moy ;*
        Heureux fuz que tel guide avoye.
        Plus tost que dire ne sçaroye
        Tous deux nous trouvasmes sans faille
        Ou devoit estre la bataille.

212.1 dit *BEFGLNRV/MX*
212.2 fut *BELNV*, fu *W* | affaire *NSW*
212.3 Et r. *L* | entrasmes *M*
212.4 Ont il eust *F*, Ont il eut *G*, Ou il eust *N*, Ou il y eut *S/M* (+*1*)
212.6 Puis la dame quest [*sic*] d. *L*
212.7 raisonner *Y* (-*1*)
212.8 Qui v. *EFGLNPQSV/MX*

213.2 Me feit p. bien a l. *V*
213.3 se mot *F/M*, ce mont [*sic*] *X* | mot en alla *BVW*
213.4 quant elle est *RW* (+*1*)
213.6 A. qui *EFGNPQ/X*, A. quil *M*
213.7 veult *X* | veulx ge espr. *V* | approuuer *B/MX*

212.　　What she said was right,
　　　　However hard to do.
　　　　Then we reentered her house
　　　　Where there was plenty of provision
　　　　For us to eat and restore ourselves.
　　　　The lady, who was gracious,
　　　　Knew so well how to converse with me
　　　　That it was worth more than the meal.

213.　　The things that she showed me
　　　　Made me muse a while.
　　　　Finally, this speech came to me:
　　　　"Madame, as for that,
　　　　I need no longer conceal my thought.
　　　　Let come what may,
　　　　I wish to try that adventure
　　　　Which no man was ever able to accomplish."

214.　　Then she said, "I will grant it to you
　　　　And I will show you that way."
　　　　Then she called for her palfrey.*
　　　　I escorted her and she me;
　　　　I was happy to have such a guide.
　　　　Sooner than I can say
　　　　We both found ourselves without a doubt
　　　　Where the battle would take place.

213.8　Quoncques ne peult ho*mm*es *W* (+*1*) | ho*m*e *M* (+*1*), ho*mm*e *R* (+*1*), hommes *V* (+*1*) | peut *AEQ*, peult *BLPV/MX*, puet *N*, peust *FGS* | escheuer *FGNPQ/MX*, eschiuer *E*

214.1　dit *BEFG*, dict *V* | je loctroy *EQRSW/M* (-*1*), t'ouctroye *B*, totroye *X*
214.2　te *om*. *S* (a celle v.) | menray *ABELPQRSTVW/YZ* (merray *N*)] menre *C*, muray [*sic*] *F/X*, mure [*sic*] *G* | telle v. *M*
214.3　Si d. *EFGNP/MX*, Et d. *LQS*
214.4　Je le *M/X* | menay *ABFGLNPRSTV/XYZ* (lamenay *EQW*)] mene *C*; menray *M* | et elle et moy *M*
214.5　quant tel *EFLS/X*, quand tel *R*, quant telle [*sic*] *GQ/M* (+*1*)
214.6　sauoye *EFGNPQS/MX*

215.　A l'aproucher j'oÿs effroy :　　　　　　　　　　[66]
　　　Grant tourbe de gens et murmure
　　　Cops ferir comme a ung tournoy.
　　　Trop douloureux fut l'esbanoy
　　　Et trop desplaisant l'envoisure.
　　　Ung perron devant la closture
　　　Trouvay, a grans lectres dorees
　　　Ou j'ay telz parolles trouvees :

216.　Cy fine le Chemin mondain
　　　Cy fine la Sente de vie ;
　　　Cy se fiert le pas inhumain
　　　Dont Atropos, juge soudain,
　　　A le pouoir et seignourie.
　　　Nulz n'y entre qui ne desvie :
　　　Deux champions a si tres fors
　　　Qu'ilz ont tous les ancestres mors.

217.　Accident combat le premier ;
　　　Peu en actaint qui luy eschappe.
　　　S'il fault, lors vient le grant murtrier
　　　Debile, Prince d'Encombrier,
　　　Qui tout occist et tout actrappe.
　　　Riens n'y vault cuirasse ne cappe :
　　　Vecy la mortelle adventure
　　　Ou prent fin toute crëature.

215.1　jouy Q, joy W | leffroy EFGNQSV/X, desfroy M
215.2　Grans turbes B/M
215.3　com L | tournay FGLQV/X, tournoye W
215.4–5　inverted, S
215.4　fut a les. B (+1) | lesbanay V, lesbauoy X. Voluntiers fusse retourne M
215.5　trop om. L (la envoisure). Pour euiter telle aduenture M
215.6　sa closture S
215.7　grant F, grand V [sic, with plural noun and adjective]
215.8　ches p. R | telles p. AEGW/M (+1), ces p. L

216.1　Cy finist QS, Cy finy V
216.2　Cy finist QS | la saincte [sic] O, la sancte V, la sante M

215.   Approaching, I heard the stir:
         The mutter of a great crowd of people,
         Blows struck as at a tourney.
         The sport was most distressful
         And the gaiety too displeasing.
         Before the pales I found a stone marker,
         Gilded in huge letters,
         Whereon I found these words:

216.   HERE ENDS THE WORLDLY ROUTE.
         HERE ENDS THE PATH OF LIFE.
         A CRUEL TOURNEY IS HELD HERE
         OVER WHICH SWIFT JUDGE ATROPOS
         HAS SWAY AND LORDSHIP.
         NO ONE ENTERS THERE WHO IS NOT LOST.
         SHE HAS TWO SUCH STALWART CHAMPIONS
         THAT THEY HAVE KILLED ALL THOSE WHO'VE GONE BEFORE.

217.   ACCIDENT DOES BATTLE FIRST;
         FEW THAT HE TOUCHES ESCAPE HIM.
         IF HE FAILS, THEN COMES THE GREAT MURDERER
         DEBILITY, PRINCE OF AFFLICTION,
         WHO ENSNARES AND KILLS EVERYONE.
         ARMOR AND HELM AVAIL NAUGHT THERE:
         HERE IS THE MORTAL ADVENTURE
         WHERE EVERY CREATURE COMES TO AN END.

216.3 Si *E* | ce f. *EL/M* | fyer *X* | le plus *EFGOQS/MX*
216.5 et la s. *W* (*+1*)
216.6 Nul *ABEFGLNPQSTVW/MX* | quil ne *M* | deuise [*sic*] *O/M*
216.8 Qui tous ont *Q* | tous *om. E* (*-1*) | les *om. R* (*-1*); noz an. *B*, leurs an. *LTV* | les
       assistans mors [*sic*] *O/M*

217.2 que luy *V*
217.3 le *om. Y* (*-1?*)
217.4 pr. de mombrier [*sic*] *W*
217.5 Qui tost *E/X* | et *om. QS* (*-1*) | et tost *EF/X* | atrappre [*sic*] *F*
217.6 Rien *A* | ne v. *EN/M* | airasse [*sic*] *E/X*, harnais ne curace *V* | c. ny chappe *FG*
217.7 Veez cy *EFGQS/X*

218.   Au perron ne fis demouree
        Ains tiray vers les lices clouses
        Pour ce que g'y viz assemblee
        Regardans debat ou meslee
        Ou aucunes estranges choses.
        La ne fus mynuctes ne poses*
        Que je viz en son eschauffault
        Atropos sëoir au plus hault.   [67]

**Cy devise la bataille faite entre
Messire Debile et le duc Phelippe de Bourgongne,
et commence la quarte partie de ce livre.**

MINIATURE 11. Atropos presides over the combat between
Debility and Philip of Burgundy

219.   **A**tropos, d'un habit divers,
             Fut paré d'estrange maniere,*
             Bendé de couleurs en travers,
        Demptelé de terre et de vers.
        Sëant en pompeuse chayere,
        Contenance monstroit tres fiere,
        Tenant ung dart de Deffiance
        Contre tel qui gueres n'y pense.

218.1   Ou *B* | demeure *S/MX* (*-1*)
218.2   Mais *LR*
218.3   g' *om. L* (*-1*) | assemblees *V*
218.4   Regardant *LQSVW/Z* | assault ou m. *T*, d. et m. *M*
218.5   Ou a au. *Z* (*+1*) | estanges [*sic*] *F*
218.6   fut *BV*, feis *M*, fis *S* | minutte *L* | pause *L*, pose *M*
218.7   a son *W*
218.8   seoit *BV*, assis *M*

Rubric. devise de la b. *NPQ/XZ* | messire *om. R/MX* | phelippes *Q/M* | la quatriesme
        AFNP/X, la quatrieme *B*, la quatreiesme [*sic*] *E*, la iiij^e *LRW/M*, la iiij. *Y*, la .iiii. *Z*
        | ce present liure *M*; de ce livre *om. LR. Rubric follows miniature in ABFGQRS;
        follows instructions in LTW/Z; follows stanza 219 in M. No rubric, V.*

218.   I did not linger at the marker
But drew near the closed lists,
For I could see the crowd
Watching the contest, the combat,
Or other strange things.
I was there no time at all
When, on her raised platform, I saw
Atropos sitting most high.

Part IV

Here is told the battle between
Sir Debility and Duke Philip of Burgundy
and here begins the fourth part of this book.

219.   Atropos, in a motley costume,
Was strangely decked out,
Filleted with crosswise colors,
Scallop-edged with dirt and worms.
Sitting on a sumptuous throne,
She displayed a very proud countenance,
Holding a javelin of Defiance
Toward someone least suspecting.

Equivalent miniature in *ABEFGR/Y*; different subject in *QS/X*.

219.1 *Line om., M.*
219.2 Feist par estrange m. *L (-1)*
219.3 Bronde *or* Broude *L* | couleur *EFGNPQS* | a tr. *M*
219.4 Demptelle *FGV/MX* | *second* de om. *V (-1)*
219.5 Et seant *M* (chaire) | pourpensee *A, L (+1)*, pompeure *M* | chiere *A*, chere *N (-1)*, chaire *S (-1)*, cheoire [*sic*] *X*
219.6 tenoit *V*
219.7 Tenant mine *M*
219.8 tiel [*sic*] qui *S* | guere *FGP*, guerre *M/X*, gaire *E*, gueire *V*

220.   Son mareschal fut Cruaulté,   [68]
        Qui tint des lices l'ordonnance.
        Son herault estoit Voulenté,
        Portant ung blason dyappré
        De couleurs de Mescougnoissance.
        Son chancelier estoit Doubtance,
        Portant le seau dont me soussye,
        Armoyez de Nulz-ne-s'y-fie.

221.   Les lices furent de Douleurs,
        Des mains Tristresse charpentees ;
        Le pavilon fut de Clameurs,
        Les banieres furent de Pleurs,
        Ou costé l'appellant plantees,
        Et les gardes des deux entrees
        Furent, je ne l'oubliay mie,
        Felle Despit et Villonnye.

222.   Le pavillon du deffendeur
        Estoit tresrichement broudé
        De Toute Bonté et Doulceur ;
        Les banieres furent d'Honneur,
        Qui moult bien paroit ce costé.
        Le herault ot nom Bien Amé,
        Qui portoit blason de Prouesse
        Couronné d'Entiere Noblesse.

220.2   tient *V* | les l. *E* | lardonnance *X*
220.4   Pourtant *F* | ung baston couloure [?] *M*
220.5   couleur *V*
220.6   Son cheualier *EW*, Son cheual [*sic*] *M* (de d.), *X* (*-1*)
220.7   Pourtant *FGPV* | le *om. V* (seel), le seel *BL* (+*1*), le feau [*sic*] *S* | dune soucye *M*
220.8   Armoye *EFGLNPQST/X*, Enuoyez *A* | En telz armes *M* | nul *LQS/M* | se fie
        EV

221.1   de doulceurs [*sic*] *X*
221.2   mains de tr. *FGNPQS/X* (+*1*) | tristresses *W*, tristesses *M*
221.3   clamours *L* (: douleurs, *l. 1*)
221.4   plours *L*

220.   Her marshal was Cruelty,
       Who had command of the lists.
       Her herald was Willfulness,
       Carrying a shield patterned
       With Ignorance's colors.
       Her chancellor was Fear,
       Carrying the seal, which worried me,
       Bearing the arms of Let No One Be Confident.

221.   The lists were of Sorrows,
       Fashioned by the hands of Sadness;
       The pavilion was of Complaints;
       The banners of Tears
       Were planted beside the challenger.
       And the guards at the two entries were
       (I couldn't forget)
       Wicked Scorn and Baseness.

222.   The defender's pavilion
       Was very richly embroidered
       With All Good and Sweetness.
       The banners were of Honor,
       Which decorated this side very well.
       The herald was called Beloved
       And carried the arms of Prowess
       Crowned by Complete Nobility.

221.5   Au coste *R/M*, Du coste *QS*, Du costel *V* | pensees [*sic*] *E*
221.6   les garde [*sic*] *M* | de deux *V/M*
221.7   lobliray *V*, loublye *X*
221.8   Felon *Q*, Filles [*sic*] *L*, Fel le d. *X*, Fiel le d. *M*, Cest le d. *V*

222.2   bourde *FG/X*, borde *Q/M*
222.4   houneur *C, corrected from* hounour
222.5   paroient *EL/X* (+*1*), *M* | se coste *E*, ceste [*sic*] c. *R* (+*1*); p. en ceste *M* | coustel
        V (: broude, ayme)
222.6   eust *FW*

223.　Voulenté en la place sault
　　　Et fist cris par toute la lice
　　　Que nulz, par signes bas ne hault,
　　　N'avantagast en cest assault,
　　　Sur paine qu'on ne le pugnisse.
　　　Puis, afin que tout se fournisse,
　　　Il cria : « Laissez les aler !
　　　Chascun pense de se monstrer. »　　　　　　[69]

224.　Lors saillit de son pavillon
　　　Debile, portant deux guisarmes :
　　　L'une fut Persecucion
　　　Et l'autre Consummacion
　　　Pour le dernier cop et fait d'armes.
　　　De sables fut sa cocte d'armes,
　　　Ou fut pourtrait et figuré
　　　Ung homme mort tout descharné.*

225.　Et pour fournir ceste besougne,
　　　Le deffendant sault d'autre part
　　　Vestu des armes de Bourgougne :
　　　Honneur le conduit et ensougne
　　　Et ne le laisse tost ne tart.
　　　Ce fut celui ou Dieu a part,
　　　Phelippe, que l'on ama tant,
　　　Le plus grant des ducs de Ponnant.

223.1　Vaillance en *E* (*-1*)
223.2　Qui f. *M* | cry *FGNPQSV*, crier *E/X* (*+1*) | parmy la *M* (*-1*) | la lite [*sic*] *X*
223.3　nul *LQS/M* | signe *QRSV/M* | ny h. *FGN*, et h. *E*
223.4　ceste as. *B*
223.5　Su *B* | que lon le *ENPQ/X*, que len le *S*, que on le *M*
223.6　ce f. *L*; que on le f. *M*
223.7　laisser *N*, laisses *S*
223.8　Ch. painne de *L* | soy m. *BNV*, ce m. *GL*

224.1　faillit [*sic*] *X*, saillant *M*
224.2　jusarmes *L*
224.5　dernier *ABFGPRSTVW/YZ*] darenier *C* (*+1*), darrier *L*, derrain *Q*, derrenier *EN*
　　　(*+1*)

223. Willfulness leapt into the open space
      And announced through all the list
      That no one, by signs low or high,
      Should have advantage in this assault,
      On pain of punishment.
      Then, so that everything might be as it should,
      He cried, "Let them come!
      Let each one think to prove himself."

224. Then from his pavilion sprang forth
      Debility, carrying two long guisarmes:*
      One was Persecution,
      The other Consummation
      For the last blow and attack.
      His coat of arms was black,
      Whereon was portrayed and represented
      A dead man, stripped clean.

225. And to further this business,
      The defender bounded forth from the other side,
      Clad in the arms of Burgundy.
      Honor escorted and coached him,
      And left him neither early or late.
      This was he in whom God had an interest,
      Philip, who was so beloved,
      The greatest of the dukes of the West.

224.6 Du s. *S* | sable *EFGLNPQSV/MX* | sur sa *FGNPQS/MX*. *Line is in eighth position, R.*

224.7 Qui fut [*sic*] *MX*

224.8 Une ho*m*me [*sic*] *S* | mort et d. *EFGNPQS/X* | descharne *EFGLNPQRSV/MXZ*] desarme *CABT/Y*, descheuele [*?*] *W* (+*1*)

225.1 furnir *BRVW* | cest *W* (-*1*) | besougne *as elsewhere in C* (besongne *ABEFGPQRT/YZ*)] besougnie [*sic*] *C*, besoingne *NSVW*, besoigne *L/X*

225.2 Le deffendeur *LQ* | fault [*sic*] *X*

225.4 enseigne *EFGLNPQ/MX*, enseigne *BS*, ensoingne *V*

225.5 le *om. W* (-*1*) | laise *X* | ny tard *FG*

225.6 eust p. *F*, eut p. *G*, ait p. *A/M*

225.7 Ph. duc quon *M* | quon *W/X* (-*1*), que len *S*; quon ayma ja tant *V*

225.8 pouuant *FG/X*. des ducz et vaillant *M*

226.   Il tenoit en sa dextre main
        Une lance de Bon Advis ;
        En l'autre je viz tout a plain
        Ung tergon tout paré et plain
        De Los, de Pouoir et d'Amis.
        Et pour le tout estre au vray mis,
        Sa hache fut de Fermeté
        Contre l'assault d'Aversité.

227.   Debile sembloit moult a craindre
        Et branloit ung dard de Grevance,
        Monstrant qu'il ne se veult pas faindre
        Et s'il peult sa partie actaindre,
        Il est mort ou mis a oultrance.
        Le bon duc paulmioit sa lance*   [70]
        Et sembloit bien ung chevalier
        Qui ne daigneroit desmarcher.*

228.   Ainsi marcherent fierement
        L'un sur l'autre les dessus dis.
        Debile tout premierement
        Jecta son dart de Griefvement
        Et cuida avoir tout conquis,
        Mais le duc, qui estoit apris
        Comme ung asseuré champion,
        Receupt le cop a son tergon.

226.3 Et en lautre vys Q | anplain W
226.4 teigon [sic] X. Line follows line 6, RS; in left margin, lines 4–7, R, letters b, c, a, d
       indicate the proper order of lines. In S a v-shaped symbol indicates the proper position
       of the displaced line.
226.5 et dauis FG, et damyer [sic] X

227.3 qui ne EFG | voult ALS/M | pas om. M (-1)
227.4 Et si V
227.5 est om. R (-1) | mort et mis BV, m. et occis M (+1) | en ou. X

226. He grasped in his right hand
 A javelin of Good Advice,
 And I saw plainly in the other
 An embellished shield full of
 Praise, Power, and Friends,
 And so that everything is truly noted,
 His battle axe was of Firmness*
 Against the assault of Adversity.

227. Debility appeared much to be feared
 And he brandished a javelin of Grievance,
 Showing that he had no desire to yield
 And that if he came to grips with his adversary,
 He was defeated or dead.
 The good duke brandished his lance
 And surely seemed a knight
 Who would not deign to give ground.

228. Thus proudly they advanced
 Toward each other, those of whom I spoke.
 Debility at the very first
 Threw his javelin of Grievance
 And thought he had won out,
 But the duke who was accomplished,
 As is a confident champion,
 Took the blow on his shield.

227.6 paulmioit *ATW/YZ* (palmioit *L*, palmyoit *B*, palmoioit *V*)] paulimoit *C*, palmiot [*sic*] *R*; demenoit *EFGNPQS/MX*

227.8 Qui neust daignie d. *T* (*-1*), ne se daignoit d. *V*

228.1 fermement *MX*

228.2 sus laultre *V* | des d. *SW/M*

228.4 Gectant *MX* | de *om. M* (*-1?*)

228.5 cuida tout avoir c. *B* | tant c. *M* | coquis [*sic*] *G*

228.6 est. tout apris *A* (*+1*)

228.8 en son t. *M*

229.   De ce cop le duc se deffit,
        Monstrant chevalereux devoir.
        Son get mist avant et parfit
        Si bien qu'a peu qu'il ne deffit
        Debile qui monstroit pouoir.
        Lors chascun se fist la valoir ;
        Chascun vouloit estre vaincqueur
        De la bataille et de l'onneur.

230.   Le duc prist son bec de faucon,
        Qui fut de Fermeté cloué,
        Et Debile le Tres Felon
        Frapoit de Persecucion
        Grans cops tous plains d'enfermeté.
        Chascun ot fiere voulenté :
        L'un fiert, l'autre rabat ou maille
        En celle cruelle bataille.

231.   Memoire monstroit esperance
        Que le duc vaincroit la journee
        Pour la tres aspre resistance
        Dont pluseurs fois fit apparance*   [71]
        Contre Accident a la meslee.
        Mais Debile par destinee
        Doubtoit, pour ce qu'il fiert et blesse
        De cops qui viennent de feblesse.

229.1 A ce S | se defendy desfit [sic] Y (+3)
229.3 mect ABELNPQRSTVW/X, | prouffit E, perfist X, partist M
229.4 a peu [sic, qu' om.] E, que peu X | qui ne EFG; qu' om. VW
229.5 quil Q | moustra S
229.6 Las M | si fit E | la om. W/M (-1); a valoir EFGLQS/X
229.8 l' om. QS (-1?)

230.4 Feroit [sic] L, Frappa X
230.5 tous om. EQ (-1); tout plain VW, tous plain [sic] F | de fermete SV/M
230.6 eust FS
230.7 fiert et lautre frappe E | et maille BEFGNPQSVW/MX

229.   The duke saved himself from this blow,
        Demonstrating his knightly readiness.
        He threw his dart forward and did so well*
        That he almost defeated
        Debility, who was displaying strength.
        Thus each one earned valor for himself;
        Each wished to be the winner
        Of both battle and honor.

230.   The duke seized his pole axe
        Which was riveted by Firmness,
        And Most Fell Debility
        With Persecution struck
        Great blows all full of infirmity.
        Each one had a fierce desire;
        One struck, the other parried or hammered back
        In that cruel battle.

231.   Memory gave signs of hope
        That the duke might win the day
        By his most sharp resistance
        Which he displayed many times
        Against Accident in this fight.
        But as ordained, he feared Debility
        Because he strikes and wounds
        With blows that come from feebleness.

Stanzas 231–235 are missing from T.

231.1   monstrant *L* | experiance *E* (+*1?*)
231.3   Par *V* | la *om. M* (-*1*) | tres *om. L* (-*1*)
231.4   fut ap. *E. Line om., M.*
231.5   en la *EFGNPQS/MX,* et la *L*
231.6   desiner [?] *V*
231.7   Doubtant *L,* Doubloit [*sic*] *M* | qui f. *F,* que f. *G*
231.8   Des c. *M,* Des corps [*sic*] *L* | quilz viengnent *V*

232.   Pour sçavoir d'armes le mestier,
       Apprendre on peult a ceste escole.
       Se l'assaillant est dur et fier,
       Le deffendeur fait a prisier :
       Se l'un mehaigne, l'autre affole.
       Hardement par my le champ vole
       Pour resbaudir les champions,*
       Qui vault d'or trente milions.

233.   Tant ont et feru et maillé,
       Chascun d'eux sans faire reprise,
       Que le plus sain fut mehaignié,
       Foullé, grevé et traveillé
       Et affebly en moult de guise.
       Mais Debile monstra maistrise,
       Car d'un cop soudain d'un quasterre
       Mist mort le noble duc par terre.

234.   Ainsi fut le duc abatu,
       Dont Atropos la foursenee
       Pour ce noble prince vaincu
       N'en tint non plus que d'un festu
       Et ne luy fut q'une risee,
       Monstrant qu'elle est acoustumee,
       Et prent son singulier plaisir,
       A voir gens finer et mourir.

232.2   On peult app. *R* | Sapprendre *FGNQS/MX* | peust *QS* | en cest *EFGQ*, en ceste
        S
232.3   Si *QS/X* | lassaillant *BLQRW/YZ*] laissaillant *CAS*, laissaillent *F*, lassaillent *GNP/*
        X, lasaillant *EV*, laissalant *M* | et dur *FG* | dure *W* | et fiert [*sic*] *V*
232.4   Le deffendre est a pr. *M*
232.5   affoule *S* (: volle)
232.6   Hardyement *M* (+*1?*) | le camp *RV*
232.7   resbaudir *BLQRSW/YZ* (rebaudir *EFGNP/MX*)] resbandir *CA*, resnandir *or* resuan-
        dir *V*
232.8   vallent dor *EPQS*, *N* (+*1*) | deux m. *Q*, xx m. *EP*, vingt m. *S*, mille millions *B*

233.1   ont feru *QS/X* (-*1*), *E* (tant ont m.); eut feru *M* (et tant m.) | maillay *NP*
233.3   sains [*sic*] *W*

232. One can learn at this school
To know the art of arms.
If the assailant is aggressive and fierce,
The defender rises to the occasion:
If one maims, the other wounds.
Audacity, who is worth thirty million,
Flits about the field
To cheer on the champions.

233. They struck and hammered so much,
Each one without pause,
That the healthiest was injured,
Bruised, scratched, and harried,
Weakened in many ways.
But Debility showed his mastery
For, with a flail's sudden blow,*
He laid the noble duke dead on the ground.

234. Thus was the duke brought low,
That noble prince defeated,
For whom mad Atropos
Cared no more than for a straw
And to whom he was laughable,
Showing that she makes it her practice
And takes her strange pleasure
In seeing people be killed and die.

233.4 Folle *FG*, Foulez *V* | greuez *V*
233.5 en maint de *FG*, en maincte g. *M*, en mainte g. *X*
233.6 monstre *Q*, monstroit *S*
233.7 souldain cop *BV* | jusqua terre *RS*
233.8 Mist le n. d. mort *W* | pour t. *R*

234.1 Aussy *X*
234.4 Ne t. *M* | t. nen plus *EFG*
234.5 que r. *Y (-1)* | rosee *S/X*, rusee *M*
234.6 quellest [*sic*] *S* | estoit *W (+1)*
234.7 Et par [*sic*] *L*, Et print *M*
234.8 veoir *BEFLNPQSV/MX*, veoyr *G*

235.   Lors heraulx comme bien appris
         Prindrent ung drap tissu de Gloire   [72]
         Et l'ont sur le noble corps mis,
         Porté en terrë et assis*
         Ou saint lieu de digne memoire,
         Ou on le trouvera encore*
         Quant le monde definera,
         Ne jamais n'en departira.

Comment le duc Charles de Bourgongne combatit Accident.

MINIATURE 12. Atropos presides over the joust between
         Charles of Burgundy and Accident

236.   A paines fut levé le corps,
           Ou du mains en sepulchre mis,
           Que j'oÿs le bruit par dehors
         De deux ostz tres puissans et fors,
         Chascun paré de ses amis.
         Accident le premier je viz   [73]
         Qui sur le renc se vint embatre,
         Monté et armé pour combatre.

237.   Cheval ot bardé d'Arrogance,
         Son harnas trempé de Couroux ;
         Malheur avoit ferré sa lance.
         L'espee fut d'Oultrecuidance,

235.1 Les *BEFG* | herault [*sic*] *W/M*
235.3 sur ce n. *R*. Et lont ainsi sur le corps mis *V*
235.4 Pourtay [*sic*] *G* | Et pourte en terre *V*
235.5 Au siege de *M* | lieu de diuine m. *L*
235.6 Ou l'on le *BELV* | encoires *V*
235.7 defmera [*sic*] *Y*. Tant que le m. durera *M*
235.8 Et j. *M* | nen partira *W/X* (*-1*)

Rubric. Comme le *FLS* | Charle [*sic*] *Y* | de Bourgongne *om. R* | comb. messire A.
         EFLNPQS/MX | *et* coment il fut vaincu *added, in a different hand, at end of rubric,*
         P. Rubric follows miniature in AFGQRS/X; follows instructions in LTW/Z. No
         rubric, V.

235.   Then the well-trained heralds
         Took a flag woven by Glory
         And put it over the noble body,
         Buried it in the ground, placed
         In a holy place of worthy memory
         Where one will still find it
         When the world ends,
         Nor will it ever leave.

How Duke Charles of Burgundy contended against Accident.

236. Scarcely had the body been picked up
              Or at least put in the sepulcher,
              When I heard a noise outside
         Of two very powerful, strong hosts,
         Each reinforced by its friends.
         I saw Accident first
         Who came to rush into the list,
         Mounted and in armor for combat.

237.   His horse was barded by Arrogance,*
         His armor tempered by Anger;
         Misfortune had tipped his lance.
         His sword was from Presumption,

Equivalent miniature in *ABEFGQRS/Y*; combatants labeled "accident" and "le cheualier delibere" in *X*.

236.1   A peine *BEFGLQTV/MX*, A poine [?] *S*
236.2   du maintz *F*, du maints *G* | ou s. *EFGLNPQRSVW*, au s. *MX* | assiz *R*
236.3   iouy *A*, jouy *Q*
236.4   ostez *R* (+*1*)
236.7   les rens *L*, les ranc [sic] *M*, le rent *S* | esbatre *EFGNPQS/MX*, combattre *R*

237.1   ot] eust *F*, et *LW/MX* | bride *ENPQS/MX*

Dont maints a batus et escoux,
Et, pour donner les rudes coups,
A son arson pend une masse
De Fortune, qui tout amasse.

238. D'autre part sault ung Bourguignon,
Charles, qui fut prince doubté,
Et resembloit bien compaignon
Qui vouloit avoir sa raison
Au plus pres de sa voulenté.
Son cheval s'appelloit Fierté
Et fut armé entierement
D'un harnas fait par Hardement.

239. Sa lance fut de Haulte Emprise,
Grant Cuer luy donna son espee :
Le forgeur s'appelloit Maistrise.
Sa dague se nommoit Franchise
Pour estre vaincqueur de l'armee.
Quant j'eux sa faczon regardee,
Vice je n'y peux percevoir*
Fors seulement de trop valoir.

240. La n'ot tente ne pavillon
Ou ses armes furent ferues ;
Ce fut a l'ombre d'un buisson.
Sans bruit ne fut pas ne sans son   [74]
L'assembler de ces deux venues.

237.5 mains *BLN/YZ*, moins *MX* | a batu *FG*, abbatus *R*, abbatuz *V/X*, a abatus *W*
        (+*1*); fut batu *M*
237.8 qui tant amasse *M*

238.1 sort *E*, sourt *FGL* | bourguiguon [*sic*] *Y*
238.2 double [*sic*] *W*
238.3 compaiguon [*sic*] *Y*
238.4 sa rainson *V*, sa ranson *X*
238.8 de H. *BVW*

With which he had battered and shaken many,
And to deliver harsh blows
From his saddle bows there hung a mace
Of Fortune who gathers up everything.

238.   From another side leapt a Burgundian,
        Charles, a redoubtable prince.
        He truly seemed a knight
        Who wanted to have his way
        As near as possible to his desire.
        His horse was named Pride
        And was fully equipped
        With armor made by Audacity.

239.   High Endeavor had given him his lance,
        Great Heart his sword:
        The armorer was named Mastery.
        His dagger was called Nobility,
        In order to be the army's victor.
        When I had looked him over,
        I could find no fault
        Other than an excess of valor.

240.   There was neither tent nor pavilion
        Where his arms were struck;
        It was in the shade of a bush.
        There was no lack of racket or clatter
        When these two met in battle.

239.1 La lance *AE* | fut et *V* | hault em. *AV*
239.7 Visce *B* | je ne *M.*
239.8 vouloir *EFGNPQS/MXZ*

240.1 neust *FGNPS*
240.2 Ou ses tentes *T* | armes ne f. *Q* (+*1*) | feussent *EQS* | feaies [*sic*] *X*, pendues *M*;
       furent ferues *L modified (later hand) to* ne furent [fucent?] veues (+*1*)
240.3 en lombre *BEFGNPQSVW/MX*
240.4 et sans *ABLRTW/YZ*
240.5 Lassemblee *QSV/M* (+*1*) | ses deux *ANV/X*

Les lances qui furent agües
Coucherent tous deux d'un desir :*
Pour myeulx et actaindre et ferir.

241.   Accident hurta par despit
Sur le duc a toute puissance :
Trois fois son cheval abatit,
Dont pourtant ne se desconfit
Mais ot cueur de sa recouvrance.
Ainsi passa le cours de lance,
Qui ne fut pas a l'avantaige
De ce duc ne de son barnaige.

242.   Les espees furent saisies
Pour mieulx assouvir ce debat ;
La monstroit chascun ses envyes—
Le jeu ne touchoit que a leurs vies !*
En tel peril est qui combat :
Art, escremie ne rabat
Ne peut ad ce besoing servir ;*
En fin fault ou vaincre ou morir.

243.   Le duc, qui fut vaillant et fier,
Mist son corps a toute deffense,
Mais Accident pour le dernier
Empoigna son baston murdrier :
C'est la masse de Malveullance

240.6   f. rompues FG
240.7   Coucherent BEFGLNP/MXZ] Toucherent CART/Y; Couchoient QS, Coucheirent
         V, Trencherent W | deux om. M (-1)
240.8   Pour trop mieulx at. M | first et om. BEFGNPQRSVW/X (-1?)

241.2   Sus Y
241.4   ne fut FG/M, ne le [?] E
241.6   le cour V
241.8   son breuaige [sic] X

242.1   La espees L
242.2   assuiuir FG, assommer E/MX | se d. E

The finely honed lances
They both couched with one desire:
To reach out and strike best.

241.   Accident struck spitefully
At the duke with all his might:
Three times he knocked down his horse,
Whereby, however, he was not undone
But had the courage to recover.
Thus passed the course of the lance
Which was of no advantage
To this duke or to his followers.

242.   Swords were seized
To better satisfy this strife;
Each one made known his desires there—
The "sport" only involved their lives!
In such peril is he who fights:
No skill in attack or defense
Can meet this need;
In the end one must win or die.

243.   The duke, who was courageous and bold,
Took up a defensive stance,
But in the end Accident
Seized his murderous cudgel;
This was the mace of Malevolence

242.4 n'atouchoit *B* | que leurs *V/MX*, que aux v. *L* (*-1*) | leurs *ABEFGNPQSTVW/ MXYZ*] leus [*sic*] *C*, leur *R*
242.5 peril *ABEFGLNPQRSTVW/YZ*] pril [*sic*] *C* (*-1*); telz perilz *MX*
242.6 Arc [*sic*] *FS*, Aye [*sic*] *X* | nescremye *E*, estremye *X. Line om., M.*
242.7 a *BEFGLNPQRSTVW/XYZ*
242.8 En fin y fault v. *V* | *first* ou *om. NQS/M* (*-1*)

243.1 et fiert [*sic*] *V*
243.3 le darrenier *L* (*+1*), le derrenier *NQS* (*+1*)
243.4 Empoigua [*sic*] *Y*
243.5 Et la m. *M*

Que Fortune par excellance
Luy donna pour ceulx desmonter
Qui se veulent hault eslever.

244. Le duc Accident rebouta
Jousques Fortune vint en place,   [75]
Dont Accident tel cop donna
Que mort a terre trebucha
Le duc, a qui pardon Dieu face.*
De ce malheur je me solace
Qu'il mourut pour non faire faille
Dedens le champ de la bataille.

245. Se la guerre fait a louer
Pour ung honnourable excercite,
Gens d'armes bien devez plourer,
Plaindre, gemir et lamenter
Le duc Charles dont je m'acquite,
Et m'est confort que je recite
Que mon maistre ne fut vaincu
Par nul homme qui l'ait valu.

246. Mais Fortune tient en ses mains,
Par la tres divine puissance,
Tous les affaires des humains,
Tant de mauvais comme de sains.
A son plaisir en fiert et lance,

243.7 pour eulx *S*
243.8 se vouloient *L* (+*1*) | trop es. *R.*
[No significant variants, *ABEFGPTW/XZ.*]

244.1 Se duc *A*
244.2 Jusquez que F. *R* (+*1*) | vint *om. W* (-*2*)
244.4 tresbucha *BEFGLNPV/MX*
244.5 a *om. S* (-*1*) | dieu *om. R* (-*1*) | dieu pardon f. *ABEFGLNPQSTVW/MXYZ*
244.6 ce *om. R* (-*1*)
244.7 Qui m. *EFGPSV/MX* | pour ne f. *B*
244.8 le champs [*sic*] *W*

Which Fortune, as is her wont,
Had given him in order to cast down
Those who wish to raise themselves too high.

244.   The duke drove Accident back
Until Fortune came on the scene,
Whereby Accident gave such a blow
That the duke, may God forgive him,
Fell dead upon the ground.
I take comfort regarding this misfortune
Since, rather than be a coward, he died
Upon the field of battle.

245.   If war merits praise
As an honorable calling,
You men at arms must indeed weep,
Pine, mourn, and lament for
Duke Charles, to whom I pay my debt,
And it is a comfort to me that I may relate
That my master was not vanquished
By any man of equal worth.

246.   But Fortune holds in her hands
Through the most divine power
All human affairs,
The wicked as well as the upright.
She strikes and flings her darts at will,

245.1   Sa *N*, Et *S*, Ce *E* | fut *ENPS/M*, feust *Q*, fust *X*
245.2   Par *ENPQS/MX* | excercice *Q/MX* (: macquite, recite)
245.6   je *om. M* (*-1*)
245.7   ne fust *X*
245.8   quil ait *W*, qui tant *M* | vaillu *L*, voulu *V*

246.2   tresdigne *W* (*-1*)
246.3   affaire *F*
246.4   Tant des *BEFGNPSV/MX*, dez *R* | comme des *BEFGNPRV/MX*, dez *S* | saincts *Q*, sainctz *V*
246.5   plaisirt [*sic*] *G* | et fiert *R*, on f. *MX*

Car du ciel ne de l'influance
Or fust il Aristobolés
Nous n'en sçavons que par les fes.

247.   Quant on a des biens a planté
Et que le tout vient a plaisir,
On se dit de bonne heure né
Et que l'omme est bien destiné,
Car il a tout a son desir.
Mais s'il est povre au definir
Ou diffamé aucunement,
On en juge tout autrement.

248.   Dont qui veult son mal destourner   [76]
Selon la divine doctrine,
Il nous fault nos cuers retourner
A Dieu, qui peult le ciel tourner,
Qui la lune croist et decline.
C'est celuy, comme dist le Pline,*
Qui ou secret de ses ydees
Se joue de nos destinees.

249.   Ainsi ot Accident victoyre
Sur ce prince fier et puissant.
Il vivra en noble memoyre
Et sera nommé en histoire

246.6 de linfernance [*sic*] *E. Line om, M.*
246.7 Et fut *L* | fut *BEFGLNPSV/X* | ores Ari. *L* (+*1*), et A. *V.* De quoy parle A. *M*
       | aristotiles *LQVW/YZ*
246.8 le*urs* f. *L*

247.1 Q. lon *B*
247.3 Lon se *FG,* Qui se *E,* On le *V* | dist *T*
247.4 Que lhonneur est *L;* lomme *repeated A.*
247.5 Et quil a *L*
247.6 Et quil est *L* | definer *L,* destiner *M*
247.7 On [*sic*] *R* | aucunent [*sic*] *W* (-*1*)
247.8 tout *om. W* (-*1*)

Stanzas 248–262 (15 stanzas) missing, A, copied from "l'Imprimé," fol. 47ʳ–48ᵛ.

For neither from Heaven nor stars' influence,
Nor even from Aristobolus,
Do we know about her except by deeds.

247.   When someone has plenty of possessions
And everything comes at his pleasure,
He declares himself born under a lucky star,
And destiny favors that man,
For he has everything he desires.
But if he is poor at the end
Or in any way dishonored,
One judges it quite otherwise.

248.   Therefore, wishing to avert ill fortune,
According to divine doctrine
We must turn back our inner thoughts
To God who makes the Heavens go round,
Who makes the moon wax and wane.
He is the one, as Pliny says,
Who in the secrecy of His mind
Toys with our destinies.

249.   Thus did Accident prevail
Over this bold and powerful prince.
He will live in noble memory
And be called in history

248.1 destourne [*sic*] *Ai*
248.3 nous cuers [*sic*] *W* | retourne [*sic*] *Ai*
248.4 Vers celuy qui fait tout tourner *AiM. Line om., X.*
248.5–8 *A blot obscures a few letters in each of these lines, W.*
248.5 croit *R* | ou d. *W*
248.6 Cest cil *EFGNP/AiMX* | dit *BFGLNPQRSV/AiMXZ* | le proline *EFGNP/AiMX,*
     S (+1); proline *Q*
248.7 Que ou [*sic*] *FG,* Qui au *VW/AiMX*
248.8 Ce joue *E* | Se jour [*sic*] *M (-1)*

249.1 eust ac. *FNP* | accident ot v. *R*
249.2 fiert [*sic*] *V/M*
249.3 viuera *R (+1)*

Le duc Charles le Traveillant.*
De luy nous cesserons a tant
Et reviendrons par poins et pas
Ad ce qu'il advint en ce pas.

250.   Accident se voult arrester
Pour actandre nouvelle proye
Et se fit de novel armer
D'un harnas de Desesperer.
Afin que de loings on le voye,
A pied se tint en my la voye
A tout ung glave de Mesure
Que l'on nomme Male Adventure.*

251.   Ung poingnant met a son costé
Fait de Soudaine Maladie ;
Mains en a occis et tué.
Et pour avoir le champ oultré
Et plus tost vaincre sa partie,
De Secrete Merencolie
Avoit une dague affillee
Qui mainte personne a tuee.   [77]

252.   J'oÿs menestriers et clerons,
Harpes, tambourins et vïelles,
Orgues et magnicordions
Faisans obades et grans sons.

249.5   *second* le *om. AiM (-1)* | tresuaillant *BEFGLNQSV/AiMX*
249.7   pointz *E*, points *R*; pons *AiX*, ponts *M*
249.8   A ce *BQSTV/AiMY* | qui *M* | aduient *V* | a ce p. *B* | ce cas *W/M*

250.1   si v. *M*, ce v. *N* | voulut *AiMX (+1)*, voulst *N*, se veult [?] *W*
250.2   attaindre *FGS/AiMX*
250.3   se *om. R (-1)*; ce fit *E*, se mist [*sic*] *AiM*
250.4   faict de d. *M (+1)* | de desesperance *X*, de deseper [*sic*] *Ai*
250.5   de loing *BEFGQSV/AiMX*, de loint [*sic*] *L* | en le voye *W*
250.6   Apres *FQS/AiMX*, A pres *E* | ce t. *G* | ta voye [*sic*] *X*
250.7   de immesure *FG*, desmesure *S/M*
250.8   nommoit *ENPQS/AiMX*

Duke Charles the Diligent.
Now we will leave off speaking of him
And return apace
To what came about in this tourney.

250.   Accident wanted to stay
        To wait for new prey,
        And had himself armed afresh
        With an armor of Hopelessness.
        So that he might be seen from afar,
        He remained standing in the middle of the course,
        With a sword of Moderation
        Which was called Ill Luck.

251.   At his side he placed a dagger
        Made by Sudden Illness;
        Many had he slain and killed with it.
        To clear the field
        And sooner overcome his adversary,
        From Secret Melancholy
        He had a sharpened dagger
        Which has killed many a person.

252.   I heard minstrels and clarions,*
        Harps, tambourines and fiddles,
        Organs and clavichords
        Making morning serenades and mighty sounds.

251.1   son coustel *V* (: tue, oultre)
251.3   et tuez *X*
251.5   A plustost *V* | vaincu *FG*
251.8   maintes personnes *RV* (+*1*) | a tue [*sic*] *V*

252.1–4 *A blot obscures a few letters in each of these lines, W.*
252.1   Vayz m. [*sic*] *X* | menestrelz *Q*, menestretz *S*, menestries *FGR*, menestreux *L*. La
        estoient menestrelz clerons *AiM* (+*1*)
252.4   Faisant *E/M* | ambades *S*

Tout triumphoit au son d'icelles :
Chascun couroit a ces nouvelles,
Chascun demandoit que c'estoit,
Car la matiere le valoit.

253. La viz venir une lictiere
De deux licornes soustenue,
Dont l'une fut Bonté Entiere;
L'autre si fut Doulce Maniere,
La plus qui fust oncques cougneue.
Toute d'or se monstroit a veue
La lictiere et le parement,
Qui cousta mervilleusement.

254. Les deux licornes par le frain
Quatre grans princes adestroient :
Fleur de Jours fut le souverain*
Et Bon Renon Qui N'est Pas Vain —
Ces deux la premiere menoient.
Les autres deux qui la suyvoient,*
L'un fut Noble Cuer Sans Envie
Et Desdaing Contre Vilonnye.

255. Aprés suyvoit grant baronnye
Et dames a grant quantité :
Chascun triumphoit a l'envie.
Moult fut belle la compagnie

252.5 aux sons *B*
252.6 a ses n. *BENV/X*, au son dicelles *FG. Line om., AiM.*
252.8 vailloit *BLV*

253.2 soustenue *LQST/AiM* (sostenue *Z*)] soustenues *CBEFGNPRVW/X*, sostenne [*sic*] *Y*
253.3 fut om. *M* (*-1*)
253.4 Et lautre fut *EFGNPQS/AiMX*
253.5 fut *BEFGLNPQS/AiMX*, fu *W*. Plus belles que onques cogneuz *V*
253.6 Tout dor *R* (*-1*) | si se m. *V* (*+1*) | monstra *T* | a vehue *FG*
253.7 ·a ce parlement [*sic*] *Ai*

There was great rejoicing at these sounds:
Everyone went running at this novel noise,
Each one asking what it might be,
For the affair warranted it.

253.   I saw a litter come there
Borne by two unicorns,
One of which was Total Goodness
And the other Gentle Manner,
The best ever known.
The litter and all its trappings,
Which cost wondrously,
On sight appeared all gold.

254.   Four great princes led
The two unicorns by the bridle.
Flower of Days was foremost
And then Good Repute Which is No Small Thing—
These two led the first.
The two others who came after were
Noble Heart Without Spite
And Disdain for Baseness.

255.   Next came a great company of lords
And a great many ladies;
Each was striving to outshine the others.
The company was most fair,

254.1 Ces deux *E* | deux cornes [*sic*] *X* (*-1*) | le fram [*sic*] *Y*
254.2 grans prince [*sic*] *W* | demonstroient *EFGS/AiMX*, demonstroit *Q* (*-1*)
254.3 jour *RS* | le primerain *LQ/MXZ*
254.4 Au bon r. *FGQS/AiMX*, Le bon r. *V*
254.5 Ses deux *E* | la premiere memoire [*sic*] *AiM*
254.6 Les deux autres *E/M* | qui la *QT/Z*] qui le *CBEFGNPRSVW/XY*, qui les *L; no pronoun AiM* (*-1*)

255.1 grande b. *B* (*+1*)
255.2 De dames *AiX*, Des [?] d. *M* | cantitie *W*
255.4 fut *om. S* (*-1*) | sa c. *G*.

Et de richesse et de beauté.
Or est temps d'avoir racompté   [78]
De la lictiere le droit voir,
Qui vault bien le ramentevoir.

**Comment Accident combatit la duchesse d'Ostrice et,
elle vaincue, l'Acteur se veult presenter pour faire son devoir.
Et comment Atropos l'envoya contremander par Respit son herault.**

MINIATURE 13. Arrival of the Duchess of Austria;
Atropos, Accident, the Author, Fresh Memory

256.   *C* a sëoit en magnificence
         Une princesse toute armee
         Qui venoit pour prendre vengeance
     Du grief et de la desplaisance
     Que ce pas luy avoit donnee.   [79]
     Celle sembloit Penthasillee
     Qui vint la mort d'Hector venger
     Mais elle le compara chier.*

257.   Son harnas fut fait de Plaisir
        Et lui donna Bonne Pensee
        Son bacinet pour garantir
        Tout ce qui pouoit survenir
        A l'assault de celle meslee.
        Elle ot une trenchant espee*

255.7 dr. veoir *E/AiMX* (*+1?*)
255.8 la r. *R/M*, se [*sic*] r. *Ai*

Rubric. Co*mme* S | combast *B*, combat *Q*, combati *R* | a la d. *W* | vaincut [*sic*] *X* |
     l'acteur *om.* S | se voult *S/YZ*, se voulut *AiMX*; se pr*e*senta *Q* | Atropos le
     contremanda *Q* | par repos son h. *N* | par R. le h. *B*, par son h. nomme r. *L*. Et
     . . . herault *om. R*; par . . . herault *om. Q. Rubric follows miniature in FGRS; follows
     instructions in LTW/Z. No rubric, V.*
Equivalent miniature in *BFR*; different subject in *EQS/X*; miniature presumably removed,
     A.

Wealthy and handsome.
Now it is time to recount
The full truth about the litter,
Which is well worth remembering.

How Accident fought the Duchess of Austria and when
she was vanquished, the Author wished to step forward to do his duty.
And how Atropos sent her herald Delay to stop him.

256. U pon it there sat in magnificence,
       In full armor, a princess
       Who came to claim vengeance
For the injury and anguish
Which this tourney had given her.
She seemed like Penthesilea
Who came to avenge Hector's death,
But she paid dearly for it.

257. Her armor was made by Pleasure
And Good Thought had given her
Her helm to safeguard against
Everything that could come about
From the assault in this fray.
In order to best wound her adversary,

256.1 La *BEGLPQRSTVW/AiXZ*] la *CF*
256.4 Au gr. *X*
256.5 Que*n* ce *E* | ce pas ne luy *M* (+*1*) | donne *V/Ai*
256.6 Elle *QSW* | la pen. *X* (+*1*); Pantafile *Ai*, pantalisee *M*
256.7 dhector *EGRTV/YZ* (de hector *BLSW/X*, dhettor *F*, dector *N*, Dector *Ai*, d'hector
       M)] decthor *C*, dethor [*sic*] *P*; la mort hettor *Q*

257.1 fait de desplaisir *R* (+*1*)
257.4 ce quil p. *FG/M* | souuenir *LV*, souruenir *R/X*
257.5 De lassault *R* | dicelle m. *E*, de ceste *QS*, de cette *Ai*
257.6 eust *FPS* | tranchante *B*, trainchante *V*

Nommee Desir de Bien Faire
Pour mieulx grever son adversaire.

258.   Ung gavrelot ot pour gecter
Qui se nomme Plaisant Requeul*
Et le tergon pour soy garder
S'appelloit Loyaument Amer
Sans Changer ne de Cuer ne d'Eul.
Et puis, qu'oublier je ne veul,
Sa cocte d'armes je persus
Plaine de cent mille vertus.

259.   La dame de son curre sault,
Preste d'Accident rencontrer,
Et fist publier au plus hault
Par Loyauté son bon herault :
« Vecy qui se vient presenter
Au jour qu'on luy fist assigner :
C'est d'Austerice la duchesse,
Qui veult tenir foy et promesse. »

260.   Quant Accident vid sa partie
En telle beauté et valeur,
S'il ot peur je n'en doubte mie   [80]
Doubtant son emprise faillie
Et qu'il n'en saillist a honneur.
Il vëoit pouoir et hault cuer
En vingt et quatre ans seulement;
Cela l'esbahit durement.

258.1 javelot *AiM* | eust *EFGNS* | pour guetter *Q*
258.2 Et se *B* | nommoit *BEFGLNPQSVW/AiXZ* | pl. acueil *E*
258.4 loyallement *B* (+*1*)
258.5 *first* ne *om. YZ* (-*1*) | *second* ne *om. Q* (-*1*) | ne de doeil *S* (+*1*)
258.6 *Line om., M.*
258.7 Sa crete *W* | darme *T* | japperceuz *EFGNPQS/AiMX*

259.1 son chariot *L* (+*1?*), son bon gre *EFGNPQS/AiMX*, son court *et V*
259.2 recontrer *Y*
259.5 Veecy *F*, Veez cy *EGNPQS*, Veez sy *X* (*all* +*1?*), Voicy *M* | Vecy qu'il *B*

She had a keen-edged sword
Named Desire To Do Well.

258.   She had a small javelin to throw
Which was called Pleasant Harvest
And the shield to protect herself
Was named To Love Faithfully
With Unchanging Heart or Eye.
And then, something I don't want to forget,
I saw her coat of arms
Full of a hundred thousand virtues.

259.   The lady leapt from her chariot
Ready to confront Accident,
And had Loyalty, her good herald,
Proclaim most loudly:
"See who comes to present herself
On the day which was appointed to her:
It is the Duchess of Austria
Who wishes to keep faith and promise."

260.   When Accident saw his adversary
In such beauty and worth,
He was frightened, I have no doubt,
Fearing that his enterprise had failed
And that he would not come out of it with honor.
He saw before him strength and great courage
In only four and twenty years;
This dismayed him greatly.

259.7 dostriche *Ai, ELNP* (*-1*), d'Austriche *B* (*-1*), daustrice *RSVW* (*-1*), dautriche *M*,
    Q (*-1*), doctriche *X* (*-1*) | la vraye d. *AiM* (*+1*)

260.1 vid *corrected from* vit, *C*; viz *W* | la p. *X*
260.3 Cil *FGN/X* | eust *EFNP* | pour [*sic*] *E*, paour *L/Z* (je *om.*), *Q* (*+1*)
260.5 Et qui *V*, Ce quil *M* | saillit *BLPV*
260.6 Il voit *V* (*-1*), Il veit *X* (*-1*); Il vit grant p. *AiM* | et haulteur *LQST*
260.7 vingt quatre *B/Y* (*-1*), ving *et* quatre *X*
260.8 lembahit [*sic*] *V*

261.   Mais Foursenez son conseillier
        Luy dist : « Te fauldra le courage :
        Jone arbre peut on bien ployer,
        Jonesse se peut esmayer
        Par fermeté et par visage,
        Et si trouveras par usage
        Que qui l'assault de maladie,
        Mort est ains qu'il y remedie. »*

262.   Accident honteux saut avant
        Comme cil que Despit argüe.
        La dame luy vint au devant.
        Lors la navra soudainement
        D'un get de fievres continue.*
        De ce cop l'avons nous perdue,
        Halas, de Bourgougne Marie,
        Qui laisse maint ame marie.*

263.   Accident cruel et felon
        Par ce murtre desordonné
        A robé le Paladion,
        Le sort, la benediction
        Soubz qui la Bourgougne a regné.
        Ce nom est failly et finé
        Au trespas de la noble dame.
        Je prie a Dieu qu'il en ait l'ame.

261.1 foursene (for-; -senne, -cene, -cenne) *EFGLNPQRSTV/AiX*, foursenet *W*, forcené *B*,
       force ne *M*
261.2 dit *EFGPV/Ai*
261.3 peult lon *L*; on *om. G (-1)*
261.4 ce peult *L*
261.5 enfermete *Q (+1)* | par vsaige [*i.e.*, usaige] *V/AiMX*
261.6 Et cy *M*
261.8 Mors *S* | ains qu'on y r. *BP*, ains qui luy r. *EFG/X*, ains que luy *N*. Mort est tost
       qui ny remedye *AiM*

262.1 saulte *E*
262.2 cil qui *BEFGNPQRST/AiM*, sil qui [*sic*] *L*
262.3 luy vient *S*

261.   But Madness, his counselor, said to him
         "You will need to have heart:
         A young tree can easily be bent,
         Youth can be thrown off balance
         By strength and by outward show,
         And so you will find in practice
         That, when assailed by Malady,
         It will be dead before there is help."

262.   Ashamed, Accident sprang forward
         Like one whom Spite spurs on.
         The lady came to meet him
         Then he wounded her swiftly
         With a shaft of unremitting fever.
         From this blow we lost her,
         Alas, Mary of Burgundy,
         Which leaves many people sad.

263.   Cruel and wicked Accident
         By this wanton murder
         Stole away the Palladium,*
         The fortune, the blessing
         Under which Burgundy had lived.
         That name is over and done
         With the death of the noble lady.
         I pray that God may have her soul.

262.5   fievre *BLPQRSTV/Z*, fiebure *M* | continues *EFGN*
262.7   La bonne duchesse m. *BV*
262.8   laissa *MV/AiX* | mainte *QRST/AiXZ*, maincte *M*; mainctz ames merries *V*

263.1   *A's original text resumes, after a 15-stanza gap.*
263.2   Pour ce *BV*
263.3   paladium *M*
263.4   Le fort *EL/MX*
263.5   a rene *E*, sa regne [*sic*] *X*
263.6   a failly *V*, est faillit *W*
263.7   dune n. d. *A* | la bonne d. *BEFGNPQSVW/MX* | Marie de Bourgogne *added in right margin (post-medieval hand), A.*
263.8   Je pry *FGLS*, Je pri *R* | a *om. S (-1)*, a Dieu *om. M (-1)*

264.   C'estoit pour nous le Troïllus   [81]
        Dont Troyes fut reconfortee,
        Qui les Troyens a soustenus
        En couraiges et en vertus
        Puis Hector en longue duree,
        Car s'elle nous fust demeuree,
        En nous estoit de soustenir
        Ce qui nous pouoit advenir.

265.   O vous qui ce livre lisés,
        Assavourez ceste adventure.
        En ce beau miroir vous mirez :
        Par ce trespas vous passerez ;
        Beauté deviendra pouriture.
        La Mort, guerriere de Nature,
        A charge de mener a fin
        Son ennemy et son affin.

266.   Et peult chascun lisant entendre
        Que ce m'est desplaisance dure
        De voir mors et en terre estandre
        Iceulx troys a qui je doy rendre
        Amour, foy, hommaige, droicture,
        Car soubz eulx j'ay pris nouriture ;
        Ilz m'ont nourry et eslevé,
        Qui ne doibt pas estre oublié.

264.2   desconfortee [*sic!*] Q
264.4   A c. V | couraige EFGLNPQSV/X (-1). En couraige et en grands v. M
264.5   Pour L
264.6   selle ANPQRTVW/YZ, se [= s'] elle L, s'elle B] celle CEFGS/X; s' *om.* M | fut
        BFGLP, fu W
264.7   le s. V
264.8   Ce que L, Ce quil FGN

265.1   Ou vous F, Or vous M, A vous S | se liure E | lirez BV
265.2   Pensez bien a EFGNPQS/MX, Asseurez V (-1?) | cest EFGNPQ
265.3   ce bel m. FG | manoir [*sic*] QS
265.4   Car ce MX, Par cest tr. FG

264. She was our Troilus
By whom Troy was comforted,
Who sustained the Trojans
In courage and in strength
For a long time after Hector;
For if she had remained with us,
We could have endured
Whatever might come to us.

265. O you who read this book,
Take well into account this adventure.
Look at yourself in this fine mirror:
Through this transition you shall go;
Beauty will become decay.
Death, Nature's assailant,
Is charged with bringing to an end
Her enemy and her friend.

266. And each reader can understand
That for me there is fierce sorrow
In seeing laid out in the ground
Those three to whom I owe
Love, faith, homage, duty,
For from them I took sustenance;
They nurtured and raised me,
Which must not be forgot.

265.5 reuiendra [*sic*] *QS*
265.6 guerroye *EFGNPQS/MX*, guerira [*sic*] *V*
265.7 Et charche de *E*, A charger *MX* | demener [*sic*] *X*, *et* mener *M*
265.8 afin *ES*

266.1 liseur *QS*
266.2 Ce que *W* | ce nest *M*
266.3 veoir *ABEGLNPQRSV/MX*, veoirs [*sic*] *F*, voirs *W* | mort *BLV* | et *om. V (-1?)*
266.4 Ces trois la a qui (la *inserted above line*) *L*, Cez trois . et a qui *R*
266.5 foy *om. V (-1)*; Amour fait [*sic*] *X* | h. et dr. *BEFGNPQSTVW/X*
266.6 Soubz iceulx jay *LR* | ie prins *G/M*
266.7 Il *R*

267.   Quant je viz la bataille oultree
        De ceulx a qui subget je fuz,
        J'ay toute crainte despitee
        Sy ay ma visiere baissee,
        Com cil qui ne veult vivre plus.*
        Sans craindre qui me courra sus,
        A chascun en donnay le choix,
        Ou a tous deux en une fois.*   [82]

268.   Fresche Memoyre m'ynduisoit
        Qu'a Dieu je me recommandasse :
        Chascun ne fait pas ce qu'il doit,
        Car qui sent le ceur en destroit*
        La regle de raison tost passe.
        Si me mis en renc et en plasse*
        Pour l'assault d'Accident souffrir
        Ou Debille s'il veult venir.

269.   Mais il vint ung herault petit
        Qui portoit ung blason d'Actente ;
        Son nom fut En Armes Respit.
        Doulcement me parla et dit :*
        « Amis, donnez a moy entente.
        Atropos, qui droit cy regente,
        Vous mande que vous departez
        Jousqu'a ce que mandé serez. »*

267.3   Jay crainte toute d. [*sic*] *A*
267.4   baissie *W*
267.5   Comme cil *ALRV* (*+1*), Co*m*me cilz [*sic*] *W* (*+1*) | qui viure ne veult plus *LV*
267.6   me courre *MX*
267.7   en donne *G/M* | de choiz *X*
267.8   Qua *M* | deux *om. M* (*-1*) | a une f. *ABFGLNPQRSTVW/MXYZ*, par une f. *E*

268.1   mynduisoit *AFGPS/YZ* (me in- *BELQ*, min- *RTVW*, mynduysoit *N*)] myduisoit [*sic*]
        C, my duisoit *X*, me disoit *M*
268.2   je *om. L* (*-1*)
268.4   sens [*sic*] *W* | a destroit *Q*
268.5   la rigle [*sic*] *X* | raison tost *ABFGLRSTVW/MYZ*] r. trop tost *C* (*+1*); tout passe
        ENPQ/X

267.   When I saw the deadly combat
       Of those whose subject I was,
       I scorned all fear
       And lowered my visor
       Like someone who no longer cares to live.
       Without fearing who would have at me,
       To each I gave the choice
       Or to both at the same time.

268.   Fresh Memory persuaded me
       To commend myself to God:
       Each does not do what he ought,
       For he who feels his heart to be distressed
       Soon passes the bounds of reason.
       So I positioned myself
       To withstand Accident's assault
       Or else Debility's, if he chose to come.

269.   But there came a small herald
       Carrying a shield of Postponement;
       His name was Respite of Arms.
       He spoke to me kindly and said,
       "Friend, give me heed.
       Atropos, who makes the rules here,
       Sends word for you to go away
       Until you are sent for."

268.6   Se *W* | en rengs *BV*, en rue [*sic*] *L*
268.8   sy v. *E*

269.2   Quil *V*
269.3   nom *om. R* (*-1*)
269.4   ma parla [*sic*] *R* | et dist *QRSW*
269.5   Amy *ALQ* | donne a *AV* (*-1?*), donnes *LS/X* | a *om. M* (*-1*)
269.6   droit sy *E*
269.7   depportez *B*, deppourtez *V*, desportiez [*sic*] *E*, despartiez *P*
269.8   Jusques a ce *BEFLNPQRW/X* (*+1*); Jusques mandez a ce *V* | ce quamende *M* |
        soiez *EN*, soyes *S*, soyez *PQ/MX*

270.   Respit, qui n'est pas des plus grans,
        Me fist departir et retraire,
        Car Atropos en celuy temps
        Avoit assés de combatans
        Et me fault sa voulenté faire.
        Fresche Memoire debonnaire,
        Que tant je trouvay amoureuse,
        Se monstra de ce moult joyeuse.

**Comment Fresche Memoire ramaine l'Acteur en sa maison et
lui devise en chemin de ses nouvelles.**

MINIATURE 14. Fresh Memory and the Author, on horseback   [83]

271.   **E**t conclud qu'elle me menroit
           Au lieu ou trouvé je l'avoye
           Et qu'Entendement manderoit
        Qui moult bien me conseilleroit
        Pour les armes qu'empris avoye.
        Ainsi nous mismes a la voye
        Pour aler a sa demourance
        Par le doux chemin d'Alegance.

272.   Memoire, qui me vit muser,
        M'entretint de beaux ditz et comptes.
        Moult bien luy sëoit a parler;
        Le chemin me fist oublier*

270.1 Despit *E* | de plus *FGR* | plusgrant [*sic*] *W*
270.2 partir *V* (et me r.), *M* (-*1*)
270.3 Atropos sui en [*sic*] *Y* (+*1*)
270.6 de bonne ayre *B*, de bonnaire *EL*, de bonnayre *X*
270.7 trouue *E/X*
270.8 Ce *GL*, Si *V* | ce mot j. [*sic*] *ES/MX*. De ce mot se trouua joyeuse *Q*

Rubric. Comme *LS/M* | emmaine *M* | maison *repeated B* | ou chemin *R* | dez n. *R*.
       Rubric follows miniature in FS; follows instructions in LTW/Z. No rubric, V.
       Equivalent miniature in *ABFGQRS/XY*; none in *E*.
271.1 couclud [*sic*] *X* | elle men [*sic*] m. *Q* | menroit *ABGLQRSTVW/MYZ*] mainroit
       C, menrroit *FP*, meroit *E*, meneroit *N/X* (+*1*)

270.   Respite, who is not very large,
Made me pull back and leave,
For at that time Atropos
Had enough combatants
And I had to do as she wished.
Noble Fresh Memory,
Whom I found so amiable,
Showed great joy at that.

How Fresh Memory leads the Author back to her house and shares her news with him along the way.

271.   **A**nd she decided that she would lead me
To the place where I had found her
And that she would send for Understanding
Who would counsel me very well
About the martial skills to which I had turned.
Thus we set out on the way
To her dwelling
By the gentle Road of Consolation.

272.   Memory, who saw me reflecting,
Spoke to me with fine maxims and tales;
She spoke so well that
She made me forget the road,

271.2   Ou lieu *FGV* | ou trouuee je *FG* (+*1*), ou trouuee lauoye *ELPQS*, ou trouuay [*sic*] lauoye *N* (-*1*), ou trouue lauoye *X* (-*1*)
271.3   qu' *om LR*
271.5   jauoye *RV*
271.6   meismes *BLQVW* | en la *BEFGL/M*
271.7   en sa *BEFGNPQS/MX*
271.8   Pour le *X*

272.1   quil me *A* | musser [*sic*] *M*
272.2   dix [*sic*] *R* | contes *LRW*
272.3   seroit [*sic*] *W* | le parler *EFGNPQS/MX*, de p. *LR*

Et me dist entre ses racontes :
« Je sçay roys, ducs, barons et contes   [84]
Sepulturez nouvellement
Depuis nostre departement.

273. Loÿs, filz du duc de Bourbon,
      Evesque de Liege tant digne,
      Conte de Loz, duc de Buillon,
      De royal sanc prince tant bon,
      Qui des parens ot une myne :*
      Accident, qui la vie myne,
      L'a n'a gueres mort et tué
      Ou fort de sa meilleur cité.

274. Le conte de Chimay tant sage,
      Tant plaisant et tant extimé,
      Tant aggrëable parsonnage —
      Tant de vertus ot en partage
      Que de chascun fut desiré —
      Accident l'a mort et maté
      D'une fievre soudainement
      Avant qu'on peust sçavoir comment.

275. De Luxembourg le conte Pierre,
      Qui six fois conte se nommoit —
      Accident lui a fait la guerre
      Et ala Debile requerre,

272.5 dit *BEFGLV*

272.6 roix *R*; *om. W* (-*1*) | ducs *om. R* (-*1*); duc *Y* | barons ducs et *S*

273.1 du *om. Y* (-*1*); filz au duc *T* | roy de B. *M*

273.2 du liege *EFGNPQS/MX*

273.3 du loz *M* | loothz *Q*, looz *L*, los *B*, lotz *SV*

273.4 Le sang royal prince [*sic*] *E* | tresbon *R*

273.5 de *BEFGLNPQSVW/XZ* | est [*sic*] une m. *L*, eust une m. *F*

273.6 la vid [*sic*] myne *R* (-*1*). *Line om., M.*

273.8 Au *M* | meilleure *W/MX* (+*1*)

And among her stories she said to me,
"I know kings, dukes, barons, and counts
Newly entombed
Since our departure.

273.   Louis, the Duke of Bourbon's son,
Most noble Bishop of Liege,
Count of Loz, Duke of Buillon,
Such a good prince of royal blood,
Who had a host of kinsmen:
Accident, who saps life,
Not long ago killed him dead
In the fortress of his best city.

274.   The most wise Count of Chimay,
So delightful and so esteemed,
Such an agreeable person
Who had his share of so many virtues
That everyone wanted his company,
Accident checked and killed him
With a sudden fever
Before anyone could know how.

275.   Count Pierre of Luxembourg
Who called himself six times a count—
Accident waged war on him
And brought Debility into it,

274.1 de chunay *X*, de chauny *M*
274.4 eust *EFN* | en *om. W (-1)*
274.6 mort a mate [*sic*] *X*
274.8 que lon *L (+1)* | peult *BFGLV*, pault [*?*] *W*; sceust sauoir [*sic*] *MX*

275.3 Ac. si luy *M (om.* la)
275.4 Et lala [*sic*] *V*, Et a la *Y* | debilite *A (+1)*

Car jone mater le vouloit.
Ces deux l'ont mis en tel destroit
Par maladie decrepite
Qu'ilz en ont fait le monde quitte.

276.   Edouard, le beau roy angloix,
       Si valereux et renommé,
       Qui fut extimé des François,
       En crainte tint les Escoçois,   [85]
       En son royaulme redoubté :
       Accident l'a a mort bouté
       Soubit d'une fievre soudaine
       Comme du trait d'une dondaine.

277.   Febus, jone roy de Navare
       Que chascun si fort extimoit,
       Accident, qui trop volt conquerre,
       A rompu comme ung petit verre*
       Sa vie qui tant flourissoit.
       L'un deffie, l'autre deçoit,
       Et a le dard si tres a destre
       Que nulz ne scet ou seur puist estre.

278.   Michel de Bergues tant vaillant,*
       En jones jours plain de prudance —

275.5 Pour ce que m. *W* | master *B*; matiere [*sic*] voulloit *M*
275.6 Ses deux *E* | sont mis *G* | tel desroy *V*
275.7 decrepitine *V* (+*1*), m. decrepye munde *M* (+*2?*)
275.8 lamende quitte [*sic*] *L*, ont laisse le monde *M* (-*1*)

276.1 Le beau roy edouard anglois *T* | le bel r. *FGNQS/X*
276.2 Cheualereux et r. *BQ/M*, Si cheualereux et *R* (+*1*), *N* (Si *lined out by a later hand*)
       | si r. *L*
276.3 Quil fut *V* | fut *om. R* (-*1*) | de fr. *FG*
276.4 craint *R* (-*1*)
276.6 bonte [*sic*] *Y*
276.7 une figure s. *M* (+*1*)
276.8 Comme dung tr. *FGV* | dardaine *MX*

Wishing to cut him down young.
Those two put him in such straits
By means of enfeebling illness
That they deprived the world of him.

276.   Edward, the fine English king,
So valorous and renowned,
Who was esteemed by the French,
Feared by the Scots,
Held in awe in his realm:
Accident drove him to his death
Suddenly, with a swift fever
Like a catapulted missile.*

277.   Phebus, the young king of Navarre
Whom everyone esteemed so highly,
Accident, who wished greatly to prevail,
Snapped as if it were a tiny glass
His life which was so flourishing.
He defeats one, another thwarts,
And with such a skillful shaft
That no one knows where he can be safe.

278.   Michel de Berghes, so valiant,
Full of discretion in youth—

277.1   nauerre *LW/M*
277.3   veult *ABFGLVW/M*; volut *R* (+*1*), vouloit *X* (+*1*)
277.4   voirre *BEPQR*, voerre *F*, voyre *X*
277.5   tant se fl. *V* (+*1*)
277.6   Lun defait *EQS/X*, Lung desfaut *M* | et lautre *E/M*; et *om. S/X* (-*1*)
277.7   tresadextre *BELW*, tresadestre *AFGT* (*bound forms*)
277.8   nul *AELNPQST/MX* | nen scait *M*, ne vit *V*, ne sceust *X* | ou asseur estre *ES*, ou bien seur estre *Q*, on seul p. e. *V*, puist *om. NP/X* (-*1?*); oncques seur estre *M* | peult *FGLV*, puisse *R*

278.1   bergues *ABQ/YZ* (berguez *ER*, berghes *LW*, berghe *V*, berghuez *NP/X*, berghues *FG*)] bergnes *C*, bargnies *S* (+*1*); *T is ambiguous and could be read as either* bergues *or* bergnes; *M begins* Bergh *but the ending is unclear.*
278.2   jeusne jours *B*, josne jours *V*, jeune jours *EFGP* | plains *S/X*

De ce temps ne cent ans devant
Tel chevalier n'ot en Brabant
Pour grande vertu et vaillance.
Accident a rompu sa chance
L'an de sa vie vingt et six
En combatant pour son paÿs. »

279.   Ainsi Memoire m'entretint
De motz sages et a planté
Et me fist comptes plus de vingt
Qui valent que bien en souvint
Et que chascun soit bien noté.
Soubit trouvasmes son hosté,*
Ou nous fusmes bien recueillis,
Logiez a souhet et servis.

280.   Memoire promptement manda
Le bon hermite souverain   [86]
Entendement, qui ne tarda
Mais fit ce qu'elle commanda
Et vint comme prompt et soudain
Avant le jour le lendemain.
C'est cil ou l'on peult conseil prendre
De tout ce que l'on veult emprendre.

278.3 De cent ans ne *MX* | cent devant *M* (-*1*)
278.4 neust *EFLS*
278.5 Pour garder *M* | grande vertuz *E*, grandes vertus *S*; Pour sa grand vertu *V*
278.6 sa lance *G/YZ*
278.7 En lan *V* (+*1*) | ving et *X*

279.1 mentretient *W*
279.2 et *om. BV* (a grant pl.), *W* (-*1*)
279.3 contes *L*, compte *W* | vingtz *V*
279.4 valloient *EFGLNPQ/Z* (+*1*), *S* (*om.* en); valoit *T*, valeut [*sic*] *Y* | qui b. *ENP* | en souuenist *R* (+*1*). Qui tant vaillent quil en souuient *V*.
279.6 hostel *LV* (: plante, notte)

Not for a hundred years
Has there been in Brabant such a knight
For great integrity and valor.
Accident snapped his good fortune
In his twenty-sixth year
As he fought for his country."

279.   Thus did Memory speak to me
In wise and plentiful discourse
And accounted to me more than twenty
Well worth remembering,
Each one notable.
Suddenly we found her residence,
Where we were well received,
Lodged and served as we would wish.

280.   Memory promptly sent for
The excellent hermit
Understanding, who did not delay
But did as she commanded
And came promptly and swiftly
Before dawn broke the next day.
He is the one from whom to get advice
About everything one wishes to undertake.

279.7 O nous *G* | recueillis *BL/YZ* (recoeullis *R*, recueilliz *AFGPQT*, recuilliz *ES/X*, reculliz *V*)] recueillez *CW*

279.8 a souhaitz *V* | et bien s. *W* (+*1*) | servis *LR* (seruis *BRSTW/YZ*, seruiz *AEFGNPQV/X*)] seruir [*sic*] *C*

280.3 qui me t. [*sic*] *Q/X*
280.4 fis *S* | celle quelle [*sic*] *X* (+*1*)
280.5 Et vingt [*sic*] *A*
280.6 jour de l. *Q*; *second* le *om. R* (-*1*)
280.7 ou len *S/MX*
280.8 ce *om. R* (-*1*) | que len *S/X* | veult comprendre *ENPQS/MX*

281.   Dont me fut donné pour conseil
        Entendement, que moult j'amay.
        Jamais je ne viz son pareil
        Pour donner de confort resveil ;
        Plus prudent nulle part ne sçay,
        Et ou grant affaire que j'ay,
        Je croy que Dieu si le m'envoye
        Pour le resconfort de ma joye.

MINIATURE 15. The Author in his bed,
instructed by the hermit Understanding

**Comment Entendement enseigne l'Acteur a se   [87]
conduire a faire ses armes.
Et comment il se doit armer et parer.***
Et commence la cincquiesme partie et la derreniere de ce present livre.

282.   **L** ors s'assist sur une chayere
        Le preudhomme devant mon lit.
        Son parler, sa belle maniere,
        Je l'oz tant aggrëant et chiere
        Que je n'eux oncques tel delit.
        Entendement commence et lit
        Leçon ou on peut moult apprendre,
        Qui le veult oÿr et entendre.*

281.1   Donc *A Q*, [D]out *Y* | donnay *M* | par c. *EFGLNPQSV/MX*
281.2   qui moult [*sic*] *E* | j' *om. Q*
281.3   je *om. S* (*-1*)
281.4   raueil *FG*
281.5   Plus preudhomme *V* (*+1*) | nulle par *G*
281.6   au gr. *BV/MX*; Ou plus grand aff. *R. Line is in eighth position, R.*

Equivalent miniature in *ABFGR/XY*; different subject in *S*; no miniature, *EQ*.
Rubric. Co*m*me *S* | a soy conduire *FGLNSW* | c. *et* a f. *R*, c. et f. *YZ* | c. en faicts
        darmes *M*, c. en fait darmes *NPS/X* | Et comment . . . parer *ABFGLNPRSTW/*
        MXYZ] *om. C* | commence *modified from* comment, *C*; et co*m*e *S* | et preparer
        T | Et commence . . . livre *om. R* | commece [*sic*] *X* | le cincquiesme [*sic*] *BM*,

281.   Then I was given for counselling
       Understanding, whom I loved so much.
       Never have I seen his like
       In giving the reawakening of comfort;
       I know none more prudent anywhere,
       And, in my great undertaking,
       I believe that God sent him to me
       To be the comfort of my joy.

Part V

**How Understanding instructs the Author about
conducting himself in using his martial skills.
And how he must don his armor and equip himself.
And here begins the fifth and last part of this present book.**

282.   *T*hen the estimable man sat
       On a chair before my bed.
       His speech, his fine manner
       I found so agreeable and welcome
       That I had never before felt such delight.
       Understanding began by reading
       A lesson where much can be learned
       By one who wishes to hear and understand it.

---

la v *Y* | c. partie et darreniere *L* | c. et derniere partie *ABFGNPSTW/MXYZ* | present *om. LS/MXYZ* | de ce liure present *NP.* Comment entendement presche lacteur Touchant le combat qui [*sic*] vieult entreprendre *E. Rubric precedes miniature in AB/Y; no rubric QV.*
282.1 La sassist *BEFGNPQSW/MX,* La saisit [*sic*] *V* | sus *Y* | vne chaire *S/M (-1),* une cheoire [*sic*] *X*
282.4 Je la os *L (+1),* Je leu [*sic*] *X* | agreante [*sic*] *ENPQS/X,* aggreable *ALV/M*
282.6 list *Q,* lict *V*
282.7 ou lon *EFGLNPV,* ou len *QS/MX* | peust *S.* L. ou peult moult fort app. *R*
282.8 Qui la *S*

283.   « Amis, qui veult en lice entrer,
        Qui est bataille perilleuse,
        Tout premiers il doibt bien penser
        S'il a corps pour le fais porter
        Contre sa partie haynneuse.
        C'est une espreuve tres doubteuse,
        Tempter Dieu, et est deffendu
        Par le saint canon de vertu.

284.   Bien est vray, qui est assailly
        Et de son droit fort oppressé,
        On tiendroit celuy pour failly,
        Lache, recrant et deffailly*
        Se le gage n'estoit levé,
        S'autrement il n'estoit prouvé.
        Sur ce moult belle usance tint
        Le sage roy Charles le Quint.

285.   Mais ton fait c'est une autre chose,   [88]
        C'est une bataille commune,
        A la fois faite en lice close
        Ou, selon qu'Atropos propose,
        En plains champs sans closture aucune.
        Soit en plain jour ou a la lune,
        Riens n'y vault respit ou actente :
        Payer fault a la Mort sa rente.

283.1   Amy *LPQ* | veulx *ENPS* | en che l. *R* (+*1*) | lices *EFGNPQSV* (+*1*) | entiere
        M
283.3   premier *ABEFGLNPQRSV/MX*
283.4   Si la *P* | faict *B/M*, fait *FGNPVW/X*
283.6   Ceste *W* | une *ABEFGLNPQRSTVW/MXYZ*] *om. C* (-*1*) | esprouue *P/MX* |
        trop d. *FG*
283.7   dieu il est *B*; et *om. M* (-*1*)
283.8   sain *W*

284.1   quil est *V*
284.3   Lon t. *ENQ/X*, Len *S*
284.4   recreu *AENPQS/MX*, rescreu *FG*; recreant *Z* (+*1*). *Line om., W.*

283.   "Friend, whosoever wishes to enter the lists,
Which is a risky battle,
First of all must think
Whether he has the constitution to hold out
Against his hateful adversary.
It is a very dangerous test,
To try God, and is forbidden
By the holy canon of virtue.

284.   It is certainly true that he who is assailed
And harassed in his rights
Would be deemed a coward,
Slacker, faintheart and feeble
If the pledge were not taken up
Or otherwise not satisfied.
Wise King Charles the Fifth
Held to this most excellent custom.

285.   But your situation is something else,
It is a battle common to all,
Sometimes made in the barred lists
Or, depending on what Atropos proposes,
In a flat field without any barrier.
Whether in daylight or by the moon,
Nothing serves for respite or delay:
Death's rent must be paid.

284.5   Si le *EFGNPQSV/X*
284.6   il *om. L (-1)*
284.7   belle usante [*sic*] *G*, m. b. ordonnance *S (+1)*; moult *lined through*, belle ordonnance tint *L*

285.1   c' *om. ABEFGR*
285.2   betaille [*sic*] *Y*
285.3   fait *EFGNS/MX* | lices closes *FG*
285.4   Et selon *BV*, Oys selon [*sic*] *L*
285.5   plain champ *V/X*, plain champs [*sic*] *B* | sans *om. A (-1)*
285.6   En plain jour soit ou *Q* | a plain *L*, au plain *W* | en la lune *R*
285.7   Rien *QST* | r. ne a. *EFGS*, ny a. *NPQ/MX* | attaincte *V*

286.   Puis que c'est ung faire le fault
        Et que le jour brief tu actens,
        Pour doubte qu'il n'y ait deffault,
        Preparer et armer te fault
        Sans perdre jour ne nuyt ne temps.
        S'estre bien armé tu pretens,
        Il te fault avoir Repentir,
        L'armurier de Divin Desir.

287.   Pieces si sodés te fera
        De tel art et de tel trempure
        Que vice n'y attachera
        Ne jamais pechié n'y prendra
        Pour faire sur ton corps grevure.
        Ung harnas te fault de Mesure
        Fait d'acier de Ferme Propos
        D'Amer Dieu, et ce je te loz.

288.   De Force prens tes brasseletz
        Que l'on dit Magnanimité
        Et pour estre prompt en tes faiz,
        Avoir te convient ganteletz
        De Charitable Voulenté.
        D'ung bassinet soyes armé
        Fait des mains de Dame Actrempance,
        Qui vault plus que l'omme ne pense.   [89]

286.3   qui ny *V*
286.4   Prendre et *Q* (-2)
286.5   Sans prendre *R/M* | jour heure ne *V*
286.6   Cestre [*sic*] *G*, Destre [*sic*] *L/MX*
286.7   Il ne fault [*sic*] *Y* | auoir et tenir *Q*
286.8   Larmusier *FG/M*, Larmoier [*sic*] *R*

287.1   sodees *EFGNPQSV/MX* (+1)
287.2   tel dart [*sic*] *W* | et telle tr. *V*, et de telle tr. *E* (+1)
287.3   Que vince [*sic*] *Y*. Que vne tache ny aura *Q* (-1?)
287.4   Ne *om. W* (-1)
287.5   sur son c. *Q* | naurure [= navrure] *L*; greure *R*, greuvure *V*

286.   Since that must be done
       And you expect the day soon,
       Lest you be found wanting
       You must prepare and put on your armor,
       Wasting neither day, night, nor season.
       If you intend to be well-armored,
       You must have Repentance,
       The armorer of Divine Desire.

287.   He will weld your pieces of armor
       With such art and temper
       That vice cannot stick to them
       Nor will sin ever take hold there
       To wound your body.
       You need armor of Moderation
       Made from the steel of Firm Intent
       To Love God, and this I commend to you.

288.   From Strength take your wristguards
       Which are called Generosity
       And to be quick in your actions,
       You should have gauntlets
       From Charitable Will.
       You should be armed with a helm
       Made by the hands of Dame Temperance,
       Which is worth more than men think.

287.6   te faul [sic] G | desmesure [sic] E
287.7   dacier et ferme E
287.8   et se X. Daymer dieu pour viure a repos M

288.1   Defforce S | les br. B
288.2   Que len S | dist TW/Y | maganimite [sic] X
288.3   promptz B | a tes fais T, en telz faiz Q/MX
288.4   gautelz [sic] Y
288.5   charitables volunte V
288.6   soyez BFGNPW/MY, soye V (-1)
288.7   de mains N | de om. L (-1) | dames [sic] V (+1), diuine Q (+1)
288.8   pence AEL, panse R

289.   Cuissos, braconniere de maille,
        Te fault de Chasteté Parfaite,
        Et affin que l'omme mieulx vaille,
        Avoir te fault et n'y fais faille
        Greves de Bonne Labeur faite.
        Et pour faire chemin et traicte,
        Solerés te fault une paire
        De Diligence de Bien Faire.

290.   Tu te dois couvrir et parer
        De tes armes esquartelees
        Qui vaillent qu'on les doit porter.
        Celles sont, a les blasonner,
        De Foy et de Bonnes Pensees,
        Et doivent estre dyaprees,
        Pour monstrer seignourie acquise,
        Du saint baptesme de l'eglise.

291.   Or es tu armé et paré
        Comme a champion appartient,
        Mais pour plus estre redoubté,
        Il te fault estre embastonné ;
        Ainsi le fault et le convient.
        Il ne pert pas temps qui retient
        Les bastons te pense bailler,*
        Dont tu as le plus grant mestier.

292.   Entendre te fault et sçavoir
        Que qui combat en fait de gage

289.1 Cuisses [*sic*] *VW*, Cuissetz *X* | braconnierez *R*, braconieres *V*, branconniere *BS*,
     braconnerie *W* (+*1*); braconnier *X* (-*1*), et braconnier *M*, et brayiere [*sic*] *E*
289.3 Et *om.* Q (-*1*); Ea fin [*sic*] *Y* | que mieulx lo*m*me *S*
289.5 bonne largeur *EQ*, bonnes labeurs *V*; de tresbon [*sic*] labeur *M*
289.7 Solers *ARW/Y* (-*1*), Soliers *V* (-*1*)

290.3 quon le [*sic*] *M*
290.5 De soy [*sic*] *S* | bo*n*ne pensee *W*
290.6 Et donnent estre [*sic*] *X*, Et si doibuent e. *M* | dryappees *E*, drapprees [*sic*] *FG* (-*1*),
     drappees *M*, *NS/X* (-*1*)

289.   Tassets, vambraces of mail,*
       You need of Consummate Chastity,
       And, so that you better prevail,
       You must without fail have
       Greaves made by Good Work.*
       And to go by road and path,
       You need a pair of sollerets*
       From Diligence in Doing Well.

290.   You must outfit and protect yourself
       With your quartered arms
       Which merit being carried.
       They are, to describe their heraldry,
       Faith and Good Thoughts,
       And should be luminously figured
       To show acquired nobility
       From the holy baptism of the Church.

291.   Now you have armor and are prepared
       As befits a champion,
       But to be more feared,
       You must be provided with weapons;
       This is necessary and proper.
       He does not lose opportunity who holds
       The arms I intend to give you,
       Of which you have the greatest need.

292.   It is necessary that you hear and know
       That whoever takes up challenges

290.7 Pour monstre [sic] FG
290.8 Ou s. M

291.1 Or est [sic] tu N/M, Or tu es V
291.5 second le om. X (-1)
[No significant variants, ABEFGLPQRSTW/YZ.]

292.2 de charge EFGNPQS; combat de bon couraige M

Il a faculté et pouoir
D'estre a pied ou cheval avoir,
Chascun selon son advantage ;
Mais par commun droit et usage,   [90]
Combatre a pied est plus honneste
Que soy fïer en une beste.

293.   Et si peut telz bastons porter
Chascun comme il a de plaisir,
Guisarmes ou maillet de fer,
Haches ou lances pour bouter
Ou de get lancier ou ferir,
Ainsi te peux a choix garnir,
Si prens bastons de tel valeur
Que mieulx en vaille ton honneur.

294.   Celle franchise signifie,
Et se doit en ce point noter,
Que Dieu par bonté infinie
Nous a donné avec la vie
Le franc arbitre de regner,
Et pouons venir et aler
Par la voye de Sauvement
Ou le sentier de Dampnement.

295.   Quant ad ce que conseil je donne
Qu'en cheval ne prende asseurance,
Il s'entent que nulle personne,

292.3   Il a faulte *M* (-*1*)
292.6   Mais pour *ABEFGNPRSTW/X*, Et pour *V*
292.7   Comdatre [*sic*] *X* | est le plus h. *Y* (+*1*)
292.8   Qui *Y* | se fyer *R*

293.1   Et sil *V* | peuz *E* | tes b. *EL*, tel baston *FG*
293.2   commil [*sic*] *V*
293.3   Jusarmes *L* | mailletz *EFGLNQRSV*, martelletz *X* (+*1*), marteaulx *M*
293.4   Et haiches *V* (+*1*) | et lances *EFGNQS/MX*
293.5   de guet *LNPS/M*, deguet *X* | et ferir *E/M*
293.6   p. aincois g. *M*
293.7   baston *L* | telz valleur *M*

Has the privilege and option
To be on foot or have a horse,
Each according to his advantage;
But by general right and usage
It is more correct to fight on foot
Than to rely on a dumb animal.

293.   And as each man can carry
Such clubs as he may wish,
Guisarmes or iron hammer,
Axes or lances for thrusting,
Or a javelin for hurling or striking,
Thus you can furnish yourself as you will,
And take clubs of such value
Which your honor deems better.

294.   This freedom of choice signifies,
And should be noted at this point,
That God, through His infinite goodness,
Has given us, along with life,
The free will of direction
And we can come and go
By the Road to Salvation
Or the Path to Damnation.

295.   As for this advice I give you,
Not to count on a horse,
It is understood that no one,

293.8 "+ a" *in right-hand margin following this line,* F; *significance unknown.*

294.1 Telle fr. *E,* Ceste fr. *Q* | "+ b" *in right-hand margin following this line,* F; *significance unknown.*

294.2 ce doit *LNP* | se point *X*

294.3 Que die par *F*

294.8 le saultier *X*

295.1 a ce *BELPQSV/M* | que *om. V* (je te); quen c. *R* | te donne *L/M*

295.2 En ce val [*sic*] *M* | prendre *EFGNPQS/X,* prens *V/M,* preigne *B*

295.3 quen nulle *FG;* que mille [*sic*] *Y*

Soit d'aulcuns biensfais ou d'aulmosne,*
Ne doit prendre en autruy fiance.
Chascun pour soy si sougne et pense,
Car espoir que les heritiers
L'oublïeront et voulentiers.

296.   Tu peus demander advoué
Pour tenir pour toy lieu et place :
C'est le saint baptesme voué
Qui ne soit pas desadvoué   [91]
Pour quelque chose que tu face.
C'est cil qui esbahit la face
De l'ennemy honteusement
Par la vertu du sacrement.

297.   Et puis pour tes armes furnir
Tu prendras lance pour gecter
Ferree de Devot Desir.
Le fust sera de souvenir
De la mort que Dieu voult porter
Et si fais ungne dague ouvrer*
Telle qu'elle morde et si picque
De la sainte foy catholicque.

295.4 daulcung *V*, daucun *MX* | bien fais *L*, bien faictz *V*, bien fait *MX* | ou aulmosne *FGLSW/MX*, et aumosne *ENPQ*

295.5 en nultruy [*sic*] *W*

295.6 a soy *V* | se [?] songne *M* | soigne *BLV*, songe *EFGNPQS/X* | pence *E*, pause *X*

295.7 Esperant que [*sic*] *M*, espoir est que *V* (+*1*) | les charrestiers [*sic!*] *Q*

295.8 Loublierent [*sic*] *A*, Loubliront *RW* (-*1*) | et tresuoulontiers *V* (+*1?*), assez vol. *M* (+*1?*)

296.1 peult [*sic*] *W*

296.2 pour toy *om. W* (-*2*)

296.4 Quil ne *FGLNQ*, Que ne *M*

296.5 Par *S* | que lon f. *EFGNP*, que len f. *S/X*, que on f. *Q/M* (-*1?*)

296.6–7 *inverted R*

Either from any kindness or charity,
Should rely on another.
Each person should look to and think of himself,
For perhaps his heirs
Will easily forget him.

296.   You can request a champion
To take your place:
It is avowed holy baptism
Which is not to be disavowed,
For anything you may do.
That is what brings fear
To the shamefaced enemy
By virtue of the sacrament.

297.   And then, to complete your arms,
You will take a spear to throw,
Steel-tipped by Devout Desire.
The staff will be by memory
Of the death which God was willing to bear.
And also have a dagger made
So that it bites and pricks
With the Holy Catholic faith.

296.6 embahy *V*

296.7 lennemys *V* | entierement *AEFGNPQS/MX*

296.8 Pour *EQ*. En faisant viure seurement *M*. *Line om.*, *X*.

297.1 les a. *B*

297.2 lances *EFGNPQV/MX*

297.3 Ferrees *EFGNPQ/MX*, Ferrures *S*, Ferre *W* (*-1*) | de ardant d. *L* (*-1*), et par d. d. *V*

297.4 fustz *F* | sera adsouuenir [*sic*] *W*

297.5 veult *W/X*, voullut *M* (*+1*)

297.6 si scay [*sic*] *L*

297.7 Telle que m. *R* (*-1*); Telle que m. et p. *S* (*-2*), Telle quel [*sic*] m. bien et p. *M* | si *om. BEFGNPQ/MX* (*-1*), se picque [*sic*] *L*

297.8 s. loy c. *R*

298.   Or as la lance en la main dextre
        Pour injure a l'ennemy faire.
        Targe te fault en la senestre
        Pour plus seur de ta personne estre
        Qui sera de Bon Exemplaire,
        Et te fault et est neccessaire
        L'espee trenchant de Justice :
        Celle te sera moult propice.

299.   Et n'as plus qu'actendre ou targer
        Ou temps pour faire tes apprestes.
        Mande Repentir l'armurier ;
        Fais luy diligemment forgier*
        Tes pieces pour estre plus prestes.
        N'espargne avoir comptant ne debtes !
        Prens en soing : ce n'est pas pour moy,
        Car nulz ne combatra pour toy. »

300.   En ce point me sollicitoit
        Entendement par la raison   [92]
        Et mes apprestez conseilloit*
        Comme celuy qui moult doubtoit
        De perdre le temps et saison,
        Et me dist pour comparison
        Le surplus a le double entendre,*
        Car il fault s'armer et deffendre.

298.1 Or as tu l. *L*, Or as lance *M* (*-1*)
298.3 Targer [*sic*] *MX* | te sault [*sic*] *Y* | la fenestre [*sic!*] *MX*
298.5 Et qui sera *A* (*+1*) | de *om. R* (*-1*) | de bonne [*sic*] *BV*
298.6 Ce te f. *V*
298.7 Car lespee *V* (*+1*)
298.8 C'elle [*sic*] *B*

299.1 Or nas *M*, Et na *X* | qu' *om. B* | a t. *ENPQS/X*, et t. *M* | tarder *FGV*, terger *E*
299.2 Au t. *X* | les a. *ENPQS/MX*
299.3 Madame r. [*sic!*] *X* (*+1*); Repentir sera *M* | larmusier *FGNP/X*
299.4 Fay *Q* | Faictz le *V* | diligemment *BFGLNPQT/XYZ* (dilli- *E/M*, diligenment
       ASV, diligamment *R*, dilliganment *W*)] diligeaument *C* | fourgier *F*
299.5 Des pieces *V* | estres [*sic*] *F*

298.   Now you have your lance in your right hand
        To cause harm to your enemy.
        You need a shield in the left
        To keep yourself safe
        Which will be from Good Example.
        And you need, it is essential,
        The keen cutting sword of Justice—
        That will be most favorable for you.

299.   There is no longer stay or delay
        Or time to make your preparations.
        Send for Repentance the armorer;
        Have him forge diligently your pieces of armor
        So that you will be more ready.
        Do not spare cost or indebtedness!
        Take care in this: it is not for me,
        For no one will fight in your stead."

300.   On this point Understanding
        Entreated me with reason
        And directed my preparations
        Like someone who was fearful
        Of losing opportunity and season,
        And for comparison he told me
        The rest figuratively,
        For I needed to arm and defend myself.

299.6 Nespargnes *SV*, Nespergne *X* | content [*sic*] *GQ*, contend *S*, contans *N*, comptans *V* | ne doubtes [*sic*] *N*, ne doubte *M*, ne debte *X*
299.7 soing que ce nest pour *Q* | pas *om. NPS/X* (*-1*)
299.8 nul *BEFGLNPQSTV/MX* | pour moy *N*

300.2 pour la *FG* | sa r. *Q*
300.3 mes appostres [*sic*] *V*
300.5 De prandre *M* | le *om. B* (*-1*) | a saison *M*
300.6 dit *BEFGLPV* | par c. *ENPQS/MX*
300.7 surplus *ALQV/MXYZ* (seurplus *E*)] surpris *CBRTW*, seurprins *N*, surprins *FGPS* | te donne a entendre *L*, a celle doubte en. *Q* (*+1*), a le tout en. *V*, a' le doubte en. *M*
300.8 Que il [= Qu'il] te fault armer *L*

301.   Je luy demanday plus avant :
       « Or sont mes pieces ordonnees,
       Mon harnas et mon parement :
       Tout se fait ordonneement —
       Mes besougnes vont preparees
       A quoy convient temps et journees.
       Tout n'est pas forgié en ung jour ;
       Que doy je faire en ce sejour ? »

302.   Entendement me respondit :
       « Amis, tu fais demande bonne.
       Ce n'est pas tout que de l'abit ;
       Il fault labourer a prouffit
       Pour la santé de ta personne,
       Si te conseille et le t'ordonne
       Que tu rendes traveil et paine
       D'estre legier et en alaine.

303.   Tu te dois le matin lever
       Et estouper et nez et bouche ;
       Courir montaignez et ramper,*
       Peu menger et biaucop juner,*
       Peu dormir sur lit et sur couche,
       Estre chaste — ce point moult touche —
       Fuïr vicïeuse pensee*
       Et avoir la langue actrempee.

301.1 demande *EFGNPS*, demandoy [*sic*] *X*
301.4 Tout ce f. *BGLNQS/X* | tresordonneement *V* (*+1*). *Line om.*, *M.*
301.5 sont *BFGQVW/M*
301.6 journee *F*
301.7 Car tout *BEFGNPQSVW/MX* | nest f. *BENPQSVW/X*, est f. *M*; ne se fait *FG* |
       forgie *EPRTVW/YZ* (forgié *B*; forge *LMNQS/X*)] forgier *CA* | a ung *ENPQS/MX*
301.8 je plus f. *M* | ce jour *M*, *AV/X* (*-1*), ce *om. EQW* (*-1*)

302.1 Antendement *A*
302.2 Amy *AFGLQ/M* | tu fait [*sic*] *W*
302.3 Et nest pas *A*
302.4 Il ne f. *B* (*+1*) | au pr. *BV*
302.5 de sa p. *BV*, de la p. *M*

301. I asked him further,
"Now my equipment is in order,
My armor and surcoat,
Everything as it should be—
My affairs will be arranged
For what suits the occasion and day—
Everything is not forged in one day:
What should I do in the meantime?"

302. Understanding replied,
"Friend, you ask a good question.
The outer trappings are not everything.
It is necessary to work profitably
For the health of your body,
And I advise and direct you
To exert toil and effort
To be swift and in good condition.

303. You must rise in the morning
And stop up your nose and mouth,
Course up and down mountains.
Eat sparingly and fast frequently,
Sleep but little on bed or couch.
Be chaste (this point is of great concern),
Flee sinful thought,
And have a temperate tongue.

302.6 Je te *V/M*, Si le te *R* (+*1*) | et te l'ordonne *B*
302.7 tu rende [*sic*] *BV*, tu rendez [= rendes (?)] *FGR*
302.8 legiere *W*

303.2 Et *om. M* (-*1*) | estoupez *A* | *second* et *om. S* (-*1*)
303.3 et raper [*sic*] *Q*
303.4 biaucop *as elsewhere*] biacop *C*
303.5 sus l. *Z* | d. et sur *A* (+*1*) | sus c. *FG/Z* | coche *S* (: touche)
303.6 m. te touche *FGNQ/X* (+*1*), fort te touche *S* (+*1*); se poinct te t. *M*
303.7 Fouir *X* | vicieuse *ABRTVW/YZ*] vicieuses *CL*, venimeuse pensee *ENPQS/MX*,
       venimeuses pensees *FG*
303.8 auoir lalainne *L*

304.   Et dois ung haubergon d'acier   [93]
        Pesant trente livres porter,
        Tes souliers de plonc renforcier
        Afin que soyes plus ligier*
        Ou harnas que tu doix armer.*
        Et dois ung gros baston plomber
        Pesant manïer et tenir
        Pour plus delivre devenir.

305.   Souvent tu te dois esprouver
        A gens fors soubtilz et puissans
        Pour soustenir et rebouter
        Tout ce qui te pourroit grever
        Et pourvëoir aux accidens.
        Telz essaiz sont asseuremens
        Contre l'effroy qui pourroit poindre
        Quant on doit son ennemy joindre.

306.   Telles doctrines et apprises
        Ne sont pas sans raison fondees,
        Mais sont par experiment prises
        Et par neccessité requises
        Pour les doubtes d'estre portees ;
        Et sont figures figurees
        A entendre legierement
        Pour prendre bon gouvernement.

304.1 Et auoir auberjon *L* | doit *B* | ung h. des*faire M*
304.2 Trente liures pesant p. *L* | Poisant *EFGNQS*
304.3 sollers *R*, sorlers *T*, soles *X*, soullier [*sic*] *M* | plombz *V*
304.4 que soyez *NW*; que tu soye *V* (+*1*), que tu soyes *M* (+*1*)
304.5 Au h. *Q/MX* | dois auoir *S*
304.6 doibtz auoir bastons *V* | plombe *L*
304.7 Poisant *EFGNPQS* | P. et maniere t. *M*

305.1 approuuer [*sic*] *X*
305.2 fors *om. M* (-*1*)
305.3 et redoubter [*sic*] *M*

304.   And you must wear a steel habergeon*
       Weighing thirty pounds,
       Reinforce your shoes with lead
       So that you may be quicker
       In the armor which you must put on.
       And you must hold and wield
       A large lead-weighted club,
       In order to grow more agile.

305.   You must prove yourself often
       Against very cunning and powerful people,
       In order to sustain and ward off
       Everything which might wound you
       And to protect yourself against accidents.
       Such trials are safeguards
       Against the fright which can stab
       When one must do battle with one's enemy.

306.   Such doctrines and teachings
       Are not based without reason,
       But are learned by experiment
       And required by necessity
       In order for fears to be borne.
       And they are images fashioned
       To be easily understood
       So as to secure good direction.

305.4   ce quil *FGNP*, ce que *L*
305.5   Et de p. *Q* (+*1*) | pourueir *R/X*, pourroit nuyre [*sic*] *M* | es ac. *FG*
305.6   assais *BLR*, assaiz *GV*, asses *P*, assez *EN/X*, assotz *S* | asseurement *M*
305.7   C. le froit [*sic*] *MX* | que *V*
305.8   son ennemy poindre [*sic*] *M*

306.1   et *om. S/Y* (-*1*). Telz doctrines et telz apprises *L*
306.2   raisons *BV*
306.3   experimens *FGNPS*; exprimens prisees *X*
306.5   le doubte *Q/Z*, les doubter [*sic*] *E* | d' *om. BEFGLNPRSV/MX*

307.   Estouper la bouche et le nez
       S'entent que l'on ne doit sentir*
       Ou gouter nullez vanités*
       Mais fuïr les mondanitez,
       Qui veult a victoire venir.
       Et le pesant haubert vestir
       Nous donne la signifiance
       De porter fais de Penitance.   [94]

308.   Et debvons courre a confesseur
       Par tres contricte voulenté
       Pour nous mondifier le cuer
       De tous pechés de toute erreur
       Et que riens ne soit oublié.
       Et ce qui sera ordonné
       Pour la penitance estre faite
       Soit brief, par bon effect parfaite.

309.   Les essaiz et les appertises
       Qui se font pour soy adestrer,
       Ce sont les devotes emprises
       Qui sont pour batailler requises
       Contre le Sauldoyer d'Enfer.
       Doncques dois tu continuer
       A mater la char perilleuse
       Par mener vie vertueuse.

307.1 Estouppant *V*
307.2 S'entent *QT/MXZ* (Sentend *BEFGLNPS*)] Sentant *CARVW/Y* | que len *MX* |
       sentier *Y*
307.3 Ne gouster *B* | nulle *F* | vamtez [*sic*] *Y*
307.4 fouir *X* | vani *lined through, between* les *and* mondanitez *C*
307.6 poisant *EFGNPQS/X*, present *L*
307.7 d. vraye s. *R* (+*1*); la *om. L*, Il *inserted, later hand, left margin.*
307.8 faitz *F*, faictz *M*, faiz *GNPV/X* | par p. *B*

308.1 Et *om. L* (courir) | au conf. *BEFGLNPQRSV/MXZ*
308.2 trescontriste *EV*
308.3 modiffier *V*
308.4 tout pechie *ENPQS/MX*, tous pechie *V* | et de *M* (+*1*) | tout erreur *EFGPQS/*
       MX

307.   Stopping up the mouth and nose
       Means that one should not scent
       Or sample any vanities,
       But flee worldly pleasures
       If one wants to come to victory.
       Donning the heavy hauberk*
       Signifies for us
       Carrying the burden of Penitence.

308.   And we should run to a confessor
       From most contrite volition,
       That our hearts may be purified
       From all sins, all error,
       And let nothing be left out.
       And let whatever is required
       To be done for penance
       Be brief, perfected by good effort.

309.   The trials and exercises
       Which are made to keep oneself right
       Are holy enterprises,
       Required to wage combat
       Against the Soldier of Hell.
       Therefore you must continue
       To foil the risk-seeking flesh
       By leading a virtuous life.

308.6   A ce *A* | ce qui *ABEFLNPQRSTVW/XYZ*] ce que *CG, M* [*?*]
308.7   Pour sa p. *V* | estre fait *L*
308.8   bon espoir p. *MX* | parfait *L*

309.1   assais *R*, assaiz *X*, assaulx *M*, excetz *G*; Le [*sic*] excetz *F* | appatises *L*, appartises *M*,
        aprestises *Q*
309.2   ce font *LN* | pour son *Q*, pour toy *MX* | adrecer *NQ*, adrecier *FG*, adrescier *P*,
        adresser *LS/MX*, adressier *E*
309.3   aprises *BEFGNQS/MX*, apprisez *P*
309.4   par *S* | bataille *Q*, batailles *EFGLNSV/X*
309.5   le souldier *X* (*-1?*)
309.7   Et m. *A* | la chair *BEFGNPQV/MX*
309.8   Pour mener *FGLS* | voye v. [*sic*] *FGN/MX*

310. Tu ne dois sans bon conseil estre,
      C'est a dire clercs et docteurs,
      Qui sont fondés comme on doit estre
      En foy et en la sainte lectre
      Venant des sains et des acteurs.
      Telz sont les saiges confesseurs ;
      La peut on apprendre scïence
      Pour deffendre la conscïence.

311. Se tu peulx ma leçon comprendre,
      Mectre en euvre et l'executer,
      Tu es digne pour l'art apprendre
      Pour la grant Cité de Dieu prendre
      Et pour les sains cieulx escheler,
      Pour Lucifer vaincre et mater   [95]
      Et te bouter en Paradis
      Maulgré tous les faulx esperis. »

312. « Sire, dis je, moult grant confort
      Me donnez et qui bien m'agree,
      Mais au primes vient le plus fort
      Et qui moult me point et me mord
      En souvenance redoublee :
      Quant j'aray fait au champ entree,
      Comment me doi ge gouverner ?
      Ce point vault bien le demander. »

310.1 b. c. astre [*sic*] *X*
310.2 Cestassauoir *L* | ou doc. *B*; clerc ne docteur *V* (: -eurs, lines 5–6)
310.3 Qui soyent *Q* (+*1*) | fonde comme doibt *V*
310.4 En la foy et en s. l. *L* | la *om. Q/M* (-*1*)
310.5 Venans *BLSVW/X* | aucteurs *T*
310.6 sont *om. V* (-*1*)

311.1 Ci *E*, Sy *F*, Si *GNPQ*
311.2 et *om. V*, et l' *om. M* (-*1*)
311.3 es *om. M* (-*1*) | dignes [*sic*] *W* | pour larc [?] *E*, pour art [*sic*] *M*
311.5 les cieulx beaux *Q*, les sains lieux *W* | eschiller *B*, exceller *V*

310.   You must not be without good counsel,
        That is, scholars and doctors,
        Who are grounded as one should be
        In faith and in the holy texts
        That come from the saints and authors.
        These are wise confessors;
        Knowledge can be learned there
        To preserve one's conscience.

311.   If you can understand my lesson,
        Put it to work and carry it out,
        You are worthy of learning the mystery
        Of how to attain the great City of God
        And to scale the holy Heavens,
        To check and foil Lucifer
        And enter into Paradise
        In spite of all the false spirits."

312.   "My Lord," said I, "you give me great comfort
        And it pleases me well,
        But the most painful thing comes first
        And pricks and gnaws at me
        Twice as much in memory:
        When at last I enter the field,
        How must I conduct myself?
        This point certainly must be raised."

311.7 Et toy b. *N*, Et pour b. *R*, Et le b. [*sic*] *X*. En gaingnant sainsi est conduys *M*
311.8 esperilz *FP*. Le hault siege de paradis *M*. *Line om., X.*

312.2 donnes *FGS* | a qui *R* | bien *om. W* (*-1*); qui moult *N*
312.3 prime *LT/YZ*; Mais maintenant *EFGNPQS/MX*
312.4 *Second* me *om. M* (*-1*)
312.5 redoubtee *BEFGNPQS/MX*
312.6 ou *LT* | camp *V*
312.7 Comme me *EFGNPSV/MX* | ge *om. M* (*-1*) | gonuerner *F*
312.8 Le point *MX*

313.   « Ta question est bien causee,
        Et demandes par bon advis,
        Car sur toy seul tombe l'armee :
        Tu n'auras nulz a ta sauldee*
        Qui pour toy voulsist estre mis.
        La faillent parens et amis.
        Confort tu n'aras en ce fais
        Fors seulement de tes biensfais.*

314.   Avoir te fault ung pavillon
        Ou soit mis en vëable lieu
        Ung escu par Devocion
        Ou soit la presentacion
        De la Vierge Mere de Dieu.
        Ainsi te monsterras tu tieu*
        Comme champion de haulteur
        Qui combat pour le Crëateur.

315.   Et pour entrer en telz destrois
        Il te fault une banerolle
        Qui sera faite de la croix,
        Pour te seigner deux fois ou troix   [96]
        Contre charme, sort ou parole.
        Apprens et retiens mon escole
        Et je t'asseure par me croire
        D'avoir ta part de la victoire.

313.1 La qu. *BE* | bien fondee *T*
313.2 demande *BLNPQS/MX*, demandee *EV* (*+1*), demandez [= demandes] *R* | par ton
        ad. *MX*
313.3 sus *T* | tumbe *N/X*
313.4 nul *BEFGTV* | soubdee *EFG*
313.5 par toy *FG* | volzisse *W*
313.6 parens y amis [*sic*] *S*
313.7 ses f. *E*, ces f. *GNPQSV/X*, chez f. *R*, tes f. *M*

314.2 Qui soit *Q/MX* | voyable *M*

313.   "Your question is well founded
And you ask it advisedly,
For the host will fall on you alone.
You will have no one in your pay
Who would wish to take your place.
Relatives and friends are missing there.
You will have no comfort in that action
Except solely from your gallantry.

314.   You must have a pavilion
Where a shield of Devotion
May be set in plain view
With a representation
Of the Virgin Mother of God.
Thus you will announce yourself
As the lofty champion
Who fights for the Creator.

315.   And to enter into such straits
You must have a pennon
Which will be made of the cross,
That you may make its sign twice or thrice
Against charm, incantation, or spell.
Learn and keep close my teaching
And I assure you that by believing me
You will have your share of victory.

314.6 m. ton lieu *EQ*, en lieu *MX*, tu tieux *V*

315.1 en tes *L*, en tous *R* | estroitz *EQ*; en tel destroict *V/M*
315.3 fait *R (-1)*
315.4 Pour tenseigner [*sic*] *EQ*, Pour toy seigner *N*, Pour te soigner *SV*, Pour te seruir [*sic*]
      MX
315.5 ch. soit *S*, ch. fort *V*; charmasot *M* | parolles *M*
315.6 retien *Q*, retient [*sic*] *W*
315.7 par moy cr. *ENPQS/MX*
315.8 part *ABEFGLNPQRSTVW/MXYZ*] par *C* | victore *R*

316.   Foy et moy a te faire adresse
        Requerras pour te conseiller.
        Nous deux te tiendrons en prouesse,
        En ferme cuer et en haultesse ;
        Sur tous nous te pouons aider.
        Ung siege pour te solagier*
        Et reposer t'est neccessaire
        Qui soit paré de Satisfaire.

317.   Et a faire le serement
        Sur le messel et sur le livre,
        Jures que voluntairement
        Tu as pris le baptisement
        Pour Chrestïen mourir et vivre
        Et que ton corps presente et livre*
        Pour soustenir ceste droicture
        Contre l'ennemy de Nature.

318.   Car ta partie jurera
        Et vouldra soustenir, en somme,
        Qu'Adam, qui premiers engendra,
        A la mort tous nous obliga
        Par la morsure de la pomme
        Et que le Filz de Dieu comme homme
        Mesmes en paya le pëage
        Pour rachater l'umain lignage.

316.1 Eoy [sic] E | a toy f. N | adrece Q, de dresse V (+1)
316.2 Requerans [sic] Q, requerrans [sic] W | pour toy c. ENPQ, pour ton c. [sic] S
316.3 le t. M, te tiendras G
316.6 Vng sage [sic] R | pour toy ELNPQSV
316.7 t' om. B
316.8 Qui pare soit V

317.1 Et puis a f. E, Et aussi f. Q (+1) | le serment E, AW/X (-1). Et present en faisant
       serment M
317.2 Sus … sus T | sur le om. M (-2)
317.3 Jure EFGNPQS/X, Jurés B

316.   For direction you will seek out
        Faith and me to counsel you.
        We will both sustain you in valiance,
        In firm heart and excellence:
        We can help you above all else.
        You need a chair for your ease
        And your rest
        Furnished with Satisfaction.

317.   And, making an oath
        On the missal and on the Bible,
        You will swear that
        You have willingly accepted baptism,
        In order to live and die a Christian,
        And that you proffer and commit your body
        To uphold this obligation
        Against the enemy of Nature.

318.   For your adversary will swear
        And, in short, will want to maintain,
        That Adam, who first begot,
        Bound us all to death
        By the bite of the apple,
        And for which the Son of God as man
        Himself paid the toll
        To redeem the human race.

317.6   ton corps present tu liure *V*
317.8   de droicture *S*; et nature [*sic*] *W*

318.1   partie te jurera *S* (+*1*)
318.3   Quadam que *S/X* | premier *AEFGLNPQSVW/X*; Q'u [*sic*] Adam le premier en.
        B, Qu'adam le premier dieu forma *M*
318.5   Pour *QS*
318.6   que *om. L* (-*1*)
318.7   paya *ABFGLPQRSTW/MYZ* (paia *N/X*)] poya [*sic*] *CE* (*V's reading is uncertain.*) |
        le truaige *B*, le treuaige [?] *V*
318.8   rechapter *S*

319.   Tu orras cryer et deffendre
         Par les quatre coings du champ cloz   [97]
         Que nulz, sur peine de mesprendre,
         Sur doubte de la vie offendre
         A la voulenté d'Atropos
         Par signes, par toussis, par motz,
         Ne donne part në advantage
         A ceulx qui combatent ce gage.

320.   Puis qu'il fault que sur ce responde,
         Les appostres n'ont ilz preschié
         Par les quatre pars de ce monde
         Que nulz ne s'actende ou se fonde
         D'estre franc ou desempeschié
         Par autruy main de son pechié,
         Et que chascun pour son plus beau
         Sougne du fais de son fardeau ?

321.   Garde toy bien et je le veul,
         Quant pour combatre marcheras,
         Que n'ayes le souleil en l'eul :
         De tresgrant destourbier et deul
         Par ce faire te garderas.
         C'est a dire que ne mectras
         Le souleul de Divine Essence
         Contre toy par luy faire offence.

319.1 Et orras *V* | crier dire et *L* (+*1*)
319.2 Pour *NP* | le quatre [*sic*] *L*; les quatres *B* | du champs *NW*
319.3 nul *BST* | sus *T/Y*
319.4 Sus *RT/Y* | la vye de off. *M* (+*1?*)
319.5 d' *om. EFGLNPQS/X*
319.6 signe *FG*, signer *Q* | toussir *ABEFGLNPQRST/Y*, tossir *W*; parolles *M* | ou motz
       ENPQS/MX
319.7 Ne donnent p. *ENPQS/MX* | p. ou a. *Q*
319.8 se gage *EFG*

320.1 Puis qui *X* | sus ce *Y*
320.2 nont il *EFG/X*; nout [*sic*] ilz *Y* | preschiéz *B*, presche *FLNQS/MX*
320.3 quatres *B* | pars du m. *R* (-*1*); corons du m. *T*

319. You will hear proclaimed and forbidden
      From the four corners of the closed field
      That no one, on pain of transgressing,
      For fear of attack on his life
      According to the wish of Atropos,
      By signs, by coughs, or by words,
      May give any advantage
      To those who take up this challenge.

320. Since you must answer to this,
      Haven't the Apostles preached
      In the four corners of the world
      That no one should anticipate or count on
      Being redeemed or cleared
      Of his sin by another's hand,
      And that each in his own best interest
      Should think about the weight of his burden?

321. I want you to take good care that,
      When you march to fight,
      You don't have the sun in your eyes,
      For by doing so you will protect yourself
      From great difficulty and grief.
      That is, you shouldn't set
      The sun of Divine Essence
      Against you by offending Him.

320.4 nul *BFGLQW/MX* | ne sa tende [*sic*] *X*, ne sattend *M* | ne satende ne f. *E* | ou fonde *LQR* (*-1*)

320.5 frant [*sic*] *Y* | franc ne d. *V* | empeschie *EFGNPS* (*-1*). Destre franchement depesche *M*, Destre franc en peche [*sic!*] *X* (*-2*)

320.6 main *om. A* (*-1*) | pechiez *B*, pesche *X*

320.8 Songe *EFGNPQS/X*, Soigne *BLV*, Songue [*sic*] *Y*; Prendra le f. *M* | des faiz *ENPQ/X*, des faitz *FG*, dez fais *S*, du faict *BVW*

321.3 Que naye *V*, nayez *NRW*; Que tu nayes *M* | le *om. M, X* (*-1*) | le soeil [*sic*] *Y* | a lueil *L/MX*

321.5 Pour ce *S*; Par ce fait tu te g. *V*

321.6 metteras *RW* (*+1*)

321.7 Les vueil [*sic*] *Q* (*-1*)

321.8 pour luy *BEFGLNQPRSVW/MX*

322.   Le Juge tu honnoureras
        Et luy seras obedïent :
        C'est Dieu a qui tu te rendras
        Et ses commandemens tiendras
        En crëant en lui fermement.
        La est le seur affermement ;
        Celui te tiendra en surté*
        Encontre toute adversité.

323.   Et se tu te treuves soupris   [98]
        Ou en effroy, comme il peut estre,
        Pour avoir mieulx ton sens repris,
        Penses ou dernierement viz*
        Ton Dieu entre les mains du prestre.
        C'est le Crëateur, c'est le Maistre,
        C'est cil ou l'on doit retourner
        Pour tous les cinq sens asseurer.

324.   Mais que Jhesucrist on n'oublie,
        On ne pourroit estre vaincu,
        Car l'escripture certiffie
        Loyer perpetuel de vie
        Se l'on a loyaument vescu.
        Ce mot note bien, l'entens tu :
        Il n'est pas mort qui vit et regne
        La ou est le glorieux regne.

322.1 le juge *A* | honneras [*sic*] *M* (*-1*)
322.2 obeissant *BEFGLNPQRVW/X*, obeissans *S*. En obeissant entierement *M* (+*1*)
322.3 Ce dieu [*sic*] *FG/M* | renderas *R* (+*1*)
322.5 croyant *ALQV/MX*
322.7 tu tiendras [*sic*] *S* | sceurete *R* (+*1*)
322.8 En contre *B*, Et contre *E*, Encoutre [*sic*] *X*

323.1 Et si *BEFGNQS* | treuue *V*, trouuuez [*sic*] *X*
323.3 son sang r. *E*, son sens *Q*, to*n* sang *MX*
323.4 Pense *BFGPR/MX* (*-1*), *ENQTV/YZ*; Pence *L*, Pensez *W* | que d. *M*, au d. *X* | dernierement *BFGPRVW/MX*] darenierement *C* (+*1*), derrenierement *AS* (+*1*), *ENQT/Z*; darrierement *L*, derremerement [*sic*] *Y* | tu v. *LV*, *E* (+*1*)

322.   You will honor the Judge
        And be obedient to Him:
        It is God to whom you will surrender yourself,
        And you will uphold His commandments,
        Believing steadfastly in Him.
        There is sure support in Him;
        He will keep you safe
        Against all adversity.

323.   And if you should find yourself taken by surprise
        Or frightened, as may happen,
        To best regain your senses
        Think where you last saw
        Your God in the hands of the priest.
        He is the Creator, He is the Master;
        It is to Him that one must return
        To reassure all five senses.

324.   Provided one does not forget Jesus Christ,
        One cannot be vanquished,
        For Scripture bears witness to
        The reward of perpetual life
        If one has lived faithfully.
        These words note well, listen to them:
        He is not dead who lives and reigns
        There in the realm of glory.

323.6 le cr. et le m. *FG*
323.7 Cest celluy *S* (+*1*) | l' *om. EFGNPRTW/MX*
323.8 tout *MX* | les cinq cens [*sic*] *LV*, le sainct sens [*sic*] *MX*

324.1 on oublie [*sic*] *E*, on uoublie [*sic*] *Y*
324.2 Lon ne *ENPSV/MX*
324.3 signifie *FG*
324.4 Loyal [*sic*] *MX*
324.5 Cy *N*, Sen [*sic*] *R*; Selon *X* | l' *om. EQ* (-*1?*) | loyallement *B* (+*1*)
324.6 notes *B*, nottes *L* | mentens tu *B*, lententu *VW*
324.7 vid *R*
324.8 La ont [*sic*] *FG* | le tresglorieux r. *L* (+*1*)

325.   Au partir marche doulcement,
        Monstrant voulenté asseuree,
        Mais aborde robustement,
        Deffens froit, assaulx vivement !*
        Ne pers nulz cops a la volee,
        Et se l'alaine t'est grevee,
        Ne t'en esbahis ou soussye,
        Car tu n'as pas saine partie.

326.   Il s'entent que d'umble cremeur
        Les sains sacremens recevras.
        Lors seras de tous poins asseur
        D'estre le champion victeur
        De l'ennemy que tu verras.
        Pour luy tu ne te changeras,
        Mais demourras sans prendre change
        Obeïssant a ton bon ange.   [99]

327.   Et se tes bastons peulx tenir
        Sans estre brisiez ne rompus,
        Je t'asseure de parvenir
        Au bien parfait de ton desir,
        C'est d'avoir l'onneur de lassus.
        Retiens ; je n'en parleray plus.
        Par me croire, tu es sauvé
        Ou par contraire condampné. »

325.1 A partir *M* | marches *E*
325.4 De sens *L* | fort *EFGNPQST/MX*, frois *B*, toy *V*
325.6 Et si *ENQS/MX* | la lame [*sic*] *GP/X*, *R* [*?*] | t' *om. X* (*-1*); si lame est trop gr. *M* (*-1*)
325.7 ten tieng es. *R* (*+1*) | ne soucie *EFGNPQS/MX*
325.8 tu na [*sic*] *BS* | same [*sic*] p. *Y*

326.1 cemeur [*sic*] *G*
326.2 Le saint sacrement *L* | receueras *W* (*+1*)
326.3 de tout point *L/MX*, de tout pointz *N*
326.4 Destre de ch. *N*
326.5 qui tu [*sic*] *W*

325.   At the outset tread softly,
Demonstrating confirmed will,
But confront your opponent stoutly,
Defend yourself coolly, attack vigorously!
Do not rashly waste any blows,
And if your breath troubles you,
Do not be frightened or concerned,
For you do not have a healthy opponent.

326.   It is understood that, with humble dread,
You will receive the holy sacraments.
Then you will be assured on all counts
Of being the victorious champion over
The enemy whom you will see.
You will never change because of him,
But will remain unaltered,
Obedient to your good angel.

327.   And if you can keep your weapons
From being broken or shattered,
I can promise you success
To the fulfillment of your desire,
Which is to have glory on high.
Keep this in mind, I will speak of it no further,
For by believing me you are saved
Or, on the contrary, damned."

326.7 demouras *ER*, donneras *FG* | sans faire ch. *MX* | prendre charge *S*
326.8 Obeissance *FG*

327.1 Et ce *P*, Et si *FGN* | telz *FG*, ces b. *Y*
327.2 brisiez *EFGPRTW/YZ* (brisiés *B*, brisies *S*, brisez *ALNQV/MX*)] briser [*sic*] *C* | ou r. *B*
327.3 tasseur [*sic*] *W* (-*1*)
327.5 la sus *L*
327.6 Retien *Q* | et je *M* (+*1*) | parlere [*sic*] *X*
327.7 Par moy *N* | tu est [*sic*] *M* | sauuez *W*

328.   Ainsi Entendement faisoit
        Grant devoir de me bien apprendre,
        Mais sçavoir ung point me failloit
        Qui le fait de mon cas toucheoit :
        C'est de sçavoir et de comprendre
        Le temps qu'Atropos vouldra prendre,
        Ou le jour limité sera
        Que combatre me conviendra.

329.   Lors me dist que des mesagers*
        De par Debile me vendroient,
        Pas a pas de pluseurs quartiers,
        Mais Accident a les legiers,*
        Qui peult estre me surprendroient,
        Dont mes apprestes se perdroient,
        Me conseillant que je labeure
        D'estre tout prest et a toute heure.

330.   « Premiers seront les anonceurs
        Les yeulx qui bericles demandent
        (Ce sont des dames espanteurs),
        Car Nature n'est plus des leurs
        Par ce qu'en declinant se rendent,
        Et sont bien folz ceulx qui n'entendent   [100]
        Que le corps fera brief default
        Puis que la lumiere luy fault.

328.2   de moy *ENPQS/MX* | bien *om. S* (*-1*)
328.6   vouloit *FG*, voldras [*sic*] *W*. Le tamps vouldra prendre *R* (*-3*); *line is in eighth
        position, R.*

Stanzas 329 and 330 om. M.
329.1   dit *EFGLPV*
329.2   viendront *EFGNPQS/X*
329.3   par pl. *X*
329.4   les legiets [*sic*] *Y*. Ac. les a legiers *LQ*
329.5   supprandront [*sic*] *F*, surprendront *ELNPQS/X*
329.6   apprestres [*sic*] *F*, apostres [*sic!*] *X* | perdront *ELNPQS/X*, perdoient [*sic*] *R*
329.8   preste [*sic*] *W* | et *om. LR/XZ* (*-1*)

328.　Thus did Understanding make
　　　A great endeavor to teach me well,
　　　But I needed to know one thing
　　　Which touched on the essence of my cause:
　　　It was to know and understand
　　　The time which Atropos will want to seize upon,
　　　When the day will be set
　　　When I will have to fight.

329.　Then he told me that messengers
　　　Would come from Debility,
　　　Step by step, from many directions,
　　　But that Accident has the most nimble,
　　　Who perhaps might take me by surprise,
　　　Whereby my preparations would be wasted.
　　　He advised me that I should work
　　　To be completely ready at all times.

330.　"The first bearers of tidings will be
　　　The eyes which call for spectacles
　　　(These frighten off the ladies),
　　　For Nature is no longer in them,
　　　Because in weakening they surrender,
　　　And foolish indeed are those who do not realize
　　　That the body will soon fail
　　　Since its light is fading.

330.1　Premier *BEFGLQPX*. Premiers les adno ser̃ont les adnonceurs *W*, *no expunctuating dots visible.*

330.2　oeilz *EP/X* | que B. [*cap. B*] *B* | besicles *X* | qui boiettes deuiendront [*sic*] *Q* (+*1*)

330.3　espauanteurs *FGP*, espauenteurs *ENQ*, espouanteurs *L*, espouenteurs *S/X*, espoanteurs *Z* (*all* +*1*)

330.4　n'est pas plus *B* (+*1*) | de leurs *V*

330.5　Pour ce *BSV* | declinent [*sic*] *EFGP* | ce r. *L* | se rendront *Q* (+*1*)

330.6　bien *om.* *Q* (nentendront) | sotz *QS*, soz *R*

330.7　sera [*sic*] *NW* | desfault *B*

330.8　Plus que *B* | leur *Q* | default *YZ* (+*1*)

331. Puis quant les oreilles desirent
      Le cocton et estre estouppees
      Sans oÿr ainsi quë oÿrent,*
      Selon que ces deux sens empirent,
      Ce sont semonces apportees :
      Ainsi sont trompectes sonnees
      A mectre selles sans sejour
      Pour aler comparoir au jour.

332. Les mains et la teste trembler
      Sentiras : ce sont seurs mesages
      Qu'il ne te fault plus retarder
      Et ne les peux contremander
      Ne replicquer a leurs langages.
      Qui penseroit a telz ouvrages,
      L'on mectroit en Dieu sa fiance
      Et tout le monde en oubliance.

333. Les jambes qui soustenu ont
      La char si tendrement nourrie
      En leur puissance deffauldront
      Et ung baston demanderont
      Pour les soustenir en partie.
      Ce messager nous brait et crye :
      'Penses de l'ame par remors
      Et pour ensevelir le corps.'*

331.2 De c. W | Le canton [or cauton] V | et om. AW (-1)
331.3 quilz BEFGNPQSV/MX, qui R; que elles L (+1)
331.4 ses deux BNV | sens om. S (-1) | sempirent S
331.5 Et sont V; Ce sout [sic] Y | semences S, sentences M
331.6 Ainsy font [sic] FGN | sonnez N (-1)
331.7 selle V/M, celles AN, seellez G (+1?)
331.8 comparer EFGNPQS/MX

332.2 se sont FGVW | seur [sic] W
332.3 Qui ne V
332.4 ne le MX

331.   Then when the ears are eager
        To be stopped up with cotton
        Without hearing as they used to,
        Just as these two senses worsen,
        These are summonses served:
        Thus are the trumpets sounded
        To saddle up without delay
        To go forth and present yourself on that day.

332.   You will feel your hands and head tremble—
        These are sure messengers
        That you should no longer delay,
        Nor can you gainsay them
        Or rebut their sermons.
        Whoever would think about such matters
        Should put his faith in God
        And put all the world aside.

333.   Your legs, which have borne
        Your flesh so tenderly nourished,
        Will fail in strength
        And demand a staff
        For partial support.
        This messenger bawls out and cries to us:
        'Think to your soul with remorse
        In order to lay your body to rest.'

332.5   a telz lan. *ENS/X*, a tes [*sic*] lan. *Q/M*
332.6   Quil p. *V*
332.7   metteroit *R* (*+1*) | a dieu *ES*

333.1   soustenus *BENPSV/M*, soustenues *QL* (*+1*); qui soustiennent tout [*sic*] *X* | tont
        ENPQS/M, te ont [= t'ont] *L*
333.2   La chair *BEFGNPQV/M*
333.6   Le m. *Q* | braye et *V*. Ces messagiers ne brayent ne cryent *L* (*+1*)
333.7   Penser *B*, Pence *L*, Pense *V*, Pensez *ENPQRT/MXYZ* | lames [*sic*] *W*
333.8   enseuely *L*, ensepuely *V*, enseuelier *YZ*, enseueillir [?] *S* | les c. *BT*. Sans trop
        obeyr a *vostre* c. *M* (*+1*)

334.   Telz messages et telz heraulx
        Sont adnonceurs de la journee,
        Avecques moult d'autres assaulx
        De maladies et de maulx   [101]
        Dont mainte personne est grevee. »
        Ainsi a sa raison finee
        Et me laissa soudainement
        Le bon hermite Entendement.

335.   Quant j'eux Entendement perdu,
        Ou tant de bon conseil trouvay,
        Je me trouvay tout esperdu
        Et ce qui me fut advenu
        Tout a par moy je recorday.*
        Diligemment je me levay
        Pour mectre suz par escriptures*
        Le droit vray de mes adventures.

336.   Dont de la matiere presente
        J'ay fait par couppletz ce traictié,
        Lequel j'envoye et le presente
        A ung chascun de bonne entente,
        Non pas par estre bien dictié,
        Mais par charitable amictié,
        Pour faire don et departie
        Du tresor de mon armoirie.

334.1 messagiers *BEFGLNPQ*, messagers *S/M*
334.3 Auec *BEFGLNPRV/MX* (*-1*) | m. diuers *Q*
334.4 Des ... des *MX* | maladie *N* (*-1*) | aussi de m. *V* (*+1*)
334.6 Ainsi par *R* | sa *om. W* (*-1*)
334.7 soudainement *ANPQRSTW/XYZ* (soub- *BEFGV/M*, soudainne- *L*)] soudament *or*
        soudainent *C* (*-1*)
334.8 Le bon homme en. *FG* (*-1*)

335.3 trouue *EFGP/X*
335.4 ce quil *NPS/MX*

334.   Such messengers and heralds
       Are proclaimers of the day,
       Along with many other assaults
       Of maladies and ills,
       By which many a person is vexed."
       Thus the good hermit Understanding
       Finished his discourse
       And abruptly left me.

335.   When I had lost Understanding,
       In whom I found such good counsel,
       I felt completely lost.
       I reflected all alone
       On what had happened to me,
       And got up hastily
       To put down in writing
       The true account of my adventures.

336.   Consequently, concerning the present matter,
       I have made this treatise in stanzas,
       Which I send and offer
       To anyone of good will,
       Not because it is well phrased
       But through affectionate friendship,
       To make a gift and sharing
       From the treasure of my armory.*

335.5   a part *FGLNP/M* | recorde *F*, recordoye *G*.
335.6   et me [*sic*] *FG*

336.1   de *om. BRW* (*-1*) | presentee *S* (+*1*)
336.2   faiz *S* | couples *FGPSV*, couplet *M*, complectz *R*, complets *W* | et traittie [*sic*] *L*,
        et traictiez *W*. Je faitz pour complect se traicte *X*
336.3   Laquelle [*sic*] *V* | j' *om. MY*; jauoie [*sic*] *L* | le *om. V, M* (*-1*)
336.5   pour estre *EFGNPQS/MX* | dicte *S/MX*
336.6   par la ch. *N* (+*1*), pour ch. *X*
336.7   despartie *S*
336.8   armoisie *NS*

337.   En la marche de ma pensee*
         Et ou paÿs d'Avise Toy
         Est ceste queste commencee.
         Dieu doint qu'elle soit achevee
         Au prouffit de tous et de moy.
         Ce livret j'ay nommé de soy
         Pour estre de tiltre paré
         Le Chevalier deliberé.

338.   Ce traictié fut parfait l'an mil
         Quatre cens quatre vings et trois,   [102]
         Ainsi que sur la fin d'avril*
         Que l'yver est en son exil
         Et que l'esté fait ses exploix.
         Au bien soit pris en tous endroix
         De ceulx a qui il est offert
         Par cellui qui tant a souffert.
                   La Marche

337.1 la merche *X*
337.2 ou tampz *R* (*-1*)
337.3 Et ceste *V*, En ceste *M* | queste *om. V* (*-2*)
337.4 dont *N*, doient *V* (*+1*) | a*n*chevee *N*
337.5 de vo*us* et *M*
337.6 liure *BV/MX* | je nomme *MX* | de foy *L*
337.8 de libere *W*

In A this stanza is arranged in run-on lines, with periods after the words ending lines 3, 4, 6, 7, and 8.
338.1 [E]t tr. *Y* | fut fait *V* (*-1*). Ce traicté faict lan mil *O* (*-2*)
338.3–4 *inverted L*

337.   This quest was begun
        In the marches of my mind
        And in the land of Look To Yourself.
        May God grant that it be accomplished
        To everyone's profit and to mine.
        This little book I have named for itself,
        To be furnished with the title:
        The Resolute Knight.

338.   This treatise was completed
        In the year 1483,
        At the end of April,
        When winter is in its exile
        And when summer does its work.
        May it be well received everywhere
        By those to whom it is offered
        By him who has suffered so much.
                    La Marche

338.3 Enuyron sur *MO* | sur *om. W (-1)*; fut *L*, sus *PR*
338.4 lhiuer entre en *O*
338.5 *Line om., MO.*
338.6 Et bien *B*, A bien *V*
338.6-7 *are collapsed into a single line, MO:* Au bien soit prins en to*us* offert *M*, Ou bien
        sont prins en font offertz *O*.
338.7 a quil il *P*
338.8 Pour *W* | qui a tant *MO*

La marche *CBORTW/YZ*, Amen *LM*, Deo gratias *G*, Et sic est finis hui*us* libri *E*, *followed
        by faint but legible initials* "AV"; *nothing following st. 338 in AFNPQSV. Explicit
        follows* Lamarche *in R.*

Notes and Other Material Following the Text

A, fol. 63r, facing stanzas 337–338, 2 paragraphs, different hands:

(1) Ce liure a esté composé par Oliuier de la Marche, designé sous le nom du cheualier deliberé : il estoit gentilhomme Bourguignon, et eut plusieurs emplois considerables a la cour de Philippe, et Charles derniers ducs de Bourgogne ; et aprés leur mort, a celle de l'Empereur Maximilien. Il mourut l'an 1501. dix huit ans aprés qu'il eut fait ce liure. Il laissa encore d'autres écritz concernans les ducs de Bourgogne. Sa deuise estoit TANT A SOUFERT. [*This may be the same hand (17th–18th c.?) that supplied the missing lines on fol. 4v and 16r.*]

(2) Ce Roman a été imprimé a Paris par Michel Le Noir en goth. L'Edition est remplie de fautes, de vers obmis, et de noms estropiés ou même differents de ce manuscrit dans le quel se trouvent trois strophes entieres qui ne sont point dans l'impression. On a cependant été obligé de restituer sur l'Imp.^{é} grand nombre de strophes qui avoient été dechirées et enlevées du mss. [*This hand is similar to the one that supplied the missing material from "l'Imprimé."*]

C: note facing p. 102 (stanza 338), post-medieval hand (18th–19th c.?), cursive, few accents visible. The letters in brackets are missing, at the edge of the leaf.

Le chevalier deliberé

toutes les avantures contenuës dans ce
livre sont allegoriques. et ont pour objet
les infirmites et les differentes catastrophes
de la vie humaine qui conduisent a la mort
par débilité ou par accident.
L'autheur est le même que celuy des
Chroniques, c'est adire [*sic*] Olivier de la March[e]
Gentilhomme Bourguignon né en 1435
et mort en 1501. tout ce qui fait le merite
de cet ouvrage est son ancienneté et
d'avoir été fait par un homme célêbre
et ecrit de sa propre main selon toutes

les apparences dans un tems ou l'imprime[rie]
n'etoit pas encor connuë en france.

M, colophon: Cy finist le liure intitule le chevalier delibere | imprime nouuelle-
ment a Paris pour Pierre Sergent | libraire demeurant en la rue noefue
nostre dame a lenseigne | saint Nicollas a Paris

P: note to 338.2, with a sort of asterisk after troys*, *in a more recent hand (17th
c.?),*
*il y a quelqu'apparence, par le premier Maitre
D'hotel du duc Charles de Bourgogne, Olivier
De la Marche. Voyez le 1ʳ feuillet, autour de la figue [*sic, for* figure] tres
rare.
[*The words* la Marche, feuillet, *and* figue *are underlined with a solid line. The
words* autour de la *are underlined with dots.*]

R: The words Tant a souffert *and* Lamarche *are in red, with* Explicit *(also in red)
below.*

*S: on the verso of the leaf containing the last 3 strophes, the title, in large black
letters decorated with red.*

X, colophon: Explicit le cheualier delibere im | prime a paris le viiiᵉ.iour
Daoust mil | quatre cens quatre vings et huyt sur le | pont nostredame
a lymaige sainct iehan | leuangeliste ou au palays au premier | pillier
empres la chappelle ou len chan | te la messe de messeigneurs les presidens

Y, colophon: Imprime en la ville de Schiedam en hollande

Textual Notes

We indicate the contents of each miniature as it appears in our base manuscript. Black-and-white photographs of miniatures 9 and 10 appear on unnumbered pages following page 53.

Headings printed in boldface are rubrics (written in red ink) in the manuscript.

Opening rubric. "*Ai*" indicates readings from the portions of ms. *A* which are copied from the printed text ("*l'Imprimé*"). See Introduction (p. 15).

2.1. For the elided form of the possessive adjective, see Introduction (p. 33).

2.7–8. According to some of the tables of rhymes in the *Recueil d'arts de seconde rhétorique* (subsequently referred to as "*Recueil*"), *-ine* and *-igne* constituted an acceptable rhyme (Part III, 137a–b; Part VII, 366–67).

5.1. The form *soye*, chosen for the rhyme, is one of many cases of poetic license (see Introduction, p. 13). Elsewhere we find the usual form *soyes* (three occurrences).

5.5. Amé de Montgesoie's *Le Pas de la Mort* accompanies *Le Chevalier deliberé* in manuscripts *BRV* (see Introduction for details).

5.6. In the majority of cases (14 occurrences), *C*'s spelling is *scauoir* (rendered in our text as *sçavoir*), but we also find three occurrences of *sauoir*. Apart from changing *u* to *v*, we have retained *C*'s spelling in each case.

6.1. Though *C*'s predominant spelling is *deux* (35 occurrences), we also find five occurrences of *deulx*. We have retained *C*'s spelling in all cases.

7.4. The non-agreement of the adjective, for reasons of rhyme, may be considered a case of poetic license.

7.8. The use of *nulz* may be a remnant of the Old French declensional system (see Introduction, p. 32). As might be expected in a Middle French text, it is not always used correctly, and *nul* also occurs as a singular subject. We have retained *C*'s spelling in all cases (14 occurrences of *nulz*, five of *nul*).

13.7–8. These lines echo a formula frequently found in 12th- and 13th-century romances, as in *mesires Gauvain . . . erra toute jor sans aventure trover qui a raconter fache*: "Sir Gawain . . . rode all day without finding any adventure worth recounting." (*Lancelot, roman en prose du XIIIe siècle*, ed. Alexandre Micha, VIII, 217, beginning of chapter LXa; trans. Carleton W. Carroll in *Lancelot-Grail: The Old French Arthurian Vulgate and Post-Vulgate in Translation*, II, 171.)

14.2. In the verb *reposer* and related forms, *C* presents both *-o-* (5 occurrences, e.g., 6.5) and *-ou-* (3). We have retained *C*'s spellings.

16.1. *C* consistently uses *amis* for the vocative singular; the other examples are in 113.3, 140.6, 269.5, 283.1, and 302.2.

18.7. Both *glave* and *lance* usually refer to the same type of weapon: in 19.1 the narrator, referring to the encounter related here, refers to *nos lances*. For a similar example, see 84.6, where *ma lance* seems to refer to the same weapon as *mon glave* in 82.6. On the other hand, the *espee "Trop de Jours,"* first mentioned in 84.2-3, is called a *glave* in 90.1.

18.8. The form *faillit* occurs in 131.5 (*fallut*, p.s. 3 of *falloir*, 103.6).

19.7. Communal bathing parties were social functions, a chance to exchange stories.

20.1-2 follow st. 15 in *A*, added at the bottom of fol. 4ᵛ, along with the catchwords *de cops*. The hand, though relatively early and possibly medieval in form, is much less careful than the original text of *A*; this material was presumably added some time after the following leaf, containing st. 16-19, a miniature, probably a rubric, and lines 20.1-2, had been removed.

20.3. The word *esteuf* comes from the game of *longue paume*, where *courir apres l'esteuf* means "to run after a ball that is getting away." The form in *C* presumably resulted from a misreading of *f* as long *s*. The word clearly puzzled several of the scribes.

20.4. Despite the high degree of agreement among the manuscripts, the syntax of this line remains puzzling.

22.6. Although one would expect *J'en suis content*, this reading is relatively poorly supported and we have decided not to emend.

22.7. The form *loings* occurs here and in 250.5, whereas *loing* appears in 25.7.

23.2. *C*'s predominant spelling is *luy* (41 occurrences), but *lui* is found about 30 percent of the time (17 occurrences).

Stanza 24. *M* adds the following stanza between stanzas 24 and 25 (fol. 299ᵛ, bottom). This stanza is not in *CABEFGLNPQRSTVW/XY*, nor does it appear in the text printed by Jehan Lambert (Paris, 1493). It is found in *Ai* and in the text printed by Martin Havard (Lyon, undated, c. 1498 according to Picot-Stein) and by Jehan Treperel (Paris, 1500). Spellings, including capital letters, punctuation, and accents, are as in *M*.

> Quand Hutin se fut departi
> Et jeunesse sen fut allée
> Je me trouué en tel parti
> Qu'a peine fusse je sorty
> Du champ ne de ceste vallée
> Ne scay ou jeunesse est allée
> Mais je me trouvay le matin
> Dans le couuent d'un jaccopin

> [When Quarreler had departed
> And Youth had gone,
> I found myself in such a state
> That with difficulty did I leave
> The field of battle and that valley.
> I don't know where Youth went,
> But in the morning I found myself
> In the convent of a Jacobin.]

Substantive variants (*mh* = Martin Havard; *jt* = Jehan Treperel).

Line 4. On a peine *jt* | pouoye partir *mh, jt, Ai*; pouuoie je partir *lined through and followed by* fusse je sorty, *M*.

Line 5. celle v. *mh, jt, Ai*.

Line 8. En vng c. *mh, jt* | de iacopin *mh*

Veinant (Z) cites these lines in his afterword, with the comment that they are in « Le plus moderne des quatre manuscrits consultés, et c'est le moins correct ». Veinant does not identify this manuscript, but adds the following:

> Ce même manuscrit, si fautif, et dont l'existence ne paraît pas remonter au delà de 1540, présente une particularité que nous croyons devoir signaler. Il se termine par : *Cy finist le liure intitule le cheualier delibere Imprime nouuellement a Paris pour Pierre sergent demeurant en la rue neufue Nostre dame a lenseigne saint Nicolas a Paris.* Cette suscription, exactement la même que celle mise à la fin de plusieurs publications de cet ancien libraire, ferait croire à l'existence d'une édition ignorée des meilleurs bibliographes, et par conséquent fort rare.

The transcription given by A.V. is accurate except that *libraire* follows the name of *Pierre sergent*.

27.6. C uses five spellings for the first-person *passé simple* of *avoir*: eulx (1), eux (7), euz (1), otz (1), oz (4). We have retained C's spellings in all cases.

27.8. The scribe of C seems to have had a slight preference for *fuz* (6 occurrences), but *fus* occurs four times, as here. We have retained both forms.

28.8. One would expect *plaisante*, but the distribution of readings suggests that Olivier wrote *plaisant* and that the feminine form found in some manuscripts and incunabula is a later correction. The masculine form may be explained by the pronunciation: the linking of the final *t* to the initial vowel of the following word would produce a pronunciation identical to that of the feminine.

31.4. Although the spellings *veoie* and *veoye* are more usual (the latter occurs in 150.5), the form *voyoie* can be seen as an acceptable variant spelling and we have decided not to emend.

32.8. C most often uses *veul* for the first-person singular present indicative of *voloir* (12 occurrences), but *veulx* (2), *veil* (1), *ueul* (1), and *uel* (1) are also found. We have changed initial *u* to *v* here and in 35.2, but have otherwise retained *C*'s spellings.

33.6. *C* regularly shortens *que* to *q* before *un* or *une*: *qune* 33.6 and 234.5; *Qung* 44.7. Several other manuscripts follow the same practice in each case, although not always the same ones.

35.6. For the use of *riens*, see Introduction (p. 32).

Stanza 36. The hermit used *vous* to the Author in 32.7–8; he uses *tu* in stanzas 36–41, resumes using *vous* in 42.6–7, but returns to *tu* in 51.7–8 and continues using it throughout the remainder of Part I.

36.4. *C* uses both *j'* (53 occ.) and *g'* (5), but systematically reserves the latter for the combination *gy*, i.e., *g'y*.

36.2, 5, 6. Olivier plays on his own name. Cf. 37.1 and 39.1–2. This word-play or allusion is at least partially eliminated in *L/AiM*.

36.6. Marches: large frontier political entities under dukes, etc.

37.4. The usual form is *comme* (31 occurrences); this shortened form, presumably chosen for metrical reasons, occurs only twice, here and in 267.5.

37.7. Elsewhere (9 occurrences) the initial *e* of *eage* counts as a separate syllable, but here the word must be read as though it were spelled *age* (an alternate form found in 60.5 and 91.1). However, since all other manuscripts present equivalent spellings (*ea-*, *eai-*, *aa-*) in this line, emendation does not appear justified.

38.1. *C*'s usual spelling is *sur* (33 occurrences); *sus* occurs twice as a preposition (here and in 172.2) and *suz* occurs once (93.5).

39.3. The form *rien* occurs only twice in manuscript *C*, here and in 155.6, whereas *riens* occurs 13 times (see Introduction, p. 32). The present phrase occurs with *Riens* in 211.4, 217.6, 285.7, and, with a minor variation (*Riens ne vault*), in 36.3.

40.1–3–4. Though *-igne* and *-ine* constituted an acceptable rhyme (see note to 2.7–8), *regime* must here be considered an approximate rhyme or assonance, as none of the tables in the *Recueil* mixes *-ime* and *-ine/-igne*.

41.1–3–4. The various tables in the *Recueil* separate *-er* rhymes from those in *-ier*. Manuscript *C* does not systematically observe this distinction, though others appear to do so: *EFGNQSV/AiM* have *-er* endings in these three lines, whereas *TW/YZ* have *-ier* endings and *BLP*, like *C*, mix the two. *R* has *-ier* in lines 1 and 3 and abbreviates the ending of *traueill(i)er*. Since this sort of hesitation is found in various 15th-century texts (M.-N., pp. 211–12), we have retained *C*'s spellings in all such cases.

41.4. Although the form *angel* is attested (e.g., in the *Livre du chevalier de la Tour Landry*, ed. Montaiglon, p. 104: "... un pechié d'orgueil, par quel les angels cheyrent du ciel, ..."), we have decided to emend, on the grounds that the *l* seems to have been added subsequent to the initial copying. The word appears as *ange* in 326.8, in rhyme position; both *ange* and *angle* occur in *Le Triumphe des dames*.

41.7. Manuscript *C* presents three spellings: *cuer* (7 occurrences, plus one of the plural *cuers*), *cueur* (6), and *ceur* (2). We have retained *C*'s spelling in all cases.

42.6. The third-person singular *passé simple* of the verb *dire* in *C* is normally *dist* (22 occurrences), but *dit* occurs four times in past-tense contexts (42.6, 100.1, 141.2, 269.4), as well as being used for the present tense (4). Since the *dist-dit* confusion already existed in Old French manuscripts, we have decided not to emend, but list variants for the four cases of *dit* in past-tense contexts.

42.7. Elsewhere *C*'s scribe uniformly uses *-st-* in all forms of the verb *monstrer*, of which there are 26 occurrences. There is no doubt, however, that the manuscript reads *montreray* in this line.

42.8. Given the multiple objects which the hermit shows the narrator in stanzas 52–71, the plural seems necessary here.

43.1–3–4. *BFGLPRTW/YZ* have *-ier* in these three lines, whereas *ES/AiMX* have *-er*, and *NQV*, like *C*, mix the two. On the subject of rhymes in *-er* and *-ier*, see note to 41.1–3–4.

43.7. Although *C*'s reading, *si plaisant*, is shared only by manuscript *S*, it seems unnecessary to emend.

44.6. *C*'s *trouue* may represent a variant spelling (= *trouvé*) of the first-person singular simple past (usually spelled *-ay*, as in lines 1, 3, and 4). *X*'s *men alle* in 44.1 (= *m'en allé*) may be an example of the same phenomenon, as may *FG*'s *laue* (= *lavé*) in 44.4. In 24a (the stanza found only in *M* and in some of the incunabula) we find both *trouué* (with an acute accent), line 3, and *trouuay*, line 7. Similar spellings occur elsewhere, e.g., 47.8, *loue* (= *loué*) *E/X*; 103.3, *devale* (= *devalé*) *X*; 114.1, *retire* (= *retiré*) *EFPQ/X*; 270.7, *trouue* (= *trouvé*) *E/X*; etc. We have emended because *C* does not normally use the *-é* spelling.

44.7. *Cordeliers* were Franciscan monks, so called because of the rope which girdled their habits; this one belonged to the reformed order called Observant Friars on the Continent and Recollects in England.

47.1. The form *autel* may have been pronounced /ote/ so as to rhyme with the *-té* endings in lines 3 and 4. Considering, however, that elsewhere *-tel* rhymes with other words in *-el* (see, e.g., stanzas 27 and 65), the emendation seems advisable here.

47.3. *C* presents just six occurrences of *-ez* instead of unstressed final *-es*: *Faictez*; *Oncquez* in 47.6 and 60.8 (compared to 9 occurrences of *oncques*); *apprestez*, 300.3; *montaignez*, 303.3; *nullez*, 307.3.

47.6. The text of *C* presents six occurrences of *tel* rather than *telle* in conjunction with a feminine noun, and one case of *telz* with a feminine plural. Since *telle* and *telles* also occur, we must assume that metrical considerations influenced the choice. See M.-N., pp. 102–103.

47.8. The first-person singular *passé simple* of the verb *voir* is normally *viz* (27 occurrences), with the occasional variant *vis* (2). The form *vy* is used only in rhyme position, here and in 133.2.

50.1–3–4. The rhymes in *C* are approximate in the same way as those in *-ine* and *-igne* (see note to 2.7–8). *BEFGNPRSTVW/YZ* have *-iengne* in all three lines, whereas *LQ/AiM* have *-ienne*.

50.8. Part III of the *Recueil*, 153c, lists *mirouar* [*sic*] among the *Aultres rimes en* OIR. *FGS* share *C*'s spelling; other forms are *miroir* (*BELNPRTVW/XY*), *mirouer* (*Ai*), and *myrouer* (*Q/M*).

Miniature 6. *B*: Entendement gives a lance to the Author, as in Min. 7. *S*: The hermit holds two objects, possibly relics, in his hands; the scene is out-doors; there is no cloister. *Q/X* show a cloister but only a single reliquary.

53.5. There is a very small " + " sign above the space between the *a* and the *m* of *fame* in *C*. Elsewhere, *C* presents one occurrence of *fames* (207.4, with no such sign) and four occurrences of *femme* (62.4, 62.7, 65.2, and 163.3).

54.2. Since *peult* is normally a present-tense form (19 occurrences), we have de-cided to emend to *pot*, supported by *BLRT* (also found in 112.5 and 213.8).

54.8. *La Nativité des dieux* is Boccaccio's *La Généalogie des dieux*, according to Picot and Stein, p. 312, n. 8.

55.2. While Olivier states that the killers used styluses, other sources indicate that Caesar suffered 23 knife wounds.

56.2–5–6. *BFGNPRTW/YZ* have *-ier* in these three lines, whereas *AELQSV/ MX*, like *C*, mix the two endings. On the subject of rhymes in *-er* and *-ier*, see note to 41.1–3–4.

60.5. This is one of the rare spots where Olivier makes a *rime équivoquée* (see Introduction, p. 12). This particular one had been used before, by Michault Taillevent in *Le Passe Temps* (c. 1440):

> J'ay temps passé et voyagié
> Sans aller jusques a Cartaige.
> Dieu mercy que me voy aagié
> Et venus jusques au quart age.
> Encore passé le quart ai je
> Et suis au quint tost arrivé :
> Viellesse ung clou tost a rivé.
>
> ed. R. Deschaux, p. 155 (st. LXXVI)

60.7. The singular *prince*, presumably chosen for the rhyme, can be seen as another case of poetic license.

60.8. For the form *oncquez*, see note to 47.3.

61.2. *C*'s *Mar* may indicate that the name was pronounced without a final /k/ sound. We have restored the more familiar form found in the majority of manuscripts.

63.1. Unlike the frequent substitution of *ou* for *on* (see Introduction, p. 35), *C* normally distinguishes *au* and *an*. Since *branc* occurs in 82.4, we have decided to adopt that form here.

67.2–5–6. C uses the form *moult* throughout (36 occurrences), unlike other manuscripts which sometimes use *mont*. This is the only line in which it is the rhyme-word. There is some evidence that the two forms were pronounced alike, or closely enough to allow *moult* to rhyme with *-ont* forms, as here, so we have decided not to emend. Amé de Montgesoie plays on the similarity of pronunciation in order to incorporate a reference to his own name in the last line of his *Pas de la Mort*:

> Sy requiers Dieu qui doint espace
> Aux chrestiens d'eulx sy bien armer,
> Que chascun a son salut passe
> Sans sa conscience entamer,
> Ce pas, pour ung mors tant amer,
> Et que je me puisse sommer
> Des bons, et pour combler ma joie
> Sans fin *amé de moult je soye*. (Walton ed.)

The table of rhymes in Part VII of the *Recueil*, 414a–b, includes *il a moult* among the rhymes in OUT, which also includes spellings *-out*, *-oust*, and *-ould*. This set of rhymes does not occur in any of the other tables, according to the *Index des tables de rimes*, p. 492a. *Moult* does not appear in any of the lists of rhymes in ONT, ON, or OT. Those in *-ont*, p. 416a–b, include both *mont* and *profond*.

67.7–8. For the rhyme, see note to 2.7–8.

68.1. This seems to be a case of auditory confusion, resulting in the substitution of one homophonic form for another. Since a boar does not kill by biting, the emendation seems called for. We have used *seure* (rather than *sure*) because that is C's primary spelling (see note to 73.6–7). We may note in passing that *morsure*, used correctly, occurs in 318.5.

68.4 C's usual spelling is *aduenture* (16 occ.). We find *auen-* 3 times: *auenture* here and in 213.7; *auenturer* in 12.6.

71.5. Since a singular form is called for in the context, we have decided to emend.

72.7–8. Another case of *rime équivoquée*.

73.6–7. C's predominant spelling is *seur(-)*: 20 occurrences (including forms beginning *asseur-*), compared to just 2 occurrences of forms using *(as)sur-*. The more usual form would be *seureté*; presumably the shorter *seurté*, like *surté* in 322.7, was chosen for metrical reasons.

74.5. Elsewhere (117.8, 119.5, 152.5), *veu* is monosyllabic, as is *veue* (in rhyme position, 253.6), but here it must count for two syllables. Since the monosyllabic form was already the norm by the middle of the century (M.-N., 58–59), we may consider that Olivier deliberately used an archaic form for metrical reasons.

76.1. Elsewhere C uses *-ss-* for the forms of this verb, e.g., *laissa*, 23.7; *laissay*, 118.6 (seven occurrences with spelling *-ss-*).

77.3. C most often uses *ot* for the third-person *passé simple* of *avoir* (33 occur-
rences); only two cases of other spellings are found, here and *eult* in 173.6.
We have retained C's spellings.

78.7–8. *ABEFGPRTVW/YZ* have *-gier* in both of these lines, whereas *LNQS/X*,
like C, have *-ger* : *-gier* and *M* has *-ger* in both. On the subject of rhymes in
-er and *-ier*, see note to 41.1–3–4.

80.5. C uses both *vid* (here and in 260.1) and *vit* (272.1). We have retained C's
spellings.

80.7. Elsewhere in C (142.2, 147.6) *veoir* counts for two syllables. The infinitive
appears five times as *voir*: 22.5, 31.2, 151.2, 234.8, 266.3. We have emended
to *voir* in order to prevent the line from being misread.

80.8. Since either the indicative or the subjunctive could be used after verbs of
opinion such as *sembler* (M.-N., 343), there seems no need to emend, despite
the preponderance of manuscripts reading *venist*.

81.6. This verb appears with the spelling *faillit* in 131.5.

82.3. In the vast majority of cases (198 occurrences), C uses *je* (usually written
ie, less frequently *je*); there are just two instances of *ge*, here and in 312.7. In
both cases the pronoun follows the verb; however, we also find *je* and *ie* in
this position (2 occurrences of each form).

82.4. The *passé simple* would fit better with the other verbs (*fut, saillit, fi, mis*),
but *LQS* do not constitute sufficient support for such an emendation.

82.6. Although only *ATW* share C's reading, and are heavily outnumbered by
BEFGLNPQRSV/MXYZ, there seems no reason to emend.

82.6. Here he fights on foot, although the most frequent use of the lance was
on a horse.

83.1–3–4. For the rhymes, see notes to 2.7–8 and 40.1–3–4.

85.2. This wording may be compared to that of 18.8, *Que nulz de nous ne faillit
point*, where *nulz* appears to be the Old French nominative singular. See
note to 7.8.

85.3. Hauberk: The long coat of mail worn over a quilted body covering.

86.1. Although C is unique in presenting *euz* with no subject pronoun, we have
not emended, since the first-person subject pronoun is often omitted, as in
11.3, 11.4, 18.7, 26.1, 26.2, 37.1, 42.3, etc.

88.1. The scribe of C generally uses *nulz* as singular subject pronoun (7.8 and
eight other occurrences). See note to 7.8.

90.1. Trop de Jours is referred to as Age's *espee* in 84.2–3. See note to 18.7.

91.7–8. *ABEFGLPRTVW/MXYZ* have *-ier* in both of these lines, whereas *NQS*,
like C, have *-ger* : *-gier*. On the subject of rhymes in *-er* and *-ier*, see note to
41.1–3–4.

93.5. On the distribution of *suz, sus,* and *sur*, see the note to 38.1.

93.8. In the left margin opposite this line, in C, there is a "#", quite faint, possi-
bly in pencil, significance unclear.

94.2. For the form *boute*, see note to 99.2.

95.2 and .6. For the forms *traverse* and *converse*, see note to 99.2.

95.6. Elsewhere *C*'s scribe writes *aussi* (4 occurrences).

98.5. Although manuscript support is minimal, the emendation seems indispensible for the sense of the passage.

99.2. Age's speech contains three previous occurrences of *veul* or *veil* followed by *que tu* (94.2, 95.2, and 95.6), and in all three the following verb ends in *e* rather than *es*. All four such verbs occur at the rhyme, as do two other presumably subjunctive forms without *s* (148.1, 296.5). On the other hand, such forms occur with final *s* in 8.6 and 302.7, also at the rhyme. This suggests that the spelling could be varied in order to produce a visual rhyme; considering the rhyme words *grace* and *face* in the present stanza, we have decided to emend. (The scribe of *C* may have been influenced by the -*es* rhymes of lines 1, 3, and 4.)

100.1. For *dit* as a past-tense form, see note to 42.6.

101.3. As noted for 42.6, *dist* is *C*'s predominant spelling for the third-person singular *passé simple* of *dire* (22 occurrences), with *dit* occurring just four times in past-tense contexts. We have decided to adopt that form here, however, because of the visual aspect of the rhyme; *dit* occurs in rhyme-position in 269.4 (*petit : respit : dit*). Both spellings apparently represented the same pronunciation.

104.8. Veinant (*Z*) was apparently following *Q* and/or *S* for *deceuz*. Given the balance of manuscript evidence, emendation does not seem necessary. This is not the first time that *QS* present a reading at variance with all others.

107.3. In the left margin opposite this line, in *C*, there is a sort of "H", quite faint, possibly in pencil, significance unclear.

108.1. This is the unique occurrence of *ny*; elsewhere in *C* the negative conjunction is always *ne*.

109.1:3. This seems to be a case of identical rhyme, but since there are no significant variants, we must assume that this is what Olivier wrote.

109.4. *C*'s *Quen*, i.e., *Qu'en*, is well supported by other manuscripts; *BV/M*'s *Que* is a possible variant and *X*'s *Quant* a somewhat typical homophonic substitution. According to Godefroy (10:718), *en soubit* is a variant on the adverb *soubit*, *subit*.

109.5–6. The rhymes suggest that *fist* and *sist* were pronounced /fi/ and /si/.

109.6. Even though *C*'s reading, like that of *AENQR*, looks more like *et fist*, we assume that *et sist* is the intended reading, since *est fait et fist* would make no sense. Some of the manuscripts listed as reading *fist* may in fact have *sist*: it is often difficult to be absolutely sure of the difference between *f* and "long" *s*. *FGNPQRSV* clearly have a form beginning with *f*; *AE* are fairly certainly *f*; *BL* are clearly *s* (*L* corrected from *f* to *s*); *W* is fairly certainly *s*; *CT* are doubtful.

110.5. The form *merveil*, chosen for the rhyme, may be considered another ves-
tige of an earlier stage of the language. See M.-N., p. 200.

111.7. The singular *Maint* does not seem correct here, given the plural verb *fail-
loient*. The error may have resulted from the identical singular and plural
forms of the noun *gorgias*. Elsewhere in *C* we find two occurrences of
mains with a plural noun (*mains lieux*, 54.7; *Mains bons ... chevaliers*, 196.5)
and one of *maint* with a singular noun (*maint contraire*, 90.2); other occur-
rences of *mains* are as a pronoun, e.g., 169.6, *Debille qui mains en mehaigne*.

113.5. Confusion between *qui* and *qu'il* was frequent (see M.-N., pp. 160 and
174; Brown, *Ressource*, 63), though it is exceptional in *C*. In this case, we
interpret *C*'s *Qui* as the equivalent of *Qu'il*.

116.7. A penciled note, on the back of the first flyleaf, *C*: « f. 39 deux mots [*sic*,
in fact four words] légèrement grattés : au cul au con fault renoncer. » The
four words are underlined thus in the note; the third word is clearly *et* in
the manuscript. *T* has abbreviations for the two indelicate nouns: the first
is similar in shape to the letter *j*, but less developed at the top and with no
loop at the bottom; the second is the typical "*9*", normally used to replace
com and *con* in longer words, and here apparently standing for the word *con*.

116.7–8. *ABEFRSTW/XYZ* have *-ier* in these two lines, whereas *LQ* (with a dif-
ferent rhyme-word in line 7) and *V*, like *C*, have *-er* and *-ier*. On the subject
of rhymes in *-er* and *-ier*, see note to 41.1–3–4.

118.1–3–4. Since none of the tables in the *Recueil* mixes *-ayme* (or *-aime*) and
-aine, *ayme* must here be considered an approximate rhyme or assonance.

118.2. *Nasse*: A basket made of willow into which a fish may swim but from
which it cannot exit and, fig., a trap easily fallen into but from which
escape is difficult. Traditionally called a "weel." The term occurs again in
128.1.

119.7. There are two occurrences of *quel* with a feminine noun (the other is in
157.2), a situation similar to that of *tel*. See note to 47.6.

121.3. There is a sort of accent over the *i* of *bruineux*, *C*, darker than the usual
oblique stroke marking an *i*.

122.1. The spelling *abres* may indicate a weakening of the first /r/ sound; com-
pare *marbre* in 48.3, but *mabre* in 201.5, rhyming with *Calabre*. Since nearly
all manuscripts are one syllable short in this line, some correction seems
necessary, poorly supported though it may be.

122.3. Although the spelling *saches* may merely indicate a dialectal trait (see
following note), we have decided to emend, both to furnish a more recog-
nizable form and because *C* uses *secq* in 3.7.

122.4. The spelling *arbes* (for *herbes*) may indicate a dialectal trait; cf. *parucque*
129.7, *parsonnaige* 156.4, and *parsonnage* 274.3. Zumthor says the spell-
ing *-ar-* reflects Parisian pronunciation (*Anthologie*, p. 22).

122.8. Pears of anguish: bitter choke pears. Also a name for a gag.

123.1-3-4. None of the tables in the *Recueil* mixes *-une* and *-ume*, so *lune* must here be considered an approximate rhyme or assonance.

124.1-3-4. The table of rhymes in Part VII of the *Recueil*, 363d, includes *regne* under the heading ENE, although words ending in *-aine* are grouped under a separate heading, 363b-d.

124.4. A small oblique stroke in C between *Maladie* and *a* suggests the distinct pronunciation of the final *e*.

126.4. C's predominant usage is like that of modern French, reducing *que* to *qu* before a vowel sound (123 occurrences), compared to just six occurrences of the full form *que* followed by a vowel sound. In all but the present line, the word *que* is spelled out in full; here it is abbreviated to *q* with a bar above. In four cases (*que hercules*, 9.2; *que honneur*, 93.8; *Que en*, 120.7; *que a*, 242.4), there is no doubt that the line must be read as though it contained the elided form *qu'*; in the fifth, *que oyrent*, 331.3, the *-e* retains full syllabic value. This is the only occurrence of *que on*; elsewhere C uses *que l'on* (28.4, 36.3, and fifteen other lines). There are four occurrences of the form *jousqu-* in C, always with that spelling. As a conjunction, C has *Jousques Fortune vint en place*, 244.2, and *Jousqu'a ce que mandé serez*, 269.8, but this is the only case of *jousque* + *que*. The abundance of variants suggests that this line was a problem for many scribes. Various emendations would be possible; we have followed what seem to be the most generally reliable manuscripts.

127.3. C's text may have been intended to convey the idea of *quant [on] peult*, with an implied impersonal pronoun, but since no other manuscripts share this reading, we are inclined to consider *quant* an error and have emended accordingly.

128.5. C normally elides, writing *s* [= *s'*] before a following vowel (40 occurrences, 4 of them *sen* for *s'en* (23.8, 108.2, 143.5, 213.3). We have therefore concluded that the line is -1 in C and have emended accordingly. There are only two other occurrences of *se* followed by a vowel: *se occist*, 53.6, where *se* represents *s'*, and *se encoffre*, 145.4, where the *-e* must be given full syllabic value.

128.7. We interpret C's *que* as the equivalent of *qu'il*, with an implied impersonal pronoun. Since many manuscripts frequently confuse *qui* and *quil* (see note to 113.5), the forms *que*, *qui*, and *quil* can be considered equivalent.

129.8. Obviously for attracting the opposite sex, an early reference to "bunnies."

130.8. The substitution of *Et* for *Est* may be evidence of similar or identical pronunciation of the two words.

131.1. Though the present-tense form *taisons* could stand, we have chosen to adopt the reading shared by the generally reliable manuscripts.

133.6. Although *recreu* is not especially well supported (it is shared by *ENPQS/MX*), it is a possible form of *recroire* and we have decided to keep it. The related form *recreant*, already well attested in Old French, is likely behind the various variants, which may be seen as reduced forms, adopted for metrical reasons.

133.8. *C*'s usual spelling is *meruei-* (9 occurrences), but the manuscript clearly reads *-uai-* here. We also find *meruilleusement* in 253.8. Apart from changing *u* to *v*, we have retained *C*'s spelling in all cases.

134.6. For the use of *nul* and *nulz*, see notes to 7.8 and 88.1.

135.6. In the thirteenth century, Alain de Lille wrote: "Learn as if you were going to live forever." *Summa de arte praedicatoria* 36: *Exhortatio ad doctrinam*: Sic disce, quasi semper victurus. *PL* 210.179 D.

138.1-3-4. On the subject of rhymes in *-er* and *-ier*, see note to 41.1-3-4.

139.3. In 37.7 *poult* is a *passé simple*, equivalent to *pot* (112.5, 213.8). Although Olivier's tense usage is far from consistent, the present tense seems more appropriate here. It is possible that the two forms, *peult* and *pot/poult*, were pronounced similarly, creating confusion in the mind of some scribes. Compare 54.2, where we have emended in the opposite direction.

139.6. On the subject of rhymes in *-er* and *-ier*, see note to 41.1-3-4.

141.2. For *dit* as a past-tense form, see the note to 42.6.

141.3. *Begude*: « En Provence, au XVᵉ s., bouchon, auberge modeste hors d'une agglomération » (Lachiver, *Dictionnaire du monde rural*).

142.2. For the forms *veoir* and *voir*, see note to 80.7.

145.4. *C*'s predominant usage is like that of modern French, reducing *se* to *s* before a vowel sound (41 occurrences), compared to just two occurrences of the full form *se* followed by a vowel sound (*se occist*, 53.6; *Se en*, 128.5), where the line must be read as though it contained the elided form *s'*. In this line, on the other hand, the *-e* must retain syllabic value.

145.2-5-6. Rhymes comprising a consonant plus *r* and the same consonant without *r* were very frequent in Middle French. See M.-N., 85. The same rhyme, *treuve : recoeuvre*, occurs in 146.7-8.

146.7. The use of *qu'en*, instead of *qui en*, is supported by all manuscripts except *L*. M.-N., 161: « *qui* n'est pas le seul relatif possible en fonction de sujet ; en effet, dans nombre de textes, *que* le concurrence fortement. »

146.8. *C*'s reading, with *la* (presumably referring to *viellesse*), is unsatisfactory, since the man who finds himself in Old Age does not "obtain" or "find" it; we have therefore decided to emend.

147.2. To be grammatically correct, the verb should be *trouvay*, as in *FGNPQS/X*, or *l'ay trouvee*, as in *M*; *trouva*, needed for the rhyme, must be considered another example of poetic license.

147.5. For the use of *nul* and *nulz*, see notes to 7.8 and 88.1.

147.6. For the forms *veoir* and *voir*, see note to 80.7.

148.1. For the use of *tu* forms without final *s*, see note to 99.2.

150.8. The form *lut*, present also in *BLNPRTVW/XYZ*, is puzzling; we feel

Olivier must have used it to replace *lire*, a form found in ms. *Q* but which makes the line hypermetric. It appears that some scribes were also puzzled by this form.

151.2. For the forms *veoir* and *voir*, see the note to 80.7.

152.2. Without exception, the spelling *viellesse* is used elsewhere in *C* (18 occurrences).

152.3. *C* presents a defective rhyme; the emendation is supported by almost all the other manuscripts.

152.6. Although the forms *cuer* and *cueur* occur more often in *C* (see note to 41.7), *ceur* is the predominant form in *Le Triumphe des dames*, occurring 58 times (e.g., 4.3, 5.2, 5.6, etc.), compared to 18 occurrences of *coeur*.

152.7. We interpret *C*'s *quil* as the equivalent of *qui*, corresponding to the modern French *ce qui*. On the subject of confusion between *qui* and *qu'il*, see note to 113.5.

153.1. Although *C* is unique in presenting *oÿz* with no subject pronoun, there seems no need to emend. See note to 86.1.

154.1. Although *C*'s reading, *et m'achemine*, is unique, there seems to be no compelling reason to emend.

154.6. Concerning the forms *deux* and *deulx*, see note to 6.1.

156.7–8. Since *C*'s *demoura* could be misread as a past-tense form, we have emended, future-tense forms being needed in these two lines.

157.7. The form *eul* occurs four times, *ueil* three times, and *oeil* once. We have retained *C*'s spelling throughout.

158.1. Considering the forms found in other manuscripts (*oeuure ARTV/YZ, oeure W, euure E*), it seems that *C*'s *euure* can be considered a "free" variant of *ouure* (*ouvre*, as in *BFGNPQS/MX*) and that no emendation is necessary.

162.2. The word *speurs*, though not to be found in any dictionary of Old or Middle French, appears nonetheless genuine; *C*'s reading is shared by *ANPQRST/XYZ*. The word may have been relatively rare, however, given the diverse readings found in eight other manuscripts. It seems probable that it was a form of *sepelire*, with *r* replacing *l* (hypothesis advanced by Christiane Marchello-Nizia in a personal communication), and our translation reflects this interpretation.

165.6. The rhyme suggests that /v/ was not pronounced in the *-yvre* endings of lines 2 and 5.

166.1. Although *CART* generally have more reliable readings than the *EFGNPQS* group (which *B* and *V* join, here), the absence of a first-person subject pronoun in line 2 suggests that the same subject applies to both *mettre* in line 1 and *voir* in line 2.

Note to fragment *O*: We have not noted most of the erroneous, aberrant, or otherwise incorrect (hypo- and hypermetric, mis-rhymed) lines. Divergent forms of proper names are generally not noted, unless *O* presents or seems

to present a completely different name. Omissions are noted, as are variants
for problem lines. As elsewhere, uncertain readings are indicated by brack-
eted question marks.

Text of first stanza in O, corresponding in part to stanza 167:

> Du sorty de mon reueil de somme [?]
> Las je vis epitaphes [?] sans nombre [*cf. 167.1*]
> Par debille et accident qui tue [*sic*] les hommes
> Si men tais pour fuir dencombre [*cf. 167.3*]
> Et me monstra pluseurs morts [*cf. 167.5*]
> Dont de tous je nauoye recours [*cf. 167.6*]
> Fresche memoire plus cassee [*sic!*] [*167.7*]
> De ceulx de mon temps mors [?] *et* passez. [*167.8*]

167.4. Monosyllabic words like *me*, even when written in full, do not normally
constitute a separate syllable when followed by a vowel. In the vast majori-
ty of cases (56 occurrences), *C* elides to *m* (i.e., *m'*) before a vowel, and
presents only one other incidence of *me, me estoit*, 20.8, which must be read
as if it were *m'estoit*. The form presented by *RS, massista*, supports this
interpretation. Since all manuscripts besides *QRS* (and *O/M*) have *me assista*,
we may assume that that is what Olivier wrote.

170.8. The adverbial use of *petit de* continued well into the sixteenth century (Littré
and G.-K. cite an example from Du Bellay). Although *a petite deffense* may also
have been correct, we see no need to emend *C*'s reading, supported by *ARTW*.
(The poem presents no other similar occurrences of *petit*.)

171.1–6. In Part VII of the *Recueil*, 415–16, we find two groups: all the rhymes
in the first set end in *-oy*, apart from *quoi* (in addition to *quoy*); the second
set, entitled *Item, d'autres en* OY, includes rhymes in both *-oys* and *-oix*, sug-
gesting that the two spellings represented the same sounds. Nonetheless,
Olivier keeps them clearly separate here, using *-oix* in 1–3–4 and *-oy* in 2–5–6.
Two of the earlier treatises in the *Recueil*, Parts III and IV, list rhymes in *-oy*
(pp. 149a and 213b), but Part VII alone lists rhymes in *-oix*.

171.6. The expression *au milieu* occurs in 79.5. According to M.-N. (p. 114),
"dès le XIVe siècle on rencontre assez souvent des cas de confusion entre *au*
et *ou*." We have retained *C*'s readings.

172.2. On the distribution of *suz, sus*, and *sur*, see the note to 38.1.

173.5. Since none of the tables in the *Recueil* mixes *-esme* and *-aine/-ene*, *mesme*
must here be considered an approximate rhyme or assonance.

176.5. Observant Friar: A member of a reformed order of Franciscans. See note
to 44.7.

178.5. *CT* are at variance with all other manuscripts, but *baillant* fits perfectly
well in the context.

179.2–5–6. For the rhyme *-ine : -igne*, see note to 2.7–8.

181.5. Although the line appears hypermetric (+1), there is no manuscript evidence to support an emendation, and we must assume that this is what Olivier wrote. Elsewhere (63.4 and 191.5), *messire* followed by a consonant has the expected three-syllable value. (All other occurrences of *messire* are pre-vocalic.)

182.1-3-4. According to some of the tables, *-oigne* and *-ongne* constituted an acceptable rhyme (*Recueil*, Part II, 96a–b; Part III, 145c). *C*'s *-ougne* is a consistent graphic variation on *-ongne* (see Introduction, p. 35).

182.7. For *par my* (as opposed to *parmy*), we follow Brault, p. 58, in writing *par mi* for the prepositional phrase. For other (non-heraldic) uses of *par my*, see 100.5 and 232.6.

Following 182 *O* inserts the following stanza, not found elsewhere.

> Ung [...] bourguignon
> que on neust [?] jamais [...]
> Ayant este bon champion
> Mourust a la bataille de [...]ssy
> Je le vis mort parmy les aultres
> Ayant escriteaul sur sa fosse
> En ses armes [...] et lion
> Et de martigny son sournom.

The rhymes do not follow the usual pattern: line 4 should rhyme with lines 1 and 3, and lines 5 and 6 should rhyme together.

184.1:4. On the subject of equivocal rhyme, see Introduction (p. 12).

185.8. *C*'s *fist* may be an incorrect repetition from the previous line. Since all other manuscripts except *O* read *prist* or a variant spelling thereof, we have decided to emend. For the expression, cf. *prist sur lui sa reste*, 190.7.

186.1. Elsewhere *C* uses the form *jut* (188.2, 197.1, 198.2).

186.6. *C* literally reads *Teruant*. Since the name is historically identifiable as *Ternant*, we have adopted that form.

188.3. Rhymes in *-an(s)* are normally distinct from those in *ien(s)*, as, for example, *reviens : engiens : terrïens*, stanza 75, and *ans : temps : lisans*, stanza 206. The form *Oriens* (*Orlïens*) also occurs in *Triumphe*, 173.1, rhyming with *biens* and *lyëns*.

189.2. According to M.-N., "*O* et *od* ... se rencontrent encore dans la première moitié du XVe siècle," but she adds that this preposition was "pratiquement morte au XVIe siècle" (p. 274). This is the unique occurrence of the form in our text; elsewhere Olivier uses *avec* once and *avecques* twice.

189.5. *C* has *Jhn̄*. The name appears in full in 204.6. It is monosyllabic in both cases.

Stanzas 193–195. There is a large *X* in the margin to the left of these stanzas, *C*.

193.2. Although *C* seems to be hypermetric (*+1*), the great majority of manuscripts present parallel readings.

194.7. *ouvrier* must count for just 2 syllables. Similarly, *murdrier* (2 syllables),

203.7, *murtrier* (2), 217.3, and *encombrier* (3), 217.4. The spellings *sangler* for *sanglier*, 67.4 and 68.1, and *templers* for *templiers*, 196.6, suggest the same phenomenon. See Morier, pp. 365 (*diérèse*) and 1063 (*syllabe*).

195.1. Unless *C's Vuaruick* can be read as a 3-syllable form, *Vüaruick* or *Vuaruïck*, the line is one syllable short, an error shared by most of the more reliable manuscripts. However, we have found no other instances where *tant* is used without *de* before a noun, whereas there are at least four occurrences of *tant de*. We have therefore preferred to treat the name as bisyllabic and adopt the reading *tant … de* shared by *L* and several manuscripts of the other family.

196.2-5-6. With the possible exception of *O*, all other texts consulted have *templiers*. On the subject of rhymes in *-er* and *-ier*, see note to 41.1-3-4.

198.1 and 2. Completely different readings permit the division of the texts into two families, *CABLRTVW/YZ* vs. *EFGNOPQS/MX*. See Introduction (p. 28).

198.5. The tables do not mix rhymes in *-té* with those in *-tié* (*Recueil*, Part II, 95b–d; Part III, 130c–d and 131a; Part VII, 425a–d, ITÉ, 425d, TIÉ). *C* generally maintains this separation, apart from st. 233 (*maillé : mehaignié : travaillé*), and *oublié*, rhyming with words in *-é*, st. 104, 266, and 308, which must be considered a different situation. In st. 211, 320, and 336 we find words in *-ié* rhyming together. In st. 38, *C* rhymes *armé : pité : passé*. The form *pitié* occurs once, in non-rhyme position, 148.6. Considering the evidence of other generally reliable manuscripts for this line, we have decided to emend.

199.3-4. Olivier's syntax is not quite standard here: the two verbs *tint* and *enfouït* should theoretically have the same subject, but the subject of *enfouït* can only be *Accident*.

201.2-5-6. The table in Part VII of the *Recueil*, 389a, under the heading ABRE, lists *arbre*, *marbre*, and *Calabre* (with just one other word, *candelabre*), suggesting that all were pronounced /-abr/. No manuscript has *Calarbre; V* has (-)*abre* in all three lines. *ABEFGLMNPQSTW/XYZ* have *marbre*. The same set of rhymes, *Calabre : marbre : arbre*, occurs in *Triumphe*, stanza 167. On the weakening and disappearance of *-r-* before consonant, see M.-N., 83–84.

202.6. On the form *Nez*, see Introduction (p. 32).

207.3. Some of the tables of rhymes in the *Recueil* (Part II, 86d; Part IV, 211d; Part VII, 366d) include *royne* among the rhymes in *-ine*. Langlois says that this is characteristic of the speech of Lorraine and other eastern areas (p. XLIV). Both *roÿne(s)* and *royne(s)* occur in *Triumphe* (the former five times, the latter twice). A similar line, with similar syllabic divisions, occurs in *Triumphe*, 13.1: *Empereÿs, roÿnes et princesses; empereÿs* also occurs in 160.1, *empereïs* in 165.1. *Empereis*, again with quadrasyllabic value, also occurs in the "*Humble supplique*," line 9.

208.2. Lay brothers (like lay sisters, 210.1) were lay members of a convent. Also called *conversi, conversæ*.

209.6. Although we might expect *tous*, manuscript evidence suggests that Olivier probably wrote *tout*.

213.8. This is the unique occurrence of the form *hons* in our text (*homs ABEFGNPQST/XYZ; hons CL; RVW/M* have *+1* forms.) It is likely that it was chosen for metrical reasons, rather than as a distant echo of the O.F. nominative case.

214.2. *C*'s *menre* may be another instance of the use of *-e* instead of *-ay*, as discussed in connection with 44.6. Since the usual ending for first-person future-tense verbs is *-ay* (9 occurrences: 11.5, 42.7, 76.7, 99.8, 156.4, 156.6, 157.7, 312.6, 327.6), we have decided to emend.

214.3. Palfreys were riding horses, as distinct from chargers.

214.4. Given the variable spacing between words in manuscripts, and the fact that what we consider two separate words are sometimes run together, this line can be interpreted as either *Je l'amenay*, "I brought it," i.e., her palfrey, or *Je la menay*, "I led her," i.e., Fresche Memoire. We have chosen the latter interpretation. Most manuscripts (*ABFGLNPRSTV*) have at least a slight space, as do *XYZ*; *EQW* have the bound form *lamenay*; *C*'s reading is unique and does not seem acceptable, unless *mene* can be read as *mené*, an alternate spelling for *menay* (see notes to 44.6 and 214.2).

218.6. The syntax of this line is somewhat strange, but the more reliable manuscripts all support *C*'s *fus*.

219.2. This is another case of non-agreement of an adjective, for metrical reasons: *paré* modifies *Atropos*, f. sing. (*Bendé*, line 3, and *Demptelé*, line 4, must agree with *habit*.)

224.2. Guisarme: a pole weapon with a slender incurved sword blade from the back of which issues a sharp hook.

224.8. This emendation is supported by the indications for the illustration (Min. 11), where Debile is described as having "*une cotte d'armes de sable semee d'ossemens de gens mors.*"

226.7. Battle axe: probably the most used weapon at this time.

227.6. *C* literally reads "*paulimoit,*" though there is an extremely faint oblique stroke above the last minim of what otherwise looks like an *m*. There is little doubt that *-mioit* was intended: Godefroy gives the forms *paumoier, palmoier* (6:47–48), as does Sainte-Palaye (8:231).

227.7-8. On the subject of rhymes in *-er* and *-ier*, see note to 41.1-3-4.

229.3. Dart: Clearly a missile of some kind, but unidentifiable.

231.4. *C*'s predominant spelling is *fist*: 48 occurrences, compared to just 3 occurrences of the form *fit*.

232.7. Although *C*'s *resbandir* may merely be another case of what looks like an *n* written where the letter *u* is in fact intended, we have decided to emend to the more familiar form.

233.7. Flails were specifically designed to be used in battle.

235.4. Since all manuscripts but *V* share the same reading (this stanza is missing in *T*), the word *terre* is likely to have counted for two syllables. The variant reading of *V* avoids the problem, assuming that *pourte* is to be read as *pourté*.

235.5–6. The rhyme words are *memoire : encoire* in *ABFGL/Y* (*encoires, V*), *memore : encoire* in *R*, and *memoire : encore* in *CENPQSW/MX*. H. Chatelain, p. 38, cites examples of both *encore : memoire* and *encoire : memoire*, adding "A consulter les tables de rimes des *Arts de rhétorique* [*sic*], on constate que pouvaient rimer en *ore* des mots comme : *memoire* [etc.]." The table in Part II of the *Recueil*, 79c, lists *memoire* (and also *histoire*) under the rhymes in ORE; Part III, 127a, lists *memore, istore*, and other words now spelled *-oire* under the heading ORE.

237.1. Barded, or bardings: protective coverings or armor for horses.

239.7. *C*'s spelling of verb forms is highly variable. Here, *peux* must be interpreted as a *passé simple*; elsewhere we find *pos* (32.1, 131.4) and *poz* (160.6, in rhyme position) for the first-person singular *passé simple* of *pouoir*. We have retained *C*'s spellings in all such cases. Other manuscripts show an even greater variety of forms: *peu W, peus BQT/YZ, peulz FG, peuz AENPSV/X, peulx L* (*R/M*, like *C*, have *peux*).

240.7. We have emended to *Coucherent*, given *actaindre et ferir* in l. 8.

242.4. *C*'s *leus* for *leurs* may indicate the absence or a very weak articulation of the sound /r/ in the scribe's dialect or usage.

242.7. *C* presents just three occurrences of *ad* (here, 249.8, 295.1), each time followed by *ce*. We also find three occurrences of *a ce*: 39.5, 127.3, 295.1.

244.5. Although *C*'s word order is unique, it is not impossible, and we have decided not to emend.

248.6. On the substitution of *dit* for *dist*, see note to 42.6. Here, the reverse phenomenon occurs, *dist* replacing the present-tense *dit*.

249.5. This name for Charles is explained in Olivier's *Memoires*, I, 147: "*pour riens n'a pas esté nommé Charles le Traveillant, car d'autant qu'il regna aultre homme ne traveilla tant en sa personne qu'il fist....*" According to Vaughan (*Charles the Bold*, 167), the nickname *le Téméraire* ("the Bold") is an ill-fitting 19th-century invention. The adjective *traveillant* appears in a different context in 124.1.

250.8. Since manuscripts *BFGLRTVW* agree with *C*, and since Olivier's tense-usage is quite variable, we do not feel it is necessary to emend.

252.1. Clarion: a valveless brass instrument like a bugle.

254.3. Although one might expect *le premerain*, the distribution of readings suggests that this may be a case of *lectio difficilior*, and we have decided to retain *C*'s reading, shared by most of the other generally reliable manuscripts.

254.6. Although *la* is poorly supported, it seems grammatically necessary and we have emended accordingly. *L*'s *les* would also be possible, referring to *Ces deux* of the previous line.

256.7–8. On the subject of rhymes in *-er* and *-ier*, see note to 41.1-3-4.

256.8. All sources consulted, both manuscripts and books, read *elle le compara*, rather than the expected *la*, referring to *la mort d'Hector*. This may be a sort of "neuter" pronoun, referring to the action (= "for doing so") rather than to the specific noun *mort*.

257.6. For the use of the masculine form *trenchant*, supported by nearly all other manuscripts, see note to 28.8.

258.2. Although only *R* and *T* support *C*'s reading *nomme*, we have decided not to emend. Compare 250.8.

261.7–8. These lines present an anacoluthon, since the subject of *est* in line 8 must be the young opponent, not the assailant referred to in line 7. We have tried to compensate for this syntactic problem in our translation.

262.5. There is fairly good support for both the singular *fievre* and the plural *fievres*. We have decided to retain *C*'s reading, considering it another instance of non-agreement between an adjective in rhyme position and a preceding noun. See Introduction (p. 13) and note to 7.4.

262.8. For the use of the masculine form *maint*, see note to 28.8.

263.3. Palladium: the sacred image of Pallas Athena considered to have the power to preserve Troy.

267.5. For *com* instead of *comme*, see note to 37.4.

267.8. Although *C* alone reads *en une fois*, there seems no need to emend. Variation between *a* and *en* is frequently observed in the variants.

268.4. For the form *ceur*, see notes to 41.7 and 152.6.

268.6. This is the only occurrence of *plasse* in *C*, compared to ten occurrences of *place*. Seven of these occur at the rhyme, sometimes rhyming with other words in *-ace* but also with *-asse* and *-ache*. We have therefore decided not to emend, but to consider this just one more example of variable spelling.

269.4. For *dit* in a past-tense context, see note to 42.6. The rhyme-words in *-it* may have influenced the choice of *dit* rather than the expected *dist*.

269.7–8. Apparently indicative forms could be used (or at least tolerated) where subjunctive forms would be required in Modern French. For the case of *jousqu'a ce que*, see M.-N., 296: "Quelques locutions marquent ... le point final du procès principal : *jusques*, ... *jusqu'a ce que* ..., suivis en général du subjonctif, parfois de l'indicatif." For verbs of volition, see note to 32.8.

272.1-3-4. On the subject of rhymes in *-er* and *-ier*, see note to 41.1-3-4.

272.6–8. The subjects of five of the next six stanzas, 273–278, all died in 1482 or 1483. We have been unable to confirm the dates of Michel de Berghes.

273.5. The use of *des*, where modern French would use *de*, linking a quantifying noun with the noun quantified, is similar to that of 129.1, *La congneuz des gens une mer*. On the subject of rhymes in *-ine* and *-igne*, see note to 2.7–8.

276.8. *Dondaine*: a catapult machine used in sieges.

277.1-3-4. Olivier's rhymes caused problems for some scribes, who tried to compensate: *conquerre : voirre B*; *nauerre : conquerre LW/M (nauarre : con- querre ABEFGPQRSTV/YZ = C)*. The table of rhymes in Part VII of the *Recueil* separates those in ARE (*Navarre*, 385c) from those in ERRE (*verre*, 387b; *conquerre*, 387c).

278.1. *C* literally reads *bergnes*, but this is likely another case of *n/u* confusion; the spellings in other manuscripts suggest that *u* was intended.

279.6. The form *houstel* appears in 27.2 (rhyming with *bel* and *tel*).

Rubric preceding st. 282. The omission can be explained as a case of eye-skip resulting from the similarity between *Et comment* and *Et commence*.

282.8. Although one would expect *la*, referring to *Leçon* in line 7, the manu- script evidence suggests that Olivier probably wrote *le* and we have decided not to emend.

284.4. The form *recrant* may be considered a shortened variant of *recreant*, used here for metrical reasons. Since *C*'s reading is shared by *BLRTV* and *Y*, we have decided not to emend.

289.1. Tassets: laminated skirts for armor. Vambraces: armor for the arms.

289.5. Greaves: armor for the legs below the knee.

289.7. Sollerets: articulated armor for the feet.

291.7. We interpret this line as meaning "les bastons [que je] pense te bailler."

293.3. Guisarme: see note to 224.2.

295.4. The word *biensfais* appears as two words here in *C*, with a round *s* and a slight space, whereas it appears as a bound form, with a long *s* and no space, in 313.8. Scribal usage varies considerably: in addition to the variants given, *BRSW* have *biens fais* whereas *AEFGNPQT* have bound forms and *YZ* print *bienfais*. (In 313.8 *BLRW* have *biens fais* and *AEFGMNPQSTV*, like *C*, have bound forms. *YZ* again print *bienfais*.) The term seems to have been considered a single word, and we have chosen to print it accordingly.

297.6. The form "*ungne*" does not occur elsewhere in *C*, nor in any other manuscript at this point, whereas *une dague* appears in 251.7. The scribe may have initially written *ung*, then realized he needed a feminine form and improvised one.

299.1-3-4. On the subject of rhymes in *-er* and *-ier*, see note to 41.1-3-4.

299.4. *C*'s *diligeaument* may be another case of *u* written where *n* would be normal and, perhaps, intended (compare *brauch*, 63.1). Since *diligemment* occurs in 335.6, we have decided to adopt that form here (compare *diligence* in 28.1 and 289.8).

300.3. For the form *apprestez* (cf. *apprestes*, 299.2 and 329.6), see note to 47.3.

300.7. The reading *surpris* probably resulted from a misreading of the model. Since it does not fit the context, we have emended to *surplus*. Although *a le double entendre* seems odd, it is supported by all manuscripts except *LQV*.

303.3. For the form *montaignez*, see note to 47.3.

303.4. *C*'s *biacop* [*sic*] is unique; elsewhere *biaucop* is the prevalent form (4 occurrences: 24.3, 74.2, 103.4, 118.3), though *beaucop* also occurs (2 occ.: 86.3, 99.3). (Other mss., this line: beaulcop *B/M* [the *l* possibly a later addition in *B*], beaucop *AFGLPQRSTVW/XYZ*, beaucoup *EN*.)

303.7. The scribe of *C* may have originally written *pensees*: there is evidence of *grattage* following *ee*.

304.1. habergeon: short coat of mail.

304.4. Elsewhere *C* writes *le-*: *legier* (78.8, 302.8), *legiers* (329.4), *legierement* (306.7).

304.5. This is the unique occurrence of *doix*; elsewhere (as in 304.1 and 304.6) *C* uses *dois* (9 occ.).

307.2. Elsewhere (295.3 and 326.1) *C* has *sentent* for the pr.ind. 3 of *entendre*, used reflexively. All other occurrences of this verb, as well as those of the related nouns *entente* and *Entendement*, have the spelling *-ten-*. Further, since the unusual spelling here may reflect a misunderstanding on the part of the scribe, influenced by the presence of the verb *sentir* in the same line, we have decided to emend.

307.3. For the form *nullez*, see note to 47.3.

307.6. Hauberk: see note to 85.3.

313.4. According to the case system used in Old French, the correct form for this context would be *nul*, not *nulz*. See Introduction (p. 32) and note to 7.8.

313.8. For *biensfais*, see note to 295.4.

314.6. Although *C* uses *-strer-* in other future-tense forms of this verb (42.7 and 157.7), we have not judged it necessary to regularize the verb here, apart from the usual change from *C*'s *mou-* to *mon-*.

316.2–5–6. *ABLT* have *-ier* in all three of these lines, whereas *EQS/M* have *-er* in all three (and *V* probably does, but *conseiller* is unclear). *FGNPW*, like *C*, mix the two endings. (*R* abbreviates the ending of *conseill(i)er* and has *-ier* in lines 5–6.) For more on this subject, see note to 41.1–3–4.

317.6. These are second-person singular present indicative forms, the sentence being the equivalent of *Et [jures, l. 3] que [tu] presente(s) et livre(s) ton corps.*

322.7. *C*'s predominant spelling is *seur(-)*, as in the immediately preceding line. See note to 73.6–7. (This line: seurte *ABEFGLNPQST/XYZ*, sheurte [*sic*] *V*, sceurte *W*; sceurete *R*, +*1*).

323.4. The variants suggest two possible corrections for *C*'s hypermetric line: replace *Penses* by *Pense*, or replace *darenierement* by *dernierement*. We have chosen the second option, since *C* uses *penses* as a second-person singular imperative in 98.4 and 333.7. The adverb is not found elsewhere in the poem, but the adjective *dernier* occurs in 224.5 and 243.3. On the subject of imperative verb forms, see M.-N., 211.

325.4. Olivier seems to have used the adjectival form *froit* where the adverb would be expected, presumably for metrical reasons (cf. *doulx*, 49.5). Further, the object of *deffens* is implied rather than explicit. Our translation reflects this interpretation.

329.1. Spelling in *C* varies: *mes-* here and 332.2 but *mess-* in 333.6 and 334.1. We have retained *C*'s spelling in each case (even though *ABEFGLNPQRSTVW/ MXYZ* use *-ss-* forms consistently). See Introduction (p. 36).

329.1-3-4. *C* again mixes rhymes, *-ers* in line 1 and *-iers* in lines 3 and 4. See note to 41.1-3-4.

331.3. There are just four occurrences in *C* of the full form *que* followed by a vowel sound, and in each case the line must be read as though it contained the elided form *qu'* (see note to 126.4). The support of *ATW* suggests, however, that *que* should have full syllabic value in the present case, and we have decided not to emend. The alternative would be to adopt *quilz*, the reading shared by the other family of manuscripts. (The pronoun *ilz* could be either masculine or feminine in Middle French; its use as a feminine was far from rare, according to M.-N., 175; a well-known example occurs in Villon's *Ballade des dames du temps jadis*, line 351 of the *Testament*. See also Moignet, 129-31.)

333.7-8. The syntax is somewhat irregular in these two lines; we have tried to compensate for this in our translation.

335.5. The phrase *a par moy* can perhaps be seen as an echo of 1.5, creating a sort of "frame" for the whole poem.

335.7. This is the only occurrence of *suz* as an adverb; *sus* occurs twice, 82.2 and 267.6. (For prepositional usage, see note to 38.1.)

336.8. *Armoire* also came to mean a place for storing books, and a library.

337.1. On the allusion to the author's name, see Introduction (p. 14).

338.3. *Ainsi que* with a reference to the month of April can be seen as an echo of the opening line of the poem, *Ainsi qu'a l'arriere saison*.

Index of Proper Names

All names in the poem appear in this list as they are in the English translation: to give them in both languages would make an unwieldy document. Further, because some people held multiple positions and many times it seemed pertinent to show their true importance, we have compressed the few who were councillors, chamberlains, and chevaliers into CCC. If no other ruler is mentioned, it may be assumed that these positions were held in the Burgundian court. Similarly, the knights of the Golden Fleece, *chevaliers de la Toison d'or*, become CTO.

For the sake of conformity, Olivier's spelling of names has been modernized and appears in the list only under this spelling. We have included information about each person in the hope that this will be both relevant and interesting. Every effort has been made for correct identification, but Olivier has been found to be less than fastidious in this regard and the difficulty was further compounded by the occasional brevity of his description: someone's nephew, for example. Consequently, we hope that these identifications are accurate but they are not absolutely guaranteed as such. Dates are included where verifiable.

Allegorical names appear in SMALL CAPITALS. Biblical references have been included with their books and brief explanations given where it was thought helpful. References to God, Christ, the Virgin, etc., are not included, nor is the Bible itself listed. Geographical names are likewise omitted. All names are referenced with the line(s) in which they occur in the translation.

250.1, 259.2, 260.1, 262.1, 263.2, 268.7, 273.6, 274.6, 275.3, 276.3, 277.3, 278.6, 329.3.

Achilles: Trojan hero, son of Peleus and Thetis, slew Hector, killed at Troy. 57.2, 58.3.

Adam: eater of Forbidden Fruit and Biblical progenitor of man. Genesis. 318.3.

Adonis: beautiful youth loved by Aphrodite, killed hunting boar. 68.2.

ADVERSITY: *Aversité.* 226.8.

Agamemnon: King of Argos, commander in chief of the Greek host at Troy; husband of Clytemnestra. 62.3.

AGE: *Eage.* 87.6, 91.1, 92.2, 94.7, 97.7, 102.1, 104.5, 115.3.

Albert of Austria: Albert II, King of Germany; tutored by Philip of Burgundy, first Hapsburg Holy Roman Emperor, 1397–1439. 178.3

Alexander: third son of Cassander, shared throne, with brother Antipater, 297–294 B.C., murdered by order of Demetrius. 56.5.

Alfonso: Alfonso V, The Wise and Magnanimous, son of Ferdinand I, King of Aragon, Sicily and Naples, 1385–1458. 190.3.

ALL GOOD: *Toute Bonté.* 222.3.

Alvaro de Luna: Constable of Castile, favorite of John II, died on scaffold, 1388?–1453. 193.2.

Amasa: rival of, killed by Joab. II Samuel. 69.3.

Amazons: nation of women warriors, supposed to live in the Caucasus, fought Greeks during Trojan War. 164.7.

Amé de Montgesoie: contemporary French writer famous for *Le Pas de la Mort.* 5.3.

Amurat: Sultan Amurat (Murad) II, Ottoman leader, extended Turkish conquests in southwestern Europe, 1403–1451. 205.7.

ANGER: *Couroux.* 237.2.

Antioch: Jean of Portugal, son of John I, said to be from Coimbra, Prince of Antioch, regent of Cyprus, CTO, d. 1457. 199.1.

Antipater: son of Cassander, shared throne with brother Alexander. 56.3.

Aristobolus: related to the Maccabees, lived 1st century B.C. 246.7.

Armagnac: Bernard of, count of Pardiac, son of Bernard VII, d. 1462. 200.3.

ARROGANCE: *Arrogance.* 237.1.

Arthur: 6th-century legendary or real king of the Britons. 63.3.

Arthur: duke of Brittany, Constable of France, so-called genius behind military reforms of Charles VII, d. 1458. 175.7.

ATONEMENT: *Satisfaction.* 29.3.

Atropos: *Atropos,* Goddess of Death; one of the three Fates, she cuts the thread of life. See also DEATH. 6.1, 154.2, 160.2, 163.2, 168.2, 216.4, 218.8, 219.1, 234.3, 269.6, 270.3, 285.4, 319.5, 328.6.

AUDACITY: *Hardement.* 232.6, 238.8.

Austria, duchess of: Mary of Burgundy, archduchess of Austria, only daughter of Charles the Bold, wife of Emperor Maximilian of Austria, 1457–1482. 259.7, 262.7.

AUTHORITY: *Regime.* 40.4, 77.4, 82.7, 83.3, 90.3.

Auxy: Jean, lord and count of Auxy, CTO, d. 1474. 191.4.

BASENESS: *Vilonnye.* 221.8.

BELOVED: *Bien Aimé.* 222.6.

Berghes: Michel de, one of Emperor Maximilian's closest advisors. 278.1.

BITTERNESS, FOUNTAINS OF: *Fontaines d'Amertume.* 123.1.

Brederode: Lord of Renaud and Viane, CTO, d. 1473. 196.1.

Brézé, Pierre de: Lord of La Varenne and Brissac, grand seneschal of Poitou, Anjou, and Normandy, killed at Montlhéry, d. 1465, 183.1.

Brimeu: Guy de, lord of Humbercourt, count of Meghen, imprisoned and decapitated by Ghents, CCC, CTO, d. 1477. 191.4.

Bueil, Louis de: younger brother of Jean V, chamberlain to Louis XI, killed in a tourney. 172.3.

Caesar, Gaius Julius: Roman dictator, general, consul, 100–44 B.C. 55.3.

Cain: son of Adam, killed brother Abel. Genesis. 52.3.

Calabria: dukes of. 201.6.

    1. John, son of René I, d. 1470.

    2. Possibly Nicolas, grandson of René I, d. 1473.

Calatravans: Members of an order founded in 1158 to protect the fortress of Calatrava (Spain). Originally a Cistercian order, it became purely military in 1164 and the members were released from their vow of chastity. 196.6.

Chalant, Jacques de: lord of Aymeville, Chatillon, Ussel, count of Chalant. 180.8.

CHANCE: *Fortune.* 36.7.

CHARITABLE WILL: *Charitable Voulenté.* 288.5.

CHARITY: *Charité.* 45.5.

Charles: the Bold, count and duke of Burgundy and Charolais, called *Le Traveillant* by Olivier (*Mémoires*, I, 122), grand chamberlain of France, died at third battle of Nancy, 1433–1477. 238.2, 245.5, 249.5.

Charles V: king of France, the Wise, confirmed donation of duchy of Burgundy to Philip the Good, 1337–1380. 284.8.

Charles VII: king of France, the Victorious, 1403–1461. 203.3.

Charny: Pierre de Bauffrement, CCC under Philip the Good, governor, captain general, hereditary seneschal of Burgundy, CTO, died at Poitiers bearing the Oriflamme, the banner of Saint-Denis, 1473. 191.1.

Chimay, conte de: Jean, lord and count of Chimay, CCC, CTO, grand master of France, d. 1473. (Brother of Antoine, 274.1) 189.5.

Chimay, Philippe de: Philippe de Croy, baron of Quievrain, count of Chimay, premier chamberlain of Maximilian, grand bailiff and governor of Holland, CTO, d. 1482. 274.1.

Cicero: Marcus Tullius Cicero, Roman orator, statesman, philosopher, 106–43 B.C. 162.4.

Clarence: George, son of Richard of York, brother of Edward IV, allied with Warwick in the War of the Roses, died Tower of London, 1449–1478. 195.3.

Cleves, Jehan, duc de: Jehan I, son of Adolphe IV, CTO, d. 1481. 204.6.

CLOISTER OF MEMORY: *Cloistre de Souvenance.* 73.2.

Cœur, Jacques: the leading businessman of France, became master of the mint, treasurer to king, arrested for embezzlement, fled to Rome, 1395–1456. 192.4.

Coimbra: John of Portugal, duke of Coimbra, archbishop and cardinal of Lisbon, d. Florence, 1459. 171.2.

COMPLAINTS: *Clameurs.* 221.3.

COMPLETE NOBILITY: *Entiere Noblesse.* 222.8.

Conches: Thibaut, bastard of, lord of Chamilley and Conflans, son of Jean de Neufchatel-Montagu, d. 1450. 196.1.

CONSOLATION, ROAD OF: *Chemin d'Alegance.* 271.8.

CONSTANCY: *Loyauté.* 45.6.

CONSUMMATE CHASTITY: *Chasteté Parfaitte.* 289.2.

CONSUMMATION: *Comsummacion.* 224.4.

CONTEMPLATION: *Estudier.* 138.1.

CONTRITION: *Contriction.* 29.4.

Cornille: bastard of Burgundy, called the Great Bastard, son of Philip the Good, head pierced by lance at battle of Rupelmonde, 1452. 182.4.

COURAGE: *Courage.* 12.8.

CREDENCE: *Creance.* 46.2.

Crequy: Jean V, lord of Crequy and Canaple, CCC, CTO, d. 1474. 191.3.

Croy: Antoine, count of Porcien, CCC, CTO, governor of Namur and duchy of Luxembourg, d. 1475. 189.1.

CRUELTY: *Cruaulté.* 220.1.

DAME TEMPERANCE: *Dame Attrempance.* 288.7.

David: King of Judah, Israel, killed Goliath. I Samuel, I Kings, I Chronicles. 70.2.

DEATH: *Mort.* 5.5, 163.5, 164.6, 164.8, 165.7, 185.8, 207.8, 208.6, 209.6, 210.6, 211.3, 256.6, 285.8. See also ATROPOS.

DEBILITY: *Debile.* 5.7, 7.3, 17.2, 38.4, 38.7, 74.7, 75.4, 154.8, 159.8, 163.1, 168.4, 169.6, 170.6, 173.7, 175.6, 176.6, 177.6, 180.2, 184.8, 185.7, 186.4, 187.8, 188.8, 189.8, 190.7, 191.8, 192.7, 194.7, 196.8, 197.6, 198.2, 199.6, 201.3, 203.8, 204.8, 205.8, 217.4, 224,2, 227.1, 228.3, 229.5, 230.3, 231.6, 233.6, 268.8, 275.4, 329.2. (Prince of Affliction, 217.4.)

EXCESS: *Excés*. 8.1.

FAITH: *Foy*. 290.5, 316.2.
FEAR: *Doubtance*. 220.6.
FEEBLENESS: *Feblesse*. 231.8.
Felix: Felix V, antipope elected by Council of Basel, 1439, excommunicated by Pope Eugenius IV; renounced claim, became cardinal, 1383–1451. 173.2.
Filippo Maria: Visconti, Duke of Milan, last Visconti to rule as duke, daughter married F. Sforza, 1392–1447. 184.1.
FIRM INTENT TO LOVE GOD: *Ferme Propos d'Amer Dieu*. 287.7–8.
FIRMNESS: Fermeté. 226.7, 230.2.
FLOWER OF DAYS: *Fleur de Jours*. 254.3.
Forest of Time Lost: *Forest de Temps Perdu*. 97.1.
FORTHRIGHT: *Franchise*. 239.4.
FORTUNE: *Fortune*. 237.8, 243.6, 244.2, 246.1.
Francesco: Sforza, won fame as soldier, son-in-law of duke of Milan, 1401–1466. 184.7.
FRESH MEMORY: *Fresche Memoire*. 142.8, 143.7, 144.3, 145.2, 145.5, 146.8, 147.6, 149.1, 151.7, 152.8, 157.1, 161.1, 167.4, 211.2, 231.1, 268.1, 270.6, 272.1, 279.1, 280.1.
Fribourg: Jean, count, marshal. 186.1.
FRIENDS: *Amis*. 226.5.
Fromont: count Aymery, uncle of Remondin. 67.2.

Gawain: knight of King Arthur's Round Table. 63.4.
GENEROSITY: *Magnanimité*. 288.2.
GENTLE MANNER: *Doulce Maniere*. 253.4.
Giles of Brittany: Lord of Chantoce, Order of the Garter, brother of Duke Francis I, d. 1450. 175.3.
GLADNESS: *Liesse*. 34.3.
GLORY: *Gloire*. 235.2
GLUTTONY: *Gourmandise*. 16.8.
Goliath: Biblical giant killed by David. I Samuel. 70.3.
GOOD ADVICE: *Bon Advis*. 118.7, 226.2.
GOOD EXAMPLE: *Bon Exemplaire*. 298.5.
GOOD EXHORTATION: *Bon Enhortment*. 46.8.
GOOD FORTUNE: *Bonne Adventure*. 134.8.
GOOD HOPE: *Bon Espoir*. 12.4. See also HOPE.
GOOD INTENTION: *Bonne Intention*. 48.4.
GOOD LAW: *Bonne Loy*. 46.3.
GOOD LIFE: *Bonne Vie*. 34.2.

GOOD REPUTE WHICH IS NO SMALL THING: *Bon Renom Qui N'est Pas Vain.* 254.3.
GOOD THINKING: *Bon Pensement.* 137.8.
GOOD THOUGHT: *Bonne Pensee.* 257.2.
GOOD THOUGHTS: *Bonnes Pensees.* 290.5.
GOOD WILL: *Bonne Voulenté.* 45.2.
GOOD WORK: *Bonne Labeur.* 289.5.
GOOD YOUTH: *Bonne Enfance.* 28.4.
GRACE: *Grace.* 46.5.
GRATIFICATION: *Plaisir.* 36.7.
GREAT HEART: *Grant Cuer.* 239.2.
GREAT PLEASURE: *Grant Plaisir.* 138.6.
GRIEF: *Douleur.* 36.7.
GRIEVANCE: *Grevance.* 227.2; *Griefvement.* 228.4.
Guienne: Charles of Berri, duke of, d. 1472. 204.1.

Haman: chief minister of Ahasuerus, enemy of Jews, hanged on gibbet intended for Mordecai. Esther. 71.2.
Hannibal: Carthaginian general, committed suicide at court of Prusias II of Bithynia rather than be turned over to the Romans. 60.2.
HARMONY: *Concorde.* 48.2.
Hautbourdin: Jean, bastard of Luxembourg, called Hennequin, lord of Hautbourdin, councilor and chamberlain, CTO, son of Valerand, marshal of France, d. 1466. 191.3.
Hector: son of Priam, brother of Paris; Trojan hero killed by Achilles before Trojan walls. 57.3, 256.7, 264.5.
Henry, VI: King of England. Olivier says he was more devoted to God than to defending his realm and his baronage (*Mémoires* II, 209), 1421–1471. 202.2.
Hercules: son of Zeus and Alcmene, maddened by wearing poisoned shirt, puts self on funeral pyre. 9.2, 54.5.
HIGH ENDEAVOR: *Haulte Emprise.* 239.1.
Holofernes: General of Nebuchadnezzar, killed by Judith. Apocrypha, Judith. 64.2.
Homer: ancient Greek poet. 162.1.
HONOR: *Honneur.* 222.4.
HOPE: *Espoir.* 90.7; *Esperance.* 91.2. See also GOOD HOPE.
HOPELESSNESS: *Desesperer.* 250.4.

IDLENESS: *Oyseuse.* 95.8, 139.1.
IGNORANCE: *Ignorance.* 141.5.
ILL LUCK: *Male Adventure.* 250.8.

ILLUSION: *Abusion.* 113.2.
INNOCENCE: *Innocence.* 46.4.
INQUIRY: *Enquerir.* 138.2.
INSTRUCTION: *Ensonnier.* 138.3.
ISLE OF INFIRMITY: *Ysle d'Enfermeté.* 125.2.

Jacques de Bourbon: count of La Marche and Castres, grand chamberlain of
    France, king of Naples, Hungary, Sicily and Jerusalem, died a Franciscan,
    Besançon, 1438. 176.1.
Jacques de Bourbon: knight of Saint Michel, CTO, son of Charles I, d. 1468.
Jael: killed Canaanite general Sisera who sought refuge with her. Judges. 65.2.
Joab: nephew of David, killed rival Amasa (II Samuel), executed by Solomon.
    I Kings. 69.2.
Judas: Judas Iscariot, betrayed Jesus. Matthew. 69.5.
Judith: heroine who killed Holofernes and delivered her people. Apocrypha,
    Judith. 64.3.
JUSTICE: *Justice.* 298.7.
Ladislas: V or VI Posthumus, King of Hungary and Bohemia, murdered his
    regent, died of plague, 1440–1457. 179.3.
La Hire: Etienne de Vignolles, captain general of Ile-de-France, Picardy, Beau-
    voisis, etc., companion Joan of Arc at Orléans, celebrated soldier of for-
    tune, 1390–1443. 177.4.
Lalain, Jacques de: CCC of Philip the Good, CTO, considered the knightly
    paragon of the court, suffered accidental mortal wound at siege of
    Poucques, d. 1453. 181.5.
Lalain: Simon de, lord of Hantes and Montigny, CCC, CTO, bailliff of
    Amiens, d. 1476. 191.5.
La Vere: according to Stein, Henri de Borsele, lord of la Vere, CTO, councilor
    and chamberlain to the king, d. 1471. 191.3.
Le Blanc de La Valaquie: John Hunyady, national hero of Hungary, and regent;
    defended Belgrade against Turkish army of Mohammed II, 1456; died of
    plague, 1387–1456. 197.3.
LET NO ONE BE CONFIDENT: *Nulz-ne-s'y-fie.* 220.8.
Ligny: Jean II of Luxembourg, count of Ligny, lord of Beaurevoir, first cham-
    berlain, CTO, d. 1440. 170.1.
LITTLE SENSE: *Peu de Sens.* 18.2.
LOOK TO YOURSELF: *Avise Toy.* 337.2.
Louis de Bourbon: duke of Bourbon, count of Vendome and Chartres, grand
    chamberlain and grand master of France, d. 1446. 198.1.
Louis de Bourbon: Bishop of Liege, son of Duke Charles I, d. 1482. 273.1.
Louis, Prince of Orange: The Good, lord of Arguel and Montfaucon, prince,
    count of Chalon, CCC, d. 1463. 199.8.

PAIN: *Peine.* 80.2.

PALACE OF LOVE: *Palais d'Amours.* 113.8.

Palladium: sacred image of Pallas Athena with power to preserve Troy. 263.3. See Diomedes.

Paris: son of Priam, king of Troy, stole Helen and precipitated the Trojan War. 58.5.

PATH OF GOOD COUNSEL: *Sente Bon Advis.* 118.7.

PATH OF ILL WILL: *Sente de Malveullance.* 96.7.

PATH OF LIFE: *Sente de Vie.* 216.2.

PATH OF LITTLE PROFIT: *Sente Peu de Proffit.* 109.2.

PATH TO DAMNATION: *Sentier de Damnement.* 294.8.

PATIENCE: *Pacience.* 127.5.

PEACE: *Union.* 48.1.

PENITENCE: *Penitance.* 29.5.

Penthesilea: Queen of the Amazons, fought in Trojan War. 256.6.

Perceval the Gaul: Perceval, knight of the Round Table. 87.4.

PERFECTION: *Perfection.* 48.3.

PERSECUTION: *Persecucion.* 224.3, 230.4.

Philip: of Bourbon, lord and count of Beaujeu, second son of Charles I, died young. 198.6.

Philip: the Good, Duke of Burgundy, called the *grand duc de Ponant* (Great Duke of the West) by Chastellain, d. 1467. 225.7.

Phoebus: François Phoebus, count of Foix, inherited kingdom of Navarre, d. 1483. 277.1.

Plato: Greek philosopher, disciple of Socrates. 144.1.

PLEASANT HARVEST: *Plaisant Requel.* 258.2.

PLEASURE: *Plaisance.* 137.5.

Pliny: Roman scholar in history, rhetoric, military science, and natural science, died during eruption of Mt. Vesuvius. 23-79 A.D. 248.6.

Polynices: son of Oedipus, gained throne of Thebes and rejected co-regency with brother Eteocles, whom he slew. 66.4.

Pompey: the Great, contempory of Julius Caesar, murdered by Ptolemy, 106–48 B.C. 59.2.

POSTPONEMENT: *Actente.* 269.2.

Poton: Xaintrailles, called Poton, lord of, knight, marshal of France, friend of La Hire and Joan of Arc, d. 1461. 177.4.

POWER: *Pouvoir.* 12.3, 226.5.

PRAISE: *Los.* 226.5.

PRESUMPTION: *Oultrecuidance.* 237.4.

PROMISE: *Promesse.* 47.5.

PROWESS: *Proesse.* 222.7.

PRUDENCE: *Pourveance.* 27.4.

Sigismond: King of Hungary and Bohemia, Holy Roman Emperor, house of Luxembourg, emperor of Germany, 1368–1437. 169.3.

Simon: See Lalain.

Sisera: Canaanite general of Jabin's army, killed by Jael in her tent where he sought refuge. Judges 4. 65.3.

SLEEP: *Sommeil.* 80.4.

Socrates: Athenian philosopher, 470?–399 B.C. 144.1.

SOLDIER OF HELL: *Sauldoyer d'Enfer.* 309.5.

Solomon: King of Israel, 973–933 B.C. 9.3.

SORROWS: *Douleurs.* 221.1.

SPITE: *Despit.* 262.2.

STRENGTH: *Force.* 288.1.

STUDY: *Estude.* 141.4.

SUDDEN ILLNESS: *Soudaine Maladie.* 251.2.

SUFFERING: *Souffrir.* 80.6.

SUFFICIENCY: *Soufissance.* 34.4.

SURFEIT OF DAYS: *Trop de Jours.* 84.3.

SWEETNESS: *Doulceur.* 222.3.

Talbot: John II, first Count of Shrewsbury, Lord Lieutenant of Ireland, Governor of Normandy, Marshal of France, Count Waterford, Lord Dungarin, killed at Castillon, 1388?–1453. 174.6.

TEARS: *Pleurs.* 221.4.

TEMPERANCE: *Sobresse.* 34.1.

Templars: a knightly chivalric and religious group founded in 1118; originally for protection of Christians in the Holy Land, it became wealthy and corrupt and was suppressed. 196.6.

Ternant: Philip, lord of Ternant and La Motte de Thoisy, provost-marshal of Paris, CCC, CTO; named La Marche pantler to the duke, d. 1456. 186.6.

Thibault: Thibaut IX of Neuchatel, lord of Blamont and Chastel-sur-Moselle, CTO, marshal, d. 1469. 185.1.

THOUGHT: *Pensee.* 1.5, 11.1, 25.2.

TIME, LAND OF: *Temps, la lande:* 78.2, 88.1, 102.5.

TO LOVE FAITHFULLY WITH UNCHANGING HEART OR EYE: *Loyaument Amer Sans Changier ne de Cuer ne d'Eul.* 258.4–5.

TOTAL GOODNESS: *Bonté Entiere.* 253.3.

Toulongeon: possibly Claude and Tristan, sons of Antoine, and Jean, nephew of Antoine, CCC, governor of Champagne, marshal, and captain general, CTO, d. 1472. 186.2.

TRAVAIL: *Traveil.* 80.1.

Tristan: Nephew of King Mark of Cornwall, enamoured of Mark's wife, Isolde. 61.4.

Troilus: son of Priam. 264.1.
TRUE FAITH: *Vraie Foy*. 46.1.
TRUTH: *Verité*. 47.4.

UNDERSTANDING: *Entendement*. 33.3, 51.6, 72.6, 75.1, 271.3, 280.3, 281.2, 282.6, 300.1, 302.1, 328.1, 334.7, 335.1.
UNTAINTED CHASTITY: *Chasteté Pure*. 45.4.

VALE OF MARRIAGE: *Val de Mariage*. 95.1.
Valerius Maximus: 1st-century Roman historian, wrote *Memorable Words and Deeds*. 162.3.
VALIANCE: *Preudommye*. 45.8.
Varembon: François de la Palu, lord of Varembon, knight of the order of Savoy, councilor and chamberlain of duke of Burgundy, d. 1456. 180.3.
VENTURE: *Aventurer*. 12.6.
Venus: goddess of love. 58.4.
Vergy: Guillaume de Vergy according to Stein. The *Mémoires* mention: Jean IV, d. 1460; Charles, d. 1467; Jean, bastard, d. 1457; Antoine, d. 1454. 196.1.
Vienne: Guillaume V of, lord of Saint-Georges and Bussy, etc., CCC, d. 1456. 168.3.

WAKEFULNESS: *Veillier*. 80.4.
Waleram: of Soissons, lord of Poix and Moreuil, etc., CCC, CTO, d. 1473. 194.1.
Warwick: Richard Neville, Count of Warwick, Grand Chamberlain of England, the "kingmaker," killed at Barnet, 1428–1471. 195.1.
WICKED SCORN: *Felle Despit*. 221.8.
WILLFULNESS: *Voulenté*. 220.3, 223.1.
WILLING: *Vouloir*. 12.1, 79.1.
WORLDLY PLEASURE: *Plaisance Mondaine*. 14.8.
WORLDLY ROUTE: *Chemin Mondain*. 216.1.

YOUTH. See RELICS OF YOUTH.

Appendix: Instructions to Artists for Illustrating the Text

Base text: *L* (B.n.F., fr. 1606); variants from *T* and *W*. Manuscript *T* is so badly damaged (see Introduction) that some readings can only be conjectural; these are set in brackets. We have not judged it necessary to indicate all the unreadable or missing portions of *T*. As in the case of the poem itself, many variants are quite minor. They are nonetheless included, in the belief that they demonstrate something of the *mouvance* of a text of this type. When *T* and *W* present the same wording, however, minor spelling variations between them are not indicated. The same editorial conventions (distinction of *i* and *j*, *u* and *v*; expansion of abbreviations) are observed here as in the text of the poem. The cedilla and the acute accent are added following the usage of the poem; the *tréma* is limited to a single case where it is used in present-day French, the word *aguës* (Miniature 12). Variations in capitalization are not noted. Punctuation follows the rules for modern French. Emendations and passages for which variants are given are marked by superscript numbers in the text; asterisks indicate explanatory notes.

It should be noted that surviving sets of written instructions of this type are relatively uncommon. (Sandra Hindman mentions those for a few other texts: "Roles of Author and Artist," pp. 38–41; *Christine de Pizan's "Epistre Othéa,"* pp. 64–65.) An examination of the various manuscripts and incunabula reveals that some illustrators must have been aware of these instructions. Of the nine illustrated manuscripts, the artist of *C* is definitely the one who most scrupulously respected the author's wishes in this respect. The miniatures of manuscripts *A, B, F, G,* and *R,* as well as the woodcuts in *Y,* generally follow the instructions, but all depart from them to some extent. Those of *E, Q,* and *S,* and the woodcuts of *X,* are at times so different from the specific instructions that we must conclude that the artists either knew nothing of them, or deliberately chose to ignore them.

The text of these instructions was included in Veinant's 1842 edition and was printed by Picot and Stein, pp. 313–19; an English translation, based on Veinant's transcription, was included in the 1898 London edition of the poem, pp. xiii–xx.

MINIATURE 1 (1^{r-v} L; 12^r T; 142^r W). Precedes stanza 1.

[E]n[1] ceste histoire[2] aura ung manoir en façon d'ung chasteaul, et tenant a icellui aura une plainne arbue, et ou milieu d'icelle plainne aura ung chevalier vestu d'ugne longue robbe noire sanglé,[3] et unes pate-nostres[4] pendans a sa sainture au dextre costé, et seront estoffees de houppes et de saingnaulx d'or. Ledit[5] chevalier aura une chainne d'or au col et tiendra ung long baston[6] en sa main dextre et en son chief aura ung chappeaul noir a une petitte enseigne d'or, et une cornette devant son visaige et a l'entour de[7] son col, et le plus en forme d'homme[8] pensif que faire se[9] peult.[10] Et emprés[11] lui aura une femme vestue d'ung drap d'or bleu, l'abilement et l'atour en maniere [1^v L] d'une sebille, et tien-dra maniere de diviser audit chevalier. Et sur la robe du chevalier aura escript L'ACTEUR, et sur celle de la dame aura escript en lieu veable[12] PENSEE.

Variants:
Only a few words are guessable in T; nothing is legible prior to Et emprés lui *in the second-last sentence.*
1. Space left for decorated initial, not executed, L.
2. ceste premiere histoire W
3. robe chainte W
4. une [*sic*] patrenostes W
5. Ce ch. W
6. ung baston noir W
7. et autour de W
8. dun homme W
9. se W] ce L
10. se polra W
11. Et dempres W
12. en lieu veable *om.* W

Translation: In this scene there will be a manor house fashioned like a chateau, and contiguous to it a grassy plain, and in the middle of this plain will be a knight dressed in a long black robe, girt up, with a rosary hanging at his belt on the right side, which will be furnished with tassels and beads of gold. The aforesaid knight will have a gold chain at his neck and will hold a long club in his right hand; on his head he will have a black hat with a small golden emblem, and a small scarf in front of his face and around his neck, and he shall have the most pensive pose possible. And near him will be a woman dressed in a robe of blue cloth of gold, her habit and ornaments like a sibyl's and she will appear to be speaking with the knight previously mentioned. And on the knight's robe will be written AUTHOR, and on the lady's will be written where easily seen THOUGHT.

MINIATURE 2 (4^r–5^r L; 14^r T; 143^v–144^r W). Precedes stanza 12.

Ceste histoire sera en[1] une champaigne seiche, et a l'entour aura arbres secz et fueilles abbattues. Et ou milieu sera l'Acteur en porpoint, et aura deux varletz vestuz de paletos partis de gris et de vermeil. Et tiendra maniere l'ung de armer l'Acteur[2] d'unes curasses, et l'autre tiendra ung heaulme a la façon de chevalier errant.[3] Et sera Pensee en son premier habilement emprés ledit Acteur, tenant en sa main droitte[4] une lance droitte, ferree a ung petit pannonceaul vermeil, et en cedit pannonceaul aura escript en lettres[5] d'or ADVANTURER. Et a l'autre main tiendra la dame[6] ung escu qui sera [4^v L] mesparty de gris et de vermeil. Et dedans aura[7] escript en lettres d'argent BON ESPOIR. Sur la curasse aura escript en lettres vermeilles POVOIR. Et le varlet qui tiendra le heaulme en la main dextre, tiendra en la senestre[8] une espee dedans le foureau,[9] et sur la gainne aura escript COURAIGE. Et d'emprés iceulx aura ung panier ouvert ou par semblance aura plusieurs pieces de harnas. Le chappeaul, cornette et la robe, la[10] sainture, le baston et les patenostres de l'Acteur seront semees parmy le champ. Et assez prez d'iceulx aura ung cheval gris pommeley ensellé d'une petitte selle en façon de selle de chevalier errant, harnacee[11] d'ung harnas estroit noir a deux bosses dorees. Et sur le flang du cheval en lieu veable aura escript [5^r L] en lettres noires VOULOIR. Et sera tenu ledit cheval par ung petit paige a pied par la longe, vestu[12] comme les autres serviteurs.

Variants:
1. sera fondee en W
2. ledit acteur TW
3. f. des cheualliers errans TW
4. main dextre TW
5. de lettres TW

6. lad*ite* dame *T*
7. aura *om. T*
8. dextre dedens la senestre tiendra *W*
9. foureau *W*, fourrea[u] *T*] four *L*
10. la cornette la robbe et la *W*
11. d'une petitte selle ... harnacee *om. TW*
12. longe lequel page sera vestu *TW*

Translation: This scene will be in an arid countryside and all around there will be dry trees and fallen leaves. And the Author will be in the middle in a doublet, and there will be two grooms dressed in tunics, half gray and half crimson; and one will seem to arm the knight with a cuirass and the other will hold a knight errant's helm. And Thought as first dressed will be near the aforesaid Author, holding in her right hand a straight lance, tipped with a small crimson pennon; and on this pennon will be written in gold letters VENTURE. And in her other hand the lady will hold a shield that will be half gray and half crimson; and thereon will be written in silver letters GOOD HOPE. On the breastplate there will be written in crimson letters POWER. And the groom who holds the helm in his right hand will hold a sheathed sword in his left, and on the scabbard will be written COURAGE. And near these there will be an open hamper where there would seem to be many pieces of armor. The hat, scarf, and robe, the belt, club and rosary of the Author will be strewn about the field. And quite near them will be a dapple gray horse saddled with a small saddle such as used by a knight errant, caparisoned with a slender black harness with two gold bosses; and on a visible spot on the horse's flank will be written in black letters WILLING. And the aforesaid horse will be held on a lead by a small page on foot, dressed like the other servants.

MINIATURE 3 (6^v–7^v *L*; 15^v *T*; 145^{r-v} *W*). Precedes stanza 20.
     Ceste histoire sera fondee sur une plainne sans arbres, et aura escript sur icelle en lieu veable en lettres d'asur C'EST[1] LA TERRE DE PLAISANCE MONDAINNE. Et ou[2] milieu d'icelle aura deux hommes d'armes a cheval qui se combattront d'espees, dont l'ung sera l'entrepreneur monté sur tel cheval qu'il est premier devisé. Et l'autre sera ung aultre [3] [7^r *L*] chevalier errant monté sur ung cheval pye, bay et blanc. Et aura cest autre chevalier une cotte verde sur son harnas, et son espee saincte pardessus. Et sur ladite cotte aura escript en lettres d'or

HUTIN. Ilz auront tous deux esperons dorez. Et en l'espee de l'Acteur et en celle de Hutin, en toutes deux[4] aura escript en lettres vermeilles[5] FOLIE. Et ou milieu du[6] champ[7] aura deux lances[8] rompues, dont l'une sera vermeille et l'autre blanche, et en la vermeille aura[9] escript ADVAN-TURER. Et en la blanche en[10] lettres d'or PEU DE SENS. Et entre eulx deux viendra une damoiselle sur ung blanc paleffroy, qui tiendra maniere de soy mettre entre les deux chevaliers et de departir[11] la bataille. Et aura en sa main dextre ung tergon grant tout[12] blanc dont elle tiendra maniere de recevoir les cops des espees pour garantir les chevaliers. Celle damoiselle sera vestue d'ung drap [7ᵛ L] d'or blanc. Et sur sa robe[13] aura escript en lettres d'azur RELIQUES DE JEUNESSE.[14] Et sur le harnas ou sur le cheval de l'Acteur aura escript en lieu veable L'ACTEUR.

Variants:
1. escript en lieu veable en celle plaine. Cest *T*; escript en lieu veable en celle plaine en *lettres* dazur, Cest *W*
2. au *TW*
3. aultre *om. TW*
4. en toutes deux *om. T*
5. Et en ch*a*scune de leurs espees ara escript de *lettre* [*sic*] v. *W*
6. Et emmy le ch. *TW*
7. le champs [*sic*] *W*
8. deux lance [*sic*] *W*
9. et lautre sera blanche. En la vermeille lance aura *T*; dont lune sera blance et lautre vermeille. En la vermeille ara *W*
10. en la blance aura escript en *T*
11. de departir *TW*] deppartira *L*
12. grant qui sera tout *T*
13. sur la robbe *W*
14. jeunesses *W*

Translation: This scene will be set in a treeless plain and it will have written thereon in azure letters where easily seen THIS IS THE LAND OF WORLDLY PLEASURE; and in its center there will be two men-at-arms on horseback who will fight each other with swords, one of whom will be the venturer on such a horse as already described. The other will be another knight errant mounted on a bay and white piebald horse. This second knight will have a green tunic over his armor and his sword hung therefrom; and on his aforesaid tunic will be inscribed in golden letters QUARRELER. They will both have golden spurs; and on each of their

swords will be written in crimson letters: FOLLY; and in the middle of
the field there will be two broken lances, one crimson and the other
white. On the crimson will be written VENTURE, and on the white one
in golden letters LITTLE SENSE. And between them will come a maiden
on a white palfrey, who will seem to place herself between the two
knights, and who will stop the fight; and she will have in her right hand
a large shield, all white, with which she will seem to take the sword
strokes to protect the knights. This maiden will be robed in white cloth
of gold; and on her robe will be written in azure letters: REMNANTS OF
YOUTH. And on the armor or on the horse of the Author will be writ-
ten in a visible place AUTHOR.

MINIATURE 4 (8^v–9^r L; 17^r T; 146^r W). Precedes stanza 26.
      Ceste histoire sera fondee en maniere d'une forest, et en icelle[1] aura
ung hermitaige et devant icellui[2] ung[3] hermite [9^r L] vestu de gris en son
habilement atout[4] une barbe grise et sera ung grant homme. Et l'Acteur
sera a pied tout armé, et tiendra maniere de parler a l'ermite, et le chev-
al de l'Acteur sera tenu[5] par ung pettit novisse dudit hermite par le frain
comme se il le menoit en l'estable.[6] Et tiendront l'hermite et l'Acteur
maniere de deviser[7] l'ung a l'autre,[8] et ne doit point avoir l'Acteur de
lance.

Variants:
   1. en celle W
   2. deuant ico [?] W
   3. ara vng TW
   4. atout TW] a tout L
   5. sera mene TW
   6. en une estable TW
   7. toucher [?] *added, in smaller letters, above* deuiser, *and lined out*, L;
      touchier TW
   8. lun lautre W [T]

Translation: This scene will be set in a kind of forest, and in it will be
a hermitage, and before it a hermit dressed in gray complete with a gray
beard, and he will be tall. And the Author will be on foot, in full ar-
mor, and he will appear to be speaking with the hermit, and the Auth-
or's horse will be held by the rein by a small novice of the aforesaid her-
mit as if he were leading it to the stable. And the hermit and the Author

will seem to be conversing together; and the Author should not have any lance.

MINIATURE 5 (10^v–11^r *L*; 18^{r-v} *T*; 147^{r-v} *W*). Precedes stanza 33.

Ceste histoire sera fondee sur ung jardin ouquel aura une petitte traille, et soubz icelle traille aura une table[1,a] mise, et de la viande sus en pettis platz de bois, moyenneement, et deux verres et une aiguiere. Et a celle table seront assis l'Acteur vestu d'ung mantel de sattin cramoisy fouré de menuz vairs et sera ledit mantel tout long,[2] les manches fandues et le porpoint noir, et en son chief[3] ung chappel a une ymaige[4] d'or, et[5] de son costé aura escript en lieu veable L'ACTEUR. Et emprés[6] lui sera[7] assis l'hermite [11^r *L*] en son habilement, et de son costé aura escript ENTENDEMENT. Et tiendront maniere de parler l'ung a l'autre, et assez prez[8] d'eulx aura ung pettit novisse pour les servir,[9] en l'abilement[10] que dessus.

Variants:

1. aura une petitte traille, et soubz icelle traille aura une table *TW*]
   aura une petitte table *L*
2. vairs (vaires *W*) et que led*it* manteau soit tout long *TW*
3. Et sur son chief *TW*
4. a vng ymage [*sic*] *W*
5. et *repeated W*
6. Et dempres *W*
7. seras [*sic*] *W*
8. assez loings *TW*
9. seruir de ce quil leur [fauldra] *T*
10. en habillement *W*

Translation: This scene will be set in a garden which will have a small trellis, and beneath the trellis a small table will be set, upon which there is meat, on small wooden plates in the middle, and two glasses and a water jug. And at this table will be seated the Author dressed in a robe of scarlet satin, trimmed with miniver, and the aforesaid cloak will be

---

[a] It seems likely that the phrase concerning the *traille* was present in the original instructions, and was omitted from *L*. The repeated words could lead to eye-skip on the part of a scribe. The presence of a trellis in the illustration of manuscript *C*, whose artist is generally extremely faithful to the instructions, constitutes indirect support for this emendation.

full length, the sleeves split and the doublet black; and on his head a hat with a golden emblem, and beside him written where easily seen AU-THOR. And near him the hermit will be seated in his attire and beside him will be written UNDERSTANDING. And they will seem to be speaking together, and near them will be a small novice to serve them, in costume already described.

MINIATURE 6 (14^v–15^r L; 21^v T; 149^v–150^r W). Precedes stanza 51.

Ceste histoire sera fondee en maniere d'ung cloistre et ouvert par grans huys.[1] Et la sera veu par maniere de reliquiaire pluiseurs piesses, assavoir[2] : le soc[3] d'une charrue, ung gros pillier[4] de pierre rompu, une chemise plainne de feu, ung estuy[5] plain de grephes et verra l'on[6] les testes descouvertes, une boitte close, ung arc turquois et des flesches,[7] une espee, ung espieu,[8] ung badelaire,[9] ung sangler,[10] une pierre et une fonde,[11] ung chevestre de corde.[12] Et devant icelles reliques seront l'hermite et l'Acteur, chascun en l'abilement qu'ilz estoient a table. Et contre le cloistre aura escript en lieu veable[13] en lettres d'or C'EST LE CLOISTRE DE SOUVENANCE. Et monstrera icellui hermite lesdites reliques[14] au [15^r L] doit, faisant semblant de les enseigner et monstrer[15] a l'Acteur.

Variants:
1. grant huisse W
2. Assauoir premierement W
3. le soc TW] le fer L ; cf. 52.1
4. gros pillier W, [T]] gros pile L; cf. 53.1
5. escuy W
6. et les verra on TW
7. flesches T (fleches W)] feshes L
8. vng espieu vne espee W
9. badelaire TW] basselaire L; cf. 64.1
10. sangler T (sengler W)] sangle L; cf. 68.1
11. vne espee [sic] et vne fonde W
12. et vng cheuestre fait de corde W
13. en lieu veable om. W
14. icelles relicques W
15. et monstrer om. TW

Translation: This scene will be set in a kind of cloister, with great open portals. And therein will be seen, as in a reliquary, many objects, that is to say: a ploughshare, an enormous stone pillar, broken off, a shirt full of fire, a small case full of styluses, seen with their heads exposed, a closed box, a Turkish bow and some arrows, a sword, a pike, a scimitar, a boar, a stone and a sling, a rope halter. And in front of these relics will be the hermit and the Author, each in the same dress as when dining. And on the cloister will be written where easily seen, in golden letters, THIS IS THE CLOISTER OF MEMORY. And the hermit will point to the aforementioned relics, seeming to show them to the Author and to educate him about them.

MINIATURE 7 (19ᵛ-20ʳ *L*; 26ʳ *T*; 153ʳ⁻ᵛ *W*). Precedes stanza 77.

Ceste histoire sera fondee sur telle fondacion que [20ʳ *L*] l'hermitaige aura premier[1] esté veu. Et devant la porte sera l'Acteur a cheval, armé de toutes armes ainsi que paravant, et l'hermite lui mettra en sa main dextre une lance noire dont le fer sera d'argent et tiendra maniere de la[2] mettre sur[3] la cuisse.[4] Et a l'entour[5] de la lance aura escript en lettres d'or REGIME.

Variants:
1. premiers *TW*
2. la *om. W*
3. sus *T*
4. sur sa cuisse *W*
5. Et entour *W*

Translation: This scene will be set in such a way as the hermitage was first seen. And the Author will be in front of the door on horseback, in full armor as before; and the hermit will place in his right hand a black lance, whose tip will be silver, and will appear to place it on his thigh. And around the lance shall be written in gold letters AUTHORITY.

MINIATURE 8 (22ᵛ-23ᵛ *L*; 28ᵛ *T*; 155ʳ *W*). Precedes stanza 90.

Ceste histoire sera fondee [23ʳ *L*] sur une grant champaigne. Et au milieu[1] d'icelle aura deux chevaliers a pied, armés de toutes armes, qui se combattront d'espees. L'ung des chevaliers sera l'Acteur en son[2] harnas accoustumé. Et l'autre chevalier sera grant et sera vestu[3] sur ses armes[4] d'une robe[5] d'armes[6] toute dessainte,[7] et son escu descoulouré, et sur[8] sa[9] cotte aura escript en lettres d'or EAIGE.[10] Et sur son espee, en lettres vermeilles,[11] TROP DE JOURS. La lance de l'Acteur, ou sera[12] escript REGIME, sera rompue emmy le champ. Et au dessus des chevaliers[13] aura deux chevaulx ensellez, dont l'ung sera le cheval de l'Acteur et l'autre le[14] cheval de l'autre chevalier, et tiendront maniere de ruer l'ung a l'autre.[15] Et doibvent[16,b] lesditz deux chevaliers estre esperonnez de deux cours esperons dorez. Le cheval du chevalier sera noir,[17] sur lequel aura[18] escript en lieu veable et[19] en lettres d'argent PAINNE, et sa lance, qui sera blanche, couchee[20] emmy le champ sans estre rompue. Et aura [23ᵛ L] escript en la champaigne en lieu veable en lettres d'azur LE TEMPS.

Variants:
1. ou milieu *TW*
2. son *om. W*
3. vestus *W*
4. ses armures *W*
5. dune cotte *TW*
6. darme [*sic*] *W*
7. destainte *W*, *T* [?] (deffaite, PS)
8. sus *T*
9. la cotte *TW*
10. escript eaige en [lettres] dor *T* (*W* = *L*)
11. vermeille *W*
12. ou ara *T*
13. des deux ch. *TW*
14. et lautre sera le *T*
15. lun lautre *TW*
16. Et doibvent ... dorez *follows* Le cheval ... Painne, *LTW*.
17. [Et] sera noir le cheual du cheualier *T*
18. et sur ledit cheual aura *TW*
19. et *om. TW*
20. sera couchee *TW*

Translation: This scene will be set in a wide field, in the middle of which will be two knights on foot, in full armor, fighting with swords. One of the knights will be the Author in his usual armor, and the other knight will be very tall, and will be dressed over his armor with a sur-

---

    b *Et doivent ... dorez.* We have interchanged this sentence and *Le cheval ... Painne*, following Veinant and Picot-Stein, in order to provide a more logical sequence of ideas.

coat all uncinched, and his shield will be faded, and on his coat will be written in golden letters AGE, and on his sword, in crimson letters SURFEIT OF DAYS. The Author's lance, on which will be written AUTHORITY, will be broken on the field. And behind the knights there will be two saddled horses, one of which is the Author's horse, and the other the other knight's. And they will appear to lash out at each other. And the aforesaid two knights should be spurred with two short golden spurs. The knight's horse will be black, on which will be written in plain sight in silver letters PAIN and his lance, which will be white, lying unbroken on the field. And there will be written on the field in an easily seen place, in azure letters, TIME.

MINIATURE 9 (28[r-v] *L*; 33[r] *T*; 158[v] *W*). Precedes stanza 114.

Ceste histoire sera fondee en[1] ung pays plain[2] de verdeurs et de fleurs. Et la aura ung palais tout refflamboiant d'or, d'argent et d'azur, et pardessus[3] aura terrasses a l'entour,[4] toutes plainnes[5] de tamborins, trompettes et menestreux.[6] Et les fenestres seront toutes plainnes de dames et de gorgias richement vestus[7] de diverses couleurs. La porte sera fermee, et au dessus aura escript en ung tableau d'or et de lettres d'azur C'EST LE PALAIS D'AMOURS. Devant la porte aura ung grant homme habilé comme ung fol, et sur[8] sa robe aura escript en lettres jaunes[9] ABUSION. Et tiendra en ses mains [28[v] *L*] les cleifz[10] dudit palais. L'Acteur sera a cheval devant la porte, monté et armé comme il a accoustumé, reserve qu'il n'ara point de lance, et tiendra maniere d'arrester son cheval sur le cul. Et viendront[11] deux personnaiges audevant de lui, dont l'ung sera ung gorgias vestu d'une courte robe[12] verde decouppee et enchatuee,[13,c] et au long de sa[14] chausse[15] aura[16] escript en lettres d'argent, en maniere de brodure, DESIR. Et prandra le cheval de l'Acteur par la bride, comme se il le[17] vouloit mener ou palais.[18] L'autre personnaige sera ung homme habilé en managier, et[19] en la[20] maniere de homme d'eaige, et sera vestu d'une robe rouge. Et sur sa manche aura escript SOUVENIR, et tiendra en ses mains ung grant miroir, lequel il presentera devant la face de l'Acteur.

---

[c] *Enchatuee.* This word appears thus in Veinant's 1842 edition (based on *L*); the manuscript could also be read as *enchatriee.* Neither form occurs in the dictionaries we have consulted. The word in *W* might be read either as *enchamee* or as *enchainee*; *T* has no corresponding term. Picot-Stein have *enchatisée* (p. 316), but in no manuscript does the word have anything identifiable as an *s.* Our translation is that of the London 1898 printing.

Variants:

1. fondee sur *W*
2. vng plain pays plain *TW*
3. par le dessus *W*
4. aura tours assez a lentour *TW*
5. touttes plaine [*sic*] *W*
6. menestriers *TW*
7. de dames et de damoiselles ... vestues *W*
8. et contre *TW*
9. en lectre [*sic*] jaunes *W*
10. les clef [*sic*] *W*
11. et viendra *TW*
12. cotte *T*; une court [*sic*] robe *W*
13. et ench. *om. T*, et enchamee [?] *W*
14. de la *W*
15. de sa cuisse sur sa chausse *T*
16. aura *repeated, T*
17. le *om. W*
18. au palais *T*
19. et *om. T*
20. la *om. TW*

Translation: This scene will be set in a region full of greenery and flowers. And there will be a palace all shining in gold, silver, and azure, and up above terraces all around, completely filled with drummers, trumpeters, and minstrels. And the windows will be full of ladies and gallants, richly apparelled in many colors. The door will be closed and above it will be written on a gold panel in azure letters THIS IS THE PALACE OF LOVE. Before the door there will be a tall man dressed as a fool, and on his robe will be written ILLUSION in yellow letters, and he will hold the keys to the aforementioned palace in his hands. The Author will be on his horse in front of the door, mounted and in armor as usual, except that he has no lance, and will seem to be pulling his horse back on its haunches. And two persons will come before him, one of whom will be a gallant dressed in a short green robe, slashed and puffed, and along his legging will be written in silver letters, as if embroidered, DESIRE. And he will take the Author's horse by the bridle, as if wishing to lead him into the palace. The other person will be a man dressed as a steward, and like a man of advanced years, and he will be attired in a red robe. And on his sleeve will be written REMEMBRANCE, and in his hands he will hold a large mirror, which he will place before the Author's face.

MINIATURE 10 (37^{r-v} *L*; 40^v–41^r *T*; 164^v *W*). Precedes stanza 158.

Ceste histoire sera fondee sur une champaigne toute plainne, sans arbres ne montaigne,[1] excepté que, a[2] l'ung des coings,[3] l'on verra, comme a dangier, ung pettit chasteaul richement fait, et contre icellui chasteaul aura escript en lettres d'or BONNE ADVANTURE. Ceste champaigne sera plainne de toutes pars de sepultures haultes, basses et moyennes, richement faittes et[4] de diverses façons et representacions sur l'ancienne mode.[5] Icelles sepultures [seront][6] armoyees d'estranges armoyeries et diverses escriptures, excepté que,[7] sur le quartier dextre d'icelle champaigne, aura sepultures, representacions et armoieries selon le temps present. Et au bout, comme tout hors des autres et separé d'icellui cymetiere, aura une sepulture toute d'or ou sera, tout droit et[8] en grant triumphe assis, ung roy armé, l'espee ou poing toute nue, et sera habilé a la façon sarrazine. Cellui roy aura en[9] sa teste deux couronnes d'empereur[10] l'une sur l'autre, [37^v *L*] et douze couronnes de roy a l'entour de[11] sa sepulture. Et en son escu aura escript en lettres d'azur LE GRANT TURQ. Et ou[12] milieu d'icelles sepultures a la nouvelle façon sera l'Acteur habilé ou mesme[13] habilement que premierement il est habilé[14] en la mesme histoire.[15] Et d'emprés lui sera une jeusne dame[16] et belle, habilee a l'ancienne façon[17] et[18] de diverses couleurs. Et aura a l'entour[19] de son chief ung chappeaul plain de perles[20] et de pierres[21] precieuses,[22] et contre sa robe aura escript FRESCHE MEMOIRE. Celle dame tiendra maniere de monstrer a l'Acteur les sepultures[23] et quelles elles[24] sont.

Variants:
1. montaignes *TW*
2. a *om. W*
3. qcoings [*sic*] *W*
4. faites et parees *W*
5. et … mode *follows* escriptures (*next sentence*) *T*
6. *The verb, necessary for the sentence, is not present in any of the three mss.*
7. de diuerses fachons et armoyees de diuerses armoyries et destranges escriptures et repr*es*entation [*sic*] sur lancienne mode excepte que *W*
8. et *om. TW*
9. sur *TW*

10. couronnes dor dempereur *T*
11. allencontre de *W*
12. au milieu *W*
13. mesmes *T*, meisme *W*
14. habillement quil est (habilé *om.*) *W*
15. en la premiere histoire *TW*
16. vne da*m*me [*sic*] jone *W*
17. a lancienne mode *T*
18. et *om.* *W*
19. aura entour *T*, aura autour *W*
20. pieres *W*
21. pierries [*sic*] *T*, pieries [*sic*] *W*
22. precieuses *om.* *TW*
23. Celle dame viendra a lacte*u*r et tiendra maniere de lui monstrer les s. *T*
24. elle [*sic*] *W*

Translation: This scene will be set on a completely flat plain, without trees or mountains, except that in one corner there can barely be seen a richly built small castle, and on this castle will be written in gold letters GOOD FORTUNE. This plain will be filled in all parts by tombs, high, low, and medium, richly made and of different styles and depictions according to the manner of the past. These tombs will be emblazoned with strange arms and diverse inscriptions, except that on the righthand quarter of this plain, there will be tombs, figures and arms of the present time. And at the end, as if outside the others and separate from this cemetery, there will be a tomb entirely of gold where there will be, seated upright in great triumph, a king in armor, his sword unsheathed, dressed as a Saracen. This king will have on his head two emperor's crowns, one on top of the other, and twelve king's crowns around his tomb. And on his shield will be written in azure letters THE GREAT TURK. And, in the middle of these tombs in the new style, there will be the Author dressed as he was in the first scene. And near him will be a beautiful young lady, dressed in an older style and in many colors. And she will have around her head a turban full of pearls and precious stones, and on her gown will be written FRESH MEMORY. This lady will appear to be showing the Author the tombs and to whom they belong.

MINIATURE 11 (49ᵛ–51ᵛ *L*; 51ʳ⁻ᵛ *T*; 173ʳ⁻ᵛ *W*). Precedes stanza 219.

Ceste histoire sera fondee sur ung grand pays sech et sablonneux. Et la aura unes lisses closes,[1] et au milieu sur cottiere[2] aura ung eschaffault richement paré. Et en icellui aura une chaiere toute d'or, ou sera assise la Mort, [50ʳ *L*] ayant une couronne toute[3] d'or en la teste. Et sera affublee d'ung manteaul getté a la mode[4] d'Espaigne, lequel manteaul sera fait de pluiseurs couleurs, et mesmes[5] de couleur[6] de terre. Et sera ledit manteaul semé de vers[7] en maniere de brodure. Et sur sa chayere aura escript en lettres d'azur en lieu veable ATTROPPOS, DEESSE DE MORT. Et tiendra en sa main dextre[8] ung darc d'argent et[9] le fer sera rouge. A l'entour[10] d'icellui darc aura escript DEFFIANCE. Les lisses seront noires[11] et de l'ung des costés seront bannieres plaines de larmes et de l'autre costé bannieres[12,d] toutes d'or.[13] Et au milieu du champ[14] aura deux champions qui tiendront maniere de marcher l'ung contre l'autre, dont l'ung sera grant personnaige[15] estrangement armé, et aura une cotte d'armes de sable[16] semee d'ossemens[17] de gens mors. Sur sa senestre espaule[18] portera deux jusarmes[19] estrangement faittes, [50ᵛ *L*] l'une envers l'autre. Et portera en sa main dextre ung darc tout noir a ung grant fer. Et d'autre part sera ung homme d'armes[20] armé de toutes pieces et[21] cotte[22] d'armes[23] de Bourgoigne vestue, telle que la portoit le duc Phelippe, l'espee[24] sainte et la courte dague. Il tiendra en sa main dextre une lance pour joutter,[25] et en la senestre aura une targe mespartie d'or et d'argent, et ou[26] milieu ung fuzil d'azur. Il aura en icelle main une haiche d'armes[27] dont la teste, les bandes[28] et la pointe seront d'or. Et tiendra maniere d'assembler contre sa partie. Les lisses seront a l'entour plainnes[29] de beaulcop de gens a pied et a cheval, et en lieu[30] veable sera l'Acteur qui regardera la bataille, et emprés[31] lui Fresche Memoire sur ung blancq paleffroy[32] et en son habilement comme paravant. [51ʳ *L*] Et tiendront maniere de deviser l'ung a l'autre. Et d'icellui costé ung peu sur le champ et sur le chemin[33] sera ung grant perron et contre icellui perron aura certainnes lettres d'or gregoises.

Variants:
1. vne [*sic*] liches closes *W*
2. sur coustiere *W*
3. toute *om. TW*
4. gecte sur lespaule a [la] mode *T*

---

[d] The omission likely resulted from eye-skip.

5. et meisme *W*
6. couleurs *T*
7. et sera seme ledit manteau de vers *TW*
8. dextre *om. TW*
9. dont le fer *TW*
10. Et alentour *TW*
11. seront toutes noires *TW*
12. plaines ... banieres *TW*] *om. L*
13. toutes d'or *T*] toute dor *L*, tout dor *W*
14. du champs [*sic*] *W*
15. sera vng grant p. *TW*
16. de sable *inserted above line, apparently by the original scribe, L*; de sables *TW*
17. dosselemens *W*
18. sur la senestre espaul [*sic*] *W*
19. guisarmes *TW*
20. d'armes *om. W*
21. et *om. W*
22. la cotte *T*, la coste *W*
23. darmes *T*] darme *LW*
24. l'espee *om. T*, chaint despee et *W*
25. pour gecter *TW*
26. au milieu *TW*
27. d'armes *om. TW*
28. des bendes *W*
29. toutes plaines *W*
30. en vng lieu *TW*
31. dempres *W*
32. sur son bl. p. *TW*
33. coste vng [...] du champ sur le chemin *T*, coste vng pou en sus de champs sur le ch. *W*

Translation: This scene will be set in a great dry and sandy region. And there will be an enclosed list, and in the middle to one side there will be a richly prepared platform. And on it will be a throne entirely of gold, where Death will be seated, having a crown all of gold on her head, and she will be wrapped in a cloak, draped in the Spanish style, which will be made of many colors and even the color of earth; and the aforementioned cloak will be strewn with worms as if embroidered. And on her throne will be written in azure letters, easily seen, ATROPOS, GODDESS

OF DEATH; and she will hold in her right hand a silver javelin and its tip will be red; around this javelin will be written DEFIANCE. The lists will be black and on one side will be banners full of tears and on the other side banners all of gold. And in the middle of the field will be two champions who will seem to march toward each other; one of these will be a tall person in strange armor, and he will have a black surcoat whose arms are strewn with bones of dead people; on his left shoulder he will bear two strangely made guisarmes,[e] one facing the other; and he will carry in his right hand a totally black javelin with a large tip. And on the other side there will be a man-at-arms in full armor and wearing the Burgundian coat of arms, such as those which Duke Philip bore, with sword and short dagger girded. He will hold in his right hand a jousting lance, and in the left he will have a targe half gold, half silver, and an azure steel[f] in the center. He will have in this hand a battleaxe whose head, bindings and point will be of gold, and he will seem to attack his adversary. The lists, all around, will be full of many people, afoot and on horseback; and the author will be in plain sight watching the combat, and near him, Fresh Memory on a white palfrey, and dressed as before; and they will seem to be conversing together. And on this side, partly on the field and on the road, will be a large stone marker, and on this marker will be certain Greek letters in gold.

MINIATURE 12 (54[r]–55[r] L; 54[r] T; 176[r] W). Precedes stanza 236.

Ceste histoire sera fondee sur ung plain champ, excepté que il y aura apparance de aucunes hayes et buissons.[1] Et n'y aura nulles lisses closes,[2] mais Attroppos sera en sa[3] chaiere en la maniere accoustumee et des deux costez aura deux grosses batailles a pied et a cheval. Et entre les deux[4] batailles, deux champions[5] [54[v] L] qui tiendront maniere de vouloir courir l'ung sur l'aultre.[6] L'ung sera armé de toutes pieces estrangement,[7] sur ung cheval grant de poil noir, bardé[8] pardevant d'une barde d'acier, a grans dagues aguës. Et sur le corps de l'homme d'armes[9] aura escript ACCIDENT, en lettres d'azur. Sur[10] le cheval aura escript ARROGANCE, en lettres d'argent. Il aura en sa main ung bourdon vert et

---

[e] Guisarme: a very popular pole arm with a sword blade having a sharp hook that issues from its back.

[f] Steel: a piece of steel for striking sparks from flint. Philip the Good, founder of the knightly Order of the Golden Fleece in 1429, used his personal emblem to decorate the Order's collar: alternating steels and flints. These steels are in the shape of the letter B.

le fer d'or, et sur la lance aura escript[11] en lettres d'argent MALHEUR. Il
aura sainte[12] une espee, et sur la gainne aura escript OULTRECUIDANCE.
Et a son arson aura une grosse masse[13] pendant, sur laquelle aura escript
FORTUNE. Et d'aultre part sera ung chevalier armé de toutes armes. Le
harnas et la barde seront[14] tout d'or,[15] et sur le cheval aura escript en
lettres d'azur FIERTÉ, et sur le[16] harnas ARDEMENT. Sa lance sera noire
et ferree d'or, et dessus aura escript HAULTE EMPRISE. [55ʳ L] Il aura
espee et dague sainte. Et seront l'ung devant l'aultre, comme pour com-
mencer la bataille. Et a l'ung des lez veable[17] seront l'Acteur et Fresche
Memoire regardans[18] la bataille.

Variants:
*The first part of this set of instructions, through the first occurrence of the
    word* lettres *(preceding* d'azur*) missing, T.*
1. ara aucune aparence de hayes et de b. *W*
2. closes *om. W*
3. en la *W*
4. entre les deux *W*] entre deux *L*
5. ara deux ch. *W*
6. courir sus lun a lautre *W*
7. bien estrangement *W*
8. sur vng grant cheual noir barde *W*
9. darme [*sic*] *W*
10. et sus *T*, et sur *W*
11. et dessus ara escript *W*
12. sainte *om. TW*
13. masse *written above* chaine [?], *lined out, T*
14. sera [*sic*] *TW*
15. toutte [*sic*] dor *W*
16. sur son h. *TW*
17. lez en lieu veable *T*
18. regardant *W*

Translation: This scene will be set on a flat terrain, except that there
will seem to be some hedges and bushes. And there will be no closed
list, but Atropos will be on her throne in the usual manner and on both
sides there will be two great armies afoot and ahorse. And between the
two armies, two champions who will seem to want to attack each other.
One will be in full armor of a strange sort, on a big black horse,

barded[g] in front with bardings of steel having great sharp spikes. And on the body of the man-at-arms will be written ACCIDENT in azure letters. On the horse will be written in silver letters ARROGANCE. The knight will have in his hand a green, large-pommeled, lance, its tip of gold, and on the lance will be written in silver letters MISFORTUNE. He will have a sword girded on and on its sheath will be written PRESUMPTION; and from his saddle-bow will hang a huge mace, on which will be written FORTUNE. And on the other side there will be a knight in full armor, his armor and bardings entirely of gold. And on his horse will be written in azure letters PRIDE, and on the harness AUDACITY. His lance will be black, tipped with gold, and on it will be written HIGH ENDEAVOR. He will have girt a sword and dagger. And they will be facing each other as if to begin fighting. And to one side in plain view will be the Author and Fresh Memory watching the battle.

MINIATURE 13 (58[v]–60[r] L; 57[v]–58[r] T; 179[r-v] W). Precedes stanza 256.

Ceste histoire sera fondee sur[1] une grant plainne [59[r] L] ou sera une grande[2] lisse, et a costiere sera la chaiere[3] Attroppos[4] habilee comme devant. Et[5] de[6] l'ung des coustez en[7] ladite lisse sera Accident, les jambes armees et les bras et les esperons chaussez, et deux serviteurs[8] a l'entour de[9] lui, en maniere de Sarrazins,[10] qui tiendront maniere de lui armer ung harnas fait[11] d'estrange façon. Et d'emprés[12] lui aura ung conseillier vestu de rouge et ung chapperon[13] fouré,[14] et sur sa robbe[15] aura[16] escript en lettres d'argent FORSENNE. Et[17] a l'opposite, dedans ladite lice, et au lieu[18] ou se doit mettre le pavilon, aura une littiere[19] toute d'or, laquelle[20] sera portee par deux licornes blanches. Sur[21] la premiere aura escript en lettres d'azur BONTÉ,[22] et sur l'aultre pareillement[23] DOULCE MANIERE. Et seront icelles licornes[24] harnacees[25] richement, et chascune licorne[26] menee [59[v] L] par le frain par deux chevaliers, chascun[27] vestuz[28] de drap d'or et en[29] couleurs diverses.[30] Sur la robe du premier aura escript FLEUR DE JOURS,[31] et aura[32] ung chappeaul de fleurs sur sa teste et les[33] cheveulz d'Alemaigne. Sur[34] le second[35] aura escript BON RENOM, et ung[36] bonnet sur sa teste a la guise de France. Sur la robe du tiers aura escript NOBLE CUEUR. Et sur la robe du quatriesme[37] aura escript[38] DESDAING CONTRE VILLONNIE. Et dedans icelle littiere[39] aura une dame armee richement, excepté la teste qui sera atout[40] les cheveulz

---

[g] Barded: Bards or bardings were armor protection for a horse.

pendans, et atout[41] ung chappeaul de duchesse en sa teste. A l'entour[42] d'elle aura pluiseurs nobles hommes qui tiendront[43] maniere de la descendre[44] de ladite[45] littiere, et l'ung tiendra[46] ung gavrelot tout[47] d'or, a l'entour[48] duquel aura escript en lettres noires[49] PLAISANT [60ʳ L] RECUEIL. Ung autre portera le tergon, qui sera d'azur, et dedans escript en lettres d'argent LOYAULMENT AMER. Et[50] ung autre tiendra ung bacinet qui sera[51] d'or ; dessus[52] aura escript BONNE PENSEE. La sieutte sera [53] de[54] pluiseurs dames en charrettes et haguenees,[55] et de pluiseurs gorgias fort en point. Et sera[56] de son costé toute la lisse paree[57] de trompettes, menestreux et de divers instrumens,[58] et[59] les bannieres d'icelles[60] trompettes seront[61] faittes[62] des armes[63] d'Ostriche et de Bourgoigne. Et[64] en lieu veable sera l'Acteur monté et armé de[65] lance sur la[66] cuisse ; et Fresche Memoire emprés[67] lui sur son paleffroy, qui tiendra maniere[68] de parler a lui. Et ung pettit herault tiendra l'Acteur par la bride et tiendra maniere de parler audit Acteur, une verge blanche en la main, et aura une cotte d'armes d'argent ou il[69] aura escript en lettres noires RESPIT.

Variants:

1. en *W*
2. grant *W*
3. la littiere *T*
4. dattropos *TW*
5. Et *om. W*
6. a lun *TW*
7. de laditte *W*
8. deux seruiteur [*sic*] *W*
9. ent*ou*r lui *T*, enthour de luy *W*
10. de deux sarasins *W*
11. fait *om. W*
12. ·Et d' *om. W*
13. rouge a vng ch. *T*, rouge vng ch. *W*
14. fourez *W*
15. et sur lad*ite* robe *T*
16. aura *om. W*
17. Et *om. W*
18. dedens la liche au lieu *W*
19. vne le*ttre* [*sic, the normal abbreviation for* lettre] *W*
20. qui *W*
21. Sus *T*

22. Et sera sur la premiere escript bonte *W*
23. pareillement *om. TW*
24. Et seront icelles licornes *LT]* elles seront *W*
25. aharnechees *T*, aharneschees *W*
26. licorne *om. W*
27. chascun *om. W*
28. vestu *T*
29. en drap dor ou c. *W*
30. couleur diuerse *TW*
31. fleurs de jour *W*
32. et icellui aura *T*
33. les *om. W*
34. Sus *T*
35. le seconde [*sic*] *W*
36. et ung bonnet *TW]* et bonnet *L*
37. du quart *T*, du grant [*sic*] *W*
38. aura escript *om. W*
39. En celle lictiere *W*
40. a tout *L*; qui sera atout *om. TW*
41. a tout *L*; et *om. T*, et atout *om. W*
42. Autour *W*
43. hommes tenans m. *W*
44. descende [*sic*] *W*
45. de celle l. *W*
46. Et aucuns tiendront *TW*
47. tout *om. W*
48. autour *W*
49. en lettres noires *om. W*
50. Et *om. W*
51. qui sera *om. W*
52. et dessus *TW*
53. sera *TW]* *om. L*
54. sera grande de *T*
55. en chariots et en h. *T*, en charios et h. *W*
56. Et sera *om. W*
57. la lice sera paree *W*
58. trompettes et menestriers et dautres diuers instr. *T*, tr. menestriers et diuers inst. *W*
59. et *om. W*
60. b. des tr. *W*

61. seront] sera *L*
62. seront faittes *om. TW*
63. aux armes *TW*
64. Et *om. W*
65. arme la lance *TW*
66. sa cuisse *W*
67. dempres luy *W, T* [?]
68. palfroy. Ten*ant* maniere *W*
69. il *om. W*

Translation: This scene will be set on a great plain where there will be a large list, and at one side will be Atropos' throne decked out as before. And on one side of the aforementioned list will be Accident, his arms and legs in armor, spurred, and two servants around him, dressed as Saracens, who will appear to be arming him with strangely made armor. And near him there will be a counselor dressed in red with a fur hood; and on his robe will be written in letters of silver MADNESS. And opposite in the aforesaid list, and in the place where a pavilion should be placed, will be a litter entirely of gold, which will be borne by two white unicorns. On the first will be written in azure letters GOODNESS, and on the other, likewise, GENTLE MANNER. And these two unicorns will be richly harnessed, and each unicorn led by the rein by two knights, each dressed in cloth of gold and in different colors. On the robe of the first will be written FLOWER OF DAYS and he will have a chaplet of flowers on his head and his hair in the German manner. On the second will be written GOOD REPUTE and a bonnet in the French mode on his head; on the robe of the third will be written NOBLE HEART; and on the robe of the fourth will be written DISDAIN FOR BASENESS. And in this litter there will be a lady, in rich armor, except her head which will have her hair hanging freely, and on top of all a duchess' hat on her head. Around her will be several noble men who will appear to help her out of the aforementioned litter, and one will hold a golden javelin, around which will be written in black letters PLEASANT HARVEST. Another will carry a shield, which will be azure, and thereon will be written in silver letters TO LOVE FAITHFULLY; and another will hold a basinet[h] of gold; on it will be written GOOD THOUGHT. Her entourage will be of several ladies in hackney-drawn

---

[h] Basinet: the most popular visored helmet of the 14th century.

carts, and of several well turned out gallants. And on her side all the list will be furnished with trumpets, minstrels and various instruments, and the banners of these trumpets will bear the arms of Austria and Burgundy. And in plain view will be the Author mounted and armed with his lance on his thigh; and Fresh Memory near him on her palfrey, who will seem to be speaking with him. And a small herald will hold the Author's bridle and appear to speak with him, a white baton in his hand, and he will have a surcoat with silvered arms, whereon will be written in black letters RESPITE.

MINIATURE 14 (63^v L; 61^r T; 181^v W). Precedes stanza 271.

Ceste^1 histoire sera fondee sur ung plain^2 pays plain de buissons et de hayes. Et par ung grant chemin tiendront maniere de cheminer^3 l'Acteur, monté, armé, habilé^4 et embastonné comme devant, et Fresche Memoire sur^5 son paleffroy emprés lui, et^6 tiendra maniere de deviser a lui.^{7} Et au bout^8 d'icelle histoire aura en maniere d'une touche^9 de bois ouquel lieu apperra ung petit manoir par maniere d'ung chasteaul^{10} paré et richement fait. Et tiendront maniere^{11} d'aler celle part.^{12}

Variants:

1. *Initial E, the cross-bar lightly barred, L (rubricator's error, possibly arising from the fact that a large initial E was needed to begin stanza 271, at the bottom of the same leaf).*
2. plain *om.* W
3. cheminer] chemine L, cheuauchier W, [T]
4. arme et habile L, *the* et *lightly barred;* habilé *om.* TW
5. sus T
6. dempres lui qui tiendra TW
7. a lacteur TW
8. bout T (boult W)] debout L
9. dune couche [*sic*] W
10. dun petit chasteau T
11. Et tiendront iceulx maniere W
12. et daler celle part tiendront maniere T

Translation: This scene will be set on an open plain, full of bushes and hedges. And appearing to travel along a wide road, the Author, mounted, in armor and fully armed as before, and Fresh Memory on her palfrey near him, and she will seem to be conversing with him. And in

the background of this scene there will be a bit of woods in which will
appear a small manor like a castle, ornamented and sumptuously built.
And they will seem to be going in that direction.

MINIATURE 15 (66ʳ L; 63ʳ T; 183ᵛ W). Precedes stanza 282.

Ceste histoire sera faicte comme une¹ chambre tendue, et le lit cou-
vert et encourtiné² de couleur vermeille. Et du travers de chascun pan
aura escript de grans lettres jaunes TANT A SOUFFERT. La curtine³ de
devant sera tiree, et la sera veu l'Acteur couché en son lit, la teste
haulte⁴ sur⁵ l'oreillier.⁶ Et devant lui sera assis en une chayere ung her-
mite qui tiendra maniere de parler audit Acteur.⁷

Variants:
1. sera fondee sus vne ch. T, sera fondee en vne ch. W
2. engourdine TW
3. La gourdine TW
4. hault [sic] TW
5. sus T
6. sur lorlier W
7. a lacteur TW

Translation: This scene will be set in a room hung with tapestries, and
the bed covered and curtained in crimson; and across each panel will be
written in large yellow letters HE HAS SUFFERED SO MUCH. The cur-
tain in front will be drawn back, and there the Author will be seen
lying in his bed, his head raised on the pillow. And before him, seated
in a chair, a hermit who will appear to be talking with the aforesaid
Author.

MRTS

MEDIEVAL & RENAISSANCE TEXTS & STUDIES
is the major publishing program of the
Arizona Center for Medieval and Renaissance Studies
at Arizona State University, Tempe, Arizona.

MRTS emphasizes books that are needed —
texts, translations, and major research tools.

MRTS aims to publish the highest quality scholarship
in attractive and durable format at modest cost.